To Brooklyn
with Love

Books by Gerald Green

FICTION

To Brooklyn with Love
The Legion of Noble Christians
The Heartless Light
The Lotus Eaters
The Last Angry Man
The Sword and the Sun

NON-FICTION

The Portofino PTA
His Majesty O'Keefe
(with Lawrence Klingman)

GERALD GREEN

To Brooklyn
with Love

TRIDENT   PRESS

New York   1967

c.3

Library of Congress Catalog Card Number: 67–23587

Published simultaneously in the United States and Canada
by Trident Press, a division of Simon & Schuster, Inc.,
630 Fifth Avenue, New York, N.Y. 10020

Printed in the United States of America

To my parents . . .
and the others of their generation who survived
the Depression with humor, courage and good sense.

**To Brooklyn
with Love**

The touching, eventful story of a day in the life of young Albert Abrams, a doctor's son, nearsighted and under-sized but still the best softball player in his part of Brownsville. Set in 1934

As Abrams and his children turned the corner and entered Longview Avenue, the street lights went on. The sudden discharge of light seemed to him overdramatic, a display he had staged, a trick prearranged with Consolidated Edison. Abrams had read somewhere that you could pay the City of Paris to light the Eiffel Tower or the Arc de Triomphe. Why not pay the Borough President of Brooklyn to illuminate his boyhood home?

The three of them—a small, neat man in his thirties, a girl of seven, a boy of five—walked cautiously down the cold, darkening street. Abrams appeared uncomfortable. He was fussily dressed in the manner of certain little men, affecting a pinkish overcoat of military cut (it suggested prior servitude as an envious enlisted man), clay-colored trousers and gleaming cordovan shoes.

Around them rose silvery lamp posts, flooding sidewalks and gutter with fluorescent brilliance, a presumed deterrent to muggers, thieves, the wicked poor.

"I knew something was wrong," he said. "Public School 133 is still there, and the old schoolyard, and the synagogue around the corner, but the trees are gone."

"Y'mean you had trees—in this place?" asked his daughter.

"A row on either side. Maples, catalpas, oaks. My father's tree was the biggest. About halfway down. It was a Lombardy poplar—one of the tallest trees in Brownsville. But it's gone."

"It's crummy here," she said.

"Yes, I guess it isn't much to look at now." He longed to tell them about the schoolyard where they had played salugi, punchball, stickball, boxball, Chinese handball, stoopball, association, but he could not. They were suburban children, reared in station wagons.

"My goodness, there's the old house." He tried to sound proud of his discovery. But he was a poor actor. His voice wavered.

"It's little," his son said.

"And dirty," added his daughter. "How come you could live there?"

Explanations would not help. They lived on a woodland hill and played with the sons of market research directors from North Dakota, the daughters of media men from Georgia.

In front of the yellow brick house—two-storied, narrow, crowned with a chipped cornice—a lavender Pontiac was parked. A Negro in a pale blue windbreaker was peering into its opened jaws, groping at its entrails with a wrench. It was parked adjacent to where the tree had stood. When had it been chopped down? A dignified giant, its upper branches heavy with summer leafage had brushed the upstairs window screens. In the spring it bore red-brown catkins. It had offended no one except some City Hall flunky who claimed its roots were strangling a watermain. He remembered a violent argument between his father and the public servant. His father had probably lost the argument. He usually did.

Through layers of filth, he could see the flaking number on the door—1422. On the brick wall were visible four dark holes where the old man's brass sign had been bolted. Privet bushes had long vanished from the tiny front yard; the wrought-iron rails were rusted.

"There's a kid lookin' at us," Abrams' son said apprehensively.

A shade in what had been his father's waiting room lifted. A brown face studied them. It was the window that had displayed the small illuminated sign:

2

SOLOMON ABRAMS, M.D.

There are broken toys now, he thought, in the rooms where my father listened to thousands of pulses and hearts, read innumerable thermometers, EKG's, X-rays, laboratory reports. No one could read a pulse the way his father did: head lowered, eyes intent, lips slightly parted. His fingers on your wrist had a soft touch. The touch assured you you would recover; you could feel the power of the healer.

In those rooms the old man had counted out the hours of his life in unpaid bills and unfilled hopes. Desks opened and slammed shut in Abrams' mind. He heard distantly the probing buzz of the ancient X-ray, heard again his father's hard tread— odd in a small man, but his father was all muscle—and the muffled voice coming through the closed office door: *Not a goddamn thing in the world wrong with you, go home and act like a mensch.*

"Now there's a lady," his son said.

A stout Negro woman stood behind the child. Arms folded, she stared at the three interlopers on the sidewalk. Was her gaze unfriendly? Abrams envisioned peeling walls, buckling floors, an incessant television set humming, the woman sipping beer from cans. Once his mother had sat there placidly reading Gissing and Meredith and Hardy, while from an RCA Victrola a strained Caruso sang La Juive.

"We gonna go in to see your room, like you promised?" asked his daughter.

Abrams frowned. "I don't think so. I don't want to bother those people."

There was a July day in 1934. His father surprised him with a new softball, a genuine Spalding "indoor," whiter than an angel's robe, intoxicating with its odor of bleached polished cowhide. . . .

"Lookin' for somebody?" the owner of the lavender car asked.

"Ah, no. I used to know some people here." Abrams

cleared his throat. "Fellow named Pennington. You ever know a Lee Roy Pennington?"

"Nope. I new here."

Where was Lee Roy, Lee Roy of the great brown football head and bandy legs? Lee Roy: nemesis, shadow, persecutor.

They walked slowly toward the corner. As they approached the intersection Abrams imagined he saw his father coming toward them: overcoat flapping open even in December, ruined fedora pushed back on his head, carrying the scuffed black satchel and a white bakery box, a peace offering for his wife. Something to atone for the imminent tirade about the lousy deadbeat who just done him out of a two-dollar fee. But of course it was not his father. It was only a Negro workman with a lunchbox.

"Anyway the corner grocery's still in business," he told his unheeding children. But the sign read ALIMENTACION. "I guess Benny sold it. That man had the greatest pot cheese in the world."

Through dark and silent streets they trudged toward the subway. It had been a short visit, much shorter than he had planned.

4

He awakened to the sounds of his parents' muffled conversation. Early risers, they spoke softly out of deference to him. Instantly his eyes found the softball. It rested on the chair beside his bed, a round white, shiny cowhide egg in the nest of his rumpled clothing.

"A Spalding," he whispered. He took it in his hands. Once again, his father had outdone himself. All he had asked for (nagged, his mother said) was the Reach, the cheap make. Secretly the old man had gone to Davega's and bought the best ball.

It had a life, a purpose, and he loved it. His small hands pressed the hard leather to his chest, fingers spread across the endless raised welts. How perfectly they wound about the surface, ingeniously duplicating the looped pattern! For a moment he regretted having to dirty it, scar its gleaming skin. Thrown to the cracked ceiling it fell magically. He was Len Koenecke patroling the outer garden for the Brooklyn Dodgers.

"Ah, why not give up the whole damn thing, once and for all." His father's hoarse voice, filtered through the door, upset him for a moment. *Serves me right*, he thought, *lying here feeling so great*. His joy was almost unbearable—the promise of a July day, heat, sun, sports, friends, the new ball. Dressing, he listened to his parents, each word diluting his ecstasy, involving him in matters he didn't want to know about.

". . . last week or so, trouble getting out of bed," his

father was saying. "Me, who could wrestle all day fifteen years ago. It's psychic, what they call the psychopathology of everyday life, as if I need a professor to tell me what's eating me."

And his mother: "It's hard for everyone, Sol, not just you."

"To hell with all of them."

"Sol, must you start first thing in the morning?"

"Why do I have trouble breathing? Never been sick in my life."

"It's terribly hot."

Under no circumstances could his father get sick, the boy thought, as he laced his sneakers. Doctors didn't get sick, especially his father. The old man was indestructible, always there to tape an ankle, administer a spoonful of syrup cocillana compound, jab a hypodermic into his quivering butt. (And his father gave the softest shots of anyone—they hardly hurt.) A good part of his youth had been spent in illness; one of his sharpest memories of infancy was his father's large, Indian-looking head peering over his crib.

". . . damned mistake on my part, the whole thing. Can't keep a patient anymore."

"People have no money to spend these days. We'll economize like everyone else."

"Hah. They're all running to the free clinics, to the drugstores to prescribe for them."

"You turned down the chance to make relief calls. Why you had to get up on your high horse!"

"Because I stand on my own two feet!"

But didn't the old man give in later, and start making calls for the city welfare department? Of course he did. He hollered about them all the time—the endless paper work, delays in getting paid.

"The whole practice of medicine stinks," his father proclaimed. "Why didn't I realize that years ago?"

Adjusting amber-rimmed eyeglasses, patting the adhesive binding the nosepiece, the boy thought of entering their bedroom. But it would be wrong to intrude his happiness into his father's misery.

His parents' morning conversation droned on, and he

6

drifted toward the window. It seemed terribly unfair for his father to love him so much, lavish gifts on him, cure him, tape his sprained ankles, help him with homework, give him all this so willingly, and yet have no control over his own life. *Love me less*, the boy pleaded silently, *and get the better of other people—patients, other doctors, storekeepers. . . . I'll give you back the softball right now, if you'll stop getting sore all the time.*

In the garden below his window, summer flowers shouted their glory at him. The doctor grew dahlias, hollyhocks, phlox, in haphazard profusion. Earth, seeds, tubers responded to Dr. Abrams' touch; the people of the slum did not. *That's another thing while I'm at it, you don't have to be such a great gardener, if you could only learn to keep your patients and make them pay up the way other doctors do.*

"Four calls and six lousy dollars to show for it," the doctor was saying. "I'll bleed to death here in this vile heat climbing stairs, sweating for each dollar. I'm warning you, Hannah, one of these days it'll all be over. . . ."

"What are you warning me for? Am I part of this conspiracy against you?"

"Never mind."

His father's voice had taken on a strange high timbre. It frightened him; the softball was dust in his hand. He studied his narrow bespectacled face in the mirror to make sure he looked sufficiently casual, uninterested in their dispute, and knocked at the bedroom door.

Inside, his mother, in flannel bathrobe despite the July heat (she was always chilly), was making the double bed. His father was standing at the oval mirror on the dresser, knotting a frayed maroon tie under the lumpy collar of a green sports shirt—a collar never designed to accommodate a tie.

Seeing him in the mirror, his father said, smiling, "Hey, there's Lou Gehrig."

All because he sees my dopey face and sees me holding the ball. Before he was angry with the whole world, but I walk in and he's happy. It's not fair.

The doctor beamed. The Indian face—hooked nose, protruding cheekbones, cleft chin, the shock of black-gray hair—was glowing. "Toss it here, Albert," he said—and reached for it clumsily. Baseball was not his sport. Once he had been a gymnast, a teacher of calisthenics and other formal European sports. His muscles had been developed in a young manhood dedicated to giant swings and parallel bars.

"When did you buy *that* for him?" his mother asked.

"On my own time," his father said. He winked at Albert—man-to-man. "I don't tell you everything."

"After all those complaints about how little you earned yesterday?"

"Why not?" the doctor cried. "Why the hell not? Let the kid play ball. That's important too. He told me they couldn't get a game going because nobody in this *fekokteh* neighborhood could afford a ball!"

"So Santa Claus bought one."

"You bet I did!"

Did they take twelve-year-old boys in the French Foreign Legion? He would enlist tomorrow—anything to escape. Albert Abrams, twelve-year-old drummer boy, beating the advance on Sidi-bel-Abbès.

These arguments about his father's generosity always summoned up a painful memory of a day when he was left alone with a Negro maid. He was five—a spindly, sickly kid. The colored woman was a black whale—silent as stone, reeking of perfumed grease. His father was out making calls. His mother was about to leave for an afternoon of bridge. He protested tearfully. She, never one to bribe or spoil him, agreed to buy him a present. But the old man had come home first and found him sniffling, convinced that his mother would forget. "Hah, I'll fix *her!*" his father had cried. "I'll get you a *real* present!" And he had escorted him through the snowy streets (it was dark, five o'clock of a January day) to Lieberson's candy store, where he bought him an enormous paint set, a great red and yellow cardboard box studded with cunning colored disks of watercolor, little tubes of oils, trays, cutouts, brushes. (It had been gathering dust in Lieberson's window for years; nobody on Longview Avenue could afford it.)

Later, his mother had returned with a small tin alligator from Woolworth's. You squeezed a handle, its legs moved. His selfishness, his mean distrust of his mother had earned him two presents. Surely he had humiliated her. (Although she, eternally poised and gentle, said nothing.) How could he compare that junky alligator with his father's lavish paint set? A show of loving the alligator was in order; he fussed with it and invented a game, hunting it under the radiator. But whenever he looked at it, it grieved him. After a while he stopped playing with it and conveniently lost it in the backyard. The paint set didn't last very long either. From lying around in Lieberson's sunlit window, the paints had cracked and lost pigment. A double disaster.

". . . too much to spend, Sol, that's all I'm saying. It's not his birthday. A ball like that is a luxury. And knowing him, he'll go flying into the street chasing it and get hit by a car."

"We play Indoor in the schoolyard, Ma."

"Just as bad. That's where all the *schwarzers* hang out. They'll fix your game, good."

"When we go in a whole gang it's okay," he said weakly. "They'd never pick on the Raiders when we're together."

His father yanked his tie into place; it flipped over backward, revealing the split underside. Clothes confounded him— suits bagged, hats ruffled, shoes bulged and cracked.

"Go play where you want, Albert," the doctor said irritably. "Hannah, lay off the kid. He can't go on being a mollycoddle all his life. He can't be scared of his shadow."

She smoothed the yellow chenille coverlet on the bed, willing to suspend the dispute. "Albert," she said, going to the dresser, "here's a list for Benny's. And there are two empty milk bottles in the kitchen."

At least he wasn't a complete loss to them. Walking down the narrow stairs, he had a poignant longing for tough indifferent Polack parents, like Teddy Ochab's, ham-handed peasants who belted Teddy and his brothers around regularly. In *that* household, he reflected bitterly, kids don't sit around worrying about who gave the alligator and who gave the paint set.

9

His father had not given up. ". . . have to be a sissy, a fairy? Bad enough with weak eyes and underweight, you got to give him a complex yet. I should have given him boxing lessons, like I wanted to, only you wouldn't let me, so at least he could stand up to the galoots and the *schwarzers*, the way I did when I was his age."

Albert spun around the bottom steps and trotted down the hallway of the lower floor to the kitchen. Briefly, he glanced at the sports page of last evening's *Journal*. It paid to be prepared. One never knew when an argument over a batting average would develop. He admired Hype Igoe's cartoon, picked up the bottles, and still carrying the softball, walked out into the July heat.

The hot day lay comfortably on Longview Avenue, like a fat woman's folded arms on a windowsill. Weather and street had negotiated a pact. They belonged to one another. Winter, on the other hand, was no friend of Longview Avenue. Snow remained unshoveled, garbage uncollected. The Abrams' neighbors exploded soggy refuse bags on the filthy drifts. People stayed indoors or walked the icy streets hesitantly, anticipating a fall or a lawsuit. But not in summer: everyone poured from the tenements across the street, from the two-story homes on Albert's side.

At the curb he spent a few seconds in imitation of his father, kicking junk into the gutter. At the base of the poplar a sardine tin, eggshells, a rotten half cantaloupe had blossomed during the night. Shaking his head, he booted them to the street. It was a gesture that affirmed their superiority over the neighbors. Most of the other inhabitants of Longview Avenue kicked garbage on to other people's sidewalks. You could keep score, Albert mused, two points for a tin can, one for potato peelings.

He paused a moment to survey the steamy street. Its mystery thrilled him. Each time he set foot on it, it revealed some new drama, some new horror, some joy, some subtlety. He was part of it—resident, member of the Raiders, student at P.S. 133—yet apart from it, observer, critic, outsider, *the doctor's* son. He balanced himself on the curb, treading one rubber-rimmed Keds after another, using the ball and the bottles as counterweights. (It was lucky his mother had not seen the sneakers. She would have protested. "You have weak ankles, and those canvas things will ruin your feet. Your father and I spend all that money on Coward arch-supporters, and you don't wear them." As a child he had called his arch-supporters "Oscarporches" and he was considered awfully cute. Oh, he was so cute!)

The morning's drama was not long in coming. Did the great stage of Longview Avenue ever let him down? Never! Across the gutter a fire was blazing at the curb, a foul-smelling, crackling fire. Never mind that it was July, a hot spell, early morning. *That's more like it. That's my crazy street.* He stopped to study it, and with a shivering sense of recognition, saw that a figure of some kind was sizzling in the blaze of old crates. A doll? A toy?

Three people were standing around the fire, studying it silently. One was the resident half-wit, Gorilla. How old was he? Fifteen? Twenty? Albert had no idea. As long as he could remember, he had seen Gorilla limping by, short-legged, curiously crippled, his huge head tilted to one side, his eyes flitting about suspiciously. Year in, year out, he wore a navy blue sweater with an orange V at the collar. (Years later, Albert Abrams would wonder where all the half-wits, hydrocephalics and cretins were being hidden. In his boyhood, each street had one or two of these sad mumbling creatures like Gorilla.)

Gorilla had a sawed-off broomstick in one hand. From time to time, he poked at the flaming form (which Albert deduced was a toy, an old Teddy bear or stuffed dog) and laughed. His attendants were a squat shaven-headed boy of about thirteen, known as Mockey, and Grubman, the neighborhood genius. Albert knew nothing about Mockey, except that he had moved into a tenement a few weeks ago, and spoke no English. The baldy wore peculiar European-looking shorts that came to his knees, and a collarless shirt, delicately gathered and stitched across the chest.

11

Genius Grubman paraded back and forth at the edge of the blaze, waving formless arms and proclaiming:

"Tiger, tiger, boining bright
In the forest of the night,
What immortal hand or eye
Dare frame thy fearful symmetry?"

Grubman was a great brain. Everyone said so. He was sixteen, doomed to die at an early age. He had transparent white skin and a blurred unformed face. He wore ballooning gray knickerbockers, black socks and black orthopedic shoes that laced halfway up his calf. It was a miracle that his heart survived from day to day. He did his schoolwork at home, but still got straight A's in everything. A professor from Brooklyn College had once examined him. Even in the summer he studied, as if aware that time was running out.

Albert crossed the street, and approached the unholy three, the sizzling blaze. *Sizzling!* Why did it make all that crackling noise? The breeze shifted slightly and he caught the stench of hair, flesh.

"Holy smoke, that *stinks*," Albert said. "What is it?"

"Aaah, aah," Gorilla laughed. "He ast what it is. Doncha wanna nice roast dog?"

"Dog!" he cried. "Why you burning a dog?"

"He wuz dead," Gorilla said. He rolled his eyes until they vanished. The whites horrified Albert.

Grubman, parading back and forth, addressed him. "Behold, the doctor's son! And pray tell, which doctor? Dr. Faustus? Dr. Johnson? He comes to observe our great annual sacrifice of the dog to the great God Moloch!" He tapped Gorilla on the shoulder. "Speak, Moloch!"

"Aaah, bullshid."

"Words of wisdom!" cried Grubman. "All genuflect before Moloch, burner of dogs!"

Mockey stared happily into the fire. Grubman's declamation was lost on him. Albert averted his head, as the choking smoke struck him full force. Now he could see the scorched

12

carcass, the glistening fat, the caking blood and charred flesh. What a way to start the day!

"Whose dog is it?" Albie asked. "I mean, how did it get killed?"

"Yes," said Grubman. "It was the dog that died. A stray, a waif, flotsam and jetsam. But the great God Moloch"—he patted Gorilla's head again—"decreed a sacrifice." Genius took a wide stance on the sidewalk and proclaimed:

"Who are these coming to the sacrifice?
To what green altar, O mysterious priest,
Lead'st thou that heifer lowing at the skies?
And all her silken flanks with garlands drest?"

"It sure stinks up the block," Albert said.

"Heretic, unbeliever!" Grubman orated. "Defiler of the temple! Go."

"Roast dog! Hot roast dog!" Gorilla called. "A nickel a shtickel!"

Mockey clapped his hands and danced toward the fire, kicking at the flaming crate. It collapsed in a cloud of hot embers. The burning corpse smothered under the debris. Maybe in the Ukraine or wherever the baldhead came from, Albert reflected, they burned dogs all the time.

"Oh shame!" Grubman wailed. His knickerbockers inflated as he spread his legs and raised his arms. "Oh shame—the sacrifice is dishonored, corrupted! We will have to drink libations to cleanse ourselves! All to the lustral bath!"

Gorilla chuckled and poked at the dog. Albert, eager to be rid of the stink yet fascinated by the drama, picked up his bottles and skipped off. But he was gratified: Grubman and company had gotten the day off to a good start.

In the alley of a tenement, Daisy, the local Negro handyman, slept off his nightly drunk. A polite booze-fat man of middle age, gentle as a puppy, he slept in a dusty heap at the foot of two brimming trash cans. His clothes were forever daubed with the paint with which he earned his living. Once Albert's father had engaged Daisy to paint his office. "Can't

13

stand his stink," the old man said, "but he needs the dough." It hadn't worked out. Daisy botched the job, never showed up, cheated him on the price. But Dr. Abrams wouldn't hurt his feelings—he kept him on the job and gave him a pint of his medical supply of Golden Wedding as a bonus. Daisy had adored his father ever since. "Ah a member of deh 'Merican Legion, Doc," he assured Dr. Abrams, "and Ah puts in a good word for yo' wit dem."

Gusts of steam billowed from Kupperman's tailoring shop. It was as though Mr. Kupperman was making the weather, creating heat in his cramped store, pumping out magic steam from his forge. Alongside Kupperman's, in an unlabeled shop that sometimes housed sinister gypsies, three bearded gnomes in eastern European aprons and skullcaps, worked madly looming cheap sweaters. Another mystery. Albert stopped to watch them wrestle bales of yarn from a pushcart. Where had they come from? Who told them about the empty store? Who were these bandy-legged trolls and where did they learn to knit sweaters?

An odor of smoking dog drifted by. Pleasantly disgusted, he turned and saw Gorilla stoking his infernal blaze. Grubman raised his arms in benediction again.

He walked on. What storybook could match the heart-breaking saga of Jimmy Kravitz, lightweight contender, once ranked third in his division by *Ring* magazine, a scrapper who had gone ten rounds with Lew Tendler and knocked down Bat Battalino? There was Jimmy, outside Fleishacker's poolroom, bobbing, sparring, muddled brain awash with memories of hot nights in the Coney Island Velodrome, the old Madison Square Garden, the Sunnyside Arena.

In this corner at one hundred and thirty-two pounds, the Brownsville Bad Boy, Jimmy Kravitz. . . .

Albert stopped to pay tribute to the old pug. Muttering, skipping rope, Jimmy was waiting for the poolroom to open. Fleishacker let him rack balls, sweep the floor, deliver bets. Cruel boys would call out to him: "Hey, Jimmy, what round is it?"

Kravitz would croak back at them: "Da last, an' I'm ahead

14

on pernts." Everyone would laugh. Sometimes a real tough guy like Zetz would sneak behind Jimmy and goose him. Once, Albert remembered, his father had made a call to Kravitz' flat (this wreck had an attractive wife and three little daughters, who survived, God knows how). Albert had come for the doctor there. On the wall of the apartment was a life-sized hand-tinted photograph of Jimmy at his peak, the Brownsville Belter himself. Crouching, liver-colored gloves up, the flattened face grim, hair slicked down and parted in the middle, it was Kravitz at his peak. He had slender legs and dainty feet. They used to say the Belter had the fastest left jab in the business. *And look at him now*, Albert thought.

Fists and strength should have assured Jimmy's success, thought Albert. *Just look at me. I am the block weakling. I have bad coordination. What will become of me, if Jimmy Kravitz, neighborhood hero, the toughest guy to come out of Brownsville, ends up hanging around poolrooms, where bums like Zetz can make fun of him?* It was a terrible thought.

By the time he got to Benny's Grocery he was feeling better. The street had a capacity to invigorate him, to stimulate his imagination, to offer him new possibilities.

Whistling, he bounced into Benny's narrow store. It always reminded Albert of a ship. The floor sloped. The shelves were ready to topple their tinned sardines and canned peaches. Great sacks of dried rice, beans, meal, were the stores of a Joseph Conrad merchantman, not a local grocery. Any minute Albert expected the whole place to career over, knocked galley-west, with rye breads and onion rolls sailing in aromatic flight. The first thing he would do would be get out of the way of that iceberg of halvah; it could kill him.

At the marble counter (a clutter of half-loaves, cheese boxes, odd jars and tins, and a square foot for stacking purchases) two women were ahead of him. They were both slatternly types, the "element" as his father called them, who began moving in after something terrible happened to everyone in 1929. They had ratty hair, shapeless cotton dresses, and they spoke in singsong cadences. *Petchetchas,* his father designated such women, an obscure word whose origins were lost somewhere in the marshy plains around Kishinev, or so Mrs. Abrams claimed.

"So he says to me, he says," one woman brayed, " 'Ya don't like what I told ya, go somewhere else, there's lotsa doctors'll take your type.' Such crust!"

"I could believe it," the other one, a shorter fatter woman, said. "My friend Ida had the same trouble with him. He starts yelling, giving her a lecture."

"Yeah, that's him. So I said to him, some doctor, some doctor you are, you're stuck all these years on Longview Avenue when all the other doctors moved to Crown Heights! Only you're stuck here, how come? And wait, wait, till you hear. He gets up and points to the door and says to me, 'Out, get out, the only thing wrong with this neighborhood is *tinnif* like you!' Imagine! I told my husband he oughta go over and punch him right in the mouth!"

"Yeh. It would serve him right. So what did your husband say?"

"Irving said, hmph, why waste his punches on such a slob?"

Oh try it, try it, Albert advised her silently. *My father'll wipe the floor up with your husband. But he can't stop you from telling lies about him. . . .*

"Lissen," the fat woman said, "it's better you don't start with his type. He's got that *meshugeneh* look in his eye, he's not to be trusted." Her voice became conspiratorial, filled with dark knowledge. "Who knows what he could do to you with all that machinery in there, when you don't know what he's doing?"

"Ya telling me? I wouldn't trust him as far as I could throw Brooklyn Bridge. Some doctor, to stay on Longview Avenue!"

Albert thought desperately: *But you think you're better than he is, and you're here. Does that make sense?*

"I tell you, that mouth on him," the first woman pursued. "Just because I asked him for the X-rays to take to the clinic, he acts like he owns them."

16

"He acts like he owns the block, that nut."

Shriveling, Albert pressed himself against a sack of rice. *Do they know? Do they know I am of the tyrant's blood, son of the man they hate so much?* No, it wasn't his father they were talking about; someone else; another doctor, a crazy one, far away.

Benny, his forehead flecked with flour, chewing on one of his own bagels, came from the recesses of the galley, carrying boxes of Del Monte prunes. "The kid, the kid," he whispered to his customers. They heard him not. The first woman gathered up her paper bags. Now polite and timorous, she said to the grocer, "Charge it, hah? My husband don't get paid regular. You know, he's on piecework." She waddled out, paying no attention to Albert. *Coward, coward,* Albert cried to himself. He should have leaped in her path, challenged her for evidence, accused her of lying, protected his father's good name. But he only pushed the bridge of his eyeglasses higher up on his nose, and studied the blue NRA eagle behind Benny's counter. *We do our part.*

The second woman concluded her purchases, also asked Benny to charge it, and walked by him silently. She made an effort to avoid Albert's eyes. At the door, however, thinking herself safe, she had turned and darted a shifty look at him. *The doctor's son.*

"Forget it, kid," Benny said. "A coupla *yentes.* They should pay their bills regular, the way your mother does."

He scooped butter from a great wooden vat (the Old Oaken Bucket, Albert was convinced), hacked off great slabs of farmer cheese, filled cunning white bags with pot cheese, a man at home with the good things of his trade. Benny's father, Albert remembered, was a bearded dwarf, who wore a high yarmulke in the store. Albert had always expected him to break into a few choruses of "Eli-Eli" while amputating rye bread. But Benny was a new man—he had nifty sideburns, a pencil moustache, and once waltzed in the Harvest Moon Ball.

"Yeah, don't pay 'em no attention," Benny said, fetching bottles of milk from a ship's refrigerator at the rear.

It was no consolation. So what if his family paid their bills?

17

At the moment, he was willing to be one of the great army of Depression deadbeats—as long as he did not have to listen to this slander of his father.

Laden with groceries, the softball cradled against his chest, he walked into the sizzling street. In front of Parolo's ice-dock, the Raiders were playing boxball. He heard their yells, their arguments, curses, and knew that Bushy was in the game. Everything Bushy was connected with became violent.

Albert looked carefully in both directions (Longview Avenue was a one-way street, but his mother warned him always to look both ways) and trotted toward the ice-dock and his friends.

"Hey, he crossed the street, he crossed the street all by himself!" Bimbo Wexler taunted. "Albert did it! Albert the great!"

Bushy slammed the rubber ball under Big Artie's legs. The game stopped as they applauded Albert.

"Don't you guys ever get tired of that old joke?" Albert asked. "I been crossing the street since I was eleven."

Long after the initial embarrassment, the pain lingered. His mother had declared the street off limits to him. He could not go in the gutter. He would get hit by a car. He would get maimed. He would get killed. Other boys could race around the gutter all day and never get touched. But it would be just his luck, his mother insisted, to get run over by a taxi. Never mind that cars passed by, on the average, one every fifteen minutes. Never mind that he had eyes and ears and could get out of the way. For years the Raiders had tormented him about the interdiction against the street. He had learned to live with it— barely. Now that the ban had been lifted by his mother, they still taunted him about it. At times he knew what Christ underwent, and felt sorry for him, false prophet though He was.

Bushy Feinstein, captain of the Raiders, best athlete on the block, feared chieftain, approached him, his eyes gleaming with menace. *Joking?* Albert wondered.

"Ya full of it, Alby-tross," Bushy muttered. "I think ya

lyin'. Your mother *still* won't let ya go in the gutter. I got a good mind to snitch on ya."

"Cut it out, Bushy." Albert tried to smile.

"Wow, lookit me fly, lookit me fly!" Bimbo cawed. He flapped his arms. "I'm an Alby-tross, an Alby-tross, I could fly acrost the gutter when my mother won't lemme walk in it!"

Bushy's eyes—slits in his puffed face—spied the softball. "Where'd ya git that?" he snapped—and grabbed it from Albert's hand.

Bimbo, jealous of Albert, jealous of the ball, danced around Albert, shadowboxing, throwing snappy lefts and rights, occasionally letting one land on Albert's forearm. He was a thick roly-poly boy, the same age as Albert (they were the youngest members of the Raiders) but stronger and heavier. Redheaded, with a face splotched with dime-sized freckles, he was a good athlete, a miniature tyrant. Oddly, his parents were stooped, beaten Semites, a fact that led Dr. Abrams, who knew Bimbo as one of his son's colleagues, to comment, "That redhead—he picked up some genes from a Ukrainian farmer."

The boxball game stopped and they gathered around to study the softball. Bushy stroked it, squeezed it, seemed ready to bite into its white leather hide.

"Whadja get it for, Albie?" asked Big Artie. He was a huge, slab-sided boy, gentle, slow-speaking, with a round innocent face.

"Oh, just a present."

"Ya mean it wasn't ya birthday, or anything?" Bushy asked.

"Nope." Why did he have to make so many explanations? Was he required to tell them how much the old man loved him? How his mother had complained that they couldn't afford the ball?

"He got it so he could *play,*" Bimbo singsonged. "How else would Dear Alby-tross get picked to *play* unless he brang the ball?" Did Wexler ever get tired of teasing him? One of his earliest memories was when he could not have been more than four. His father had bought him a cowboy suit, the only one ever seen in the neighborhood. The hat, Albert recalled, was more on the order of a disorderly Royal Canadian Mountie's, and there was a fringed buckskin vest, suspiciously Indian. Still it was a cowboy suit, and he had stood, humiliated, in the front yard, behind the privet hedges, as a crowd assembled to gape at the doctor's son. Bimbo had spied him, had made the sign of "shame, shame" with two fingers, and had lisped, "Albert is a boy-stout, Albert is a boy-stout!"

Albert had urgently wanted to explain to them that it was *not* a boy scout's uniform, but a *cowboy suit*, and besides, the word was *scout* not *stout*. Finally, in tears, he had fled their taunting grins and their unified chant. *Albert is a boy-stout.* Except for a few self-composed dramas in his room, he had never worn the costume again.

"Yeah, who would ever pick you for a game?" Bimbo persisted. "Gotta bring the ball, so he could get a game."

A cool disdain was indicated. Yet there was bitter truth in Bimbo's insults. Invariably he was odd-man out—the loner left on the pavement, squinting behind the eyeglasses that mangled his weak eyes, unsteady on weak ankles, as Bushy would pronounce the curse on him: "And you're playin' with ya mudder's broomstick."

"A catch. Let's have a catch!" Little Artie shouted. He was Big Artie's cousin, a wiry uncontrollable runt with a face like a shaved monkey. Rhesus, macaque or spider? Albert wondered. He and Big Artie were inseparable. Their mothers worked, their fathers were unemployed and looked for work, the two cousins made their way by themselves, gobbling cold lunches in dirty kitchens, racing the streets, children of the paralyzing poverty that had struck Longview Avenue five years ago—but not at all subdued by it. Albert liked them: in their undisciplined freedom there was kindness. They rarely teased him.

Albert set the grocery bag down and tossed the ball to the monkey-face. Little Artie scampered off, nutty with joy. He threw it to his cousin; the fat boy caught it with a man's meaty hand and whipped it back underhand.

"To me, to me!" Albert called. "Peg it down to first!"

"Some first baseman," Bimbo shouted. "He couldn't catch cold."

Albert dropped the peg. They abandoned themselves to the magic of the new ball. In a few seconds Bushy Feinstein had assumed command. That urge to rule, dominate, hurt, win, sent him flying around the front of Parolo's ice-dock, scooping up grounders, rifling shots at the others, screaming, giving orders, making plays.

Albert, ignored in the frenzied play, stood at the curb fascinated by Bushy's mania. It was always that way when Bushy was in a game. He *was* the game. He moved with the skills, the natural coordination of a great athlete—a fourteen-year-old Mercury, swift, hard, lithe, anticipating the other boys' moves, a step ahead, a touch smarter, a speck stronger. How Albert envied and feared him! His face was worth studying, too. It was not an athlete's face, Albert decided, but a round, soft, puffed face, crowned by a great crop of brown Brillo (hence his name). It was a splotchy enraged face, with no eyes—just two Oriental slits. You could never stare Bushy down, or rebuke him; *there were no eyes to meet your gaze.* His temper was a legend. Once, Big Artie had rested a Spalding Hi-Bouncer in the Brillo and said, "A egg in a nest!"—and Bushy had bloodied his nose with a savage left hook.

There was an unknown sinister force in Bushy's life, Albert felt, that made him the way he was. There was some secret in his home, some unfathomable terror in his family, that drove Bushy into vile rages—and heroic achievement. His parents were stern silent people, more prosperous than the other residents of Longview Avenue. They owned the tenement house in which they lived. Old Feinstein was fiercely Orthodox, with a long black beard. He had those same puzzling slits instead of eyes. Once on a lovely Saturday morning, Albert had witnessed a terrible confrontation between Bushy and his father.

Bushy—insatiable competitor—had been playing an early morning game of stoopball with the two Arties and Teddy Ochab. Suddenly Bushy's father, dressed for synagogue in black homburg and black topcoat, waddled angrily out of the house looking for his son. Seeing him thus engaged in vile sport on the Sabbath, he ordered him to get dressed for *schul*, and when Bushy ignored him, came at him, on stubby Orthodox legs, waving a barrel-stave. What amazed Albert—as he recalled the awful scene—was that Bushy could have outrun the old man or seized the weapon, or simply run into the house and gotten dressed. Instead a lunatic ballet unfolded. Bushy ran backward, ever the athlete, screaming, *Wait! Wait!*, executing fancy dance steps while the stave swished an inch from his head and limbs. Only once did Feinstein catch his son—smack on the behind, making a noise that could be heard a block away. And so they had danced and pirouetted around Longview Avenue, the shrieking son, cursing father, and it dawned on Albert that to Bushy Feinstein it was another game, like touch football or Chinese handball. If you counted misses, he won by a mile: Bushy 12, Mr. Feinstein 1.

"Lissen," Bushy commanded, intercepting the ball with one quick hand. "We got time for a game this morning."

They all agreed. No one consulted Albert, but he didn't care. Anything, *anything* just to play, instead of his usual fate—umpire, scorekeeper, lost-ball chaser, or spectator.

"I'll bring my bat," Albert said. "How soon you wanna play?"

"Ten minutes. Inna schoolyard." Bushy counted heads. "We need more guys."

"I'll call Teddy Ochab and his brothers," Big Artie said. Teddy Ochab was a regular member of the Raiders. A Polish boy, he lived several blocks from Longview Avenue, in a small enclave of towheads. His brothers did not belong to the gang, but could be called into service as needed—handy spare parts. Big Artie jogged off.

"Ya get too many guys," Bimbo chanted, "and Albie won't play. He'll take his ball and go home."

"Ah, shut up," Albert said. "Change the record for once, willya?" He pushed his descending glasses up his nose. Was every day of his life destined to go this way?

Little Artie sent the ball skipping over the pavement. Bimbo scooped it up, stepped on an imaginary second base,

22

pivoted and threw it to Bushy. "We got two! What a DP combination!"

Albert was fed up with him—snotty, cocky, always better than he was. He was sick with himself for having bribed his way into their favor. "You missed second base," he called to Bimbo. "By a mile."

"How could you tell, ya four-eyed fairy?" Bimbo shouted. "Ya stink anyway. I can beat you at any sport in the world."

"Blowhard," Albert countered.

Bimbo swaggered toward Albert. "Name one. Go on, name one. Name a single sport you can beat me at." He hooked a freckled hand into Albert's belt. "Salugi? Touch? Punchball? Boxball? One-wall handball? Chinese handball? Nuts? Stickball? Indoor? Hardball? Kickety-can? Go on, name one."

Bushy, scenting violence, flipped the ball to Little Artie, who let it bounce off his head into his cupped hand. "It's so good, I could bite it," he said.

"I could mopilize you if I wanted, ya sissy," Bimbo said. "Admit ya stink at everything."

The slits in Bushy Feinstein's face closed. His doughy face sniffed blood, hatred, swinging fists, tears. These invigorated him.

Bounding over to the two smaller boys, Bushy began a crazed chant: "Fight, fight, fight, the two of yez! Swing, swing, swing! Go on Bimbo, fight him, sock him! Go on Albert, swing! I'll hold ya glasses!"

"Who wants to fight?" Albert pleaded—his voice shaking. "It's nothing to fight over. Besides, you know I have weak eyes. And he's got ten pounds on me." Oh, how he hated, detested, despised himself for the coward's way.

"Yeah," Bimbo said. "His old lady won't let him."

"Leave my family out of it," Albert said. He tried desperately for the right note of dignified menace in his voice. He failed. *Oh please God, once, once in my life let me stand up to somebody and win.* . . . And the insult to his mother was the worst part. His mother was not part of his street life of punchball and baseball, curses and taunts. *No!* She read English novels and played bridge and had good manners.

23

Bimbo unhooked his hand from Albert's belt. Suddenly Albert cried at him: "I can beat you at Baseball Players!" It was a shrewd move—a move from strength. Baseball Players was not a real sport, it was an intellectual game. His memory was a fine instrument, honed through endless hours of homework, in cool libraries.

"Oh yeah?" Bimbo asked.

"I'll play him," Bushy growled, shoving Bimbo aside. "I want revenge for the last time."

"Right, right, Bushy!" Albert cried. He would settle for any kind of acceptance—even Bushy's thirst for revenge. "Shoot for who goes first, Bushy?" They thrust fingers at each other. Albert won. "I got last licks," he said.

Kneeling, Albert took a stub of white chalk from the pocket of his checked linen knickerbockers. On the eternal pavement—arena, blackboard, a second home—he wrote:

	1	2	3	R
BUSHY				
ALBERT				

"Three inning game, okay?"

Bushy scowled. "Yeah, yeah."

Wildly happy, he offered the chalk to Bushy. Confidence welled in him. Baseball Players was one game at which he was unbeatable. Relentless reader of box scores, a sponge who absorbed names endlessly, he had a natural edge on the others. His memory was phenomenal; he was an ace speller. Indeed, he was surprised that Bushy had challenged him. Was it perhaps the chieftain's notion of an act of kindness—making it up to him for bringing the softball into their lives?

Bushy frowned, trying to think of a stumper. Ever his stooge, Bimbo whispered in his ear. Emboldened, Albert cried: "No coaching from the sidelines!" Bimbo spat, moved away. Some reluctant respect was due the champion.

"Here's my first," Bushy said. On the sidewalk he wrote, H----N. And added: "Phillies."

Immediately Albert knew it was Haslin. But he did not

want to humiliate Bushy. He paused, grimaced, simulated puzzlement. Picking a scab at his elbow, the champ asked tentatively, "Haslin?"

A zero was marked down for Bushy's half of the first inning. Taking the chalk, he nursed a delicious confidence. He knew he had a winner. His glance at the *New York Journal* had rewarded him with a wonderfully obscure ballplayer. The question was *when* to spring it. Delay was indicated; perhaps he could win with an easier one, and save his jewel. For his first "at bat" he offered H– – – – –D and announced: "Cleveland." After an illegal whispered huddle with Bimbo, Bushy guessed that it was Holland. The first inning was scoreless.

In the top of the second Bushy came up with a ridiculous H– –G, Yankees. At once Albert knew it was Hoag. Everyone knew Myril Hoag. He was fast, a great fielder with a great arm, the guy who went in to play when Babe Ruth got tired.

Albert came back with S– – – – –N, Reds. Bushy guessed it was Shevlin. In his last chance at bat (unless they went into extra innings) Bushy challenged him with P– – – –R, Red Sox. Of course it was Porter. Bushy was shut out.

They were in the last of the third. A run for Albert would maintain his string of victories. Casually he wrote on the hot sidewalk:

$$D\text{–}\,\text{–}\,\text{–}\,\text{–}\,\text{–}K$$

"Tigers," he said.

The leader squinted at the letters. *Odd,* Albert marveled, *the way he's got no eyes. Slits. But they see everything. The trouble is you can't look back at him, ever. And that fat face and the Brillo hair. Who'd guess he was the best fourteen-year-old athlete in the neighborhood? Why, the Raiders were such a great punchball team because of Bushy that they had to schedule games with guys like the Hawks—who were fifteen, sixteen years old.*

Albert felt guilty. It seemed wrong to engage this great competitor in a contest of wits, memory. Not that Bushy was stupid—it was simply that no man, anywhere, could beat Albert Abrams at Baseball Players.

"Wise guy," Bimbo sneered. "All ya do is read sports pages, but ya can't even hit a punchball."

"Shaddap," Bushy commanded. "I'm concentratin'."

Runs were scored when an opponent guessed wrongly. Conceivably, Bushy might guess his way out of the enigmatic D— — — — —K.

"A?" Bushy asked.

Albert gulped. "Holy smoke, maybe you got it." It would be like Bushy to claw his way out. Winning came naturally to him. Albert filled in a blank space. The name read, D— — —A–K.

Bushy smacked a fist into his palm. Once, in a rage over losing, he had torn a Spalding punchball to bits with his teeth, screaming as he ripped at the rubber.

"C," Bushy said.

Albert filled in another blank. Now the name read, D— — —ACK.

"Diblack? Dotlack? What the hell is it?" Bushy shouted. "I swear, if you make this up, I'll mopilize ya." He grabbed Albert's forearm. "Ya makin' funna me, I'll tear you apart."

"I'm not, *I'm not!*" Albert protested. "I'll show it to you in the paper!" Actually, Bushy had lost the game already. He had no right to shout out wrong guesses of the entire name; these counted as runs. But Albert raised no objection.

Bushy released him. Red welts blossomed on Albert's arm. The chief had a grip like an alligator's jaw.

"I seen it this morning," Albert cried. Bad grammar might help; everything else seemed to fail.

Bushy was beyond conciliation. Frustrated, the senseless rage in him boiled over. *"E!"* he shouted. *"E! E! E!"*

"Wrong," Albert said. Grinning, he took the chalk and marked a one under the uncompleted name, gave himself a run in the bottom of the third inning, then completed the score to show he had won the game, 1–0. "It's *Doljack*," he said.

"Doljack?" Bushy cried. "*Doljack?* I never heard of *Doljack!*"

"He made it up," Bimbo sneered.

Kibitzing the game, Little Artie shrugged. He knew very

little about baseball players. He was always being left back in school; he could barely read.

"That's right," Bushy said. "Ya made it up, just to get the better of me, dincha?"

"No, I swear I didn't!"

The leader grabbed Albert again and jerked him upward. Mad eyes glared at the undersized boy. "Ya pull that on me again, I'll make ya lick it off the sidewalk with ya tongue!" He shook Albert as if he were a kitten; the victim's head bobbled, the glasses slipped down his nose.

"I didn't pull anything, Bushy," he pleaded. "I'll show you in the paper, in the box score. Doljack pinch-hit last night for the Detroits!"

"Ya stink, ya stink," Bimbo muttered. He circled them— jackal moving around lion.

Someday, someday, Albert mused, *I shall have to fight Bimbo once and for all, get my nose bloodied, my face bruised, but I shall have to say, yes, I will fight you.* Not Bushy, of course. He would get killed if he dared lift a fist against Bushy. But Bimbo was his age, his height (even if he had ten pounds on him). The day of reckoning was not far off; he would have to accept the challenge, take his drubbing, and have it over with. Would it hurt much? He had not had a fight for over a year—with a strange boy from a different neighborhood—not really a fight, since he had been beaten mercilessly. As he recalled it the blows hurt quite a bit. One of them had closed his eye almost immediately. How awful it had been—the eye shutting without his wanting it to, leaving him a stringy Cyclops, unable to see his dancing opponent.

"I'll go getcha the sports page right *now,*" he said to Bushy. "I'll prove it to you in black and white."

"Shove it," Bimbo said. "If we don't believe ya, that's enough; right, Bushy?" Dancing in front of Albert, he ripped a "homer" on his fly, tearing open all the buttons. "Home run!" he cried.

Buttoning up, he saw clearly the way the day was going. He didn't care for it, didn't care for it at all. "If there's anything funny about that," he informed Bimbo loftily, "I fail to see it."

Bushy flew away, intercepted a peg from Big Artie, who had returned from his call on Teddy Ochab, spun around and rifled the ball to Little Artie. The monkey-faced boy tried to handle the peg, but it bounced off his chest, into the gutter—and the path of a fruit-and-vegetable truck.

"The ball, the ball!" Big Artie shouted. He raced into the street, scooped up the ball a few inches from the front wheels and sped to the opposite side. "Missed me a mile!" Big Artie cried at the cursing driver. Grateful, Albert watched him. In nine million years he wouldn't have done that. He would have let the ball get crushed. If he did try it, even money he would have gotten hit by the truck. He thanked Big Artie, picked up the groceries, and started home.

Big Artie, with a fat man's dignity, patted Albert's head. "Yer okay, Albert." Then he pointed to Bushy, who had resumed the boxball game with Bimbo and Little Artie, once more in furious combat, bulldozing, browbeating, winning. "Nuts to him and his big mouth," Big Artie whispered. "He's got loose marbles. Hymie Slabowitz, who lives over him, says Bushy's old man beats him with a stick."

Content that there was kindness in the world (Big Artie's) and a rude justice (Bushy getting whipped) he walked home carefully, avoiding the cracks in the pavement, at peace with Longview Avenue again.

The dog had burned down to a charred chunk of bone and flesh. The stink of hair lay heavy over the pyre. Grubman pronounced his benediction. "Committed to the boining ghat! You know what is a boining ghat, Abrams?"

"Sure I do, Genius. In India."

"Correct! One hundred percent for the doctor's son."

Gorilla rotated his furred inflated head. "Yeh, yeh. We boined it good."

Ah, the mystery of them! And how good not to be any of them—Grubman, Gorilla, or the baldhead Mockey.

In the sanctuary of the kitchen, he built his breakfast with the touch of a master mason. A fresh seeded roll was halved, its insides scooped out. (That was the sign of the true sandwich-maker: the courage to tear out the soft interior and make room for the genuine articles.) One half-roll he spread with Benny's creamy butter, fresh from the old oaken bucket, the other with cold chicken fat, of the consistency of axle grease. On this side he arranged lettuce and three chunks of pungent pickled lox; on the butter side, an inch-thick slab of Velveeta cheese. "To neutralize it," Albert said proudly. "Nothin' like cheese for that." The two halves joined, he admired his artistry. Then he poured a glass of cold milk, carried the bottle with him, and settled at the tiny white-enameled kitchen table for his delayed breakfast.

The New York Times, purchased by his father at the candy store, lay crisply folded on the sideboard. Albert set the paper in front of him. A slow delicious peace descended on him. It reminded him of the way he felt when he had his appendix out and they gave him pills—a warm soft pillow enveloped him, and he felt very happy, very secure. Good food, reading material had the same effect on him.

Each exquisite sensation from the mammoth sandwich was matched by the new notions, ideas, words he absorbed from the newspaper. All his life he would find the front page of a paper, any paper, one of the most exciting things in the world.

Munching noisily, alone in the moist heat (he could hear his father raking in the yard), he scanned the headlines. Later he would read the entire paper at his leisure—sports, theater, books, the obituaries. For the present, the front page would sustain him.

Hitler To Reform Storm Troops, Chief Peril to Him. Everyone talked about Hitler, about the way he was picking on the Jews. But no one really thought he'd make any serious trouble. And how could he ever get away with that kind of thing? *Never.* They'd boycott German goods, that would fix *him.* And look what happened to Spain when they started up with the Jews! Albert felt strong, determined. Jews could be tough—like Bushy Feinstein, or Zetz, or Zetz's brother, or Jimmy Kravitz when he was young. Imagine trying to pick on tough guys like that!

Hot Wave Equals 16-Day Record. Ah, the weather report, that was most gratifying. It was decent of the *Times* to write about it, because he was personally involved with the weather. He would brave that sixteen-day record to play indoor baseball outdoors, later assume his perilous duties as scorekeeper in the great punchball play-off between the Raiders and the Hawks. At night he would race the dark streets in a wild game of ringa-levio. No heat wave would stop *him.* He was Jack London, Winchester at port arms, on the lookout for murderous Kanakas somewhere in the Line Islands.

President Motors Over Puerto Rico. Mr. Roosevelt Greets Populace. That was okay with him. Everybody liked Mr. Roosevelt, just the way everybody hated Hitler. Even his father, who disliked almost everyone, had to admit FDR was pretty good, a *mensch.* It was funny, though, two years ago, when they had an election in Albert's class in P.S. 133, Roosevelt didn't win. Neither did Herbert Hoover. Norman Thomas won. He got 32 votes, and FDR got 9 and Hoover didn't get any. Right up to election date, Albert had been convinced that Norman Thomas was going to be President, and was badly let down when he didn't come close. Even Hoover beat him.

NRA Order Strikes Garment Concern . . . Lehman

Forecasts $62,000,000 Deficit . . . General Walkout in San Francisco Blocked. It seemed to Albert that there was an awful lot of trouble in the world, but it didn't bother him at all. He had a feeling everything had to work out for the best. Why, the very presence of all this information, clearly reported in the *Times,* assured him that things *had to work out!* If you wrote about all these problems enough, he reasoned, people would think about them and solve them.

Concluding his breakfast with the happy news that *Navy Flier Hops to Coast and Back for Fourth,* he folded the newspaper and returned it to the sideboard. He picked the crumbs from his plate, poured a second glass of milk, and took a worn yellow copybook and a pencil stub from his back pocket. (The pencils were purchased by his father in huge lots from the Brooklyn Jewish Guild for the Blind and they seemed to last forever; long after Albert had graduated from college and left Longview Avenue permanently, the yellow pencils kept turning up on his desk, and years later, were used by his children. His father must have bought thousands of them.)

In the copybook he wrote the date, and under it *Things To Work At.* There were, of course, more urgent problems than NRA strikes and Hitler's reform of the storm troops, and he knew exactly what they were. Under the heading he wrote:

>   Exercises to develop muscles.
>   A calm steady look when threatened.
>   Do not run away from boogies.

He then crossed out the last word he had written and substituted *colored boys.* Then he continued:

>   Not afraid to talk back to Bushy and Bimbo.
>   Ignore ordinary insults.
>   Defy Mom on roller skates.
>   Help Pop.

The phrasing of these last two entries bothered him, but since the list was for his eyes alone, he did not amend them. *Defy Mom on roller skates* sounded as if mother were on skates, which was ridiculous. And he wasn't sure what *Help Pop* meant. Would he stand on the street corner in front of the poolroom and drag people in to be his father's patients? Would he write threatening letters to the deadbeats? Would he hire a loudspeaker and go around proclaiming what a good doctor his father was, so that mobs of eager people would jam the waiting room—that quiet room, so often empty of people during office hours?

The noise of raking roused him. *Just like him,* he thought, *out there futzing around with his garden when he should be thinking up ways to make money.* You didn't catch that chiropractor who had moved in around the corner raking a garden! No, he just yanked people off the street and pounded their spine or put them on grapefruit diets.

". . . lice who throw things into other people's yards, goddamn ill-mannered galoots."

The doctor's morning curses lanced through the screen door, more painful than the hot sun. Each curse, each malediction, saddened and weakened the boy. Oh, he had no right to his day of happiness, his softball, his *Times,* his sandwiches, his friends, and his imminent adventures!

He walked out to the small wooden porch and saw his father cleaning the remains of a rotted orange crate out of his dahlia patch. To Albert and the world at large, he declaimed: "Scum of the earth, we're forced to live with! You think they understand anything? You think they show some respect for a flower?" It was a hard question to answer. The family next door were impoverished people—the man of the house a plumber without a job. They lived on relief checks; an older son sold grapes from a pushcart. Albert did not expect them to be much concerned with flowers; his father did. It seemed a failing to the boy. The old man had no right to expect *anything* from Longview Avenue.

Abruptly, the doctor's mood changed. Amid his giant blossoms, in the dark earth, shadowed by a huge cherry tree, a gnarled green apple tree, he was happy, relaxed. The black humors would vanish in the presence of green shoots, leaves, the dazzle of a dahlia. "Ah, the hell with all of them," he laughed. "Don't pay any attention to me, kiddo. Does anything else matter when I can grow beauties like *this*?" And he turned a topheavy bloom toward his son—a spiked explosion of magenta and gold. "They call this one Garden Queen. Isn't she a corker?" Somewhere his father had picked up a variety of rural expressions—*corkers* and *humdingers* often turned up in his speech. As a young man he had worked summers on Catskill farms; he liked farmers.

"It's terrific, Pop."

"Yeah, I never saw a better one at the Botanic Gardens. What do they know about growing dahlias, those professors?"

What connection professors had with the Brooklyn Botanical Gardens eluded Albert, but he had long learned to tolerate his father's irrelevancies. He had a desire to be in the garden working alongside the old man—turning the soil (once the doctor had found an Indian arrowhead for him), caressing the sprouting tubers with horse manure, gathering debris for the ritual fire. But he had no real heart for gardening. It tired and bored him.

"Can I give you a hand, Pop?"

"Nah, nah, I'm just cleaning up a little. Wow, look at that pepper bush, is that gorgeous or not?"

A tiger swallowtail, bright-yellow and black, settled on one of the white blossoms. His father studied it a moment. It stole nectar, fluttered away.

"The ball's terrific, Pop. We tried it out already."

"That's great, kiddo. Hit a home run. Be another Ty Cobb." Sweat poured down his father's forehead. Bronzed, he looked more than ever a Cherokee or a Creek, not the son of an immigrant fruit peddler from the plains of Moldavia. "When I was a kid your age I could do a hundred push-ups. It's all in the practice."

Oh, a lie, a lie, Albert knew. Sure, his father could do all those things. He still had biceps of steel. But no amount of practice, no hours of exercise would ever put muscle on his own scrawny limbs. He knew. He had tried. He had punished

33

himself into exhaustion with push-ups, waist-bends, jumping jacks, worked out with dumbbells and elastic stretchers—and no muscle, not a lemon-sized lump of strength ever bloomed on his arms or legs. It was in the genes, he realized, and he wished his father would concede that he would never, never have a muscle in his body. It was his mother's side that was to blame, Albert thought bitterly. She and her brothers were formless people— with smooth unmolded arms and legs. And that hereditary fault predominated in him. *Ah, curse the bad luck. I'm doomed, doomed.*

". . . exercise did it. Baseball's okay, but you just stand around a lot, you don't run too much. That's why when I was a kid we used to work out with the ropes, the bars, the Indian clubs, the horses. *That's* the way you develop muscles. Teddy Roosevelt had the right idea. He was a skinny shrimp like you until he started. . . ."

Sweat soaked the physician's toxic green shirt; the tie depended loosely from the collar. Did he ever learn? Albert wondered. Did he know that the *yentes* on the block, those slatterns in the grocery store, were talking about him, how bad his temper was, how he threw people out and insulted them? And he could use a haircut. Black, thick, it grew over the nape of his neck and infringed on his ears. *Some doctor, he's still on Longview Avenue.*

"I'll see you later, Pop," he said. At least that hopeless fury of the morning was not in evidence. The yard, the flowers, the bower of trees soothed him. He should have been a gardener, a forest ranger. Once the doctor had had a classmate in high school, an immigrant boy like himself, a certain Sam Newman, who had gone off to study forestry at Cornell, a dark, round-shouldered Jewish boy from the East Side. Newman became a forest ranger, and later taught forestry. His father often told the story, admiring the good sense of Sam Newman, envious of him. A splendid fantasy grew in Albert's mind. He would write a letter to Sam Newman, Forest Ranger, and find out if there was a staff doctor's job open at the forestry school. *Dear Mr. Newman, you don't know me, but I am the son of Dr. Solomon*

*Abrams with whom you attended high school on the East Side
many years ago. . . .* Briefly, he saw his father striding happily
amidst pines and spruces, inhaling sweet mountain air, smiling
at birds and butterflies, official doctor to the rangers.

His mother was cleaning the kitchen. She moved slowly in
the enervating heat. Her skin was white and smooth and always
seemed to be faintly powdered and scented, although Albert
knew it wasn't.

"Must you wear sneakers?" she asked.

"We're playing Indoor in a little while."

"You're not playing at this moment."

"I can't keep changing shoes all day."

Serene, she wiped the kitchen table, carrying his dirty
plates to the sink. "I don't know why you insist on undermining
all the good we try to do for you. We bought you arch-
supporting shoes for a very good reason, and you refuse to wear
them."

"Mom, I can't run in them. They weigh me down."

"You won't be able to run at all if you weaken your ankles
any further."

"I got to play baseball, Mom."

"I realize that. But you can get hurt very easily."

Stop reminding me, he thought. *No more, I beg of you.*
Sedately, his mother moved about the narrow kitchen, a tall
woman of excellent bearing. She had large calm features and
deep gray eyes. But she suffered from low blood pressure, low
metabolism, and mild anemia. His father was always taking
tests of her blood, her pulse, her heart, just as he was forever
stuffing vitamins into Albert's mouth. They were two of his
favorite patients.

Depressed by his weak ankles, he slouched toward the
hallway. "Albert, there is an excellent article in *The Saturday
Evening Post* on China," she called after him. "And a nice
J. P. Marquand story."

"Yeah, Mom, I'll read 'em." Mother and son were insatiable readers. She felt herself on speaking terms with men like
Marquand and Demaree Bess. She missed not an issue of the

Post, the *Ladies' Home Journal*, the *Literary Digest*. As soon as she had read them, Albert took them over. The old man never read anything except the *Journal of the American Medical Association*, nursing a special affection for Dr. Morris Fishbein's column, "Tonics and Sedatives."

The house was disconcertingly narrow. The entire lower floor save for the kitchen and hallway was consumed by his father's office—waiting room, examining room, consultation room, places redolent of iodoform, sweat, old leather. Halfway down the narrow hall, in an alcove leading to the cellar steps, was a closet, constructed by his father in 1910 when he had opened the office. It had become a dumping place for odd possessions.

Albert opened its lower compartment, rummaged amid the junk, and found his baseball glove. It was the best on the block—a genuine Chick Hafey, burnished mahogany brown with neat's-foot oil. The bat was rather scarred and the base of the handle was chipped. But his father had wound adhesive tape around the haft and it was regarded by the Raiders as the second best bat on the block. Little Artie owned the best one— a Louisville Slugger he had found in an empty lot—an ancient gray-yellow weapon, bearing the burned signature of Lefty O'Doul.

Glove hooked around his belt, bat on shoulders, ball in hand, he left the bondage of his house, his father's fury and his mother's fears, to meet his friends again. Maybe he'd get a hit today. Or make a great catch. But at least he'd get to play.

FIRST to arrive at the schoolyard, he shoved the bat and ball under the wrought-iron railings, then backed up for a running start. Teddy Ochab had taught him how to vault the treacherous iron spikes. *Boy, if his mother ever saw him doing it!* He gathered speed, thrust one foot on a crosspiece, pulled himself higher by grasping the iron rails, and leaped over the deadly points, hitting the hot pavement. The jolt rattled him from his skull to his toes, but he was pleased with the way he had managed the vault. Retrieving bat and ball, he crossed the schoolyard to the shade of the "pavilion" and squatted there.

As long as he could remember, going back to his first day in first grade at P.S. 133 (his mother had kept him out of kindergarten because of childhood illnesses), the schoolyard had fascinated him. If Longview Avenue was a stage, a movie screen on which were acted out wild dramas—dog burnings, cruel beatings—the schoolyard was gateway to a mental institution of some kind, an arena built for nuts. P.S. 133 itself was no bargain. Liver-colored bricks and stony windows suggested a corrective home for wayward girls, a prison for Army deserters. Inside it was worse. Dark secret stairways led nowhere. There were nonfunctional alcoves where "ungraded class" villains— extortionists and thieves—lurked in wait for him.

(Once a party of Zulus had seized him in an unlit cave and emptied his pockets. He couldn't have been more than eight. A

37

year later fat Dominic Esposito, a future Mafioso, had pointed a knife at his stomach and taken a nickel from him for protection.)

But if the foul hallways and staircases of P.S. 133 terrified him, he had no such feeling about its classrooms. These were second homes to him. He had them licked. There was nothing he could do wrong in them. His report cards were an unrelieved parade of A's. No teacher's pet, he sat quietly, daydreaming, knocking off 100's in arithmetic, reading, composition, anything they had to offer. If called upon, he knew the answers. If pictures were needed, he could draw wonderfully. But he kept quiet in class, finished the examinations ten minutes before anyone else, and wished he could trade all his brains to be able to hit a punchball as far as Teddy Ochab, or fight like Bushy.

As for the schoolyard, it made no sense. Its shape was puzzling—a malformed rectangle, chopped off at one end by a twisting driveway, rounded at another by the kindergarten playground, fenced-in by the high spikes he had just vaulted. It was an enormous area, but its haphazard outlines rendered it unfit for any known game except underleg-basketball-relay, jump-rope, club-snatch, or swat-the-baron. One could not even find enough uninterrupted wall space for a good handball game. There were no baselines marked off for softball ("indoor" as it was known), nothing to delineate a touch football field, not even a foul line at the slanting iron basketball backboard. Instead the hard paving had been marked with patterns of white and red lines for games nobody understood. Perhaps they were games played by boys and girls at the turn of the century. More likely they were games that never existed anywhere on earth. It was quite possible, Albert speculated, as he squatted in the pavilion shade, that the lines had been painted arbitrarily by swarthy Italian workmen just off the pickle boat, indentured laborers under the cold eye of an Irish straw-boss. "Build it as fast as yez kin, me ginny bhoyos," Albert heard him say cheerily, " 'tis only for the use of a lot of little sheenies and niggers, so let us confuse the b'Jesus out of them."

Under the pavilion he was safely camouflaged from enemies. The shed was also irregularly shaped, a shelter for rainy days, but too long and narrow to accommodate any known game. However, it was a splendid repository for urine, vomit and an occasional bowel movement. The corners of its gum-encrusted surface reeked savagely.

Yet as horrid as the schoolyard was, it intrigued Albert. It was a jungle, desert, an uncharted sea, a wild and foreign place. Sitting there, he was Paul DuChaillu, in wait for the mountain gorilla, Captain John D. Craig, telling the world *Danger Is My Business*, a Jack London sourdough, Doc Savage himself. Somewhere out there the man-eating tiger roamed, the Ogallala Sioux had dispatched war parties.

On the opposite side of the fence four colored boys had appeared. They had drifted over on bare feet, clothed in rags, shirtless, glistening like ebony statuary in the morning sun. They surveyed the schoolyard, failed to notice him, and were now flailing at one another with old clotheslines. They flew about gracefully, black ghosts in rags, as alien to him as if they were Yap Islanders. A little worm of fear nibbled at his insides. Furtively, he moved deeper into the rank pavilion, clutching the bat. The rules were clear: *Stay away from them, don't start with them, don't provoke them, travel in groups, don't ask them into your games, and stay out of theirs.* When he had begun Hebrew lessons at night at Yussel Melnick's, he had to wait until three or four boys had finished before leaving. Group travel was mandatory; a boy alone after dark was fair game for the dark ones.

Jealous, he watched them speed about—heedless of passing cars, contemptuous, full-throated, untiring. They were a party of Melanesians on a coral beach, anticipating a dinner of long pig. Did *they* ever have to do calisthenics to develop their muscles? Certainly not. Did *they* have to worry about being left out of a touch football game? Never. He wondered if anywhere in Brooklyn there were skinny, weak, scholarly colored boys who were rotten athletes. But surely, he thought, they must have *other* problems, although at the moment he couldn't think of any. Right now, he would have traded places with them, given

39

up all his books and straight-A report cards, to be able to run, shriek, fight, go shoeless, defy everyone and scream, over and over, *sheeeeeet!*

For a moment he thought he recognized one of them, a certain Lee Roy—bandy-legged, with a football-sized head, a boy the color of a Hershey bar. Some years ago, he had tried to make friends with Lee Roy in school. He had seen him weeping, offered to help him with his work, and had suffered for it. Should he greet Lee Roy? What would he say? *Hiya, Lee Roy, 'member the time I tried to teach you long division and you stole my pencil case?*

At last he saw the Raiders turn the corner. Bushy was in the lead. Little Artie, weighed under by his huge bat, followed. Teddy Ochab had come with two of his accessory brothers. Some Italian boys from a few blocks away had been enlisted. No one looked at the Negroes, who continued their mad game, slashing at each other with the ropes, screaming fearfully. Bushy led the Raiders over the high fence.

Albert jumped up and threw the ball to Big Artie who caught it with one huge hand. He was the size of a full-grown overweight man, but he was dressed like a small boy—shorts (trimmed down from old yellow linen knickerbockers), a purple polo shirt, red kerchief knotted about his neck, and a rubber band encircling his long black hair, to keep it from flopping in his eye.

"All of yez come here!" Bushy commanded. "We'll choose up."

They gathered around the leader. Fearing him, Albert had to admire him. Without Bushy the Raiders would be nothing.

Teddy Ochab was the only one in the gang who could really challenge Bushy as an athlete. But Teddy always seemed half asleep. At the moment, he was fondling Albert's softball—his first look at it—caressing it, holding it close to his bespectacled eyes, sniffing it. He was fourteen like Bushy, but small, wiry, with a flat Polack face and a mop of yellow-white hair. Teddy had excellent manners and rarely yelled; he was never cruel.

"Neat ball, Albert," he said. "It got the real *smell*." He sniffed it again, luxuriating in the fresh leather. Behind him stood his two younger brothers, Ziggie and Stanley. They were equally blond, smaller, skinnier, faster than wind. But whereas Teddy Ochab was a "good" boy who did his homework, had his heart set on high school and maybe college, went to libraries, and never talked back to grown-ups, the two younger Ochabs were regarded as uncontrollable.

Bushy seized the big bat from Little Artie. "I'll choose up with Teddy." This was the usual procedure, Teddy being the second best athlete. Bushy tossed the Louisville Slugger to Teddy, who caught it midway up. They alternated hands to the top and Teddy won. He chose Big Artie.

"Second picks, last licks," Bushy said quickly. He was not a man to let any advantage sneak by. Teddy nodded his accord, and adjusted the rimless glasses on his nose. They were banker's glasses—discreet, octagonal, not out of place on his dignified face.

Bushy chose little Artie. They kept alternating choices. Bimbo Wexler, picked by Bushy, clapped his hands to the sides of his freckled head and cried: "Oi vay, we got last picks! We'll get stuck with Four-eyes!"

Albert tried to put himself above Bimbo's taunts; he succeeded only in squinting. To his surprise, he was not chosen last. Teddy, on last pick, announced: "I got Albert." This was Teddy's way of thanking him for the softball. Bushy was left with Ziggie Ochab who was ten and a half, but a fast runner.

"We'll play pitcher, three infielders and two outfielders, okay?" Bushy asked Teddy.

"It ain't much of a game," Big Artie said.

Shading his eyes, Albert looked at the iron fence. The Negro boys were draped on the rails in baroque patterns, black ivory in a seventeenth century church, dark Laocoöns.

"Should we ask *them?*" Albert asked timidly. "I think I know one guy, he isn't too bad. Lee Roy."

"Who? Who?" Bushy cried, spinning around. "Whah?

41

The *boogies?* Ya crazy or somethin'? They'll cockalize ya!" He laughed meanly, pleased with the prospect.

"Well, we only got six a side," Albert said.

"Ya nuts? Ya nuts?" Bushy yelled at him. "Nobody ever plays with them? They *stink!*"

Bushy led his team to their positions on the irregular diamond, the wedge they somehow had managed to squeeze into the madman's playground.

Crouched low at shortstop, Bimbo pounded his glove. "Ya scared of 'em, Abrams, that's why you asked could they play! Scared they'll beat you up, so you wanna kiss ass!"

"You're full of it, too," Albie called back—a weak response, but all he could think of under stress. "That guy Lee Roy was in my *class.*"

The strategy of an undermanned team was to let the best player pitch, enabling him to cover most of the infield. Naturally Bushy Feinstein pitched. He got Teddy's team out in order. A cyclone, he was all over the infield, batting down a line drive here, stopping a grounder there, his face contorted with rage. After Little Artie had backed up to catch a towering fly hit by Big Artie, Bushy led his team to bat. Teddy's took the field.

"We'll score a million runs!" he shouted at Teddy.

Teddy Ochab ignored him. He had the deliberate mind of an intelligent Slav. At the pitcher's mound—a chalk mark on the hot cement—he pushed his banker's eyeglasses up his forehead and squinted at the far fence. "I got an idea," he said to his five teammates. "This here brand-new ball will sail right over the fence. Big Artie *tapped* it and it flew. We oughta put one guy *over* the fence. *In the street.*"

"I don't get it," Big Artie said. "That's off the field."

"No it ain't," Teddy said. "It's just over the *fence.* We got no ground rules says it ain't. Look—a second baseman c'n play deep for short flies. The other outfielder covers left-center. The guy over the fence can get a head start on a ball hit over."

Albert marveled at Teddy Ochab's savvy. He was just as shrewd as Bushy. Everyone batted right-handed, so most balls would be hit to left or left-center; right field could be lightly patrolled.

"Who wantsa play over the fence?" He surveyed his team. It was a choice between his little brother Stanley, or Albert— the weak sisters. Stanley was picking his nose dreamily; he wasn't much of an athlete. "Albert," Teddy said, "you got that big glove. You go in the street. I'll move y'around with the batters, dependin' how they hit and what I'm throwin', okay?"

Bushy's team watched Albert run to the fence, take his running leap and haul himself over the spikes.

"Watcha doin'?" Bushy shouted. "Sendin' him home?"

"Nah, nah, the Polack wants him to play outside, I get it!" Bimbo yelled. "For long flies!"

"*Illegal!*" shrieked Bushy. "Whaddya handin' me?"

Teddy sniffed the ball, cupping it in his hands. "There's no rule says he can't."

"Wise guy!" Bushy sneered. "I'll slam it over his head! Ya hear me, Abrams? I'll belt it over ya head!" He liked the notion so much he began to laugh. "He'll have to chase it into a hallway and the boogies'll get him!"

"How can he catch it anyway?" Bimbo cried. "If he runs in the gutter, his mama'll holler at him!" Bushy's team roared at Bimbo's wit. What a jerk Ochab was! Sticking the one guy who was *afraid of cars and boogies* right in the street!

The over-the-fence outfielder barely heard them. He had other worries. Hostile stares from Lee Roy and his friends disturbed him more than the teasing. Strange, how the colored boys hadn't entered Teddy's mind. He had no fear of them, and he had assumed that Albert would not fear them. Entwined around the railings like fauns and satyrs, they looked at him with liquid eyes, eyes like sea organisms preserved in yellowing formaldehyde. He pounded the pocket of his Chick Hafey glove, hitched his belt, adjusted his eyeglasses, flexed his knees, and crouched low, ready for anything. And still they stared and still he wondered: *What have they got against me? What did I ever do to them?*

Through the morning haze he could see Teddy throwing warm-up pitches. Little Artie was swinging both bats at the plate. *Look tough, calm.* He spat, straightened up, bent over. Lee Roy whispered something to a tall boy the color of mahogany, a boy with a bullet-shaped head. Two odd tufts grew out of his forehead.

"Hi there, Lee Roy," Albert called. "Aren't you Lee Roy Pennington who was once in 4-B with me?"

The football-shaped head rotated slowly. "I ain' no Lee Roy," thick lips muttered. He nudged the tall boy. "You know Lee Roy, Madison?"

"Ain't nobody *nowhere* named Lee Roy." Some dark voodoo knowledge was shared. Something Albert could never understand. Two other boys—smaller than Lee Roy and his friend—giggled.

But of course it was Lee Roy. *Why won't he admit I tried to make friends with him one day in Four-B?* Maybe he was ashamed of the whole thing and wanted to forget it. Albert remembered finding Lee Roy at recess, sitting alone, wearing a pair of oversized shorts held up by unraveling suspenders, crying silently. Through some clerical error, Lee Roy had been placed in the smartest class in the fourth grade, the 4-B-1. The "1" signified the brightest children (Albert had always been in a "1" class). From the first day Lee Roy had been lost. He could barely read or write. Through bureaucratic delay, his transfer to the "ungraded class" had never come about. So he had lingered in Miss Shapiro's room, surrounded by brilliant Jewish boys and girls, slumped in his seat, his eyes like two spoiled eggs, his huge lips depending from his football-shaped head in dumb sorrow.

Albert had come upon him weeping and asked him what was wrong. "Cain't do none o' dis *sheeet*," Lee Roy had sniffled. " 'Rithmetic?" Albert asked, looking at the filthy dog-eared notebook in Lee Roy's lap. "None of hit, cain't do *none* of hit." So he had patiently sat down next to Lee Roy Pennington and tried to teach him long division. He had failed. Lee Roy was in no mood to learn long division or anything else. He kept crying noiselessly, his eyes getting bigger, wetter. Close by he smelled fearfully, but Albert stuck it out. "Donchoo come bother me no more," Lee Roy had murmured when the bell sounded. An hour later, Albert discovered that his beautiful pencil box, a gift from his father, a treasure chest of colored pencils, erasers, a compass, protractor, ruler, all sorts of cunning accessories, had been stolen. He couldn't prove Lee Roy had swiped it, but who else could have? He remembered going for a drink of water. Lee Roy had probably helped himself then.

Teddy Ochab waved Albert to his right, pitched to Little Artie, and Little Artie popped up to the second baseman, a tranquil boy named Frankie Udo.

Bimbo smashed a line drive through the gap between second and third base. Albert realized that Teddy's strategy was not foolproof. By moving the second baseman into the outfield, the holes in the infield had been enlarged. The next batter hit a hard grounder off Teddy's shins and beat the throw to Big Artie at first base. There were two men on and Bushy was up.

Teddy was waving at him to move deeper into the gutter and to his right. He would pitch Bushy high and hope he'd loft one into Albert's big glove—if it didn't sail right by him, over him, or bounce away. Suddenly Albert's heart was thumping against his chest. Why was he always like this when the chips were down? Why couldn't he be cool, tough, steady, like Bushy or Teddy? At the edge of the curb Lee Roy and his pals were goggling him, as if he were a freak. They had disengaged their limbs from the fence and were facing him.

"Dat him?" he heard the bullet-headed boy ask.

Lee Roy responded: "Yeah. Dat him."

Holy smoke, Albert shuddered, *don't I have enough trouble trying to play center-field, without these threats?* As the only twelve-year-old boy on Longview Avenue, perhaps in all of Brooklyn, who knew about the Zulu wars, Chaka, and Rorke's Drift, he had a right to be scared.

Pondering this, he was a second late in reacting to the hard crack of the bat against the softball. He saw Bushy fling the bat and race for first base. The other runners also took off. "*Homer! Homer!*" he heard Little Artie yelling. High, high, rose the white ball, gleaming in morning sunlight. It was the center of the world, the only thing that mattered anywhere. It ascended into the hot blue sky, in a perfect arc (Albert wondering what equation would describe its trajectory), and then started a

45

graceful descent, waxing bigger, approaching, inexorable—but *beyond him, beyond his reach!* He turned his back and ran into the gutter, heedless of cars, Lee Roy, his mother, hearing Teddy and his other teammates screaming: *"Back! Back!"*

With nothing else to do, he ran. He ran hopelessly, keeping one eye on the descending white ball, his gloved hand out, appalled that the runners had raced off. They were convinced he'd never catch it. By now he had crossed the street, stumbled on the opposite curb. The softball expanded, inflated—it was as big as a basketball. Desperately he threw out the Chick Hafey glove, heard the conclusive *splat!,* and knew that the ball had stuck in the webbing.

In triumph he collapsed against an ashcan. Tumbling, he gripped the ball. *Out! Out! I got the great Bushy Feinstein out!*

Stanley Ochab was at the fence, screaming at him: *"T'row it, t'row it, dey're taggin' up!"*

The runners were scrambling back. They would try to advance. Albert was certain he could double someone off. He got up and cocked his arm for the relay to Stanley. They swarmed over him.

Gently, Lee Roy and his friends coiled about him. With no effort, the ball was detached from his raised arm. The glove slithered off his left hand. Laughter oozed about him like oil. Lee Roy shoved him to the pavement, stepped over him as if he were a crate. In a blur of flashing teeth, glistening black domes and churning limbs, he led his guerrillas down the street.

Albert sat up. He was unhurt but terrified. Oh, his softball, his softball! A dollar twenty-nine cents worth of his father's love—from his old man, who climbed four flights of stairs for two-dollar fees!

He started to trot after the thieves—they were still in sight—then stopped. They were faster, smarter, tougher. He would be engulfed, drubbed. Lee Roy had legions uncommitted—older and meaner boys, knife-wielders, shooters.

The Raiders were also frozen into inaction. Bushy, his mind fixed only on the game, was shrieking at his players to tag up and advance. He barely noticed Albert's martyrdom.

"*Boogies! Boogies!*" Little Artie screamed. "*They got the ball!*"

"The ball! The ball!" Stanley Ochab shouted.

Across the playground raced Teddy. His courage was legendary—or was it the dumbness of a hardheaded Polack? (In regulation hard baseball, Teddy was the only man willing to catch—*without* a mask or chest protector, wearing his prim eyeglasses!) Scrawny legs pumping, he leaped over the fence and raced after the thieves. No one, no one in the world could interfere with *his* softball game, could dare steal *his* friend's softball.

"C'mon, Albert, let's get 'em!" Teddy cried.

Teddy's courage infected him. He was a Marine at Belleau Wood responding to the sergeant's challenge: *C'mon, you guys, yon wanna live forever?* For there was no doubt in his mind, as he ran breathlessly after Teddy, that he would be killed, at least maimed for life. How, he wondered, does a knife in the ribs feel?

Lee Roy and his associates had run halfway down the street and then, contemptuously, started a game of catch. They could have hidden, escaped—but they had stopped in front of the open yard of the roofer, Kalotkin. Albert understood them—it was the ultimate in defiance. *We can steal your ball and play with it under your nose, and you won't dare take it back from us.*

"Give us the ball!" Teddy shouted—and plunged into their dark ranks. He leaped for the softball as it sailed from Lee Roy to the bullet-headed boy.

Albert was looking at glory, at something he could never do. Not even Bushy, the loudmouthed tyrant, not even the awesome Zetz, who had fought in the Golden Gloves, would throw himself into such a trap. But all he could do was watch; he was paralyzed.

"Sheeet, man, yo' want the ball, we make you work fo' it," Lee Roy laughed. He threw it to one of the smaller boys.

"It ain't your ball," Teddy said. "Give it here."

"Yo' come git it," Lee Roy mocked.

Teddy threw himself on a small boy, who rolled the ball

away to Lee Roy. "Yo' don't tech me, heah?" the child said. "Dis heah boy *private* prop'ty."

Roofer Kalotkin, a hairy mammoth, plodded out of his yard. "What the hell's alla noise about?"

"They stole my ball!" Albert wailed.

"Stay away from *schwarzers*," Kalotkin advised. But he too was afraid. They would come back at night and wreck his yard. It was unfair, unfair, that in the whole world only Teddy Ochab would stand up to them. Albert gulped, hitched his belt, and ran into the street. If no one would help Teddy, he would. Lee Roy was wearing his glove.

"Attaboy, Albert," Teddy said. "You take half the street, I'll take half." He squinted at Lee Roy through his eyeglasses. "Okay, wise guy, I double dare ya to t'row it now."

Lee Roy giggled.

"I'll *kill* ya, ya don't give it to me," Teddy said carefully. "I mean it, Lee Roy."

Once more the ball was tossed—high, but not high enough, from a small boy to Lee Roy. Teddy soared, more Greek than Pole in the sunlight, tipped the edge of the softball with his fingers. As it changed course, Lee Roy raced forward on bandy legs. He and Teddy both reached for the ball. Teddy tapped it again—toward Albert—and landed on top of Lee Roy.

"Grab it and run!" Teddy cried. "I'll beat the hell outa Lee Roy!" He started to pummel the Negro, accepting some hard knocks and kicks in return.

Albert scooped up the ball. Strangely, the other three robbers let him do so. They had tired of the sport and Lee Roy needed their help. Fear jellied Albert's legs. His stomach turned to ice. But he gripped the ball and raced for the corner. Bushy and Big Artie were running toward him. Feet pattered alongside him. The smallest of Lee Roy's gang, a miniature black, was jogging insolently beside him, grinning, clawing at the ball.

"Ah cut yo' ass," he giggled.

Albert cursed his weak ankles, his underdeveloped calf muscles. He was churning, puffing, yet he hardly moved; the colored boy was trotting and was abreast of him.

48

"You-you-you better watch it," Albert gasped. "There's my gang—"

"Dey *sheeet* too," the mite said. Spying Big Artie and Bushy, the tot vanished into an alley.

Teddy Ochab was fighting the three remaining thieves. It didn't bother him. It was his assignment and he accepted it, just as he was known to take Emily Post's *Etiquette* from the library and practice good manners on his dopey brothers.

At first he had gotten the best of Lee Roy, bloodying the flat nose, hitting him hard in the gut. At that point the other two had jumped on him, and all four now rolled about the gutter filth. Finally, Kalotkin and his neighbor Dinowitz, the locksmith, intervened. The adults unglued arms, legs and heads.

"Lemme go, lemme go, I gon' *keel heem*," Lee Roy screamed. Blood gushed from his offended nose.

"Whattsamatta wit' you kids?" Kalotkin preached. "Aincha got what else to do besides tryina kill each other?" He had Teddy Ochab in a bear hug.

"We gon' ketch you by you'sef," Lee Roy warned. "We gon' kick yo' haid in."

"I'll fight yez all right now," Teddy said. "One at a time or all at oncet."

"Fight, fight, is that all you kids think about?" Kalotkin cried. "Go home and read a book, take a piece of paper and a pencil, you should make something outa yourselves, awready. Jesus, I never seen worse kids. G'wan beat it, you three guys, you ain't from this neighborhood. You too, Polack."

"We be back," Lee Roy said. He ran his brown arm against his leaking nose. Blood left an oily streak on the chocolate skin. Then they vanished.

"Lousy kids!" the roofer shouted. "Lousy boogies!"

"Nothing helps wit dem," Dinowitz said sorrowfully.

Teddy adjusted the rimless glasses on his nose (throughout the battle royal they had remained there, inviolate), picked up Albert's mitt, and jogged off.

"That Polack," the roofer said wonderingly, "some guts he's got to take on a gang of boogies."

"Whaddya expect from a Polack?" asked the locksmith. "They got no brains."

Albert watched his black pursuer disappear down an alley. Then he stumbled into Big Artie's arms and gave him the rescued ball. "Ted-Ted-Teddy got it," he gasped. "He-he-he's fightin' all of them—Lee Roy—and the other guys—"

"Holy smoke, lemme see the ball!" Bushy shouted. He grabbed it from Big Artie and began examining it. "I wanna make sure none of the black rubbed off on it."

"Ray, Teddy! Ray, Teddy!" shouted Little Artie. "Here he comes!"

Applauding, whistling, they welcomed Ochab. Running on toothpick legs, he approached them, waving Albert's glove. He was unmarked, but his shirt was torn. His mother, a hard-fisted farm woman, would beat him when he got home; but he had conquered. Albert looked at him, wondering: How brave could anyone be? And why this bespectacled, white-haired Polack? *And see the great Achilles whom we knew.*

"Ya give him his lumps?" Bushy asked.

"I give him a bloody nose," Teddy said. "He stinks. He can't fight."

"Your friend Lee Roy," Bushy said to Albert. "Your great friend."

"Yeah, you were gonna ask him to play!" Bimbo added. "What a great idea! Your buddy Lee Roy!"

"Ah, lay off," Teddy said. He adjusted his eyeglasses and gave Albert the glove.

Was there no justice anywhere in the world? Albert asked himself. Only *he* had run to assist Teddy; now, for reasons that eluded him, Bushy and Bimbo were tormenting him again. He should have been praised, lauded, cheered, the way they cheered Teddy when he returned from battle. In their guilt they had seized the initiative, making him suffer for having once known wicked Lee Roy.

Once more Albert got set in the outfield—alert, ready for anything, with the Chick Hafey glove on his left hand. He could catch *anything*. He would run forever and catch them over his

50

shoulder, off his shoelaces. He was Len Koenecke, Tris Speaker.

Professionally, he spit, backed into the street, pounded the mitt. Down the street, he saw his father approaching, walking in swift short steps—a man walking impatiently, but with a certain reluctance.

"Hey, kiddo," his father called. "Is that a way to play baseball? In the middle of the gutter?"

"I'm the center-fielder."

"Well, don't let your mother catch you there. Look out for cars. Better you should miss a ball than end up in the hospital."

"Holy smoke, does he have to?" Albert asked himself in a whisper. He watched his father's hard figure (the green shirt stained with sweat) turn into a shabby gray tenement. The ground floor displayed a scarred gold-on-black sign:

YUSSEL MELNICK
Hebrew Teacher

"Leviathan," Dr. Abrams said. "Pay a dime and see the whale." Years ago, he had taken Albert to Coney Island to see a dead sperm whale, displayed under a glass canopy on Surf Avenue. It had smelled almost as bad as the teacher.

What was one to make of Yussel Melnick? How had he survived? It seemed to the doctor that people like Melnick were nothing more than fodder for Cossacks, born pogrom victims. So fat, so old, so totally unequipped to confront the world. He was a vestige. A monument. Like finding a great auk or a hairy mammoth. He was surely something for archaeologists to ponder. He admired Melnick's library—holy texts, Talmudic marginalia, commentaries, Rashi, Maimonides, who knew what else? Wisdom cooking inside the moldy covers. Was God or at least God's Word really in those flaking volumes? Melnick must have believed it. How else could he have *shlepped* those books all the way across Europe, from *shtetl*, to *shtetl*, out of the Ukraine or Moldavia or wherever it was, all the way to some forgotten port, past mocking port officials, to Ellis Island's snide

51

customs guards, to the East Side, and now to a Brooklyn slum. Melnick, keeper of the words.

"They didn't get here in an airplane," Dr. Abrams said to himself.

There was a mystery surrounding the ancient. He was slightly insane, a *meshugeneh* given to irrational outbursts. His numbskulled students regarded him with fear, awe, wonderment, but never contempt. He was a nut, but *their* nut. Larger than life, he loomed over them in the shabby schoolroom of the Talmud Torah, beating ancient lore into minds crammed with batting averages.

For Dr. Abrams, a call on Yussel Melnick was the nearest he came to attending synagogue. The physician was an irreligious and irreverent man. Deviously, he ate oysters and clams whenever he had a call to Sheepshead Bay or Coney Island. With gleeful defiance, he munched bacon and ham at his own dining table, much to the annoyance of his wife, who although as careless of kosher prohibitions as her husband, regarded his whooping at each mouthful of Armour's pork products as an act of guilt. She was partially correct. And indeed, his visits to Melnick, while always professional, were in part redemptive. He felt somewhat holier, a little closer to some unfathomable mystery, some ancient historical evidence, after his ministrations to the legendary sage.

The doctor and the *melamed* would converse in high-blown theatrical Yiddish. They gestured: if Melnick stroked his beard, Dr. Abrams assumed a Talmudic pose, fingers pensively crossed on his iron chest. Although the doctor's Yiddish was good (his English was unaccented and, in truth, he preferred Thoreau to the Talmud), he could not match Melnick's airy phrasing. Moreover, Melnick had the voice to go with the language—a rumbling basso, a terror to thick-heads reading woodenly for their bar-mitzvah.

When Dr. Abrams entered the dark corridor leading to Melnick's meager apartment, he was assailed by a salad of foul old kitchen odors. The stench was laminated, layered, a mélange of bad aromas. Long widowed, Melnick had no wife to

52

clean for him, no children. Occasionally a neighborhood wife would volunteer to sweep and dust. The floor protested against the doctor's hard step. From the rear of the flat came the shudderings of the teacher's mighty snores. In the small bedroom, the scholar snorted beneath a ragged quilt, his gut rising and falling, his sour breath fluttering his beard.

"I know you're there. You came in with the step of a jailer."

"How do jailers walk?" asked Dr. Abrams.

"Softly, yet loud enough to warn of their arrival." One hand groped for his spectacles on a bed table. He adjusted them on his snubbed nose; a nose worn down through years of shoving it into books, the doctor thought. Melnick's eyes opened a fraction—an old land tortoise on the alert. The doctor felt like Thoreau spying on wildlife. "Why did you not awaken me?" the teacher asked peevishly.

"You looked like you were enjoying a dream."

"I stopped dreaming many years ago. Dreams are for children."

"That's not what Freud says."

"Feh. Even though he is Jewish."

"A lot of intelligent Jews, Reb Yussel, are not in agreement with your view of life. Look at Trotsky."

"On him, feh also. What kind of a Jew made himself a general of an army, hah? And went hunting and fishing when he was in the prison camp, instead of praying?"

Dr. Abrams frowned: irrefutable logic, of a sort. "That's to his credit. It helped him survive."

"Hah! Trotsky a general, a war commissar, yet. He must have had a double, some goy who did the work."

The doctor mulled this over—a good point at that, considering the unlikelihood of any Jew, Trotsky or Freud, ever commanding troops—and fished for his stethoscope. "Yes, I bet you were having a wonderful dream, dancing with Clara Bow." (Dr. Abrams always ran several years late on athletes, movie stars and politicians. His idea of a baseball player was Christy Mathewson, of a statesman, William Jennings Bryan.)

"Too old for your jokes. And what else you are talking about."

Albert's father helped Melnick into a sitting position. Propped against goosedown pillows he reminded the doctor of the Jewish King Lear as played by Jacob Adler or perhaps Boris Thomashefsky. A high black yarmulke, like a bishop's miter, crowned Melnick's ruined head. Beard and hair, unkempt, curling, radiated from his skull and his cheeks, giving him the look of a benign Medusa. Ancient texts and notebooks filled with his scrawlings in Hebrew script littered the filthy bedclothes.

"Homework?" asked the doctor.

"I always work. What else do I have to do?"

Dr. Abrams felt the teacher's pulse. "You mean you haven't learned everything yet?" Blood still pumped, the heart did its rhythmic work. How old was he? Past ninety? No one knew. A racial memory stirred the doctor. A miserable village of wood huts, a street paved with jagged stones, creaking carts and horse troughs, a smell of manure and axle grease.

The stethoscope imparted its message to the doctor's ears. *Something keeps him going.*

"Who said you're sick?" asked Dr. Abrams. "All you need is a little air. Open the window; a man could suffocate in here."

July heat flooded the room as the doctor slammed the window aloft. The ammoniated stink of an army of cats rose from the vile backyard. Piles of garbage greeted his critical eye. "Lice, vermin," the doctor said in English. "What the hell do they know about sanitation. Some place for a scholar."

"To tell the truth, I feel weak today," Melnick wheezed. "I called you you should give me a medicine to make me strong enough to go to the synagogue later today."

"No. You stay here and rest. The galoots can miss a day."

"Not the students, curse them. More important."

Where could he begin with Melnick? Everything imaginable was wrong with him—kidneys, lungs, feet, back. But he dutifully wrote a prescription—magic scrawlings, cabala. Melnick fell asleep. The doctor assembled his stethoscope, the sphygmomanometer, packed his satchel. The old man could owe him for the visit. What did his dollar matter in a day that might not bring him five dollars? *I'll go broke, but I'll have his blessing,* thought Dr. Abrams.

He was at the door when Melnick spoke again. "Oi, they beat me."

Dr. Abrams turned. "Who? Where? If you start that mumbling again you'd better explain it this time."

"Yes, it hurts."

Melnick was reputed to be mad; he had bouts of incoherence, moments of mumbling, disconcerting "fits."

"What a disgrace!" Melnick boomed. "Me, a lineal descendant of the Gaon of Kishinev, to run through the streets in my *gotkes* and get beaten with sticks!"

"I believe you," the doctor said. "But it's medically impossible for you to still hurt sixty years later."

"But it hurts," the *melamed* persisted. "Here." He tried to find some part of his back with his hand and gave up.

"I gave you something for your pain," the doctor said.

"As a matter of fact, it stopped now, where they beat me. In the street. All the *goyim.*" Melnick pointed a finger at his physician. "Abrams, do I have a low high-blood-pressure?"

To Dr. Abrams' patients, all blood pressure was high-blood-pressure. One had either high-blood-pressure or a low high-blood-pressure.

"You have an average, a middle high-blood-pressure, is that good enough?"

"Thanks God, something to be grateful for, as I approach the Angel of Death." Melnick fumbled in a small leather purse and extracted a creased dollar bill, stained, secreted, a museum piece. He gave the fee to the doctor and grasped the physician's hand warmly, wetly, as if seeking to draw life from his vigorous friend.

"How did a Jew get such muscles?" marveled Melnick.

"The same way Trotsky became a general."

Collapsed again on his pillowed throne, Melnick assumed a regal air. He looked livelier, more vigorous—Maimonides at the Moorish court, dispenser of wisdom.

"This afternoon I am going to make a parade."

"Oh yeah? Who are you, Pershing?"

"There is a new Torah to be welcomed. I must march through the streets with it, to proclaim its glory. When a Torah comes, there is a great *simchah*."

"I forbid you to go parading around in this weather, or any kind of weather. You're not Jack Dempsey." As usual, the doctor was a few years late: Max Baer would have been more apt.

"It was I who forced those donkeys at the *schul* to buy it, I who shamed them into it, Reb Yussel Ben David Melnick, descendant of the Gaon. It is a work of art, joy, wit, learning. Made in Eretz Israel."

"I believe everything you've said. You still can't go strolling around in that sun. Before your back was killing you. Where they beat you. Remember?"

"Gone! Gone like the wicked priests! We will parade!"

Dr. Abrams shook his head: he envisioned trumpets blaring, Old Glory flying high, Black Jack Pershing on a high-strutting horse, as they marched down Longview Avenue to the "Stars and Stripes Forever." Melnick in an armored car, the Torah born aloft by the men of the Yankee Division. Children would wave small paper flags. Orange ones? With lions on them and a candle at one end? Didn't Albert bring them home from Hebrew school years ago? What holiday? He dismissed a twinge of guilt. Who could remember all of that stuff with all those new pharmaceuticals and new literature, and this *fekokteh* depression, when a man couldn't earn a living?

"You'll get sunstroke in that heat. Worse."

"No. Not if God wants me to march. Just a little parade. Around the block, to show the scrolls to the heathen, the believers and the fallen sheep."

"Ah, you're impossible."

"Listen, Abrams, old friend. I don't have much time. I'm not especially anxious to be introduced to the Angel of Death, but I'm not shivering in my shoes over him. I could tell him a few things. So I'll honor the Torah, sun, heat, dirt, who cares?"

"Well, you're old enough to make up your own mind. And

old enough to be a damn fool." He picked up his black satchel again. "Remember, if you fall flat on your face in the gutter, don't blame me."

Melnick shoved his steel-rimmed spectacles on to his forehead. His reptilian eyes squinted at the doctor. "You I would never blame, Abrams. You are one of us."

"Me? I'm practically a goy."

"No, no. We understand. We *see*."

Albert's father shrugged. Enough of these cryptic Talmudic comments. He was flattered, but slightly irritated. Leaving, he heard the teacher's bass rumble following him: "In fact I feel so happy about the new Torah, that soon I might even let you see my work, it's almost finished now. . . ."

Work? What work? Melnick's meanderings bothered him. He had his own *tsuris*. Descending the stairs, he skidded clumsily on discarded peapods, caught his balance, and rested on the bannister. "Goddamn punks! Filthy lice!" he shouted. Plummeting down the stairwell came a soggy bag. Dr. Abrams heard it explode below, scattering its eggshells and orange rinds. "Lousy dirty scum! When the hell will they learn simple cleanliness?" His protest was unheard, unanswered. Yussel Melnick would live out his days amid potato parings and old sardine tins.

The street shimmered in the heat. Through the dark doorway it was a yellow, glaring rectangle standing on end. Outside, in and out of the frame, Negro children, shoeless, shirtless, raced about. Their blood boiled with energy. Melnick's Nubian retainers. Didn't King Solomon have colored servants? Hagar's dusky children, they shrieked vengeance on a world that had no use for them. *Wait, wait, they'll want to murder us all in our beds someday*, the doctor thought, *and who can blame them?*

Outside the schoolyard he saw his only begotten son, his flesh and blood, playing baseball. A sense of continuity, of things going on, remembered, honored, buoyed him. Was there some thread from Melnick—before Melnick—to himself, to Albert? Melnick was giving them something. An idea. A code.

Maybe not even that much. Maybe only a tradition, a mystique. What was it? Courage? He said he was not afraid of the Angel of Death. Dr. Abrams, stepping down to the steaming sidewalk, recalled the Passover song about the butcher who got paid off by the Angel of Death. But Melnick was no coarse butcher. "He's got something that keeps him going," he told himself, and walked toward another tenement. Five more flights, another dirty flat, a dollar in payment.

❝IT ain't balls and strikes," Teddy Ochab said patiently. "You coulda stood there all day and hit a good one, Albert."

Humiliated, he had struck out with men on second and third.

"I'm sorry," Albert said. "It's the way Bushy hollers at me when he pitches. Isn't that illegal? I never heard of a pitcher shouting when he throws."

The unbeatable Bushy had circled his arms in an exaggerated windup, thrown the ball from under his right leg and shrieked: *"Swing! Swing!"* Albert, forever the sucker, swung. And missed by a mile.

"Some athalete," Bimbo said. "Couldn't hit a basketball wit' a broomstick."

Disgrace was total. All had forgotten his pursuit of the thieves, his assistance to Teddy. *Unfair, unfair,* he thought. Was he never to get ahead? Status forever eluded him. He was eternally done in, betrayed by weak ankles, a faint heart, and a fierce intellect, not to mention "rich" parents. One day he would give up altogether, surrender, become a sidewalk intellectual like Grubman, parading up and down and reciting poetry.

Teddy Ochab, bat in hand, paraded down his rank of half-sleeping ballplayers. "C'mon, waken up there. Who's up?"

No one was sure.

"I'll fine yez all," Teddy said. "You guys stink, yer weakalings."

Egg exploded on Teddy's forehead and dripped on his prim eyeglasses. Amazing, Albert thought, how awful it stank the second it smashed on Teddy's head. Bushy, with an instinct for other people's disasters, danced at the pitcher's mark. "A hit, a hit! Someone hit him wit' a rotten egg!"

They left their positions in the field. Teddy's sleepy players got up. Another egg splattered at Albert. Gelatinous goo stained his sneakers.

"Up there! *Up there on the roof!*" screamed Little Artie.

Arrayed against the blue sky were eight or nine black heads—Lee Roy and his mobile reserve. They were older and bigger, brawny galoots, grinning, laughing, hurling rotten eggs with savage glee. One smashed on Big Artie's chest; it smelled fearfully. Another, dropped vertically, found a target on Frankie Udo's head.

"*Dis is war, man!*" screamed one of the big boys. "We keel you all *daid!*"

The Raiders retreated out of range. Only Teddy stood his ground. "C'mon down and I'll fight yez all!" he shouted. He had taken off his glasses and was wiping them on a handkerchief.

"You *sheeet*, man; we gon' keel you!" Lee Roy cackled.

Another barrage came from the roof. Their ammunition was varied. This time the eggs were accompanied by stale bagels—stolen from a bakery. One of them bounced off Teddy's head. It made a noise like a rock. He too retired to the edge of the fence, out of bombing range.

"Yah, yah!" screamed Lee Roy. "I tole you I git back at you! Zero in on dat enemy and blast 'em!"

High-arching mortar shots descended on the Raiders. But at a distance, they could dodge.

"Lousy boogie bastards," Bushy muttered. "I'll murder them! *Murder* them!" But he made no attempt to lead a foray against the war party.

"It's no use," Big Artie said plaintively. He was daintily holding his stinking shirt away from his chest. "We're outnumbered. They'd mopilize us. We couldn't have a chancet against those big guys."

"Let's charge 'em," Teddy said. He looked at the Raiders. No one moved. No one wanted to second his foolhardy courage.

"Big Artie's right, Teddy," Albert reasoned. "They'd murder us." Nothing could be gained in prolonging the battle. They had *their* rules, the Raiders had others. All you could do was avoid them, stay away, don't talk, don't get involved, make believe they weren't there, didn't exist, didn't bother you. They ran no risks, had no homes, no parents to answer to, no studies to be done, no goals to go after, no teachers to respect. Wild, free, they roamed the streets, and to hell with everything.

"We gon' come after you!" one of the biggest boys yelled. "We gon' git dat Polack *sheeet!*"

Teddy ran for the pavilion. Nothing could stop him—not death, nor maiming, nor humiliation. Bushy and Little Artie raced after him and grabbed his arms. "Don't, don't, Teddy, they'll mopilize ya, don't start with them," Bushy pleaded.

"The big guy up there," Little Artie said. "He's got a knife! He's the guy stuck up a pushcart last week."

He pointed to a great black pole of a boy, dancing, grinning, inviting Teddy to his doom. "Let him go, let him go!" the Negro called. "Ah fix *him*, Polack *sheeet!*"

They ran back to the fence. Albert, halfway over, his feet resting in the crossbar, looked at the dark invaders who had ended their softball game. It appeared (and he hoped he was wrong) that they were staring at *him*, at him *alone*, that despite the threats to Teddy, *he* was the real target.

Was it his imagination, or did he hear the tall boy, the one reputed to carry a knife, inquire of Lee Roy: "*Dat* deh one?"

Did Lee Roy's dark arm point at him, and did he hear Lee Roy say: "Yeah *dat* deh one."

There were endless levels of terror and this was surely one of the highest.

Women's voices drifted out of the living room when he got home. He was exhausted after the softball game and the defeat at the hands of the Negroes. Tiptoeing, he slithered carefully through the corridor to avoid meeting anyone, or having to explain his egg-splattered sneakers.

His mother always had female guests visiting, particularly in the summer. They were usually relatives—close, distant, obscure. Albert had no objection to them, but he was just as happy to be left out of these vague associations. For one thing, the conversations were all about *other* relatives, people who meant nothing to him. He could hear his mother's well-modulated voice. "Of course, that was Anna Bakofsky, and we were girls together on the East Side, she and her sister, the one who is a history professor now at NYU, a really brilliant girl. . . ."

No, he didn't want to be involved in any of *that*, with female relatives munching fruit and candy in the living room, leaning on his mother for a little sustenance and cheer. He had his own worries. The morning's disasters demanded solitude and reflection. Errors, omissions, failings, would have to be turned to profit. Women were of no help in these straits. They gave you nothing that armed you for the world of Bushy and Lee Roy. What did they know about the ordeals he faced every day? Could they tell him how to dodge a rotten egg? A stale bagel had bounced off his elbow during the encounter; the elbow had turned blue-black and it throbbed.

62

Although lunch was a half-hour away (he was sure that the guests had come for lunch as well as conversation) he sneaked two apples, a banana and a pear from the kitchen, arranged them neatly on his bed table, polished his eyeglasses on his yellow polo shirt, and took a library edition of *Michael Brother of Jerry* from his dresser.

But the mirror on the dresser delayed him. Study of his own image was always pleasurable, even though the final estimate was disappointing.

"My head is top-heavy," he said solemnly. It was. His dark brown hair grew thick and wiry, like his father's before it began to thin out and resemble an Indian's roach. "Big forehead, lots of brains," Albert said, "but the rest of the face is too small." Under the high brow, his eyes were mangled by powerful lenses; his nose was snubbed, his mouth well-formed but short. The ears stuck out too far, probably as a result of his father grabbing them in those fits of joy that seized him whenever he saw his beloved son.

But if the face were less than he wished it to be, the body was a total loss. Narrow-chested, thin-limbed, it would never be the physique of a Jack London hero.

The genes have eluded me, the good ones, anyway. His father was all muscle, great lumps of biceps and deltoids and hamstrings, a naturally powerful man, born tough and hard. Not a day's exercise had ever been needed to give him strength, while he, *shlemiel*, could swing clubs and do push-ups forever and still be formless and feeble. "Look at that arm, just *look* at it," he said to his mirror image. "It has no shape whatsoever, it is merely an arm." He held it aloft—no muscle bumps, an arm as straight and smooth as a pink snake. "Why don't you just give up?" he continued. "It's beyond belief. Twelve and a half years old, and underweight and I'm getting a potbelly *already*." Lifting his polo shirt he thrust out his apple-sized gut. "A paunch before my bar mitzvah."

Morose, he settled on his bed with *Michael Brother of Jerry*. For a few seconds he caressed the bloody maroon binding (solid morocco leather back, marbled pasteboard sides). Books, the mere feel and sight of books, gratified him. The gilt lettering on the cover, the well-rubbed yellow-gray pages, the bugle notes of the title page, the orderly chapter headings, the finality of the last page—all these assured him of something sensible in the world. A book, any book, had a completeness, a solidity. He envied the men who did the binding for the New York Public Library. How good to spend one's life dressing books in severe covers of maroon, dark blue, apple-green, muddy brown! Good dependable colors, for good dependable books! They rarely let him down. There were times, of a winter's night, at rest on his green chenille bedcover with a novel, after a long day of school, snowball fights, homework, disappointments, minor triumphs, his father's rantings and his mother's cautionings, that he was convinced he was possibly the happiest person in the world. At times like this, trimming the skeletal core of his fourth McIntosh apple with expert teeth, lost in Klondike gold hunts and South Sea chases, he craved a magical power to transmit his joy to his parents. They could never love Jack London the way he did; not his mother with all her *Saturday Evening Posts* or his father with all his AMA *Journals*. Oh, you could get a few laughs out of Morris Fishbein's "Tonics and Sedatives," and there was nothing wrong with a Mr. Moto story or Hercule Poirot, but magazines weren't books; they didn't last; they didn't have the heft and the feel that delighted him.

Librarians were astounded by him. Some thought him a faker. "You could not possibly have read those two Kipling novels in two days," one gray-haired lady said to him. She was one of the last of Brooklyn's good-hearted Protestants, always trying to recommend worthwhile books to slum children. "I think, Abrams, you are just taking them home and returning them for the fun of it." He didn't argue with her. Never, never would she understand the thrill of racing through *Kim* or *Soldiers Three* on a February night, his hoard of fruit close by, the frail Philco offering a hum of music and news. As it did now.

    . . . *more arrests were reported in Germany today as Chancellor Hitler moved to suppress any attempt at a revolt after his crushing of dissident elements in the semimilitary SA . . . over a hundred are reported dead. . . .*

At the moment, however, the terror in Europe (which he understood with great clarity) did not stir him. He really wanted the batteries for today's games. But suddenly he was immersed in *Michael Brother of Jerry*. That old South Sea rascal, Jack London, was weaving his magic, and Albert was in a trance, gasping, suffering, undergoing delight, terror, joy, wonder. Ah, Jack London! They were in San Francisco. Dag Daughtry had gone to the office of Dr. Emory for a checkup, bringing along his Kanaka manservant, Kwaque. Kwaque had been complaining about painful swellings in his arm; his face had become peculiarly marked. Daughtry himself had a touch of rheumatism. Albert trembled; the story was building; some horrid intelligence would soon be revealed.

"You know, Mr. Daughtry," Walter Merritt Emory went on enthusiastically, while he held the steward's eyes with his and while all the time the live end of the cigar continued to rest against Kwaque's finger, "the older I get the more I am convinced that there are too many ill-advised and hasty operations."

Still fire and flesh pressed together, and a tiny spiral of smoke began to arise from Kwaque's finger end that was different in color from the smoke of a cigar end.

Shuddering, Albert sped ahead. He had suspected it all the time. *Leprosy.* But only Jack London could scare you that way—burning a man's finger to prove the diagnosis. Nerves dead. No sensation. His eyes raced ahead; his heart thundered.

". . . it is the finest, ripest, perforating ulcer of the *bacillus leprae* order that any San Francisco doctor has had the honor of presenting to the Board of Health."

"Leprosy!" exclaimed Doctor Masters.

And all started at his pronouncement of the word.

The sergeant and the two policemen shied away from Kwaque. . . .

But good God! What was this? What next? Was there no end to the way Jack London could terrify you, no end to his hideous imagination? For not only did Kwaque have leprosy, but, but . . . Daughtry himself, Michael's master. . . .

"Gentlemen, you have seen," Doctor Emory said, "two undoubted cases of it, master and man, the man more advanced with the combination of both forms, the master with only the anesthetic form—he has a touch of it, too, in his little finger. Take them away. . . ."

The horror of it all! Soon Dr. Emory was having them marched off under police guard to the pest house. Good old Dr. Emory, who had seemed such a great guy! That was what made Jack London so superb. You never really knew.

"You gotta come to lunch now."

A girl's voice broke the spell. He peered angrily over his glasses. A slender blonde girl his own age, a girl in a blue dress, was standing in the doorway.

" 'Member me?" she asked.

Embarrassed, he gathered up the heap of banana peels and apple cores and tossed them in his wastebasket. He got up warily, displeased with her intrusion. He was still Jack London, Winchester at the ready.

"Cantcha talk? I'm your cousin. Or somethin'."

Was not life precarious enough without this intruder? Girls were a pain, a complication. In school, he never spoke to them. Other boys, like little Artie, chased them, pulled their hair, yanked up a skirt now and then. But Albert kept his distance. His life had too many pitfalls, too many genuine worries, to permit girls any place in his sorry scheme of things.

"I think I remember you," he said.

"I'm Ruthie. I was here two years ago when I was sick and your father examined me. You're Albert, my cousin."

He fussed at his bookcase, returning Michael Brother of Jerry, thumbing through other volumes. In the dresser mirror, he saw Ruthie whatever-her-name-was resting languidly, like a stupid vamp, against the doorway. Slowly, the notion formed in his resisting mind that she was pretty, perhaps beautiful. The awareness painted his neck vermilion and his ears began to tingle. Her hair was buttery-yellow, braided around a faintly protruding forehead. Her eyes were large, dark brown, and her skin pale, luminous. There was a network of tiny blue veins at her temples, and it bothered him. Once in third grade, there had been a brilliant boy named Jacob Sheer in his class, who had the same kind of pale tracery at his temples. Jacob Sheer had vanished one day, to die secretly, with no warning. He wondered if Ruthie were sick. She didn't act it.

"I live with my Aunt Molly," she said. "She's your mother's second cousin, so that makes us something. Doncha remember two years ago when we played in the backyard?"

"Maybe I do, and maybe I don't," he said. He remembered her. She was one of the strays, the lonely people, the poor relatives, friends with some old-country connection, who wandered into his mother's field of generosity. How perfectly this Ruthie fitted the role! No parents, sick, a child brought to a rich relative's house—*rich! that was a hot one!*—to be reminded that they knew esteemed people like Dr. Abrams and his wife.

"You still got the truck, the one that sprinkled water when you filled the tank?" she asked. She spoke in an East Side singsong, a lilt that evoked streets dirtier and meaner than Longview Avenue.

"What sprinkling truck?" he asked gruffly. He tried to sound like George Bancroft or Richard Dix. She had come closer to him and she smelled of Palmolive. Her legs were long, very white, and hairless. Under her sleeveless light-blue dress, two terrifying bumps distracted him. A twinge shivered his belly, a sensation utterly new to him, and one he would rather do without.

"You had one, yes you did," she persisted. "You told me you were gonna be a street cleaner when you grew up! Boy, what an idea for a doctor's son!"

"You're nuts," he said. "You made that up. I don't even remember you." But her recollection was accurate. He had not very long ago yearned for the simple life of a garbage collector.

67

It was after his father had gone through an especially savage period of tirades, headaches, chest pains. How good to be a garbage collector, and never worry about ungrateful patients, unpaid bills, and people who got sick, suffered and died!

He felt her finger tickling the nape of his scarlet neck. He leaped away. "Cut it *out!*" he cried.

"Oh, you're a genius!" she giggled. "You should hear your mother brag about you. I'm honored to have such a famous relative." And she bowed to him.

They heard Mrs. Abrams summoning them to lunch. Albert shuffled after her, convinced that somehow the redness of his neck and ears, the strange twinge in his groin, would betray him. *But what did I do? Nothing. Nothing at all.* Still his mother would be aware that he had committed some sin with Ruthie. He hitched his belt and walked pigeon-toed, Joe Stripp coming in from the infield, and brushed by her in the corridor, inhaling her soapy-sweet odor.

In the dining room, the two children sat quietly while Mrs. Abrams and the second cousin, Molly Koplik, conversed in soft voices. The doctor, Mrs. Abrams said, would not be able to join them for lunch. He wondered about it, because his father wasn't that busy.

Usually the dining room comforted Albert. He liked the sand-colored grasscloth walls, the dark oak furniture, the apple-green mosaic of foliage in the screened windows. But people like Molly Koplik and her ward, Ruthie, aggravated him. Frankly, they gave him the creeps. He knew why, and he was ashamed of himself for feeling as he did, but why deny it? *Victims.* People more vulnerable and incompetent than himself, people who needed his pity, his love, his support. They came to his house for sustenance. And he of all people was expected to cheer them up! How unhappy could anyone get?

Chewing a mammoth Swiss cheese sandwich on onion roll, he studied Molly Koplik through his eyeglasses. A garment industry worker. A woman about his mother's age, an old maid with a girlish figure in a yellow cotton dress, but a withered face. At fourteen she had been sent out to work in a dress factory. Both parents had died in the influenza epidemic after the war. Ruthie, a niece, had ended up in her care. It was Molly, or the orphanage. Molly accepted the child. The details were vague to Albert. And there they were—two lost souls.

"Isn't Ruthie a beauty?" Molly asked. "Such a face. An angel."

"She is turning into a lovely young lady," Mrs. Abrams said.

Some people, Albert thought, were without shame, utterly, totally without shame. The girl was unembarrassed by these plaudits. She grinned, sinking her white teeth into a buttered bagel.

"She wants to be an actress," Molly said. "But who knows how these things happen? You got to have money, connections."

Oh yes, she'll be an actress. Like I am destined to play shortstop for the Dodgers.

"If Tanta Avra were still alive," his mother was saying, "she'd be at least eighty-five, because she died just about the time my father did."

"Hannah, she was older than *that*," Molly Koplik said. "She always lied about her age. Once we wrote to Glebocka, to the village where she was born, and got them to find her birth certificate, because we never knew her real birthday. What a miracle! Wars, pogroms, revolutions, who knows what—and there it was! It proved she was three years older than she said. We wanted to have a big party for her, but she was angry! She said we had no right to find out how old she was! Such a woman!"

His mother laughed gently. What was so funny? Who was Tanta Avra? There was a vague cloud over all these people they talked about—Tanta Avra, Uncle Berra, Alta Mahefka—people out of some murky European past, remnants of the diaspora, who meant nothing to him. Should he be ashamed of himself? He knew all about Tony Cuccinello and Van Mungo, but nothing at all about these forebears.

"Ruthie and I paid a visit to Uncle Berra in Cleveland last

year," Molly said. "You should see him, Hannah! Past eighty and still strong like an ox! He's so funny! And all his sons made such a success, it's a pleasure to visit there. The youngest, Ira, was a big athlete by college—a football player. So a Natalian fellah in Cleveland comes to him, and he says, look I'll make from you a prizefighter, you'll make money. Ira didn't need the money, he was going to law school, and Uncle Berra takes good care of him, but for a *joke*, he becomes a fighter. He didn't tell Berra, he just went off, and he had to fight a big *schwarzer*, in front of a lot of people. Ira knocks him out, the *schwarzer*, the first time he hits him, and he wins money. Then he fights again, and again, and by now, the rabbi at Berra's temple finds out. So he calls Uncle Berra in to lecture him, and he says to him, 'Your son, Ira, who made his bar mitzvah here, and should be a blessing to you in your old age, he is fighting prizefights with *schwarzers* an Natalians and all kinds of *goyim!* How do you let him do this, a Jewish boy?'

"So Uncle Berra thinks about it, and he asks the rabbi, 'He *wins*, my Ira?' 'Yeah,' the rabbi says, 'four times he won already! I read it in the papers!' So Uncle Berra says, 'When he *loses*, I'll tell him he should stop!' "

Mrs. Abrams lifted her chin and laughed delicately. Molly and Ruthie roared. "Oh, Berra was always a character," his mother said. "When he lived here in Brooklyn years ago, we saw a lot of him. He was very fond of Dr. Abrams. They used to wrestle in the cellar, would you believe it? The doctor had an old gymnasium mat there, and he and Berra would go down there—they never told me—and try to pin one another. You wouldn't remember, Albert. It was before your time."

All those muscles, and none for him. His father, Uncle Berra, Ira, that young Jewish pugilist who knocked out Negroes—all these were superior people.

"Ruthie dear, have some more coleslaw," his mother said. The blonde girl ate like a truck driver. But her manners were good. She knew how to hold a knife and fork. Even this disturbed Albert. Who taught her? Where did she come from anyway? Who were her parents, and why was she being brought up by Cousin Molly? Albert's mind had an organizational bent. When he kept a baseball score it was accurate down to every pitch.

"By us, she's usually a picky eater," said Molly Koplik. Mrs. Abrams refilled their glasses with iced tea. "But when she visits, she eats beautifully, God bless her. And here, she likes to come better than anywhere else. She always asks when can we go by Aunt Hannah and Uncle Sol again."

"Well, you should come more often. You are always welcome, and the doctor is delighted to take care of your medical needs."

"Albert, God bless him also," Molly went on, enraptured with the environment. "Look how nice he's growing up. He's like a half year younger than Ruthie, am I right? Because he was born just after Uncle Shmulka from Providence died in the car accident."

More obscure people, people doomed to die in accidents, Albert thought. A family loaded with troubles.

"I can see he's a very good eater, not a picky eater," Molly pursued.

"Albert consumes an enormous amount of nervous energy. He is very high-strung." His mother discussed him casually, exposing him in public.

"It's nice they're the same age," Molly said. A crafty note crept into her voice. "He's still so smart in school?"

"Albert does exceptionally well," Mrs. Abrams said.

"Ruthie is smart, I mean not a genius like Albert," Molly said. "But lately, everything is with boys. Those loyzers! Boys, boys, is all she thinks about. Believe me, Hannah, I have my hands full."

Albert, studying the girl from behind his mammoth sandwich, looked for a sign of humility. None. She was wicked, corrupted. Ah, those loyzers on the East Side!

"You may take Ruthie in the yard and play checkers with her or cards," his mother said.

"I can't, Ma. I got a punchball game this afternoon."

"Since when are you such a great punchball player? I thought all you did was keep score."

Humiliation streaked his cheeks carmine. He ducked as if avoiding a blow. No longer could he look at the blonde intruder, now stuffing stewed pears into her mouth. He got up to leave.

"I'm a sub. I might get to play." A catch in his voice betrayed him.

"Ask if you may be excused. You can surely give Cousin Ruthie a few minutes of your time."

"Okay, can I be excused?" With minimal courtesy, he invited the girl to join him. She hopped from her seat.

"Hmm, so this is iced tea?" Cousin Molly asked. "So how do you make it? With the ice first or the tea first? By us, we got no ice in the house, but I could get a small piece maybe and chip it up."

As he led Ruthie out of the dining room, he tried not to think about people so miserable they had never heard of iced tea. In the corridor he saw his mitt lying at the bottom of the hall closet. He stooped to pick it up.

"We gonna play catch?" she asked.

"I don't play catch with girls."

"Well we gotta do *somethin'!* I'm your guest and you have to entertain me. Because you're rich."

He opened the lower drawer and rummaged about for a bottle of precious neat's-foot oil, vital balm. "I'm gonna oil my glove. You can watch." Was he crazy? Or was that sweet-smelling girl pushing his shoulders, leaning on him?

"I could push you right over, I'm bigger than you. Into that drawer and lock you up." She laughed.

"What a pest!" he shouted. "Hands off!" He could not find the bottle. His hands shuffled through a half-dozen *Boy Allies* books (abandoned when Kipling beckoned), a stamp album that bored him after his tenth birthday, the crumbs of an erector set he could never manage. The screwdriver gave him fits.

With great clatter a pair of roller skates were disgorged.

The girl shoved past him and seized them. "Wow, skates! Let's go roller-skating! I'm terrific! I can do the eagle and onesies!"

He took the skates away from her. "No skating. I'm gonna oil my glove."

"Ah, come on. Look, they're almost new. Lookit how they spin."

"I said no."

"Then I'll skate by myself."

There were certain advantages, he reasoned, to being an orphan, raised by a distant cousin who worked in a factory. It made you an insensitive clod, like this bare-legged vixen. You cared nothing, nothing at *all*, about the way you acted or the way people felt about you. She brushed by him, wedging her slender form against his (he backed away and slunk against the cellar door), then squatted in an unladylike way and started to attach the skates to her feet. As she did her skirt rose.

"You can't go out in the street and skate by yourself," he said. His voice rose an octave.

"We'll take turns. Boy, are these neat. They just fit." Fussing with the key, the straps, her skirt went higher and he caught a glimpse of pale green underpants. Did he see daisies on them? Little flowers? That twitching flickering sensation agitated him, just below the belly button. He must run away. Hide. Go into the backyard and oil his glove. But he stayed. The skirt rose another inch. The flowers hypnotized him.

"Whatcha lookin' at?" she asked. "You see somethin'? Free show? I can't help it if it's crowded in here."

She held her arms out to him. "Gimme a lift."

With wet palms he lifted her up. The skates rolled noisily on the corridor's linoleum and she moved expertly toward the door.

"You can go by *yourself*," he said.

She opened the door. Afternoon sun swept blindingly over them. Heat flooded in like the exhaust of a truck. "Ah, come on, Albie. Albie-Walbie," she pleaded.

"Look, I got to tell you something." He shaded his eyes. "*I can't skate.*" Saying it, he was a little proud of himself. In every

73

man's life there were moments when one must face up to the truth—no matter how awful. He might have lied his way out of it. He might have retreated to the backyard. But he had to be purged, punished, held up to contempt and ridicule. Let her know the truth about himself, with his big talk about a punchball game. Confession would wash him clean, absolve him of the sins of pride and lust.

"Whaddya mean ya can't *skate?*" she cried. Her East Side singsong soared. "So hah come ya got skates? And they're ball-bearians! Ain't they ball-bearians?"

"The word, for your information, is ball-*bearings*. I cannot skate. I do not know how. I never learned."

"Hah come?"

"My mother wouldn't let me go in the gutter on roller skates."

Ruthie pondered this. "Ya mother won't let ya go in the gutter on skates? Hah come she bought 'em for ya?"

"My father bought them."

She hooked a white arm in his and began to drag him into the vestibule. "Anyone can skate. I'll learn ya."

"No."

"I seen ya crossing the street before. Ya go in the gutter."

"But not on skates. It's my mother's rule."

His self-exposure was so damning that she could not laugh at him. Penniless, raised in a house where they didn't even know how to make iced tea, she had to pity him.

"Your mother won't see. Honest, I'll learn ya in ten minutes."

"*Teach* me." He pulled away from her. "The fact of the matter is I have weak ankles from scarlet fever when I was a baby. Somehow the infection settled in my ankles." *I was wounded in the Argonne, machine-gun nest. I carry a steel plate in my left knee, from the time I won the Silver Star.* Scarlet fever was nothing to laugh about. The truth was, he had had them all, every imaginable disease of childhood, striking him in procession, feverish assaults: scarlet fever, polio (a mild form that left him dragging a foot for a year), diphtheria, measles, influenza, scores of colds, grippes, high fevers, local infections,

74

aches and pains. At the age of twelve he was a veteran of thousands of alcohol sponge baths and bedpans.

"So ya can watch me," she said. They walked into the blinding light. Longview Avenue dozed—hot, dirty. Down the block some galoots, members of the vile Hawks, were shouting their arguments. Across the street Genius Grubman, afloat in his knickers, sashayed past the dog's pyre, mumbling equations.

Ruthie clumped down the stone steps and rolled away—lithe, graceful. He tried to suffocate his jealousy.

Yes, my dear girl, you may know how to skate, but you are not cursed with weak ankles and an inborn lack of balance, resulting from childhood ailments. Perhaps I cannot skate, but I have seen more of life than you, things normal men would cringe at, that would turn brave hearts to water. Why Albert Abrams Cannot Skate—A Story for Which the World Is Not Yet Prepared. . . .

White legs and round behind pumping, she sped down the street, came flying back, spun around impertinently, and rested against the poplar. She stuck her tongue out at him.

"I double dare ya," she said.

"Darers go first."

"I went already. I promise I won't laugh at ya, no matter how ya flop." She clattered toward him.

"I assure you it doesn't matter to me. Skating isn't the most important thing in the world."

In tenement windows across the street, sodden people seemed to be staring at him, waiting for his next move.

Inside the gate Ruthie sat down and unstrapped the skates. "Ya'll skate because I say ya'll skate," she said firmly. "I got a great idea. Ya hold on to me, and we'll go *against* the traffic. If a car is coming, I'll drag y'on to the sidewalk. Ya could never get hurt. There are hardly any cars on this street."

Two roles were offered him: invalid, maimed veteran, a man paralyzed by disease and his mother's caution, or a Doc Savage of the streets, unafraid to roller-skate, even if it meant leaning on a twelve-year-old girl from the East Side. *By God, he would skate.*

"Ya can't be a sissy all your life," she explained.

She strapped the ball-bearings on to his feet. Rising, he wobbled, and fell to the stone step.

"Useless, forget it," he said. "I have no sense of balance. Can't I make you understand that?"

With artful hands, she drew him up and escorted him through the gate, to the shade of the poplar. Her hands were gluey. They were unnatural. They guided him skillfully off the curb and into the forbidden gutter. He darted a look at the upstairs window: *Ma, don't look now, I am committing a crime against you, against your express orders. I am inviting paralysis, mutilation, sudden death.*

An invisible rope looped about his legs sent him galley-west. Supine, he sprawled in the gutter amid aromas of horse urine and rotted peelings. It was unfathomable the way his legs had sailed out from beneath him—as effortlessly as the way the colored boys had plucked glove and ball from his hands. Was not a man entitled to a certain degree of control over his acts? Ruthie helped him rise. Now he was nerveless, grim, calm—Cornelius Johnson, the world's greatest high jumper, getting ready to clear the bar at six eight. He tried a few more rolling steps. With no warning, he was down again—arms flapping, legs kicking. His spine uncoiled like a garden hose. He could have been carried home in a pail.

"Ya not *relaxed*," she said. "Just walk, *walk*, and I'll help ya."

Grubman serenaded him from across the street:

"Awake, arise or be forever fallen!
    They hoid and were abashed, and up they sprung,
    Upon the wing, as when men wont to watch
    On doody, sleeping found by whom they dread. . . ."

"Who's *that* nut?" Ruthie asked.

"One of my many admirers."

Yanked up by her gummy fingers, he steadied himself, hearing Grubman's declamation:

"Fallen Cherub, to be weak is miserable,
    Doing or suffering. . . ."

76

"Pipe down, Grubman," Albert called. "Who needs your poetry?"

They progressed slowly. Now his legs were obedient. Six, seven, eight steps forward—and he did not fall.

"I see a car," he said.

"So? It's coming at us. All we gotta do is walk by the curb. Anyway, ya mother can't see ya from here."

Sweat speckled his forehead; his glasses were fogged. "I don't think I'm making any progress." Out went his legs. She tried to catch him, but he hit the curb. A strawberry bloomed on his lower spine.

"Just when ya were getting better," she said. "Ya went real good just before you fell. Upsy-daisy." She pulled him up and wheeled him around. He spun stupidly, like a huge stuffed monkey—a millionaire's toy in Saks Fifth Avenue.

"Not in the gutter."

"Oh, for Pete's sake."

"On the sidewalk, it's safer."

Beneath the dappled shade of maples and catalpas, they returned to the house on the pitted sidewalk. It was slow going. He staggered from tree to iron railing to trash can, assisted by her sticky hands. Passion vanished. He was *achieving* something. The last few steps he barely needed her. They stopped at his father's tree.

"I think I'm getting it," he said craftily. A delicious sense of learning came upon him, like the first time he mastered a geometry problem, or memorized a page of the *Iliad*. It was a form of ecstasy. She clapped her hands.

"Was it so terrible? I knew ya could!"

He glanced at the window. No sight of his mother. She would be conversing with Molly Koplik, reminiscing about poor relatives in Providence and Cleveland.

"This time yourself," Ruthie said. "In the *gutter!*"

Once more into the imminent deadly breach. A far, far better thing that I do. . . .

They allowed a creeping Hupmobile to go by. Then she gave him a gentle push.

"Here I go," he said. Victory was imminent: *he could skate*.

Trembling, arms outstretched like the wings of a DeHaviland gypsy moth, he minced forward. His style was atrocious, but he was undeniably skating.

"I got it! *I got it!*" he cried. Life was not all bad. Life had its rewards. You could make a great catch. You could learn to skate.

Grubman, watching from the opposite curb, applauded mockingly. His doughy white hands passed one another like wounded doves. "It was a famous victory," the Genius intoned. "O wonderful son, that can so astonish a mother!"

"Nuts to you, Grubman!" he called back gaily. "And leave my family out of it!"

The riposte was too much of an exertion. His legs flew forward. He struck the hot asphalt again. But this time he was undismayed. Nothing could deter him now. He rested on one knee—Al Barabas, stopped inside the ten-yard line, but certain he'd get the TD on the next inside-tackle smash.

He heard his mother shouting at him. It was strange, that even when she shouted, she sounded calm.

"*Albert! Get out of the gutter at once! Don't you see that truck coming right at you?*"

He looked over his shoulder. His first reaction was that *she* had arranged it, that she had telephoned the coal company and ordered the truck. A huge blunted hood had come to a halt five yards in back of him. He knew the truck well: BURNS BROS. BURNS. What was it doing making a delivery in July? And cruising the wrong way down a one-way street? The driver honked at him. "Hey kid, git off da street!"

"Come up here at once!" his mother cried.

On his feet, he skipped to the sidewalk. The coal truck resumed its illegal passage down Longview Avenue. Albert had an urge to leap on the running board and shriek at the driver: *Why? Why me? Why in all of Brooklyn, on this day of this year, at this moment, did you choose to drive the wrong way on Longview Avenue, and come at my back, just as I fell, at the*

*very instant when my mother is looking out the window as I am
learning to roller-skate? Are you in league with my mother? Did
Mr. Burns and my mother arrange all of this beforehand? Have
you been hired to humiliate me?*

Ruthie helped him remove the skates. She was frightened,
implicated in his guilt. "You gonna tell Aunt Hannah it was me
made you do it?" she asked.

"Nah, you don't have to worry. You'll be able to come here
for lunch again."

In the living room Mrs. Abrams sat serenely, awaiting the
culprit. She fanned herself with a program from the Majestic
Theatre. Ruthie entered silently. Albert glanced at his mother,
at Molly Koplik's distressed face, and went to his room. He fell
on the bed and flicked on the radio.

*Senator Borah charged today that the New Deal is at-
tempting to fasten a stranglehold of bureaucracy on the American people. . . .*

His mother was standing in the doorway. Never did she
betray anger in her large-featured face. All overt displays of fury
in the Abrams household were reserved for the doctor. Her
hazel eyes were tranquil. Her white skin was unwrinkled. Not a
brown hair was out of place.

"You disobeyed me."

"It's about time, isn't it, Ma?" Only half of his voice
emerged.

"Turn off the radio." Mrs. Abrams was not a tall woman,
but her carriage was splendid. She gave the impression of
height. As a girl, she had played tennis. In her early forties she
was a sedentary bridge-player and a reader of quality novels. But
excellent bearing had remained with her. Albert could never
quite figure his mother out. What was she doing on Longview
Avenue with her good manners, her soft voice, her library of
Gissing and Meredith and Thackeray? Certainly she was the
only wife in the neighborhood who knew how to play bridge.
Her partners were lady schoolteachers from Crown Heights.
Bimbo Wexler had once hurled the taunt at him: *"Ya mudder
plays bridge!"*

79

She was an island of dignity and intelligence in the seething slum. There were times when he wished he could admire her more for these qualities. If only she'd let him grow up! He loved her, especially during his frequent illnesses, but a man had other needs besides affection, and books, and a high IQ.

"Ma, I know I did wrong. I did a terrible thing. I'm sorry, I'm sorry, I'm sorry. You want me to write it on a blackboard?"

"Don't be sarcastic."

"I'll go to my grave unable to roller-skate."

She brushed back a hair. "When your father and I forbade you to skate did you think we were being cruel parents? Did you?"

"No, no. You just have distorted values."

"Indeed. You seem to be a great authority on values."

"If every single guy in the neighborhood can roller-skate and also a lot of girls, then there is clearly something wrong with me—or with you—if I can't."

"Evidently you are convinced that it is our determination to make your life miserable."

He sat up on the edge of the bed. As far back as he could remember they had never hit him. Now *there* was something to puzzle out. Bushy's insane father would chase him around the street, beating him with a broomstick—and Bushy could do anything, *anything* in the world. But did Bushy love his parents?

"Maybe you don't intend it that way, but you're succeeding," Albert said.

"How? By lavishing books and presents on you? By buying you the best clothes of any child in this neighborhood? By that expensive baseball your father got for you? I doubt very much if he earned the *price* of that ball yesterday. Are you complaining about the vacations to Rockaway?"

"We didn't go this summer," he said desperately. He would enact to the fullest his role as ingrate.

"You know perfectly well why not. We cannot afford it. You are by far the most privileged boy around here. The least you could do is to reciprocate our good treatment of you by obeying us. You defied me when you went into the street on roller skates."

"I know, I know. I confess. Guilty. I admit it. I throw myself on the mercy of the court."

"I've warned you about that sarcastic tone."

"Okay. I won't do it again."

"Yes, but that one time might have been enough to kill you!" She said it as calmly as if advising him she were going out to shop. "Of course it would have to be you, to fall flat on your back at the moment a huge truck came rumbling by. That driver stopped no more than a few feet from you. You might have been crushed to a pulp."

"He was going five miles an hour and he stopped cold. My lousy luck, you had to be looking out the window. You must have a sixth sense or something."

"I was looking for your father." Albert did not care for the expression *your father*. More and more, his mother seemed to be using it. Until a few months ago, it was *Daddy*. "Don't get the idea," she went on, "that you are all I have on my mind. Your father and I have other things to concern ourselves with beyond whether you can roller-skate or not."

"I know, I know." He got up, blinking away meager tears of self-pity, and stared out the window at the multicolored glory of the backyard. The dahlias were like his parents—too good for the punk neighborhood, wasted and mocked by riffraff. *Ya mudder plays bridge. Ya fadder pulls out babies.*

"That's the size of it," he said flatly. "I will never learn to ride a bike, or roller-skate, or ice-skate, or do any of the important things, thanks to you."

"Yes, you certainly sound like an underprivileged child. You, with the highest IQ ever recorded at P.S. 133. Reading adult books. Your father and I have certainly been cruel to you; we surely have deprived you of everything."

Albert spun from the window. "Ma, I would throw every single book I have into the furnace, and flunk the next IQ test, if I could only skate! Or fight! Or run fast!"

"I cannot be held responsible for your childhood diseases."

"Who says you are? But you won't let me live."

"I will not permit you to do things harmful to your health. You have weak ankles."

At last, they had come to the crusher, the end of the argument, the point of no return. *He had weak ankles.* Was there anything worse than weak ankles? (They were weak. They tended to spread sideways when he stood in one place too long.) Under the pressure of his mother's inexorable logic he surrendered. A man could not fight weak ankles. Those cursed ankles said everything, left him defenseless. There had been no need to catalogue the near-fatal diseases they had nursed him through, the pained hours they had spent at his crib, the parade of esteemed specialists summoned by his father. *Horowitz is the biggest man at Brooklyn Jewish in pediatrics, and he'll set us straight.* Albert had stumbled through a childhood of burning fevers, shuddering chills, platoons of needles jabbed in his tender behind, armies of pills rammed down his trembling gullet, icy bedpans shoved under his ravaged body. Surely it was a miracle he was alive at all, his mother once told him, an absolute miracle, a tribute to his father's medical skill and her devotion. Albert believed her. His early years seemed a blur of sore throats, fevers, headaches, diarrhea, weakness. Was it to be wondered that they were determined to preserve his precious blood? Was it so outrageous that they wanted him out of the gutter where Chandlers and Essexes might crush him to death, off bikes and roller skates, which were known to cause broken limbs, fractured skulls? For that matter, was it not logical that they insisted he be back in the house at an early hour, safe in bed—while the rest of the Raiders roamed the streets in savage games of ringalevio—when it was well known that murderous Negroes prowled the streets, in search of timorous boobs like Albert Abrams? There was no point in reviewing these unarguable truths.

"Ruthie can roller-skate and she's a girl," he said.

"Ruthie has been brought up with a minimum of supervision. That is Cousin Molly's concern."

"She learned to skate in the gutter. Like any other normal

civilized human being." His mother's face became cold. "All right, I surrender. You win. You always do."

"I do not appreciate that tone. When you are finished feeling sorry for yourself, you may join us in the living room. Molly is giving Ruthie a lecture."

"It wasn't her fault. It was my idea."

When she had gone, an odor of perfumed powder lingered; he resented it. Things would be easier all around if she would smack him now and then. But this regulatory kindness, this reasoned, calm, intelligent arrangement of his life would drive him nuts, utterly, totally nuts. Between the old man's rages, and his old lady's restraints, he would end up in the booby hatch for sure.

For comfort he turned to *The New York Times*. His perfunctory reading that morning was a warm-up. Now he had time to plunge into its black and white magic, sponge up every word, wallow in every headline, each sensible paragraph. In moments of black despair he drew solace from the newspaper, by seeking out items which revealed people worse off than he was. No matter how deep his misery, how dreadful his situation (the incident of the skates and the truck was one of the worst within recent memory), the *Times* never failed him. The world was filled with wretches who had much less to be thankful for than Albert Abrams, Esq.

Right off the bat he was cheered by *Hot Wave Equals 16-Day Record; Death and Prostration Toll Rises Here as Expected Relief Fails*. Ah, the sunstroke victims collapsing on baking sidewalks, the blue-faced drowned at Coney Island, the heart failures, the heat-prostration cases gasping in the shade of a red oak in Prospect Park! The city was filled with them. How lucky he was to avoid all that! The heat never bothered him. A thorough reading of Paul DuChaillu, greatest of the gorilla hunters, had taught him how to cope with heat—*move slowly, not too much liquid intake, light clothing*. A man had many things to be grateful for. Those who did not read Paul Du-Chaillu obviously could not survive in heat waves.

Mayor Bars Idlers from City Buildings; Orders the

Courts Cleared of Hangers-On. Assuredly, this was in the category of minor things to be grateful for, but still, he was not one to turn down any advantage. He was lucky he wasn't a hanger-on, an idler, a loafer with nothing better to do than haunt the corridors of a city building. Imagine, a fellow spending his life around the Department of Sanitation! And double disgrace, to have Mayor LaGuardia throw you out! It could ruin a man's career. Scar him for life. These people were *all* worse off than he was, even if a few could ride a bicycle.

A thankful wave washed over him, as he reflected how glad he was not to live in Germany. *National Socialist Party Undermined by Events in Germany.* He read on, chilled by the account of murder, execution, shots in the night, stabbings, casual killings of storm troopers, generals, politicians, former ministers, party officials, a lot of Germans dead, gone. Good, Albert said to himself. Let them kill each other and lay off the Jews. It was the way he felt whenever he read about a gangster being killed by rivals. They should all kill each other. Yes, it was better to be a non-roller skater than dead in Germany.

The inside pages were pure gold, a Comstock Lode of disasters. *Boy, 3, Dies as Car Leaps into Group.* Not me, not me, some poor little kid in Coney Island. He was on the sidewalk, thinking he was safe and sound, so it just goes to show you!

Dr. Butler Warns of Our 1789 Lesson: He Calls Economic Nationalism Suicidal as Policy of American States. Sighing, Albert was relieved. How much better off he was than all those misguided fools, who, ignoring Dr. Butler's warnings, were prey to economic nationalism! And how better off he was than all those people who had to sit through Dr. Butler's speech!

Even the sports pages were a help. It was most reassuring not to be in the spiked shoes of Walter (Boom Boom) Beck, who, after pitching to eight men and allowing three runs in the first inning, threw the ball against the right-field wall. Poor Walter, that was *his* cross to bear. It was also pleasant to assess oneself as better off than the Boston Braves, who were beaten twice by the Giants in front of 42,000 people. And shut out 15 to zip in the second game!

There remained the reliable obituaries, columns and columns of people much less lucky than he. He read solemnly, mouthing the notices to himself in sonorous holy tones, the Reverend Abrams, D.D., murmuring silent *Lord have mercies* and *Rest in peaces* on the souls of the departed—a former Connecticut assemblyman, a retired brewer, a choral leader, an Episcopalian priest, a widely known Pacific Coast shipping man, and the Dowager Maharanee of Mysore. *Go, go, to your rewards. I live, perhaps to roller-skate someday.*

Invigorated by bad news he got up, rubbing the bruises on his back. Scars of battle. He would show them to the Raiders later. But to what avail? They would still mock him. *Ya jerk, ya can't skate.* It would be better to forget the whole malformed adventure—the lunacy of submitting himself to a girl's scheme, the ignominious way it ended.

A terrible hunger sucked at his abdomen. It demanded a visit to the refrigerator. Lunch, after all, had been a half-hour ago. The exertions of the street, the emotional upheavals, had left him weak, in need of sustenance. He walked past the living room. Forever the gracious hostess, his mother had opened a box of Loft's Parlays for the guests and was playing casino with Molly. It was a game she normally disdained. Ruthie was seated at the dining room table, using his best paint set. She painted solemnly, her face almost transparent in the filtered light. Nuts to her, he told himself.

In the kitchen he split a bagel, gave it a quick surfacing of butter and cream cheese, and sat in the white enameled chair, chewing moodily. A gap had developed in his busy day. The punchball championship was not until three. There was no baseball game on the radio until later. He found the sandwich bland, added a slice of red onion and a cross section of green pepper. His mouth flamed, so he poured a tumbler of cold milk.

Peace descended on him. Frustrated flies hummed jealously against the closed screen door. Beyond, the reds and yellows of his father's dahlias glowed fiercely. The heat was beneficial, comforting. At moments like this, he loved the cramped kitchen with its lumpy walls (an irregularity derived from years of overpainting). A good reliable place, the kitchen. Of a winter's morning, ready for another day of school, he boiled up steaming cups of cocoa and devoured bales of Shredded Wheat, while in the yard outside, in the cold darkness, snowflakes whirled and settled on dead stalks, leafless trees, the hibernating garden.

His peace was soon disturbed by voices rising from his father's office. How often he had heard these arguments, these harsh and upsetting sounds! Did he have to fight with his patients all the time?

"What the hell do you mean?" he heard his father saying. "You owe me ten bucks for three months now, and I have a right to ask for it!"

"Please, please, Doc, it's murder tryin' to earn a living," a young man's voice pleaded. "This here is worth at least fi' dollars. I'm sellin' 'em like hot cakes."

"Don't *please Doc* me! Cake-eater!" his father cried.

An old story, Albert knew. These moments had a hideous fascination for him. He hated them—but he could not resist eavesdropping. Sneakily, he crawled under the kitchen table. An unused bolted door formed part of the wall between kitchen and consultation room. He pressed his eye against the keyhole and was able to see his father seated at the desk, his Indian face furrowed. To one side of the desk sat a pale young man with slicked-down black hair. He was ill-shaven, stoop-shouldered, and filled perfectly his father's epithet—cake-eater. When the old man got angrier, he would surely call the patient a crap-artist and maybe even the worst of all, a whoremaster.

"What kind of crap is this, Levinson?" his father demanded. "What am I, a fool, a sucker for your tricks? I want ten bucks! It was twenty, and because I knew your father for years, I cut it in half. Not to mention free trips to the hospital I made to examine you. I said ten bucks, and I want it now."

The young man whined. "On my mother's grave, I swear

it, Doc, I ain't got it. Believe me, take this in exchange, at least for fi' dollars worth of what I owe you."

He was holding something up, but Albert in his cell beneath the table could not see it. The keyhole was not big enough. What was he trying to pawn off on his father?

"I want my money," his father said. "Goddammit, I have a right to be paid!"

His father's anger turned the bagel to flannel in his mouth. The part he had eaten became a clot in his esophagus.

"I'll inform you of a few other things while I'm at it, cake-eater!" the doctor raged. "You can take the X-rays I worked my ass off to make, and go run off to the lousy professors in the white coats tomorrow! No, never a nickel to pay the general practitioner, but you'll always find it for the fancy specialists!"

"I ain't goin' to no specialist."

"Like hell you're not! That's what your father was talking about last night, right in this office! Wasted an hour of my time chewing my ear off—and not a thin dime for me!"

"But look, Doc—this beautiful item of merchandise, I'll give you in exchange! I'm sellin' them all over Brooklyn. I got a monopoly on the distribution. Look, I'm chargin' everyone seven bucks for this item, but you can have it for five, so all I owe you is five. Ain't that fair?"

"No, goddammit! No!" his father roared. "I don't want that piece of crap! I don't need it! Nobody can stick me in a straitjacket and tell me what I am, or what I belong to, or what I do, get it?"

"But it's patriotic. It's your patriotic doody."

"Ten bucks, you punk, let's have it!" the doctor cried. "You're such a hot salesman, selling that junk, you must have ten bucks in your pants!"

"Doc, I give it to my old lady to buy food. Believe me, it's terrible by us. My father ain't worked in six months. And me, since I was laid off, I ain't had a regular job. Tell me, Doc, did I or did I not always pay up when I had the dough?"

Grudgingly, the doctor said, "Yeah, I guess so."

"So, gimme a break, willya? It's a depression, everyone

knows that. I'm a trained lathe operator. I made good dough all my life, since I was sixteen. But who can get a job? Doc, you know what I'm up against."

"What about me?" asked Albert's father. "You think I got it so easy?"

"I know, I know," the young man agreed. Whatever he was trying to sell, he had now placed it on the doctor's desk. Albert, stretching his neck, inviting a headache by peering downward through the keyhole, still could not discern what it was. "It's awful for a professional man, a doctor like you, a guy with all that education. Believe me, Doc, there ain't another like you in Brownsville, my parents swear by you. . . ."

He wheedled on, flattering, making excuses, invoking his elderly parents, whom the doctor had taken care of since 1910, all his relatives who loved the doctor, all the nice things people said about him. (Albert wondered: Did it include the two slatterns he had heard denouncing his father that morning in the grocery store?)

"Doc, it breaks my heart I can't pay up," the patient went on. "Look—keep the item. Keep it. It's yours. I tell ya what. You credit me for whatever you want, whatever you think it's worth against what I owe. Is that fair or not?"

"Ah the hell with it, the hell with it all," Albert heard his father say.

"Doc, you're the only gent in this lousy neighborhood," the young man went on. Sniffing surrender, he was closing in. "You keep the banner, it's yours—gen-u-wine silk, printed in sun-fast colors, an expensive silk-screen process, with gold paint on the pole. You hang it up, everyone'll take notice. Not just a crummy cardboard poster but a real classy item."

"All right, just get out of here," the doctor said wearily.

"Four bucks, okay, Doc? Three less than what I sell it for. So off the ten, I owe you six, and I promise you'll have it next week."

"Hah?" Dr. Abrams seemed to have lost interest.

"Next week. Ah, when I come for the X-rays."

"To take them to the professors, hey, Levinson?" There

was almost a gay note, a mad note of triumph in his father's voice—cheated, gulled, euchred, he was salvaging something, proven correct in his suspicions. "Go on, take them, go running off, and good riddance. I'll probably never see you or your parents again, but who cares? Patients like you I can do without."

"Don't say that, Doc. You mean a lot to us."

"Like crap I do. Go on, get out." There was no more anger in the doctor, just resignation. In a way, it was more terrifying than his rages.

The patient offered a few more flattering remarks, then left, leaving behind the "item of merchandise"—whatever it was. Albert had to find out. He crept from beneath the table, swallowed the rest of the milk, and walked down the corridor, standing a moment outside the door. He entered softly on sneakered feet and heard his father at his desk—a pen scratching, a drawer being opened and closed, the old man trying to find something in his cluttered desk.

For a moment, Albert stood in the gloom of the examining room, in the shadows of the X-ray and the metabolism apparatus, and looked at his father. In the consultation room the shades were half drawn to obscure the summer sun. The doctor wore his poisonous green shirt; he was writing something in his day book. Albert was fascinated by his father's bare arms, great oaken clubs, dark, hairy, muscled by years of gymnastic work, swings, leaps, exercises, a thousand encounters with parallel bars, leather horses, ropes, rings, Indian clubs. How he envied the old man's strength! But he was not jealous. He did not begrudge it to him. But it seemed to Albert that the power in his father's body should have given him a commensurate power to handle people, control them, make them like him, make them pay their bills, keep them from running off to professors. It worked in the street, didn't it? Bushy led the Raiders because he was the strongest. Lee Roy and his cronies could steal the ball because they were powerful and fast. Zetz, the leader of the Hawks, a savage boy of sixteen, had once fought in the Golden Gloves. All of these people turned their muscle to advantage.

Only his father seemed incapable of using his strength. It didn't appear to do him any good.

Shaking his head, he padded into the rear room, pretending to be looking for a notebook.

"Hello, kiddo," his father said. He was smiling. The devouring rage had vanished. The Indian face was relaxed, pleased. *Not fair, not fair, Albert thought miserably. He takes one look at me, one look at my skinny build and my four-eyed face and he is happy with everything, he forgets all his troubles, he isn't mad, he isn't yelling. I cannot take much more of this, I cannot accept all that love, if he is going to be angry at everything else. In fact, I will happily settle for having him hate me and ignore me, if only it would enable him to handle patients.*

"How was the ball?" his father asked. He closed the ledger and locked it in a side drawer, a secret place. Financial matters were never discussed. Albert was forbidden to look into the drawer. He did not particularly care. Often his parents, discussing bills or taxes or the mortgage, would lower their voices when he appeared, or halt the conversation.

"It was great, Pop. We played a four-inning game."

"Yeah, I saw you. When I made a call to Melnick."

"The colored kids broke it up."

"What, the *tunkeles?* What the hell do they mean breaking up your baseball game? Where do they come off doing that, those lice! I'll call the cops!"

"No, no, Pop. It won't do any good. You can't catch them. And if you do, they come back with bigger guys." Considerately, he did not add—and whenever you call the cops, you end up fighting with the police and they get sore at you, not the people you want them to get after.

"Punks. I'll go out there and teach them a lesson."

Albert rolled his eyes back in despair. "You can't, Pop. Just forget it."

He walked over to the desk. Leaning against its glass-topped edge, he tried to think of something that would cheer up the old man. Nothing occurred to him.

"Did you hit a home run?"

"I made a good catch. Teddy Ochab said he never saw a better one in the majors."

He spared his father the details about the theft of the ball and glove, the way in which the colored boys had humiliated him, his rescue by Teddy, the way Bushy had struck him out. Those were horrors with which he had to contend. His father had enough worries. Why burden him with the problem of a weakling son?

"Guess I'll go in the yard and read," Albert said. Under the desk glass was a photograph of him, aged five. It was taken in a Coney Island booth—a solemn profile. His features were blunt and babyish. He could remember the day it was made: a cold May afternoon. They had eaten Nathan's hot dogs, cotton candy. The wind on the boardwalk had blown his mother's skirts up and his father had yelled at a few staring galoots. The creased photograph disturbed him. Was he so important that he had to be stuck under the glass next to his father's license to dispense narcotics?

"Stay, stay. I'm not busy." The phone rang. It was a relief case—a welfare department call. The city paid the fee, but only after hours of red tape, weeks of waiting. "Lousy relief work," the doctor said. "The world is filled with nothing but paupers and crooks."

Don't start again, Albert begged. *If you can't stand it, quit. I don't want to listen to you eat yourself up every minute of the day. And stop smiling at me. You smile at me all the time. You hate the whole world, but you always smile at me. I am not that great.*

"I think you're getting muscles," his father said. "Here, give me a feel of your right arm."

Albert obliged. He flexed his right arm. His father's iron fingers probed the soft biceps—a shriveled prune of a muscle. "Not bad. You should work out with dumbbells, weights. Do exercises like I did when I was a kid."

"Pop, I did them a whole winter last year and I didn't get one single solitary muscle. I could do exercises forever, and still be flabby. It's in my genes. I am simply a person without muscles. I take after Mom, not you."

"Nah, it's all in the exercises. Look at Teddy Roosevelt. Look at me. Sure, I was a strong kid, but nothing to brag about. But from the minute I was in school, on the East Side, poor as hell, with my old man pushing a cart of grapes or pears or oranges, and me running after him, I used to work out." His eyes became soft, the harsh lines around them less emphatic. "Old Mr. Cooney spotted me right off. He knew I was a natural for the gym. There was a gent, Francis Xavier Cooney. No more like him. 'Abrams,' he used to say, 'you got a body that was made for the parallel bars.' And me, sixteen, a dumb greenhorn with a father who never talked to me, and living in a cold-water flat, seven flights up. That old Irishman took me into the gym and taught me what it was to have friends, to develop your body, to compete. And never a word about me being a Jew or him an Irishman or any of that crap. Too bad he died. I would have sent you around to take boxing and wrestling lessons from him. He was still running the school a few years ago, and over eighty years old. I loved that old guy."

His father's young manhood was populated with muscular teachers and coaches, most of them Irishmen, who had taken him in hand, taught him gymnastics, swimming, track and field. The doctor had worked part-time as a gym teacher while in medical school. Often, Albert wished the old man had remained a gym teacher. As a teacher he never would have had to worry about unpaid bills, patients who gossiped about him, ran out on him. Maybe it wasn't too late; maybe he could do something—*anything*—other than be a doctor.

"Yeah, once I ran into Cooney, a few years before he died," the doctor reminisced. "Your mother and I were coming out of the Majestic Theatre, and there he was, taking his constitutional at night, very erect, snow-white hair, no hat, even though it was December. He knew me right away. 'Abrams,' he said, 'Abrams, the best man on the rings I ever coached.' Was he proud when I told him I was a doctor. He felt he had a lot to do with it, and believe me, he did. I could have stayed a slob like my father, selling oranges from a pushcart. Cooney, he was one of the great ones."

They sat in silence. They had run out of topics. The doctor knew nothing about baseball. Albert was made a little uncomfortable by his recollections of better days. It made the present even worse than it was. Instead of good old Mr. Cooney, he had deadbeats like Levinson.

"Did that guy who was just here sell you something, Pop?" he asked.

"What? Oh, that punk. Look! Look at the piece of *dreck* he forced on me—four dollars worth of the ten he owes me. As if I'll ever see the other six! *Feh!*"

From a chair at the end of the desk—the chair where his corporal's guard of patients, the bits and pieces that the Depression had left him sat—he picked up a garish banner. It depended from a long gilt wooden bar. Gold-fringed, tasseled, it was the red-white-and-blue NRA sign, handsomely dyed on shiny rayon. The Blue Eagle gleamed: WE DO OUR PART.

"What a racket! What a swindle!" cried Dr. Abrams. "People can't get money to eat and this cake-eater Levinson is cheating them with fancy-shmancy fake silk eagles!" The anger darkened his face; the lines at the edge of his mouth deepened —Chief Angry Eagle Abrams, the mad Indian. "The hell with them! The hell with all of them! What did the *fekokteh* NRA ever do for me? I am my own goddamn man and they might as well know it!"

Crash went his fist on the desk. Albert paled, recoiled, certain his father had shattered the glass desk top. Terrified, he wondered: Who might as well know it? Should they take an advertisement in the *Times* telling the world that *Dr. Solomon Abrams is his own goddamn man and you, whoever you are, might as well know it?*

Scowling, the doctor settled into a seething silence. He locked his hands on the rise of his paunch—it wasn't really a belly, more like two chests—and stared at the tawdry poster. He seemed to be saying to himself: I'm not unpatriotic and I have nothing against FDR and the NRA, but why pick on me?

93

"Pop, did I see you come out of Melnick's house today?" He was impelled to get the old man to talk about something else—anything. But that was the trouble. There was hardly anything they could ever discuss. Albert didn't care for gardening or handy repair work. The old man could fix anything—he was a carpenter, electrician, upholsterer, plumber, painter; Albert could barely drive a nail.

"Hah? Yeah. The old *kocker* wanted someone to complain to."

"How old is he anyway?"

"How old? Only God knows, and I mean *God*. He and Melnick have been having a conversation for a long time. Who knows? His whiskers are probably over a hundred, but he's a kid, only ninety-two."

The doctor laughed: he found something delightful and redeeming in the old Orthodox Jews of the neighborhood. The guys with spinach on their face. He roared at the *Ballyhoo* magazine cartoon of the old bearded Jew posing for the photographer. "*Smile!*" commanded the photographer. Answer: "*I am smiling!*" But he always treated the old gents, as he called them, with great courtesy.

"I heard Grubman say that Yussel was once invited to Columbia to talk to some professors. Or maybe it was the Jewish Seminary there."

"Hah!" roared Dr. Abrams—successfully diverted from his fury over the vanished fee. "Hah! That I'd like to see! Nicholas Murray Butler and Melnick sitting down to dinner! Pork chops and lobsters! *Wow!*" The notion overwhelmed him. Dr. Butler, to Albert's father, was one of the great comic figures of the age. Albert laughed too, although he really did not understand what was so hilarious about Nicholas Murray Butler.

"Melnick's got a secret room in the basement," Albert ventured. He was ecstatic: he had moved the old man away from his violent anger.

"What's he doing? Taking in laundry?"

"It's a workshop or something. Once Little Artie peeked in and Yussel smacked him with the ruler. Little Artie saw a lot of big tables covered with what looked like painter's cloths."

94

Dr. Abrams nodded. "Sure. He's a *painter* on the side. I can see him in a Sherwin-Williams white cap and overalls. But he'll go broke on the turpentine to clean his beard! *Clean his beard!* Oh, I can see the paint on it!"

The laughter convulsed him. When he stopped, he wiped his eyes, rose suddenly from the swivel chair, and walked to his son. With almost involuntary moves, as if the boy's presence were irresistible, a magnet that drew him willy-nilly, he hugged Albert to his chest, kissed the coarse hair of his head a dozen times, and tugged lovingly at his ears.

"Ah, come on. Cut it out, Pop."

"I'm allowed to kiss you."

"But, holy smoke, Pop. . . ."

"Daddies love their little boys."

"Leggo, Pop, stop."

The warmth flowed from his father's iron hands. It settled softly on the boy's thatched head. Embarrassed, he let himself be crushed against the hard breast. *He simply cannot keep his hands off me—I'm so precious; like that photograph under the glass.* Once, in a swimming pool at Rockaway, in the presence of older boys who had spent the summer tormenting him, his father had dived into the water and begun grabbing his ears in that crazy possessive way. The older boys sneered at him. Later they bent and twisted his ears viciously until he wept. But he never told his father. What was so marvelous about his ears? All that love, all that grabbing and kissing, that soft-eyed admiration from the old man—he would trade every bit of it for an ounce of Teddy Ochab's courage.

Sated, the doctor released him. "Is mother upstairs?"

"Yeah. Her cousin Molly is here with that girl."

"Lady Bountiful. The poor slobs we worry about." He did not sound angry; he merely regretted that so many people had to be poor slobs.

"They came for lunch," Albert said.

"Why not? What have they got? Lost souls."

His father rummaged about the desk. He found a fountain pen, a prescription pad, and stuffed them in his shirt pocket. "Tell Mother I'm going to the surgical supply store."

But no calls, Albert thought. No people to call on, so he can earn money. More and more, his father seemed to be off on errands that did not involve the earning of a living—the post office, the surgical supply, the garage.

"Okay, Pop."

"You want to come along with me?"

He liked to accompany his father on calls, on long rides to places like Brighton, Sea Gate, Canarsie. He enjoyed riding with his father on a winter's evening, huddled in an old furred lap robe, silent as they sped through strange streets. He did not mind waiting (the old man gave patients a lot of time, more than they were worth, his mother said) and sometimes he would craftily leave the car to relieve himself in the gutter, sighing as his bladder eased and his urine rose in steamy clouds in the Brooklyn night. Ah, those were fun, expeditions to the distant marches of the borough—Manhattan Beach, Flatlands, Gowanus, Dyker Heights.

"We got a punchball game this afternoon. A champeenship play-off with the Hawks."

"Okay, kiddo. Knock 'em for a loop."

Albert's eyes followed the thick figure as it progressed through the darkened office, the sunny waiting room, into the foyer. He heard the door slam. Then he settled into his father's swivel chair.

The office intrigued him. His father's palace, his workshop. Everything belonged to the old man; everything was useful; everything helped people. The cumbersome X-ray with its probing snout, the hooded metabolism apparatus, the severe cabinet of the EKG, the sterilizer snorting steam, the ancient oak medicine cabinet, the examining table. *My father's office.* It had a pungent smell of iodoform, alcohol, furniture polish. But he was beginning to wonder how important it was. *Betrayed, betrayed. There is too much promised in these rooms and not enough delivered.* "People," he whispered, "people, please come here, in large groups. Please pay your bills, people. Respect him a little, he's a terrific doctor, he can help you. Try not going to the clinics and the chiropractors and the professors, give my father a break. . . ."

He halted his appeal. "Jerk," he said to himself. "Big jerk who can't help his father." Blinking, he spun in the chair a few times. Above the doctor's desk framed photographs stared at him—evidence of his father's youth, hopes, friends, idols. It pained Albert to look at them, like the old man's stories about his friend Cooney. Life must have offered him everything in those years; and he had ended up, stuck in Brownsville, with no patients and bills that were never paid.

A group of physical education instructors stared back at him—serious moustached young muscle-men in tights and jerseys. His father had been the only Jew in the class—dark-haired, Mohawk-faced. Solemn, arms folded, they confronted the world of 1908, sure of themselves, happy in their work. Who could deny them anything, those confident athletes? His father should have spent the rest of his life in tights and a jersey, teaching basketball to kids.

In dark mahogany frames and yellowed matting, the faces of some of the doctor's professors peered down at Albert—sedate, high-collared men, distinguished medical personages. *Abrams, you are the most promising young fellow to sit in my class in years. . . .* These were men who never lost their temper or had to worry about two-dollar fees. At one end of the wall a photo of Freud scowled at a print of Maimonides. His father once said enigmatically, "A couple of great guys, those two."

It seemed inconceivable to Albert that a man who had had these marvelous associations, who had come this far from a boyhood of tagging after his father's pushcart, could be denied everything. Gymnast, scholar, student, healer, a man who knew about Freud and Maimonides—surely the world had more to give him, even if there was a depression. He personalized the Depression, and hated it—the tall bony creep Rollin Kirby drew in the *World-Telegram.*

Albert puffed out his cheeks, blowing warm air into the consultation room. His eye scanned the top of his father's desk. It was a discouraging clutter of bills, paid and unpaid, medical literature from the indefatigable drug houses (the Depression didn't seem to bother *them*, his father always said), and a massive bronze desk set, a gift from his mother on their tenth wedding anniversary. Scissors, letter opener, inkwells, the items lay scattered about. On a bronze tray intended for paper clips, there were a dozen wooden identification tags for the doctor's dahlia tubers—*Queen of the Garden, Warren G. Harding, Sarah Bernhardt.*

Albert opened the middle desk drawer. It was as disorderly as the desk top—more bills, receipts, a folder of postage stamps, checkbooks, rubber bands, old Jewish New Year's cards, photographs. There was a mad assortment of keys—unlabeled, some rusty, some bent. The old man never threw anything out. His cellar was a storehouse of shovels and rakes caked with rust, blunted chisels and planes, decaying coils of rope.

One short hollow key opened the right-hand drawer where the day book was kept. How odd that anything in the house should be locked! There was nothing worth stealing. His father always carried the day's receipts in a crumpled wad in his pants pocket. Albert opened the side drawer and saw the ledgers. On top was the one in which his father had just written.

He had never been curious about the entries in the books. His father's income was of no interest to him as long as he ate, went to school, was clothed, and had a bed to sleep in. But for some reason, he was now piqued with nosiness. How much *did* the old man earn? Was his mother bluffing when she said he had barely earned the price of the softball?

He picked up the ledger. It was a hideous blood-colored account book. He opened it, looking around to make sure there were no witnesses to his peeping. He began turning pages.

His father's impatient handwriting was almost illegible. The entries were severely slanted and tended to bunch together in cramped hieroglyphs at the end of each line. He was annoyed that he had to spend so much time deciphering the old man's scratchings. What if his mother caught him? Wasn't he in enough trouble already? "If there is anything worse than a sneak roller skater," he muttered grimly, "it's a sneak accounts-book looker." And he turned the pages to July, stopping at the first of the month. There, he read:

Call, Joseph Bernstein, 781 Rower Ave., grippe	$2.00
Call, F. Calucci, 1776 St. Marks, sprained ankle	2.00
Office, Moses Kaplan, checkup	1.00
Office, Vito LoBalbo, fill out forms for city job, routine check	1.00
	$6.00

On July 1st, his father had earned six dollars. At first Albert was convinced it was a mistake. Maybe he didn't put everything down in the book. He might not include things like X-rays. Or maybe he forgot a few calls. A whiz at mathematics, he figured that his father, at that rate, earned forty-two dollars a week, or $2,184 a year. "Impossible," said Albert, addressing himself to the framed gym teachers on the wall above the desk, to Freud, Maimonides, and the assorted professors. "Absolutely impossible and I don't believe it for one minute. No doctor earns that little." His hands trembled as he turned pages in the ledger. On July 2nd the doctor had earned twelve dollars, including an eight-dollar fee for X-rays for Thomas Natale. On the 3rd, ten dollars, but that included five dollars owed to him by Samuel Tabachnikoff. On the 4th, admittedly a holiday, he had earned one dollar, *one single solitary dollar*, from an office visit by a certain Benjamin Saltz, chest pains. Albert envisioned Benjamin Saltz as a stooped garment worker, reluctantly handing his father a dollar in coins—reward for self-education, hard work, the praise of professors, and his skill on the parallel bars. If that's what college gets for you, who wants to go?

The lightning calculator was at work again. Earnings for the first days of July and the last few days of June—a full week—gave him a total of fifty-one dollars. That was a little better. Not much, but a little. *Ah, the winter, the wintertime!* The old man probably cleaned up then; he got rich on grippe, colds, flu, pneumonia, broken arms and legs. But his hand trembled as he started to riffle pages backward. It was obvious his father made more money *then*, so why look? Of course, January, February, March—they more than made up for the slow summer. They had to. Softly, he closed the accounts book—cursed Pandora's Box—and returned it to the drawer. He locked it and put the hollow key back in the middle drawer.

Involuntary tears clogged his eyes. "Stop, stop," he said. "You can't do anything about it. I told you, it's better in the winter with all those germs around and everyone getting sick." But the tears coursed down his narrow face—silent, unbelieving tears. "I should be out earning a living," he mumbled, "instead of making him buy softballs for me. Ah, I'm no good, no good at all."

He would go off into the world and make a lot of money, prevail on some rich hospital to hire his father as chief consultant, see to it that the old man shined his shoes and got haircuts regularly.

Voices in the corridor told him that his mother's guests were leaving. Ruthie and his doomed adventure on roller skates had been banished from his mind. Who cared? Who cared at all? So what if he couldn't skate—when his father had earned one dollar on July 4th?

"Hannah, if I could tell you how much these visits mean to us," he heard Molly Koplik say. "To see a real house, everything so nice, to let poor Ruthie know we got family, relatives like everyone else."

"That is not necessary, Molly," Mrs. Abrams was saying. "You are more than welcome here. I wish you would come more often. And the doctor will be happy to take care of your medical needs. Your parents were very dear to mine in the old country, Molly, and I feel obligated to help you."

It maddened Albert (for reasons he could not explain) that his mother spoke so precisely, so perfectly, without a trace of accent. Molly's singsong was positively crude next to his mother's pleasant lilt. Not a flossy, fancy accent, but a precise way of saying each word. Where'd she learn it? It was as if his mother had been *born* speaking good grammar and without any accent. Again, he imagined one of his nutty exchanges: *I will trade all her fine speech patterns for more shrewdness, toughness, cunning. Like the dentist's wife in the neighborhood who* wears a starched uniform, makes believe she's a nurse, and threatens the patients with lawsuits when they don't pay up!

"Hannah, there should be more people like you," Molly said. "You make it happy for us. Ruthie say good-bye to Aunt Hannah, and thank her for everything."

"Thanks, Aunt Hannah. I'm sorry about the skates. C'n I say good-bye to Albert?"

He dried his eyes, smearing them with dirt, and walked into the corridor. Molly and Ruthie were at the door. His mother was to one side.

"Our cousins are leaving, Albert. Come say good-bye."

He shuffled toward them.

"How did your face get so dirty?" asked his mother.

"Had something in my eye and I rubbed it." He shook hands with Molly. She kissed him, a wet garment worker's kiss. He nodded at Ruthie. She took the hint and offered no kiss.

"Such a wonderful boy," Molly said. "It should happen to Ruthie to find such a boy when she grows up."

Didn't they know about hemophilia and feeble-mindedness and all the other horrid things that happened when cousins married? Not to mention the fact that, biological and genetic pitfalls apart, he couldn't stand Ruthie Koplik, although she was admittedly a beautiful child and her gluey hands had given him the shivers.

"Ruthie will have no troubles on that score," Mrs. Abrams said. "She is turning into a beautiful young lady."

They lingered, reluctant to return to their hot flat on the East Side.

"And Hannah," Molly went on, "if you hear from a job, like with Uncle Kalman, if he needs a first-class operator, you'll get in touch with me?"

"Of course, Molly."

More people he didn't know. A mysterious Kalman. Did he own a pants factory in Bridgeport? It sounded as if Molly needed a job.

"Hannah, I'm ashamed to ask you like this, but if you got friends with girls a little older than Ruthie, who don't need some of their clothes, believe me we're not so proud both of us, we'll take and be grateful. . . ."

The street door swung open, slammed shut. Albert saw his father enter the foyer. He had not gone to the surgical supply house. Something had brought him home. With an instinct born of long hours of study of the doctor's mannerisms, Albert smelled the imminent show of fury.

Mrs. Abrams opened the interior door. The cousins stepped aside. The doctor, without breaking stride, with no greeting, no sign of recognition, stomped past them into the sunny waiting room. His dark head was lowered, his face taut. Into the midst of the waiting room (so often vacant!) he charged. Albert shuddered at the waste of all those *National Geographics*, the neat tray of white calling cards, the hard leather chairs. Crazily, his father spun about, and began to shout—not to his wife, his son and the relatives, but to an invisible audience.

"I caught him! I caught the son-of-a-bitch red-handed stealing a patient!"

"Sol! Your language!"

But he heard nothing, saw no one. A hot glaze had come over his eyes. Rage blinded him, like the invasive sunlight.

"That lousy bastard Smackowitz, that dirty charlatan, that stinking chiropractor who moved into the open store around the corner, like a goddamn gypsy! In his fancy white coat and white shoes and the whorehouse diploma in the window! I caught that son-of-a-bitch right in the act, and I had a good mind to beat his brains out! Why I didn't, I don't know."

"Sol, control yourself. There is no excuse for that kind of language, especially in front of children!"

Hideously fascinated, Molly and Ruthie watched his performance, his pacings, his wild gestures, his impassioned face. It seemed to Albert, cringing against the wall, sick to his stomach, that the miserable visitors were *enjoying* his father's convulsions. If it shattered their vision of the house as a place of wealth and comfort, it reassured them that "rich" people like Dr. Abrams and Aunt Hannah could also be miserable.

"That vile, cheating Galitzianer, that quack! That lousy bone-twister! Five minutes ago, I walk on my way to surgical supply and I see him in front of that store he opened, and he's leading old man Pergament by the arm—leading him off the street into that place! Pergament! My patient! My patient from the day I hung out the shingle! I saved that old *futz* from pneumonia twice and I've massaged his prostate until my finger got sore! Not to mention all the free calls to the hospital when his wife had her gallbladder out! And there he is—that old ingrate, smiling at Smackowitz and letting himself be led by the arm into a grocery shop!"

The guests were hypnotized. Ruthie's blue eyes were wide, her mouth open. This was better than lunch.

"Well, I told them off!" the doctor yelled. "I gave them a reading from the Torah they won't forget!"

"Them?" his wife asked. "You bawled out Mr. Pergament also? That poor old man who is almost blind?"

"That's right, side with them!" Up, up rose his voice—not louder, but thinner, in that mad tone Albert had come to dread. It was a voice that made him think of crazy people, of people who couldn't control themselves. "Yeah, you always side with them! Why, I told that whoremaster Smackowitz if I caught him stealing patients from me again, I'd tear his hands off, I'd break his skull! The nerve of that scum, in broad daylight, grabbing people off the street! He can do it, but I can't because I'm a professional man, a gentleman. And I told off Moishe Pergament also! Let him go to the devil! Let him go to that *fekokteh* chiropractor and get his behind manipulated—"

"Sol, stop that at once!" his mother cried.

"—fraud, charlatan, scoundrel, pimp, I say to hell with all of them, they all stink!"

He walked away, insensate with fury, into the inner room.

"Oi, I'm sorry, Hannah, I'm sorry," Molly moaned. "We stayed too long. Come, Ruthie."

His mother ushered them out the door.

Albert shuffled down the corridor. *You bet you did. Saw the Wild Man from Borneo, dincha? Glad you had a free show.*

In the kitchen Albert sat morosely, chewing at his unfinished bagel. Will it ever end? he asked. Drawers slammed, furniture was agitated in the office. His father moved about in a dulled rage, spitting out curses, laments, recriminations. Unafraid, his mother walked down the corridor and entered the office. She would beard the lion in his den, offer her soft words, undergo one more baptism of violence. He resolved to stop making issues about roller skates and the bicycle. He thought of her buying him the tin alligator from Woolworth's when he was five years old, of his father's paint set, and he drowned in guilt for that sensible fearless woman.

"Sol, that was uncalled for," he heard her say.

"Was it? Am I supposed to let those thieving lice walk all over me, steal my patients from under my nose?" Still in high register, his voice scared Albert. Until it got down to normal, he would suffer some dread for the old man, fear of something awful his father might do.

"I don't mean that. You certainly have a right to be distressed."

"Distressed! Woman, you know so little. Things keep up like this, where will we be?"

"I'm aware of our economic problems. We'll have to make the best of it, like everyone else does these days. I mean the way you carried on in front of Molly and the children."

"Your *shnorrer* relatives? Eating free meals here? Better they should hear about the kind of life I really lead, so they'll know for once who they're sponging on!"

"That is not like you, Sol. That is unkind."

No, take it back, Albert said, sniffling. *Take it back. You don't mean it, do you? You have to be a little sorry for them. I am, and they aren't anything to me.*

"Sol, you're overwrought. This terrible heat. . . ."

"It's not the heat, it's the stupidity."

There you go, there you go, Albert said to himself. He slumped deep in the kitchen chair. *In the middle of everything, going crazy and yelling, cursing, losing patients, insulting the whole world, you have to make a rotten joke. Can you beat that?*

". . . the heat and the relief work, I know you hate, and the competition from younger doctors and chiropractors; I know it's hard for you, Sol, but is it any secret that people have lost jobs and can't pay, or that it's hard times for everyone? You act as if you're the only one having a difficult time."

"I am a physician, dammit!" Again the voice soared. "I have worked all my life for a little respect and the right to get paid when I perform services, and every smart-aleck cake-eating bastard in the world is out to do me in! Every whoremaster and crap-artist is out to eat my guts, to destroy me! Like that *shtunk* who sold me this *fekokteh* NRA silk flag for what he owed me!"

The sight of the banner with its blue eagle drove him to new frenzy. Albert heard it being slammed to the floor.

"Tell me please, my philosophizing wife, tell me please, how do you pay the mortgage with a piece of silk *dreck* like this, with gold tassels, hah?"

"I cannot talk to you when you are overwrought."

"Just as well! No more speeches from you, my great rationalizer! I'll handle this stinking mess of my life in my own way, in my own way, on my own time! I'll settle it once and for all, and the hell with everybody!"

What will you do? Albert inquired rhetorically. *What will you do, Pop? Join the CCC? Get a WPA job like Teddy Ochab's father, swinging a pick in Prospect Park? Will you enlist in the United States Army?* This wasn't too bad an idea, at that. Captain Solomon Abrams, M.D. His father was only fifty, still a young man. They would all ship out to Hawaii or the Canal Zone. He'd make Major in a few years. He would be Albert Abrams, Army brat. He saw himself in dusty blue jeans, burned by the desert sun, treading the sandy streets of a cavalry post in New Mexico. That would be a good life! No chiropractors to rob his patients, no Bushys and Bimbos and Lee Roys to terrorize him. *Dear Mr. Secretary of War, my father is a terrific doctor who hates his life here in Brooklyn, and is anxious to start a new career in the U.S. Army Medical Corps. . . .*

The hallway door opened and his mother appeared. Walking toward him, she was immaculate, her face unlined.

"Who told you to be underfoot? I don't like you listening in on our conversations. Can't you go somewhere else when your father and I are discussing personal matters?"

"I didn't hear a word you said."

"Not much, you didn't. Big ears."

"Who cares anyway?" he asked. "You think I care? All that yelling—I don't even know what it's about."

His mother turned away. She would return to the living room and spend the afternoon with an English novel—Gissing, Meredith, or one of the new J. B. Priestleys. The English soothed her.

". . . take the whole lousy thing into my own hands," his father was muttering, "and end it once and for all! Settle it myself. . . ."

The raging voice grew hoarse. Indistinct mutterings replaced discernible words. Papers were crumpled. A desk drawer slammed. Albert could bear it no longer.

He strolled on to the screened porch, down the rickety steps into the quiet, heat-soggy garden. Midway there was an ancient weatherworn bench. Rusted iron feet were sunk in the hard earth. He sat down, shaded by the cherry tree, poplars. Head in hand, he asked aloud: "How you going to settle it, Pop? You going to rob a bank? Win a sweepstakes ticket? You going to blow up the whole house and kill us all, so you won't have to ever worry about losing patients, or earning six dollars a day?"

Albert buried his head in his crossed arms, too unnerved to cry. He tried to think about a variety of reassuring things, such as the half-pitcher of iced tea in the refrigerator, his extremely high IQ, Joe Stripp's batting average, and the championship punchball game. Nothing helped.

Sometime after his father's hysteria over the stolen patient (the outburst had deposited a lump of clay in Albert's belly), he returned to the street. He glared defiantly at the late afternoon sun: *Do your worst.* The sun had been pumping hot yellow light into the street all day. Now, half-enshadowed, half-illuminated, it had assumed the look of an amphitheater, a primitive colosseum in Iberia or Pannonia, a bush-league ballpark built by a homesick Roman proconsul.

Awaiting the great punchball championship play-off, the crowd had gathered early. They had preempted choice seats on stoops, steps, windowsills, fire escapes, fences. Others had brought fruit crates or milk bottle cases. What elegance! Albert applauded his neighbors' resourcefulness. They were every bit as wise and as good as a group of English lords and ladies, resting aristocratic behinds on shooting-sticks. (He knew about shooting-sticks from his mother's English novels.) Small children had established curbstone squatters' rights. They jammed together in agglutinized groupings along the chalked base lines. Albert was proud to be part of the famed team that had brought out such a throng. True, he was only a scorekeeper, but he was a Raider, through and through. With pardonable pride, he acknowledged that he was the finest scorekeeper in the business.

Outside Fleishacker's poolroom, beneath the orange awning, a group of older galoots loitered. Albert realized immediately that he had seen a verb visualized. They were indeed *loitering*, pure and simple, nothing else. *Alone and palely loitering*. No, Keats must have meant something else. In any case, they loitered, a jury of elder wise guys, clustered around the dreadful figure of Mutty Zetzkin. They lit his cigarettes and brought him soft drinks; he, with lizard's blinking eyes, observed the Hawks taking warm-ups. The enemy bounced and leaped on rubber Keds on the hot asphalt, prodded by the croaks of Mutty's kid brother, the mighty Zetz. His real name was Isadore, but heaven help the wretch who would so address him. The captain of the Hawks was Zetz, ruthless Zetz, Tamerlane of the streets. He was another Bushy Feinstein, two years older, many years meaner.

That first look at the monstrous Hawks shivered him, made his hairs prick up. He threaded his way along the sidewalk, looking for the Raiders. His clipboard and pad were tucked under one arm. A phalanx of pencils glittered in the pocket of his yellow polo shirt.

107

"Excuse me, Daisy, didn't mean to bump into you."

The handyman rotated his bemused black head: stoned, *shicker*, at three in the afternoon. He neither felt Albert bump into him (he was sprawled against a trash can) nor heard the apology. Who ever apologized to him?

Sobering thoughts about the permutations of terror occupied the official scorekeeper as he walked toward the ice-dock. The subject fascinated him, for it sometimes appeared that there was a fear-inducing quality in everyone—even a drunk like Daisy—although he doubted that Daisy could ever menace him. Ah, but elsewhere, elsewhere on Longview Avenue, brutality and meanness lurked about him. Why were so many people so lousy? Were there no limits to unkindness? Did everybody have to belong to the great brotherhood of bullies and bastards?

The notion skipped around his mind as he looked carefully both ways (why? no traffic) and crossed the street. There was Bimbo for example, who thought he was tough and was always abusing him. But Bimbo was a child—twelve and a half. Yet as nasty as Bimbo was, how could he possibly compare to their lord, Sir Bushy Feinstein? Driven by a lunatic need to win at everything, Bushy could mopilize Bimbo with one hand tied behind his back! He could scare the pants off Bimbo just by nailing him with those demonic eye-slits. Yet how tough was Bushy? When you got down to cases he was only fourteen years old. Move up one level of terror, one rung higher on the ladder of hell, and there stood the odious Zetz. *Oh, how monstrous he was, how awful to contemplate!*

The ferocious Isadore Zetzkin took his "runner-in," pivoted on sneakered feet, and slammed an iron fist against the Spalding Hi-Bouncer. As he streaked around the bases, Albert got a good look at him. Zetz was not much taller than Bushy but was twice as broad. His face was lumped and scarred. Its centerpiece was a huge hooked nose, which, if adorning a scholar's phiz, might have afforded dignity. But Zetz had been twice expelled from school for shouting salacious words at teachers, and his face was a masterpiece of proud stupidity. And that nose, squashed, bent, bloodied in a hundred street-fights, had assumed the appearance of a mutant banana, a botanical sport (so reasoned Luther Burbank Abrams) destined to spawn new species of malformed bananas. *Oh, Zetz!* The monster had hot pale green eyes and honey-colored hair that grew in ringlets low over his creased forehead and thick around his dried apricot ears. Vaguely he resembled certain hideous Greek statues Albert had seen in the Metropolitan Museum of Art.

"Outa my way, ya_____!" And Zetz' voice fouled the air with a string of atrocious words. He thundered around the base paths, unloosing a miasma of language so filthy that Albert felt its presence hang in the atmosphere like the exhaust from a truck or the vapors that had arisen from Gorilla's roasted dog. Like the rest of the Hawks, Zetz wore a tight blue T-shirt. A yellow flannel H was sewn to the chest. The Hawks had been the first team to sport uniforms. The Raiders looked hopelessly outclassed.

Zetz was high on the ladder of terror, Albert realized. But where did that leave Lee Roy Pennington and his associates? He thought about it a little, as he approached the Raiders—resting in the shade of the ice-dock, looking subdued. But if the ladder of nastiness went Bimbo, Bushy, Zetz, where did Lee Roy fit in—football-headed, softball-stealing Lee Roy? Lee Roy was as wolfish as they came. He might battle Bushy to a draw. But Zetz could murder Lee Roy. Zetz feared no one, except his own brother. It was widely rumored that Zetz had once knocked a colored boy's eye clean out of his head. The ambitious Negro had made the mistake of trying to steal a football from Zetz' locker at Hamilton. (Zetz had already stolen it from the gym.) Isadore Zetzkin, son of an elder of the synagogue, had given the thief one of the worst beatings in the annals of Hamilton High School. Big Artie, who had heard the story secondhand, had rendered a solemn account of it, as they all listened in awe: *That boogie's eye came right outa his head on the locker room floor and they hadda sew it back in.* Medically unlikely, Albert thought, but a good tale of terror.

Lee Roy would have to settle for a spot beneath Zetz but above Bushy, although the rankings were by no means final. A niche, too, would have to be found for Lee Roy's tufted friend. Parity with Zetz? Doubtful. Someday they would have to battle it out, the way fighters did for ratings by Nat Fleischer and *Ring* magazine. And this Zetz, this ogre, was the captain-general of the team his own Raiders dared challenge! He thrilled to Bushy's effrontery, to Teddy's courage, to all of them—Big Artie, Little Artie, Frankie Udo, even Bimbo. Heroes! His friends! Perhaps some of their bravery would rub off on him. That, and setting-up exercises might do the trick, might fool them all. He felt taller, more rugged, bouncier in his bumpered sneakers. If they could bring down the cannibal Zetz, they could beat anyone! And so could he!

Yet he wondered: Would victory over the Hawks settle anything in the long run? Talmudical details disturbed him. Perhaps a sage like Yussel Melnick might know the answer. For beyond the barbarian Zetz, blaspheming lout, there loomed the shadow of his brother Mutty. The horror of him! You wanted to get up close and study him, pat his head, pinch his arms, so you could be assured he was real, a genuine killer, a pumper of bullets and a wielder of ice picks! Shoulders hunched, eyes secreted behind smoked glasses, cigarette dangling from blubbery lips, he was to Albert an ultimate atrocity. You could not stop looking at him. *Made ya look, made ya look, made ya buy a penny book.* How had he murdered three men? For what reason? Why did he feel it his duty in life to throw stink bombs into bakeries and start fires in tailor shops? Who awarded him this satanic power and why was he allowed to get away with it?

Under Fleishacker's awning, advertising *Moxie*, Zetzkin squatted—untouchable, a lord of the earth. A human fire hydrant surrounded by loving dogs. A galoot fetched him a pack of Camels. Another was sent off for a huge paper cup of lemon ice from a Sicilian vendor who had set up his bucket-on-wheels near home plate.

But why? Albert asked himself. Why do the likes of Mutty Zetzkin and his attendants appear to have the world in their grasp? Why do things go so well for them and so badly for his father? Assuredly, something was wrong somewhere. Something was not working properly. But he abandoned gloom. This was not the time for it. Excitement overwhelmed him. The Raiders were moving from the shadow of the ice-dock, waiting their practice licks. Bushy observed the enemy slyly from behind his slits.

"They got a new guy this time," Teddy Ochab said.

"Yeah, a ringer," Bushy said. He was grim. As Albert and the others stood by, Bushy indicated a tall boy with long black hair elegantly tied with a red kerchief. "I know that guy," Bushy went on. "Pole Vault Podolsky. He played right end for Hamilton. Know how old he is? He's *seventeen*."

"Seventeen!" Albert's voice wavered.

"We shoulda made rules on how old y'could be," Big Artie said sadly. In his trimmed cotton knickers and sleeveless orange shirt he looked like a glandular fat boy, an eight-year-old grown to monstrous soft size.

"We dint think of it," Bushy snapped. It had been his responsibility to set the rules with Zetz. He had failed to protect them from ringers. "Ah, we'll moider 'em anyway," Bushy snarled. "They stink. They stink on ice. They'll try to bulldoze us, but they ain't no better. I ain't scared."

"Nobody's scared," Teddy said. "But they look bigger 'n last time."

The world was all unfairness, at least in things that counted like fist-fighting and punchball. Albert found a vacant seat on a tenement stoop and began making out the official scorecard. My goodness, Albert thought, the average age of the Raiders is thirteen and a half! The Hawks averaged a good two years older, and they were playing a seventeen-year-old giant, the mythical Pole Vault Podolsky! But the game was a holy duty. That spring the Raiders had run out of teams their own age. They were too good. They had drubbed the Atlantic Avengers, the Park Place Panthers, the Ralph Avenue Rens, the Saratoga Celtics, the Rochester Redmen. The last few games had been farces, slaughters. The hapless Maple Mohawks had lost to them 28–6. Albert could remember Bushy dancing

111

around the base paths after Teddy had smashed a homer, shrieking: "More! More!"

But the Hawks! From the crowded stoop, his linen behind drawing street dirt, his nose happily inhaling body odor, he studied the great Podolsky. The ringer was six-foot-two with a face like an antelope. He had a stately quality, the mark of a natural. Podolsky took a dainty runner-in and struck the ball. The pink rubber Spalding soared high, higher, like one of Picard's balloons, into the summer sky, over his father's poplar, far down Longview Avenue. Distantly, more than two sewers away (a sewer was the length between manhole covers), someone raced vainly for the Podolsky clout.

"And dat's only warm-ups," Albert heard Gorilla droning. "Boy, oh boy, deh'll moider you guys. Deh'll wipe da floor up wit' ya." Shuffling on shortened legs, the half-wit sidled up to him. He was grinning. His empty head was cocked to one side. Summer, winter, he wore his natty brimmed, tweed cap. It was always yanked to one side, in the manner of Kid Dropper or Monk Eastman.

"Wanna bet, Gorilla?" Albert asked. "Even money?"

"Who's rich like you? I ain't no doctor's son." Spit bubbled at the corners of his primordial mouth. A lungfish's mouth, Albert thought, the mouth of an aardvark or a three-toed sloth.

"Go chase yourself around the block, Gorilla. Three times, and come back twice."

But Gorilla lingered. He was intrigued with Albert's beautiful lettering. "You make neat box scores," he said. "You could be a sports writer. Dat's de best job in de world. You git paid for watchin' baseball." He giggled. "I could be a sports writer also. I'm loinin' to write in Ungraded Class."

"Yes, a writer!" intoned Genius Grubman. He floated toward them, airborne on knickerbockers. "The moving finger writes and having writ moves on! And whose finger, pray? Why the fickle finger of Alfred Lord Gorilla Fisloff! I am grooming this boy for the Pulitzer Prize!"

"Putzeleh?" asked Gorilla.

112

Oh, the injustice of it! Doomed, doomed to sit on a cindery tenement stoop keeping my detailed box score, with a dying prodigy and a moron for companions! A rude justice in this, he suspected. *Punishment for disobeying my mother and for failing to help my father.* Still, he knew in his heart of hearts that he welcomed the attentions of Grubman and Gorilla. They, thank goodness, were two people he did not have to fear. The pain of an unburied crime stabbed him. There was a day in first grade, a misty spring day, when he had gone hopping off to school, canvas briefcase slung over shoulder. On the way he had seen Gorilla, shuffling to his appointment in the Ungraded Class, stopping to admire his reflection in a mud puddle. Albert had never been a cruel child. But something about Gorilla's innocent back, his bent legs, had tempted him. How awful to recall it! He had shoved Gorilla face-down into the mud, and then scampered away hearing the half-wit's unearthly wails. Never, never had Gorilla mentioned the incident. It was possible that he had no idea who had victimized him. But every time Albert looked at the large head, the vague eyes, he wondered to himself: *Does he know?* Again and again Albert returned to the memory of his gratuitous maltreatment of the moron, rubbing it like an unhealed scab, picking at it, refusing to let it dry and fall. If the memory served any purpose, it helped him understand the ferocity of monsters like Zetz and even Bushy.

Grubman draped a white arm on Gorilla's shoulders. They faced Albert with great ceremony—Rosencrantz and Guildenstern. They regarded him as a species worthy of contemplation and study, the *doctor's son*, rarer than the passenger pigeon or the great auk, as elusive as the okapi.

"We shall sit in judgment, we three," Genius chanted. "We shall be the new triumvirate. The three in one, the one in three. We gather here to watch the slaughter of the innocents. Lambs led to the altar. Your colleagues, Abrams, will shortly be pronounced, by medical authority, and the official coroner of the Borough and County of Kings, that is Brooklyn, deader than Kelsey's nuts."

113

"Says you!"

"Yeah," Gorilla said, yanking at his cap. "Kelsey's nuts!"

"Now look at it this way," Albert said, pleased to have an audience. "We beat the Hawks once already this year. Okay, they spotted us three runs because we're all about two years younger on the average. But we beat 'em. The next game, they didn't spot us anything, and they won it 4–3 on a disputed play. So we're even-up. And man for man, we're just as good as they are."

"Eternal optimist!" cried Grubman.

Loyal residents of Longview Avenue, a few relatives, applauded as the Raiders started their warm-ups. They seemed like a team of midgets. But only a fool, Albert knew, would underrate them. The essence of a punchball defense was a good center, fast and fearless, and an equally fleet outfielder. In Bushy, the Raiders had a player acknowledged to be the greatest punchball center of his time, even greater than Zetz. Teddy Ochab was equally sensational in the outer garden, the cow pasture—speedy, fearless, adept at dodging cars.

Albert said to Gorilla: "Mind my seat, I got to get the Hawks lineup." He strolled toward the enemy. As he walked through the tense mob, he felt sad in the knowledge that punchball was a transitional game, a sport that must vanish someday. He would have to write an article about it and have it published somewhere.

"Basically," his essay would begin, "punchball is patterned after baseball. It is played on a diamond-shaped field, on a paved street with black asphalt surface. Like baseball, there are bases, around which the players must be moved, counterclockwise, in order to score runs. Home plate in punchball is a manhole cover, usually the one nearest a street corner. Second base is the manhole cover (or 'sewer' as it is known colloquially) next removed. The manhole cover beyond second base is usually where the outfielder stations himself. First and third bases are marked off with chalk halfway between home and second base, adjacent to the curb. Thus a long, narrow diamond forms the field.

114

"Foul lines," Professor Abrams went on, "are extended up each sidewalk from the corners of first and third base. A severe problem on any punchball field is parked cars. Often, owners have to be implored to move them. Sometimes the players themselves must push them away. It is inevitable that punchball will vanish with prosperity. The street lined with automobiles will make the game an impossibility, for what is required is a minimum stretch of three sewers of open gutter, free of cars.

"Unlike baseball, a bat is not used. (Stickball, another street variant, employs an old broomstick. Punchball is a purer, earlier game.) The fist or palm of the hand is struck against a hard hollow rubber ball. The ball is not thrown by a pitcher but tossed in the air by the batter himself and then struck. Prior to the impact, the player takes what is called his 'runner-in.' Starting at home plate, he takes a few steps gathering momentum, dribbling the ball as he moves. He then pivots to the left or right depending on whether he is left-handed or right-handed, and with the full momentum of body and arm strikes the ball. From this point on, baseball rules generally apply. A caught fly ball is out. On a grounder a player must be retired at first base."

Professor Albert Abrams, Ph.D. in American Civilization, elaborated: "It is a game of incredible skill, speed and subtle variations. It demands of its players lightning reflexes and the highest degree of coordination. For example: when the batter takes his runner-in, he is already more than a third of the way to first base! He is going at full steam. He can hit the ball high and far, or slice it, or tap it over a fielder's head, or slam it full force at a fielder's feet, or between them. He can loft it to the sidewalk, where it will get lost between trash cans and passersby. Imagine the demands made of the defense under these circumstances! And one must keep in mind the nature of the official Spalding Hi-Bouncer: bouncy, elusive, a ball that can sting, wobble crazily, or indeed, give a player a black eye, as this writer himself has witnessed."

Bushy was at his post. He was crouched low, directing

fielding practice. His hands were on his knees. His invisible eyes missed nothing. He had an athlete's cunning instincts. He went after the ball the way a green chameleon Albert had seen at the Bronx Zoo went after bugs. The poor roaches and flies never stood a chance.

Frankie Udo was batting. He hit a skidding grounder past Little Artie at third base. Bushy screamed, "I got it!", flew toward the ball, skidded on one leg, scooped the ball up with one hand and threw it viciously to Big Artie at first base. Out by a mile.

Eyes rimmed with hate, the Hawks watched the Raiders in the field. They lounged outside the poolroom—beasts of prey waiting for timid antelopes to wander to the waterhole. Under Mutty's baronial eyes, they rested and contemplated the meal they would make of the younger boys. Zetz puffed a cigarette. The smoke drifted up, infiltrating Zetz' plantain nose, drifting into his glazed green eyes. He was clearly not a member of the human race.

"Could somebody give me the lineup?" Albert asked politely. The galoots studied him with the flat eyes of future shakedown artists, second-story men. Mutty Zetzkin—toad on a throne—did not notice him. It was unnerving to Albert to even have to look at the killer.

"I'll line y'up, ya little *putz*," one of the Hawks muttered. "I'll line y'up against a wall and pull ya pants down." This one was a beauty, a work of art. Albert knew him as Flab, a corrupted miscreant, reported to have done appalling things to a thirteen-year-old girl in an abandoned car under the elevated tracks. Moreover, he had gotten away with whatever he had done. Such were the joys of being a Zetz or a Flab: a life of unpunished crime.

"I'd appreciate a little cooperation, gentlemen," Albert said. "I happen to be the official scorer."

Flab's face, a map of lumpy acne, studied him with contempt. Zetz also looked at him swinishly. The deformed mango of a nose, forged in the fires of a hundred fist-fights,

116

seemed to glow, to cast a sickly heat. *I never see thy nose but I think upon hell fire and Dives who lived in purple. . . .*

"Hey, kid," Zetz said thickly—his voice struggled upward from a garbage heap—"hey, kid, does yer old man pull out babies?"

"What has that got to do with the price of ivory in the Congo?" Albert asked.

Flab grinned through his pimples. "Ya mudder plays *bridge*."

What passed for a smile crinkled Zetz' jellied eyes. "Yer old man sticks his fingers up ladies," he croaked. The others laughed.

"I'll give you the lineup, kid," Pole Vault Podolsky said. All six-foot-two of him, he walked over to Albert with schoolyard dignity. You didn't play right-end for Alexander Hamilton without developing a little class. Once Albert had seen the great Podolsky coming home from practice in the fading sunlight of an autumn day. His uniform had been stuffed into his padded football pants which he carried on his shoulders as if bearing an amputated trunk. Pole Vault walked sedately—wearied from a long afternoon of catching passes—amid falling leaves and street cries, alone in his glory. Albert's heart had leaped when he saw him.

"Thanks, Pole Vault," Albert said. "You gonna play for Hamilton next year?"

"Sure, kid."

He dictated the enemy lineup. Albert lettered the names expertly on the scorecard.

Flabbenstein, 3b
E. Cohen, 1b
Podolsky, of
Zetzkin, c
B. Cohen, lsw
Parolo, rsw

"Hey, Four-eyes," Zetz called. "I bet yer old man sticks his fingers up niggers too."

"Is that necessary? Does that kind of thing give you pleasure?" His knees wavered. "As a matter of fact, my father took care of your family for a long time." *Until,* he wanted to add, *they stopped paying their bills.* But he said nothing else, because Zetz' tightly curled yellow head was moving toward him. But the ogre did not strike. Instead he hawked an oyster deftly between Albert's sneakers. "Next time right in yer eye, ya fairy."

"It's okay, kid," Pole Vault said. "Go on back to ya team." It appalled Albert that this manly athlete should have fallen in with such evil cronies. Well he was a ringer, a professional. No doubt he was getting paid for the game, maybe as much as a dollar. The stakes on the game were high, a half-dollar a man, three dollars wagered by each team.

This prize was held in trust by the poolroom owner, Eddie Fleishacker, who was deemed sufficiently rich and incorruptible to assume the perilous assignment. Violent fights often erupted over close decisions. The bet-holder (in this case also the chief umpire) had to make the decision as to whether the bet should be called off. Albert, retreating from the Hawks, saw Fleishacker, a gaunt pockmarked man in his late forties, sucking around Mutty Zetzkin. It was clear where *his* sympathies would lie. He operated his poolroom only with Mutty's approval; he paid protection; he hired only those whom Mutty okayed.

At the curb, Albert consulted Bushy for a final check on the lineup.

"Whattsamatta, I already gave it to ya?" Bushy snarled. He was on edge. His eyeless face quivered.

"I'll read it off, just in case," Albert said.

"*Mermelstein, first base*
Udo, left sidewalk
Ochab, outfield
Feinstein, center
Ballenberg, third base
Wexler, right sidewalk."

"Yeah. Lemme see theirs." Bushy grabbed the clipboard. "Same lousy team except for the ringer. We beat 'em oncet, we'll beat 'em again."

The others gathered around Bushy. They sweated gallons. They were tense. Bimbo Wexler, twelve and a half, matched against a team that fielded a seventeen-year-old, kept peeling his lips back and spitting. He was scared silly.

"We git last licks," Bushy said. "I won the toss yesterday. Those bastards are out to bulldoze us, 'cause they ain't any better. Stand ya ground on the bases or when ya make a tag. If ya fall okay, but *hold the ball!* Teddy, play deep for Podolsky."

Teddy sniffed his cupped hands.

"He hit one over three sewers in practice," Little Artie said.

"It don't matter," Teddy said. "It gives me more time to git under it. He puts too much height in them."

Bushy's Brillo hair stood on end. *"Let's go kill 'em!"* And he trotted out to his center position, the undone buckles of his gray knickerbockers flapping. A wild cry arose from the spectators.

Eddie Fleishacker took up his position as first base umpire. He would be in charge of decisions at first, second and the outfield. Punch-drunk Jimmy Kravitz, throwing jabs, dancing away from Leach Cross, was umpire at third.

"Play ball!" Fleishacker yelled.

The blue-shirted Hawks gathered at home plate. There was a pinging tension in the air. It permeated the heat and the layers of stench. An awareness of the Raiders' youth thrilled the crowd. They anticipated a sacrifice, a public destruction of young boys. A fat woman leaning from a window, at rest on pillowed arms and bosom, said "Oi, such liddle boys, like weak-a-lings they look by the big boys."

Flab, depraved Arnold Flabbenstein, bounced the new Spalding a few times.

"Ram it down their t'roat," Zetz whispered. "Knock 'em down when ya run."

Back at his seat on the tenement stoop Albert trembled in

anticipation. It was just like the first man up at Ebbets Field in a Dodger-Giant game. The Raiders crouched in the field, on their toes, light on the hot asphalt. The sun beat down on them, merciless, blinding. "Ready, you guys," Bushy said.

Flab rubbed the ball between his palms to give it English, bounced it, ran forward, pivoted and tossing the Spalding, slammed it with his open palm. Already, he was almost halfway to first base. The ball skidded to the space between Little Artie at third, and Bushy. Flab had done something frightening to the ball. It squirted out of Little Artie's hands and bounced toward the sidewalk. Bushy lunged for it, but Flab was already at first. Each ruby sore on his face grinned. The crowd screamed.

Ernie Cohen, one of twin brothers, was next man up for the Hawks. Both Cohen boys were revered neighborhood athletes. Ernie, an occasional "prelim-boy," had no neck. He snorted through a blunt nose, as if wearing a protective mouthpiece.

Cohen bounced the pink ball, ran forward and slapped the ball daintily over Big Artie's head. It bounced lazily to the sidewalk. Bimbo charged it, fumbled it, picked it up, dropped it, and then, terrified by Bushy's shrieks, threw it under Big Artie's legs. There were runners on first and second base.

Albert groaned. "I see what they're gonna do! They're gonna play the sidewalks and corners, and keep the ball away from Bushy and Teddy! They'll kill us."

"As learned men have said," uttered Grubman, "you can only die once."

The mob hummed. Under the orange awning, the older galoots snickered. Mutty Zetzkin nodded approval, crossing his stubby legs. He wore brown and white cake-eater's shoes, white silk socks.

Up to the plate stepped Pole Vault Podolsky. Tall and finely muscled, legs nude beneath scarlet and gray basketball shorts, he surveyed the defense and conferred with Zetz. Albert saw Zetz point to the Raiders—a fox sniffing chickens. They were looking for a weak spot.

Zetz patted Podolsky's behind. The antelope dribbled the

ball, ran, drew back his arm, and struck the tossed Spalding with his fist. Into the summer air rose the Spalding in a rising arc, the trajectory of a sure home run. The crowd howled as they saw the ball vanish, so far and so high did it travel. Ernie Cohen at first and Flab at second took off. There was no need to "tag up" on a hit like that. It could not be caught by any known human being.

Albert clapped his hands against his cheeks. "It'll be a slaughter! Three runs right off! Nobody out!"

Gorilla feigned weeping. "Baaaah. Boooo. Dey gonna moider us. Ya tink I care? Naaaah."

Bushy yelled at Little Artie to cover home plate. The monkey-face sprinted to the manhole cover. At last they saw the stricken ball descending—miles away it seemed. Flab rounded third base. Ernie Cohen was approaching second. In great prancing strides Pole Vault Podolsky had passed first.

Albert shaded his eyes, craned his neck. Distantly, almost at the end of the street, more than three sewers away, they saw the tiny figure of Teddy Ochab speeding, back-turned, zigzagging past an oncoming truck, arms and legs pumping. *Heroic Polack!* They saw his eyeglasses fly from his face, but still he ran. The rubber band holding one leg of his knickerbockers came loose; he ran on and the Spalding flew to earth.

"He got it!" screamed Bushy. *"He got it."*

The miraculous Teddy had stretched out one hand, thrown his entire skinny body forward, staggered, fallen, done a complete somersault against the curb opposite P.S. 133, but had made the catch. *In all the annals of punchball,* wrote Dan Daniel Abrams, *never have these orbs witnessed a more astounding display of patrolling the outer garden.*

On his feet, Teddy uncorked a mighty throw to Bushy, who had run out for the relay.

"Double 'em, double 'em off!" Albert screamed. Zetz bellowed at his runners to get back to their bases. Otherwise a simple throw to the bases would double them off. Slow-witted Flabbenstein was doubled off second base by Frankie Udo, who had taken the throw from Bushy. Frankie threw the ball to Big

121

Artie at first, trying to double Ernie Cohen off. But Ernie Cohen slid back a second before the play was made.

Bushy sprinted in, took the ball from Big Artie and waved it under Flab's piebald nose. "Haddya like that, huh, big shot? Pull that crap on us? Play ringers? Yer out. *Out. Out. Out.* Git off the field!"

It bothered Albert that Bushy's fury should detract from Teddy's catch. Such a catch was seen once in a lifetime. It was pure. It was beautiful. It was immortal. He knew he would remember it all his life—that vision of Ochab running like the wind across the plains of Poland, running heedless of cars and trucks, losing his eyeglasses, one pants leg undone, one bony arm reaching out for Podolsky's mighty clout, running like all the brave boys in the world.

It was Zetz' turn at bat. He smashed the ball against the asphalt. His primordial brain, Albert knew, that tiny protoplasmic organ embedded in layers of muscle, was extending itself. Teddy had ruined him.

In the field, Bushy taunted him. "Hit at me, Zetz! Right at me! Whatsa matter? Ya scared of us? Can only hit dinky little placers? We'll give you guys a lesson."

"I'll ram it down his t'roat," Zetz muttered. And he took his runner-in, crashed a fist against the ball. But anger had blinded judgment. The ball traveled in a whistling line right at Bushy's head. The chief stood his ground, made a cup of his artful hands and squeezed it. It was the third out, a ridiculously easy one.

As the teams exchanged positions Zetz slammed his shoulder into Bushy.

"Accidentally on purpose," Albert informed his aides.

"Watch it, watch it," Bushy snarled.

"I'll cockalize ya," Zetz sneered. "After we beat yez, you an' me can meet in the schoolyard."

"Yeah, bring ya whole family. You eat it, too."

The show of violence was imminent. The tribal chieftains stopped, curled lips, then trotted off. Albert saw them confront one another like angry dogs; he almost wished they'd fight it out. They deserved one another. They were born to make each other's blood flow, to inflict pain. Law of Club and Fang!

Albert explained to Genius Grubman that it would be a low-scoring game. Bushy and Teddy were the only hitters on the Raiders. "Genius," he said, "I think we're in for a defensive battle."

"Indeed. 'This battle fares like to the morning's war, when dying clouds contend wit' growing light.'"

"Now what's that from?" Albert asked.

"*Penrod and Sam*," said Grubman. "By a certain Elizabethan bard, Booth Tarkington."

"The heck it is, Genius. It's Shakespeare."

"Yes, Marvin Shakespeare."

Gorilla smiled at his friend's brilliance, licked his spatulate thumb, and pinned an imaginary medal on Genius' flabby chest.

Little Artie led off. He tried to slap the ball over their first baseman, but the big galoot stabbed it with a mighty leap.

"They stink!" taunted Zetz, crouched low at center. "Powder-puff hitters! Buncha fairies! Junkmen!"

Frankie Udo grounded out harmlessly.

Up to the manhole cover stepped Teddy Ochab. There was more applause. He looked tiny, skinnier than ever. Without his eyeglasses—one lens had smashed when they fell—he had to squint.

"Hit it a mile, Polack!"

"Give 'em good, Teddy!"

Teddy studied the defensive alignment. He smelled the ball. Twice he bounced the Spalding, ran forward, drew his arm back, and struck the ball softly. It lofted in a low arc over Zetz' curly head. Albert realized what the brilliant Teddy had done. Pole Vault Podolsky may have played football for Hamilton High, but he had lots to learn about playing the outfield in punchball. He was standing too deep. His own incredible hitting power had misguided him. Nobody could hit a ball that far. The artful Teddy had neatly dumped his hit halfway between Zetz and Podolsky.

123

The crowd howled. Zetz and Pole Vault raced toward the bouncing Spalding. Teddy lowered his white head and ran on. He did not stop at first base, but kept charging around the diamond, beating the relay to second.

Zetz studied him—contemptuous, puzzled. He could not figure this well-mannered runt. His hatred of Bushy Feinstein had a certain logic. They were of the same cloth of violence. But Teddy was beyond his primitive brain. You could not bulldoze him, razz him, unsettle him, denounce him—or provoke him into cursing. And he had more guts and savvy than any kid his size or age in Brooklyn. His purity offended Zetz, but there was nothing he could do about it.

Now Bushy was at bat, with Teddy on second and two out. Zetz motioned Pole Vault to move in. There would be no more cute hits dropped between them.

Bushy ran in, threw the ball with an odd twist, then slammed it viciously into the corner of the left sidewalk. The ball whistled over the third baseman's head, struck a trash can, then skidded away. Albert leaped up and down—puppet on a string. They'd show those bullies! Teddy flew to third. Ernie Cohen, the Hawks' first baseman raced home. It was possible the crazy Polack would try to score on an infield hit! Zetz, skinning a knee and an elbow, had made a skidding stop of the erratic ball. He saw there was no play at first; Bushy had it clean. Then he saw the Polack, head down, arms pumping, flying home with what would be the first run.

"Git ahead of him! Git ahead of him!" Zetz screamed at Ernie Cohen. The club fighter ran toward the manhole cover. The noise of the mob was deafening: it was one of those terrible moments that only a punchball game could produce. Cohen drew even with Teddy, started to run sideways as Zetz rifled the ball to him—a perfect throw. Ernie Cohen caught it and ran squarely into Teddy's path to make the tag. Teddy did not see him. He crashed into Ernie Cohen, all one hundred and two pounds of him. Cohen shoved his fist and the ball into Teddy's gut. Teddy bounced—almost three feet in the air, it seemed to Albert—hit the gutter, got to his feet again, and kept running.

"Out!" yelled Jimmy Kravitz. "Yer out!"

The ball bounced out of Cohen's hand. Teddy ran until his sneakered feet crossed the manhole cover.

"Safe!" croaked Kravitz. "Ya dropped it! Safe!"

The entire drama had taken less than ten seconds. The roar of the mob was ear-shattering. Albert expected windows to smash. At home the Raiders leaped on Teddy's back, hugged him, kissed him.

But no more runs were scored. Big Artie was thrown out. Only Bushy and Teddy could hit against the Hawks.

"As I said," Albert informed Gorilla and Genius, "a low-scoring game." As he made his pronouncement, he noticed they had been joined on the stoop by Mockey. His shaved head glinted in the afternoon sunlight. His wide eyes absorbed everything, understood nothing. Who played punchball in Kishinev?

Albert sighed. Ah, this was his life—scorekeeper for the athletes, bench-warmer, assigned to a stone seat of a filthy tenement house with an imbecile, a doomed genius and a baldheaded greenhorn. *What am I to deserve this? Who am I?* He was, he decided, a sinister figure in a Joseph Conrad novel, an outcast on an island off the Malayan archipelago, leader of a party of depraved pariahs, mysterious men who had committed crimes *not mentioned in the Bible.* Between innings Grubman took one of his promenades. He waddled in high laced boots, flapping shapeless arms, a learned penguin.

"The glory of it," Genius called out. "We drink delight of battle with our peers, high on the ringing plains of windy Troy!"

"Gaaah," Mockey gurgled.

"Whadda dope he is," Gorilla said loftily. "Dumb Mockey. Don't even know no English. Whaddya laughin' for? Ya don't know what my pal is sayin'!"

Mockey unloosed a flow of Yiddish. Genius bent an ear toward the foreign tongue. "He speaks a rare, exotic language, this newcomer. A Romano-Ukraino-Yiddish, worthy of the

125

attention of H. L. Mencken. I will decipher it or my name isn't Irving Grubman."

"Heeeeh,'" Mockey said.

Genius placed a mushroom-white hand on the shaved pate. " 'Shoot if you must this old baldhead, but spare your country's flag, she said.' "

"Ya payin' too much attention to him, Oiving," Gorilla said jealously. "Ya'll sperl him. He's just a dumb dope."

Gorilla had at last found someone to abuse. It wouldn't last. As soon as Mockey learned English, he would lord it over Gorilla.

"You're all nuts," Albert said. But he said it happily, enjoying their company. Excluded from the wrenching violence of the game, the feats of strength and speed, he luxuriated in his own party of eccentrics.

The game moved through the heat-laden afternoon. Vendors made their appearance. The Sicilian lemon-ice entrepreneur was joined by a man selling "snowballs"—flaked ice scraped from a block, over which was poured venomous nauseating sweet syrups—poison purple, bloodred, lizard green. Albert was forbidden by his mother to buy snowballs. "They are crawling with germs," she said. "That filthy block of ice is the most unsanitary thing I have ever seen." Many a time he had stood by slavering, while his friends sucked at the icy concoctions. He never saw the snowball vendor without a sense of being tempted, of witnessing something evil, desirable. Another man, a bearded elder with side-whiskers and a flat black hat appeared, hawking small bars of sesame-seed candy from a tray. This fellow puzzled Albert. Was that *all* he did? As long as he could remember he had seen this ancient with his tray of confections. Was that a proper life for an old man with whiskers?

Under the poolroom awning, Mutty Zetzkin, King Pluto of the Underworld, remained enthroned on a wire-backed chair. No one else sat in the presence of the ruler. Mutty watched the game in brooding silence, hawking gangsterish phlegm to the

126

cracked sidewalk. He was unhappy with the way those snot-nosed kids were showing up his brother's team.

On the curb in front of Albert, enfumed Daisy sat with a colleague, another Negro handyman named—enigmatically—Cowboy, and discussed baseball. More accurately it was Cowboy, a loquacious fellow, who delivered a monologue while Daisy punctuated it. Poor Daisy was always asleep or drunk. Cowboy on the other hand abstained. He was a founder of the store-front church on Rower Avenue, "The Wholy United Army of God," sometimes referred to as "The African True Church of Jesus Christ." Next to religion Cowboy adored the New York Yankees. Albert had often overheard him arguing vigorously with taunting galoots outside the poolroom. It bothered Albert that Cowboy was so earnestly involved; the clods made fun of him and he never caught on.

It was Cowboy's conviction that the other seven teams in the American League were in conspiracy against his Yankees. He watched Little Artie make a brilliant play at third and clucked approvingly. The teams changed again—no scoring.

"Dat boy lak old Joe Sewell," Cowboy told Daisy. "Dey don't stop ole Joe wit dem hard ones." He looked accusingly at Daisy.

"Do dey?" Daisy's breath was a fruity vapor. Six feet away, on the stoop, Albert could smell its alcoholic aroma.

"No! Dey tries. Y'see, Daisy, Cleveland a dirty ball club. Washington a dirty ball club. Red Sox an' White Sox is dirty ball clubs, too. Dey all try gang up on deh Yankees. Dey try to hit deh ball past Crosetti and Lazzeri and ole Lou, but dey cain't. Deh Yankees too smart and too good fo' all dem dirty ball clubs."

"Das good."

"Yeah, Detroit a dirty ball club. Dey most of dem dirty, 'cause dey all hates de Yankees."

Albert marveled: The way he's got it all figured out! It's like his religion—the Yankees are God or Jesus, and all the other teams are the devil.

"How come dey all dirty?" Daisy vaporized.

127

"Oh, dey dirty way down deep in dere hearts."

"Yeah. Like deh Howks?" They watched Buddy Cohen crash into Big Artie at first, trying to jar the ball loose. Big Artie stood his ground.

"Yeah, lak deh Howks. Dey only kids but dey dirty awready."

In the fifth inning the Hawks tied the score. Zetz' strategy of probing at the weakest men—Bimbo and Frankie Udo—produced a cheap run. Two placed hits, an infield out and a long fly sent Podolsky home with the tying run.

"We git it back!" Bushy yelled, as he led his team to bat. "We git it back!"

But the Raiders looked frightened. A sense of defeat hung in the air. They had been presumptuous to challenge the Hawks. There was no prevailing against villains like Zetz and Flab. The bad ruled the world.

Their feebleness was evident. Little Artie popped out to Zetz. Bimbo grounded out. Big Artie, trying to blast one as far as he could, put all his heft behind the ball, but it was caught by Podolsky.

"Dey gonna slaughter you guys now," Gorilla pronounced.

"Says you," Albert responded.

Once more Zetz shouldered Bushy as they exchanged positions. Bushy looked more puzzled than enraged; he could not conceive of anyone rash enough to assault him.

"We got ya, squirt," Zetz croaked. "You 'n' me c'n meet in the schoolyard."

Bushy rocked back a step; his fists jerked up. Teddy came between the madmen. "Nuts to him, Bushy. Let's beat him first."

The teams came into the seventh and last inning tied. They were exhausted by the heat. The Raiders appeared to have shrunk during the long afternoon. It was as if Bushy's desire had pumped them full of life, but that the magic infusion had leaked from their hides, and they were revealed as nervous boys.

Albert studied his clipboard. The Hawks were taking a long time before their last licks in the top of the seventh inning. Clearly a psychological move to unnerve the Raiders.

"Batter up!" called Fleishacker. "It'll be night before you guys bat! We'll be playin' extra innings. Ya think I get paid for this?"

Zetz bent low, bouncing the ball. His malformed nose was sniffing out a hole in the defense. Albert had the sensation that the nose was a weapon; a man could be beaten to a pulp with that horrid organ. Zetz struck a perfect "placer" over Little Artie's head. Rattling trash cans and iron gates, Frankie Udo raced for the ball. It evaded his fingers and came to rest under a privet hedge inside a yard.

Zetz rounded first and streaked toward second base.

"Ground rules! Ground rules!" screamed Bushy. "He's only 'llowed foist on a ball inna gate!"

"Yer ass!" shouted Zetz. "I was around foist before it went in! I take the extra base!"

Umpire Fleishacker hesitated. He scratched his long head. "Ah, I think maybe . . ."

Albert saw it! Fleishacker had glanced nervously at Mutty Zetzkin—his protector.

"He gets second," the poolroom owner pronounced.

"Robbery!" screamed Bushy. The Raiders ringed Fleishacker, demonstrating that Zetz was not at first when the ball entered the yard. Zetz was here; the ball was there.

"Ya scared stiff of his brudder!" Little Artie shrilled.

"Ya favorin' them!" Bimbo cried.

"In ya heart ya know!" taunted Bushy. "Ya know in ya heart we're right!"

Fleishacker stood his ground. "Ground rules," he said. "I followed the play. You guys git back in the field or I forfeit the game."

Albert shuddered: he was an expert on the subject of defeat, a connoisseur of losers; he could smell humiliation in the air.

But the Hawks were frustrated. The Raiders rose to heights of defensive art. Little Artie almost fractured an ankle making a sliding stop of Buddy Cohen's grounder. His leg was skinned, bloodied from ankle to knee, but he felt no pain, did not whimper. Parolo, the weakest hitter on the Hawks, attempted to slap a hit into Bimbo's vulnerable right sidewalk. But Bimbo fooled him with a twisting, leaping catch. Two men were out.

A sense of triumph stirred in the crowd. The Raiders bent low, certain that the last out would be made. Big Artie licked his fingers. Bushy's breathing was audible as the mob grew silent. The leader glanced threateningly at Zetz, who had one foot on the second base manhole cover, ready to fly home on a hit.

The formidable Ernie Cohen stood at home plate, rubbing the ball, endowing it with English. The spectators edged forward. Old *bubbas* and *zaydes* on windowsills, understanding little of the savage encounter, confounded by the violence of their sons and grandsons, appeared caught up in the tension. What did the Talmud say about punchball? The clipboard dropped from Albert's trembling knees. Was ever man witness to a more thrilling climax? No! Not in all of Ralph Henry Barbour, not even in Jack London!

Once, twice, three times Ernie Cohen bounced the ball. His head was low. Amazing, Albert thought, at the age of sixteen he already has the pronounced supraorbital ridges of the boxer, a physical trait also manifested in Australian aborigines.

Cohen advanced as if stalking an opponent, tapped the ball. It rose in a delicate loop, a perfect Texas Leaguer, a soft hit destined to drop between Bushy and Teddy. Zetz pounded toward third and home.

Bushy flew backward in a frenzy. He had started an instant too late. He screamed: *"I got it! I got it!"*—as if his frantic shrieks would bring the ball closer to him. From the outfield, Teddy came sprinting and got to the Spalding first, a second before it struck the gutter—a perfect hit. The crowd shrieked.

Zetz was a blue blur. Propelled by the engine of his powerful nose, he chugged home with the run that would put the Hawks ahead, two to one. At home plate a weeping Little Artie screamed: "I got him beat! T'row it!"

Teddy stumbled over Bushy, lost the ball, scrambled for it—*disaster, disaster!*—and threw it to Little Artie, a clothesline. But it was too late. Zetz pounded across the manhole cover seconds before Little Artie closed his fists around the ball.

The Hawks leaped on Zetz' back, slammed him, punched him, cheered him. His Etruscan head bobbed and jerked in their midst—the devil triumphant. Every now and then his long snout poked from their midst.

Albert moaned. He leaned on Gorilla's sloping shoulder. "Oh, it was so close. Teddy almost caught it."

"Oh-most don' count," Gorilla said.

Grubman rested against the wrought-iron balustrade of the stoop. " 'What's Hecuba to him or he to Hecuba that he should weep for her?' "

Retrieving his clipboard, Albert had a sudden sense of something wrong. He was not sure what was wrong, but he was disturbed. At home plate Podolsky was waiting for the noise to subside before taking his licks. But Zetz was shoving Podolsky forward, urging him to hit.

A bulb burned bright over Albert's head. It was the way the light lit up over Jerry-on-the-Job's thatched head in the comics when he got a smart idea. Quickly he scanned his scorecard.

"Yow!" Albert shrieked. "Yow!"

Catapulted he flew from the stoop, tripping on the sidewalk, vaulting over Daisy. He sped for Bushy, waving the clipboard. Fleishacker shouted at him to get off the field.

"Bushy! Teddy! All you guys!" he screamed. "He batted outa turn!"

The Raiders, stunned by their failure to stop the run, took a second to react. Then Bushy and the two Arties gathered around him.

"Look! I got it here in black and white on the clipboard! Flabbenstein was supposed to be the next man up! They forgot about him! He never hit! Ernie Cohen batted outa turn! He's automatically out!"

Bushy studied the scoreboard. It was there: irrefutable evidence in Albert's neat lettering. Deliberately or through stupidity they had skipped Flab's turn at bat. That worthy had been resting under the awning half-asleep. In the feverish atmosphere Ernie Cohen had gone to bat without thinking. Nor had any of the other Hawks noticed it. He was out, the third out. The inning was over and the Raiders would have their last licks with the score tied at one-one.

Bushy grabbed the clipboard and waved it at Fleishacker. "Call him out! Out! Whaddya waitin' for? Cancha read English? A guy bats outa turn he's *out!*"

"Wait, wait," the poolroom owner cautioned. "Not so fast."

Fleishacker's pouched eyes inspected the scorecard. But he said nothing. The Raiders ringed him: seven small boys in sneakers and flapping knickerbockers.

"I guess Flab was supposed to hit," the umpire conceded. "Hmmm. Whaddya know."

With Zetz leading them the blue-shirted horde ran toward the curb. "Wise kid," Fleishacker said, glancing at Albert. "You and yer fancy scorecards."

"As if it's my fault!" cried Albert. "Someone has to keep the official score! Why blame me for *their* mistake?"

"Whatzis all about?" croaked Zetz. "Hah? What's alla crap about? We got a run, dint we? We're ahead two-one, ain't we? Come on, Fleishacker, we're gonna score ten more."

"Cohen batted outa turn. He's out." Bushy advanced a step toward Zetz.

"G'wan Bush-ass, git your team in the field. G'wan, Mermelstein. You too, Polack. Git in the field."

He was a bad actor, Albert thought. In more ways than one. He knew he was wrong. He knew Ernie Cohen had skipped Flab's turn. Albert could tell by the way he had been hurrying Pole Vault to the plate.

Bushy lunged at Zetz. Teddy and Big Artie grabbed Bushy in time. "Wait, wait, Bushy," Big Artie pleaded. "We're right. They're wrong. Albert got the goods on 'em. Don't start a fight now."

Fleishacker dawdled. He took a few paces, studied the lowering sun, rammed his hands in his back pockets.

"The rules are clear!" Albert orated. "A man batting out of turn is automatically out." He was distressed by his voice. It betrayed his fear. He could barely look at Zetz. The misshapen

132

nose was seeking him. He felt like a termite undergoing inspection by a hungry anteater.

"Call it, Fleishacker, call it!" Bushy shouted. "Cohen's out!"

"No run, no run, the run don't count!" cried Little Artie.

Albert danced around the inflamed group, bounced in front of the umpire and waved the clipboard. "I got it here in black and white: I got the goods on 'em! *I got the evidence!*"

Poised on his toes, the clipboard aloft, his bespectacled face fixed on Fleishacker, he did not see Zetz come at him. The ogre descended on him brutally—falcon on duckling. *How swiftly it happened!* How expertly Zetz punished him! All his life Albert would never understand how Zetz got away with it, with no protest from anyone, with barely a word of disapproval. It was as if Zetz had rehearsed the moves many times before on other small boys. The moves were like ballet steps, coordinated, one blow leading to another, all of them combined in graceful sequences.

First Zetz' iron knee had jerked up swiftly and crushed his genitals against his groin. In a cloud of pain, he saw the mad green eyes, the tight honey curls, the lumpy nose. As the shock shivered him, the flat of Zetz' right palm smashed against his nose. Involuntary tears gushed from Albert's eyes. He did not want to cry, but the abused nose had no choice. Then with his left hand, Zetz lifted Albert's eyeglasses and spit full force in his eyes. He was blinded, crushed with pain, tearful, reduced to slime. And how quickly it had happened—in less than a few seconds!

Shame and pain made him weep. He doubled over, holding his insulted crotch. "Why—why'd you pick on me?" he wept. "Just because I told the truth?"

Jackknifed, he limped a few steps away from the staring mob: not a word of reproach had been directed at Zetz. For some reason, as Albert tried to suppress tears, he kept thinking about the time he had pushed Gorilla into the puddle. The sweetness of gratuitous evil! How invigorating it was to hurt someone weaker!

133

The crowd parted, as if letting a diseased dog walk by. He heard Teddy Ochab's protest—only Teddy, forever decent.

"Why'd you have to hit him?" Teddy asked Zetz. "He's half yer size. You wanna pick on somebody pick on me."

Zetz growled—part wolf, part hyena. "I'll take yez all on at once, or one at a time. Lousy punks. I'll send that fairy Abrams back to his old man in a crate, he could bandage him up. Little four-eyed putz. Him and his lousy scorecard. We're still up, get it? Ya hear, Bushy? Let's go, Fleishacker."

The pain flamed through Albert's groin; it would not disappear. Whipped, disgraced, he sought the tenement stoop. Genius Grubman put a motherly hand on his back.

"Call it! Call it!" Bushy cried. "He's out! A guy bats outa turn, he's out!"

A light winked in Fleishacker's rheumy eyes. He smiled at Bushy. "In baseball, yeah," the umpire said. "In baseball." He darted a look at Zetz and the Cohen brothers. He had given them their cue.

"Yeah," Ernie Cohen agreed, "this ain't baseball."

"The rules are the same," Teddy Ochab said.

"The hell they are!" Flabbenstein said. The teams moved closer to each other.

"You, ya big jerk," Little Artie taunted. "You were the guy fell asleep when you shoulda been up!"

Flab clenched a fist. "You wanna fat lip, monkey?"

"You gotta catch me foist." Little Artie spun away, light on his feet, elusive as a fox. He was too quick ever to be trapped and humiliated the way Albert had just been martyred by Zetz. Albert, sitting down painfully, watched Little Artie challenge the hoodlums and was jealous of him. His groin screamed. His tears cascaded.

"Should I call ya fodder?" Gorilla asked.

"Nope. I'm okay, Gorilla. I'm not crying because I'm hurt. It was the way he socked my nose. The tears won't stop."

The argument around Fleishacker intensified. There were shoves, curses. Did baseball rules apply? Was the fact that the Raiders had not called the out-of-turn batter until after the run a factor? And it was only their four-eyed scorekeeper who had caught the error. There was no official punchball rule book anyway.

"I t'ink I better call ya fodder," Gorilla repeated.

"No, no, leave him alone," Albert moaned. That was all he'd need: his poor harassed father entering this hell, cursing, flailing his arms, witnessing his son's agony. His father had worries enough. Why burden him with his own inadequacies? He envisioned his father throwing inept gymnast's punches at Zetz. Zetz and his abominable friends would swarm all over his father, beat him into the gutter, make a mockery of his muscles.

"Hand us the ball," Bushy ordered Fleishacker. "We're up. Score's still one-up."

"Da hell it is," Zetz said. His blood sizzled. He could kill, maim. He had crushed Albert the way a man stepped on an ant; no one dared impede his hunger to win. As the two captains faced the umpire, Mutty Zetzkin, walking gently on chocolate and white shoes, approached. Behind him trailed his retinue of low-lives.

"Why should he butt in?" a man called from the safety of a fire escape.

"Yeah. Fair's fair. The kids are right."

Fleishacker rolled his eyes. "Jeez, whaddam I supposed to do?"

Bushy yanked the ball from the umpire's hands. "Ya scared! Ya scareda them! Ya scareda him." He pointed at Mutty.

"Clean ball club always have trouble wit' dirty ball club," Cowboy said. "Dem big kids dirty ball club."

But Daisy was asleep.

How dutifully, observed Albert, the crowd parted to make way for their king—murderer, shakedown artist. Authority, strength, a certain wisdom suffused Zetzkin's flat face. He barely moved his lips when he spoke. His words came forth slowly, carefully selected. A man of discretion. No pain could keep Albert from witnessing this drama. He got up, knees and thighs squeezed together.

Flanked by Gorilla and Genius, with Mockey bringing up the van, they walked toward the boiling confrontation, a Conradian quartet of outcasts. *Marlow lit his pipe . . . I saw him first on the beach at Katipan, a lithe, limber youth. . . .*

"Now, ya hear what I'm saying?" Mutty began. "The way I figure, a man bats outa toin he's out." He spoke in such a hoarse rumble that his respectful audience had to remain utterly silent to catch the oracular pronouncements. "But like here, what just happened, the ump dint call it, the udder team dint call it, the next man was awready up. Derefore, the play is okay."

"Whaddya mean we dint call it?" yelled Bushy. "We called it!"

"Yeah!" Teddy shouted. "Albert right here caught it!"

"Nah, nah," Mutty Zetzkin said reasonably. "The next guy was in the batter's box awready."

"There ain't any batter's box!" cried Little Artie. "He wasn't even takin' his runner-in!"

From the edge of the crowd, Albert shouted, "He wasn't up at all! Podolsky wasn't at home plate! I saw them trying to get him up! Those guys knew it!" He skipped around the dispute, poking his head between Big Artie and Frankie Udo. No, it was impossible that Zetz would crucify him again. Someone would help. Such criminal acts could not forever go unpunished. "They knew! They knew!" Albert cried. "Boy, haven't you guys ever heard of sportsmanship or fair play? Come on, Mr. Zetzkin, be fair about this thing!"

He saw Zetz move a step toward him—or rather he saw Zetz' nose twitch in his direction, then saw Mutty wave a blunted hand at his brother. *Mr. Zetzkin?* Who, ever in the history of Brownsville, had addressed the killer as *Mr. Zetzkin?* Who but A. Abrams? Visions of Walter Camp All-Americans dotted his mind. What would they do with the Zetzkin Brothers at Harvard? How would you fit a fiend like Zetz into *The Crimson Sweater?* He would have to draw up a recommended reading list of Zetz, and make a fair-minded, sporty, good-tempered athlete out of him.

"Nah, nah," Mutty said. "The run scores. The guy was up. You know what I mean? We go back where we was. Podolsky is up. Doncha see what I mean?"

Fleishacker nodded his head. The Raiders groaned, protested.

"Give us the ball, kid," Fleishacker commanded Bushy.

The cheeks of Bushy Feinstein's face inflated. His skin was a splotchy scarlet. His body trembled. He aimed his eye slits at Zetz. They were like the apertures of an armored car.

"Ya want the ball, Zetz?" Bushy taunted. "I double dare ya to git it offa me. I triple dare ya. Know what y'are? Yer a lousy yellow-belly, shit-throwin', bulldozin' stooge. Ya need ya brudder to fight ya battles, ya *putz*." He extended his hand and rotated the pink Spalding under Zetz' nose. Albert expected the nose to seize the ball and eat it. The storm that had churned and boiled in the guts of these two madmen could no longer be contained.

Albert, wedged between Big Artie and Frankie Udo, thought his knees would melt.

Zetz hurled himself at Bushy. His fists flailed, his arms rose and fell in windmill style. Even his awful nose seemed to be landing crushing blows on the smaller boy. Bushy covered his head, backed away and assumed a classic boxer's pose—left arm out, body turned sideways, right arm on chest.

"Let 'em fight!" ordered Mutty. "Give 'em room! Git back!"

The seas parted. Sweating bodies moved away. A large black asphalt circle was left for the contestants. With a shrill noise—unearthly, inhuman—Bushy ran at Zetz, throwing vicious punches, forgetting his fancy boxer's style, eager to destroy the demon. Zetz returned them, chopping hard blows on the younger boy's head.

"Man, look at dem kids swing!" an older galoot shouted.

"Dey'll moider each udder!"

"Lemme ref, lemme ref," pleaded Jimmy Kravitz. The old

137

pro skipped to the side of the boys, tried to separate them and gave up. They were intent on killing each other.

Never, never in his life had Albert seen such a terrifying clash of monsters, of hateful unyielding men. Neither Zetz nor Bushy stopped swinging, not for a second. Fist cracked on forehead, on arm, on jaw. Blood spouted from Zetz' nose and dribbled down his blue shirt. It would bleed forever, Albert thought. That nose was a tank, a watershed, a repository for gallons of blood. The nose was central to Zetz' metabolism. Like the single spot behind an elephant's ear where he could be killed. Maybe Bushy had found the vital point. Zetz would roll over and die and Albert would spit on his corpse. But Zetz battled on. He landed a direct hit on Bushy's forehead; a great bluish lump bloomed below the Brillo. A second later another sickening crack closed Bushy's right eye; one of his slits was useless. No effort was made to defend themselves. With bone-cracking bolts, they invited mutilation, surrender.

Crack!

Thwack!

Ka-nock!

Thooomp!

The mob shrieked each time a fist landed. Albert cringed; it seemed they were hitting *him*. How easy Zetz had let him off with a knee in the groin, a slap in the nose, a faceful of spit! He found it difficult to join the Raiders in yelling encouragement to Bushy. It was too much to bear for very long. They fought like inmates of a lunatic asylum, maniacs turned loose for the amusement of a cruel warden. They fought like two huskies in a Jack London novel, tearing each other to bloody offal over a chunk of frozen seal.

Clack! Bushy's right fist struck Zetz' cheekbone. The evil one did not flinch, did not retreat. *Thoonk!* Zetz' fist pounded against Bushy's chest. And still they milled, struck, exchanged bruise for bruise, blood for blood. More terrifying to Albert than the gush of blood, the flowering bruises, was the inhuman noise that kept streaming from Bushy's tortured mouth. A reptilian hissing, a deathly buzzing, perhaps the noise made by a tarantula stung to death by a killer wasp (as depicted by Fabré), it was a sound unmeant for human ears.

There was a second's respite. The Titans circled one another. Zetz' head was low, taurine. He had not been as badly mauled as Bushy, whose face had inflated to twice its size. Purpling lumps covered his forehead, his jaw. And he wheezed . . . zzzz . . . zzzzzz.

"Why is he making that noise?" Albert asked Teddy. "Why doesn't he breathe like anyone else?" He was concerned for Bushy's sanity. He could not go through life hissing like an impaled snake.

Zetz feinted and threw a roundhouse left. It slammed against Bushy's jaw, but he did not budge. He was made of wood. Rage devoured him; nothing could hurt him. In an instant he was on top of Zetz. Both landed blows in an almost rhythmic pattern. *Thwack!* Fist on forearm. *Clunk!* Fist on side of head. *Glapp!* Fist on neck.

Again they rested. Bushy, heaving, wiped at his forehead. Zetz spat blood into the street. He pinched his nose and a flood of red spouted to the pavement. The crowd gasped. *What courage! What contempt for pain!* Like signers of a lunatic pact, they nodded at one another and charged—arms swinging, fists stinging.

"Hey, Mutty," Fleishacker said. "Maybe we oughta stop it? Those kids both are takin' a beating."

"It's good, it's good for dem," Zetzkin said softly. He was annoyed that his brother had not demolished the younger boy. *Zetzkin, you do not know the depths of my violent friend Bushy,* Albert said to himself.

"That Feinstein is dead on his feet," Mutty continued. "When he drops, we stop it. He'll drop, he'll drop. Know what I mean?"

Demonic power kept Bushy on his legs, punching, ducking, swinging, drawing pain and wonder from the adversary. It was beyond belief—he was getting the best of Zetz!

"Ya got him, ya got him!" Teddy cried. "Keep jabbin', he'll quit!"

"Man, lookit Bushy swing!" Little Artie shrieked.

As astounding as a ten-run rally was Bushy Feinstein's recovery. He was throwing punches faster, with more snap than when the historic battle had begun. A wild sideways blow caught Zetz on the neck. He wobbled, his eyes glazed. But he threw himself at Bushy, burying his head in Bushy's gut, punishing him with blows that landed suspiciously low.

"Foul! Foul!" cried Teddy. "Call 'em, Jimmy!"

Kravitz danced daintily around them. "Keep 'em up, kids, keep 'em up! I take da round from ya, ya don't." He was somewhere else—back at the Coney Island Velodrome going fifteen with Joe Gans.

"Go finish him!" Mutty commanded. "He's dead on his feet!"

"Says you!" Teddy cried.

"I'll kill the little bastid," Zetz muttered. "I'll kill him."

King of the streets, the toughest galoot in the neighborhood—undone, shamed, bested by a fourteen-year-old! He hurled himself at Bushy. They locked arms and danced like crazed lovers. Struggling, they fell to the gutter, rolling in filth, biting, cursing, refusing to let go. Bushy's hands reached for Zetz' throat.

Amidst the screams of the gratified crowd, Albert heard an agitated shouting in Yiddish, an angry voice at the edges of the mob. Suddenly the owner of the voice appeared, bursting through the spectators: an apparition, a prophet come to wreak vengeance.

"Holy smoke!" Little Artie cried. "It's Bushy's fodder!"

Old man Feinstein's eyes flamed with holy fire. He was a bearded bowlegged man, built like an oak cask. A yarmulke perched on his round head. His fringed ceremonial vest fluttered with each step. In one hand he brandished a broomstick.

"It's okay, it's okay, Mr. Feinstein!" cried Big Artie. He knew all about Mr. Feinstein's broomstick. He had felt it once after chalking a dirty word on the old man's stoop. "Bushy dint start it! The other guy did!"

"Yeah, Bushy dint do nothin'!" Bimbo wailed.

The blaze burned brightly in Feinstein's red eyes. A roaring Jeremiah, he had come to punish a sinner, his own son. He raised his terrible swift sword. Albert cringed.

"No, no!" Teddy shouted. "Don't hit him!"

Bushy, unaware of his father as he wrestled Zetz against the curb, fingers spread on Zetz' flowing beak, did not see the broomstick swing over him. It landed with a nauseating *craaaack!* on Bushy's right leg. He screamed. Avenging Yahweh, Feinstein swung again and again, as his son tried to roll out of range of the blows. Zetz, sensing the intrusion of an alien force, scrambled to his feet and stood next to Mutty. Everyone watched Bushy's martyrdom in silence. No one tried to stop the raging father, no one came to protect the tortured son. Rules of the game, Albert thought.

The Angel of Death struck again. With each crash of the bastinado he showered curses on his son.

"*Goniff!*" *Thwack!*

"*Paskudnyak!*" *Thwack!*

"*Goy!*" *Thwack!*

"*Trombonik!*" *Thwack!*

"*Gengster!*" *Thwack!*

Under the hail of blows, Bushy writhed and rose to his feet, only to be laid low by a swift stroke of the pole. It whistled in the summer air—the judgment of centuries in Feinstein's wand. In his rage the old man missed and stumbled. Bushy, begrimed and bloodied, staggered to his feet again. Curiously he did not run away. Instead he trotted off a few paces and turned to face his father.

"*Bestid!*" cried Mr. Feinstein. He waddled at Bushy, broomstick raised. No one halted him. Bushy did not run. Like certain primitive rites, reasoned Albert. Custom requires him to take his lumps.

"Can't somebody make him stop?" Albert pleaded. "Mr. Fleishacker? Teddy? He'll *kill* Bushy!"

No one moved. All understood that there existed some tribal pact between old Feinstein and young Feinstein. *This was the way it had to be.* Bushy parried a blow with his artful hands, retreated to the sidewalk. "No more, Papa. No more. He started in with me. It wasn't my fault."

He spoke without tears. His courage stunned Albert.

"Loyzer! Loafer!" screamed Feinstein. He missed Bushy's head by an inch. The breeze could be felt yards away. "Go by deh house! Wait by deh house! *Grubba ying! Bo 'van! Goyishe* bestid making fights in de street!"

Bushy obeyed. He darted a last look at Zetz as if to say—*I was winning when he butted in, but we'll settle this another day*—then skipped off. It was amazing that he could run. He had absorbed punishment like a sponge. Albert trembled. What would his father do to him in their apartment? Whips? Flails? An Iron Maiden? Bamboo shoots under the fingernails? For a moment, as Bushy's figure trotted away, Albert thought he heard a muffled gasp, a sob. Suddenly his heart ached for their captain. Who could imagine that peerless leader, the greatest punchball player of his time, *weeping*? But he was sure he had heard it. Bushy cried. It had been too much for even his hard heart.

In awe, the crowd watched Bushy vanish into the tenement, followed by the rolling figure of the old man. They savored the carnage that would follow.

A crimson handkerchief covered the lower half of Zetz' face. *Keep it there*, Albert said to himself. *It improves your appearance.* Zetz' muffled voice was directed to Teddy. "You guys gonna keep playin'? Or you gonna give it to us by forfeit?"

"We don't forfeit nothin'," Teddy said. "You know we got no subs. We can't play without Bushy." Albert cringed. What a liar he had been—pawning himself off to his mother and Ruthie Koplik that he was a substitute.

"Then we win," Zetz said. "Give us the six bucks, Fleishy."

The Raiders howled. Leadership had devolved to Teddy, but he could not match Bushy's aggressiveness. He was too well-mannered. "That ain't fair," he pleaded. "You started in with Bushy anyway. Then his old man chased him."

"Tough titty," Zetz sneered.

Albert, circling behind Big Artie, piped up: "Legally, that

comes under the heading of an Act of God. We weren't responsible." No one heard him, but he was proud of his contribution.

"Fleishy, you got to call it no contest," Teddy said. "Like in a fight. Give us each our dough back and we'll play yez tomorrow—anytime. We ain't scared."

Fleishacker extracted the wad of bills from his pants' pocket. Then he hesitated. His sad eyes were directed at Mutty Zetzkin. The hoodlum studied the forlorn group of leaderless Raiders. Albert watched him carefully. *Yes, yes, he was going to favor them!* Some movie notion of a hoodlum's heart, some appreciation of the myth of the good-hearted gangster touched him. He was Jimmy Cagney buying ice cream for the kids. "Give 'em back the dough, Fleishy," he said. "No game."

For a moment, Zetz appeared ready to turn on his older brother. Truly, he was a shark. The scent of blood turned him killer; he would attack his own kin. But the shark did not challenge the judgment. He turned away, fouling the summer air with words Albert had never heard in his life. There was a sprinkling of applause and much favorable comment on Mutty Zetzkin's generosity.

Fleishacker peeled off the three bills for Teddy. Small solace for a mighty effort, Albert thought. The Hawks should have been out. The Raiders should have batted in the last inning. Deflated, the players wandered off. Albert tucked his scorecard under his arm. The evidence, the evidence. He had called it. He had the essential knowledge, the truth. And what had it gotten him? Pain, humiliation, not a word of thanks.

As the crowd drifted away, he heard a mother yell from a tenement: "Shloimy! Come in de houze!"

And the small boy's response: "No. You'll kill me."

What bloodthirsty people! *You'll kill me.* But why not? Why should it be so hard to kill? He could kill. He could kill Zetz this minute, and not have a moment's sorrow over it. Darts of pain fluttered his tender crotch where the savage had jammed his knee. His nose and sinuses burned from the blow struck by Zetz' hand. But worst of all was Zetz' noxious spit. Long wiped from his eyes, it seemed to have left a film over his face, a sickening coating. As soon as he got home, he would scrub his face with green soap and wash away the filth.

Zetz would have to die. He would have to kill him. He would do it by stealth, by trickery. Do any of these people, dawdling away their afternoon, realize who walks in their midst? How could they? They were all inferior weak people. None had the powerful will that would propel him to the awful deed. They were drones, nonparticipants in the great game of life. Had any of them come to his defense when Zetz had brutalized him? Was he given any credit for spotting the man who batted out of turn? No. They had stared at him slack-jawed, with the bland bemused faces of the mob, studying him for the freak he was—the doctor's son.

" 'What though the field be lost?' " he heard Grubman call after him.

The Unholy Three, mysterious wanderers through the Line Islands stood in judgment on him—Gorilla, Genius, Mockey.

"May I inquire why you guys hang around me so much?" Albert whined. "What am I to you?"

" 'What though the field be lost?' " Grubman repeated elegantly. He raised one arm and braced his booted feet.

> "All is not lost—
> The unconquerable will and study of revenge,
> Immortal hate and courage never to submit or yield:
> And what is else not to be overcome?"

Ah, how much more admirable and worthy were the Grubmans of the world than the Zetzes! But look who had the power! Look at Germany! A country run by Zetzes while they arrested the Grubmans and burned their books!

Albert waved to his three buddies. Grubman had read his mind! *Study of revenge and immortal hate.* He could not let Grubman die young. How brilliant were the Genius' powers of divination! He knew, he knew, *exactly* what was in the mind of Albert Abrams, aged twelve. It was nothing less than the carefully planned and perfectly carried out murder of Isadore (Zetz) Zetzkin, sixteen.

Balancing a well-oiled Winchester repeating rifle with telescopic sight, he would climb the maple outside Zetz' house. It would be the dead of night. The streets would be empty. He would wait. He would bide his time. Perhaps he would carry a small flask of rum to sustain himself. Zetz would come home from an evening of roistering, his curly head and barbaric nose glowing with self-importance. He would drill him right between the eyes with a shot so clean it would hardly bleed. He would kill him as deftly as Jack London's young seaman in the crosstrees who had picked off several score cannibal Kanakas as they tried to board the *Mary Alice*.

No, no, there was a better way. He would disable him at first, with a blast shattering Zetz' kneecap. Smash the patella to smithereens. Then he would jump from the tree, carrying the Winchester at port arms, and approach Zetz' fallen form. In the moonlight, Zetz would see looming over him the compact figure of Al Abrams, last of the great copra traders, a man feared and loved from Palembang to the Ellice Islands, the man who had beaten Bully Hayes and had known O'Keefe. He would remind Zetz of the day he had humiliated him in front of all Longview Avenue. He would spit in Zetz' face to even the score. Mercilessly he would level the Winchester at that hateful head. *Die, Isadore Zetzkin, die. A bullet between the eyes, and you die in the gutter filth where you belong.*

He entered his home without a twinge of guilt. How pleasurable it would be! The fantasy was so real, so good! It was almost as good—no, better!—than the actual deed!

IT was half past five when he stumbled up to his room to listen to the last few innings of the game between the Dodgers and the Phillies. The Dodgers had dissipated a three-run lead and were losing emphatically. But the game did not divert him. His heroes—Al Lopez, Joe Stripp—gave him no lift. He switched off the radio.

If the real world failed to answer his needs there was always a fictional escape. From the bottom drawer of his walnut dresser he took out a multicolored metal contraption. It was a baseball game that his father had gotten for him in a toy store on Nostrand Avenue. ("It's much too expensive," his mother had said, "and he's too young to understand it anyway." She was right at the time. It took him a few years to master the game, but when he did, he embellished it and created something beyond the notions of the manufacturers.)

The game consisted of a flat metal surface on which, in lurid colors, was depicted a baseball diamond, with players dressed in a 1910 style. Their trousers suggested gym bloomers and their caps were square. At the right hand side of the diamond was a button, which, when depressed set in motion a revolving drum. On the surface of the drum was printed a variety of possibilities—*base on balls, foul out, strike out, force at second, double play, etc.* The drum would spin and come to rest beneath a circular housing on which were columns, reading from left to right: *bases empty, man on first, man on second, first and second, first and third, bases loaded.*

146

One depressed the button. The drum rolled. One released the button. The drum wobbled to a halt. The player then consulted the entry under *bases empty*. If it read *single*, or *base on balls*, he hit the button again, but this time consulted the column reading *man on first*.

It was a superb game. Albert had never seen another like it. None of his friends could afford one. But even in department stores, toy stores, at the homes of a few family friends wealthier than the Abrams, he had never encountered another *Batter Up!* It occurred to him that it was the *only game of its kind in the world*, a freak, an experimental item, a hand-fashioned once-in-a-lifetime job, offered to the public and withdrawn because of production problems or a conflict over patent rights. He had latched on to a collector's item. Someday he would donate it to the Smithsonian.

It was not merely a game, it was a way of life. For what Albert had created was his own *league*. He invented teams. He set a schedule. He kept notebooks crammed with batting averages, team standings, pitching records. He kept box scores. He was league commissioner and president. And he was also owner and manager of one team, the unbeatable Panthers. They always won the pennant. He saw to that. But he did not really cheat. However, by clever manipulation of the game, he could always insure a Panther victory.

As chief statistician of the Continental League, he assembled his dog-eared copy books. They went back several years, a legacy, something for the time capsule at the Chicago World's Fair.

The schedule called for a game between the Panthers and the Corsairs, a team that always gave him a lot of trouble. He anticipated a pitcher's battle between the Panther's ace, Freddy Mikulowski, and the Corsairs' crafty southpaw, grizzled Mose Forrest. Lettering neatly, he drew up his batting order for the day. He wallowed in power. All disturbing thoughts of Bushy, of Bimbo, of Lee Roy, of Zetz vanished. The film of spit Zetz had left on his face vaporized. What availed Zetz, that ignorant street bum, alongside his cool judgment as manager of the Panthers? And look at the team he had developed! A tribute to

147

his shrewd trading talents, his knack for working with young ballplayers, for getting the best out of them!

Vincenzo, 2b
Deems, cf
Breckenridge, lf
Mulqueen, 1b
LeGrange, 3b
Matthews, rf
Schiffman, ss
Hasselbach, c
Mikulowski, p

His own, his very own players. He knew them better than he knew the Dodgers. Tony Vincenzo was the fastest man on the double-play pivot in organized baseball. But he had a trigger temper and he scrapped a lot, maybe too much for the team's good. Abner Deems was in his late thirties, prematurely gray, a red-faced dirt farmer from Tennessee. Nobody could patrol the outer garden (or cow pasture) the way Abner did. Oh, those long smooth strides as he settled under a fly ball! Rookie Tut Breckenridge was a close-mouthed, narrow-eyed kid from Clinton, Iowa. Nobody cared much for Breckenridge—a little too cocky for a kid up from class B baseball, but he hit the long ball. Clean-up hitter Joe Mulqueen was a beet-faced jolly Irishman from Haverhill, Massachusetts. A lot of people thought that Fat Joe was past his prime, that he could be fooled by a curve ball. But canny skipper Al Abrams had faith in the Big Guy. When the chips were down, Old Joe delivered. Frenchy LaGrange was a reliable third sacker, a great glove man. No one ever slipped a bunt past Frenchy. Interestingly, he was the only French-Canadian in the League, being a native of Trois Rivières. Next in the batting order was Manager Abrams' special problem—the hateful Spider Matthews, a foul-mouthed hillbilly from Earth, Georgia. Everyone on the team detested Spider. But no one could play those rebounds off Panther Stadium's crazily-angled right-field wall the way Spider could.

Manager Abrams was concerned about him. If he didn't mend his ways, he might have to be traded. He was causing a lot of dissension.

This brought Manager Abrams' shrewd eye to his real favorite in the lineup, the fellow who was Spider's chief victim, the brilliant Sammy Schiffman. Sammy was one of the league's few Jewish ballplayers. He had gone from Thomas Jefferson High School to the Panthers as an eighteen-year-old. Now in his third year in organized baseball, he was being hailed as the greatest fielding shortstop since Honus Wagner. But he was nervous, erratic. Spider Matthews led a vicious clique of racists who made Sammy's life miserable. Although a superb athlete and not lacking in courage, Schiffman was not aggressive. He was a brooding young man who read serious novels. At times he regretted his decision to play baseball, when he could have accepted an athletic scholarship to Columbia and studied dentistry. Manager Abrams was going to try to work something out for him in the way of higher education.

The big gun of the pitching staff was Mikulowski, three times a twenty-game winner, a control artist with icewater in his veins. "Mikko," as he had been dubbed by the sports writers, was a prankster. What laughter echoed through the locker room when Big Mikko would nail Sammy's spikes to the floor! Or the day he flavored Spider Matthews' chewing tobacco with chopped rubber bands! But there was no joking around when Mikulowski toed the rubber and glared down the opposing batsman.

Enveloped in fantasy, cocooned, Albert pressed the button. The drum spun noisily. The entries became a gray blur. As he released the button, the drum jogged to a halt and settled into place. The Corsairs' leadoff man, Dave Abbott, had the option of a triple or a fly out. Albert, suddenly in a loser's mood, wanted the Panthers to share his misery. He would make them lose. Mikko would have an off-day. He would be outpitched by Mose Forrest. He awarded Abbott the triple.

Silence, enfolding heat, the rattling noise of the drum lulled him. Although the game had become routine for him—

he could knock off a low-scoring encounter in ten minutes—he kept playing. *Old Abrams, hanging in there grimly.* As long as the drum rolled, he controlled the destinies of Sammy Schiffman, and Mikko, and Spider Matthews. They became more real than the scary world of Zetz, Bushy, Lee Roy, Mutty Zetzkin—and the dark despair of his own father. He preferred his own fictional batting averages to the ciphers of failure: *Gottlieb. Remove Wart. $1.50.*

The Corsairs had jumped on Mikko for two singles and a walk. Bases were loaded. He consulted the notebook in which he kept his roster of players, casting a shrewd eye on his bullpen. Mikko might have to be yanked. He liked the master notebook. It was an old discarded one from Hebrew School, opening from right to left, and strangely lined—alternating wide and narrow bands—for Hebrew script. Was he committing a sin using it for baseball players, imaginary ones at that? Yussel Melnick's crisscrossed, whiskery face glowered at him from the lines. Yussel would never know. The notebook was pale blue, and on the front cover, under a drawing of the British Lion and a Union Jack, appeared something called "The Balfour Declaration." *His Majesty's Government View with Favor the Establishment in Palestine of a National Home for the Jewish People.* Who was Balfour?

Faintly he heard his father's voice. It filtered through to him, sounding mashed, vague. He shivered. He knew that high-pitched voice. Agony, agony: his father was suffering torment, another crisis. Albert increased the tempo of the game. He rattled the drum noisily, permitted it to roll longer than normal, depressed the button with a *clank* and released it with a *thoong.* The plays followed one another in speeded-up motion; he envisioned his athletes flying around the bases in old-movie rhythms. But his father's voice persisted. Through the screened window, through the summer foliage of the backyard it drifted to him, and he could not escape it. Occasionally he heard his mother's quiet voice in response—calming, explaining. And again his father's querulous tones.

"Enough is enough," Albert said. "Enough is sufficient."

He threw *Batter Up!* on the bed. It landed with a lazy whirr of the drum. The game was human; it protested when abandoned. He returned his notebooks and the Balfour Declaration to the bottom drawer and walked downstairs. Sneakily, he entered the rear room and concealed himself alongside a rear window.

His mother and father were seated on the slatted bench under the trees. They sat close together. Slumped, his father appeared to have lost control of his spine. His head was low. It was not like him at all—a man who walked with a gymnast's firm step. Albert could not see his mother's face. She was turned to one side, facing her husband, holding his hand. Compassion for them made him swallow, choke. *In this dark world and wide, nothing, nothing at all I can do for them. Helpless. Weak. A pain in the neck. Lodged with me useless. If only I could do something for them, anything at all. . . .*

His ears quivered; his nose twitched. He was the last of the great Nandi trackers, guiding Burton and Speke to the Albert Nyanza. Nothing could escape those sensitive ears.

"It is nothing to get upset about, Sol," his mother was saying. "This kind of thing can happen to anyone."

"This was different."

Lower your voice, Albert prayed. Your voice is too high, too thin, sickeningly unnatural. It is not your voice. You are speaking with a false voice that has somehow insinuated itself into your larynx. . . .

"I couldn't find my way," the doctor said. "I was lost, couldn't find my way."

His mother patted his hand. "It was a temporary lapse . . . nothing. . . ."

So what if you were lost? Albert asked himself. Can't people get lost in a place as big as Brooklyn? Why there were parts of Brooklyn unknown, unexplored, wild and savage littorals, fastnesses inhabited by the Canarsie Indians. His father prided himself on knowing Brooklyn like the back of his hand. He never needed a map. But still, a man had a right to get lost in the place without having a fit, and without making a big emotional act!

"How many times have I gone to Carrollton Hospital? Tell me, how many times have I driven to that *fekokteh* dump?" his father was crying. "A thousand? More than I want to think about."

"Of course you have," she said soothingly.

What was that? He got lost looking for the hospital? Albert squashed himself against the wall.

"Lost! Like some half-wit! I-I-I couldn't find it! It was as if I was somebody else. As if there was no hospital. Like a dream, where you go back to a place you knew when you were a kid, you're sure it was right there, on that block—but it isn't. And the more certain you are it was there, the more evident it becomes that it isn't."

"Oh, Sol. The heat . . . the way you fret over everything."

"Someone else. I was someone else. In a different city. I rode around for two hours . . . in circles. Looking, looking . . . up and down Eastern Parkway, side streets, all over Crown Heights. But I couldn't find it."

Why dincha ask a cop? Albert asked. *Are you helpless? Are you crazy? Don't you know if you ask people they'll tell you?*

"I stopped the car once. I forget where. I tried to think. Where is it? Where is that lousy dump with its cockroaches and the snotty nurses? No use. I had no idea where it was. And two patients waiting for me. Old man Glogauer with the splenectomy. And someone else. Some other old *kocker*. Labovitz? Belkin? Who? I can't even think of my patients' names anymore."

In his hiding place, Albert shivered. *Unfair, unfair!* The man being betrayed by unseen forces. A man that strong had no right to collapse. Those massive shoulders, the steel chest, the pulsating biceps and forearms (sometimes they looked like Popeye's) were meant for the strong-willed. In Jack London's books men built like his father were masters of their fate, courageous and determined men—sourdoughs, cowpunchers, South Sea skippers. Weaklings and cowards (like me, Albert thought) suffered. Not men of muscle like the doctor.

152

". . . in circles, down streets I can't even remember . . . two hours . . . never had any idea where Carrollton Hospital was. Did they move the dump? Tear it down? I was afraid to ask anyone, afraid to stop. They'd know. They'd know there was something wrong with me. Once a little *tunkele* threw a tin can against the car. I didn't even stop to yell at him. . . ."

Boy, you must have been sick. Any time a colored kid hits your car with a can and you don't stop to holler. . . .

"I was afraid of something."

"What were you afraid of?" asked Mrs. Abrams. "Why you know Brooklyn better than anyone. The hospital—it's a second home to you."

"Don't tell me! Didn't I put my blood and sweat into that dump so the fancy directors in white coats could crap all over me?"

Ah, that is more like it. That is my old man. Maybe he isn't so sick in the head after all.

"No, no, I was scared stiff. I was like a kid on a dark street. Lost. A neighborhood I didn't know. Wops and Micks waiting in alleys to jump on me. On the East Side when I was eight years old, the old man would send me out in the morning to go to a wholesale market by myself. Shoving the small pushcart—boards on an old baby carriage—and he'd take the big one to Brooklyn. Cold. Freeze my ass off in the dark. All that behind me, forgotten. But it was the same. Cold and dark and lost—and no way to the hospital."

"It was just a 'lapse,'" his mother said with calm determination. The way she reduced everything to flat, cool formulas! Albert marveled at her.

"What was I afraid of?" the doctor asked. "I've never been afraid of a goddamn thing in my life!"

"I'll go back with you right now. You are always more comfortable when someone accompanies you. We'll drive to the hospital and you'll make your visits."

"Nah, nah, woman. I can find my way now. What would it prove? I don't need you to lead me around."

153

"I'm not suggesting that. But people do have moments of forgetfulness."

There she is, Albert told himself. *There she is. Making it all sound so easy. Nothing is really so terrible after all, is it? The roof could collapse on them, and she would say, it's not so terrible after all, is it? It's only the roof. It can be fixed.*

"I tell you what," the doctor said hoarsely. "I couldn't find that damn place because I didn't *want* to find it. I didn't want to see the stinking hole again! Or my lousy colleagues! Or the snotty nurses! Or my cheating patients who suck my blood but never pay me! Or the whole, vile, stinking practice of medicine!"

"Sol, lower your voice. The neighbors. . . ."

"And they can kiss my foot also! Rotten seltzer-wagon drivers and halvah manufacturers! Galitzianer lice, throwing garbage bags in my yard and knocking down my fence! Mutts crapping on my peonies! Cats pissing on my dahlias! Dirty low-lives who never pay their bills and run off to the professors! Oh, I'll lower my voice for them, those *shnorrers!* Thanks a lot, my esteemed neighbors, for not letting me live! Bastards!"

Albert shut his eyes. At moments like this, he envisioned himself as an orchestra conductor, a boy Toscanini in a two-piece pearl-buttoned black velvet suit (short pants), standing on a podium, raising and lowering his elegant ivory baton in time to his father's mad outbursts. *When he hits those high notes, way way up, I raise the baton—then a crashing crescendo, and a loud, long coda on bastards.* His orations were rhythmic, symphonic, syncopated, starting modestly, then rising majestically to heights of outrage and fury. Does it ever end? he wondered. Does he have a machine built inside of him that turns out those orchestrated rages?

"I won't get back in the car, Hannah. Not today." He raised his head. It appalled Albert: lined, gray, not the head of a strong man. "I can't wander around those filthy streets in this heat trying to find a place I know as well as this yard. I'm afraid it'll happen again. No, if you come along it doesn't help. Since when am I a little snot-nosed kid who needs a woman to lead me? It'll happen, it'll happen. I'll go in circles. I won't find the hospital because I don't want to. I wanted to get rid of it, forget it, everyone in it."

"You are a physician, Sol. That hospital, whether you like it or not, is an integral part of your life."

Integral? Integral? Only his mother, that well-bred reader of Gissing and Meredith and Hardy could use such a word in a crisis—and get away with it. It glittered with decency alongside his father's bastards and goddamns.

"That's the trouble. It's wrong for me."

She placed an arm around his sloped shoulders. They were like granite, Albert knew: shoulders that had borne him as an infant and small boy, from whose hard flesh he had plunged, screaming with laughter, into Swan Lake and the Olympia Pool in Long Beach. . . .

Whistling to announce his presence (softly at first, to simulate an approach through the corridor, then rising in volume to fake his arrival), he walked out of the consultation room, into the kitchen and slammed the screen door with a resounding bang. That should tell them he had arrived; that would end that aggravating conversation.

How lovely was his father's garden! Pepper bushes swarmed with fat bees and gay butterflies. Albert could identify them all, thanks to the Book of Knowledge—Monarchs, Tiger Swallowtails, Sulphurs, Cabbages, Red Admirals, Mourning Cloaks. Once, of a fragrant August night, he had sighted a pale green Luna moth settle in ghostly splendor on the pepper bush and vanish. It had never returned. Dahlias bloomed in paintbox hues—magentas and lemon yellows, vermilions and mauves. Azaleas, weigelas, phlox, hollyhocks—all these responded to the physician's artful hands, his loving infusions of horse manure, peat moss, bone meal.

As usual, his mother frowned whenever he made one of these unannounced appearances. She seemed to be saying: who needs you, buttinsky? But the old man was smiling at him. Smiling! Was there no limit to that man's inconsistencies? Did he have to sit there smiling at him, manifesting his uncontrollable, limitless love for him—a minute after complaining that

155

he was on the verge of going off his nut? Certainly such behavior could not be considered normal. *Why am I burdened, Albert wondered, with all his love? It's too much; more than I can return.*

Still whistling, he jumped down the four wooden steps and walked the brick path toward the bench.

"Please return to the house," his mother said.

"Why? It's a free country."

"Your father and I are having a private discussion that in no way concerns you."

Your father. Albert hated it when she referred to him as *your father.* It made him sound as if that were all he was, that his entire function in life, his demonstrable existence consisted only of being the father of Albert Abrams, scorekeeper. When she referred to him thus, he was no longer her husband, or Solomon Abrams, M.D., or the former champion gymnast of Mr. Cooney's Institute for Physical Training. He was reduced to being his father, a minor personage.

"The private discussion just ended," the doctor said brightly.

Albert felt his insides jump. *That man sounds happy. He actually sounds happy.* He flopped into a faded beach chair opposite the bench. But it was marvelously comfortable. Exhaling noisily, he advertised his honest fatigue.

"Who won the game, kiddo?" asked his father. "Those galoots sure made a racket."

"It was called off. They had a big argument over a guy batting out of turn, so they called the game off. It was tied one-up."

But the physician did not hear him. He was studying his son's face and figure with joyful intensity, his eyes lingering on the wiry hair, the broad forehead, the bunched small features, the taped eyeglasses, the narrow chest, the slender limbs. Love oozed from the doctor's ravaged face, sheer disbelief that he could find so much pleasure, so much wonder in a son, a real, honest-to-goodness son. Albert fidgeted. He felt he was a smear

156

on a glass slide and his father was squinting at him through the Zeiss-Ikon microscope.

"You get any good wallops?"

"Huh?"

"Any hits. Any socks?" Ah, the ignorance of his father! He did not understand street games.

"I don't play, Pop. I'm not that good. I keep score. As a matter of fact, I was the one who found out a guy on the Hawks batted out of turn. I called it."

"That's important also."

He permitted his father to think so. But no, he would not tell him the rest. He would spare him the details of Zetz' cruel treatment of him, that swift series of moves with which Zetz had humiliated him, as the mob stood by and watched happily. Knee in crotch, flat of palm against nose, faceful of poisonous sputum. He would never, never tell him. His father had his own terrors to exorcise—wandering around Brooklyn in search of a hospital he knew as well as he knew his own home! Zetz would remain his private problem. He would settle with Isadore Zetzkin, that banana-nosed Neanderthaler on his own terms. No longer was there any doubt in Albert's mind. The deed would have to be done. Perhaps an ambush from behind a privet bush. A Colt Police .38 with silencer would do the trick. Disable him with the first shot, low in the groin. Then stand over him and remind him of a few things. The coup-de-grâce—right between the hateful eyes. Those green-jelly orbs would turn to cold marbles. Yes, he would kill Zetz with no remorse, no guilt, no pain.

"You should have seen the fight, Pop. Bushy Feinstein and that big guy Zetz from around the corner almost killed each other."

"I hope you stayed out of it," his mother said.

"Oh sure, Mom. I was right in the middle of it. That's me, Jack Sharkey."

"Yeah, why not?" his father said, indignant that his son did not weigh one hundred and ninety-five pounds and was not capable of going a fast fifteen rounds with Max Schmeling. "It's your fault, Hannah! I wanted to give him boxing lessons! But you said no. Why should he be a mollycoddle all his life?"

"Must we begin that?" she asked.

"I should have had him down at Cooney's gym once a week!"

"Pop, can't we drop that line of discussion once and for all?" Albert appealed. "It's a dead end that gets us nowhere." His father had talked for years about taking him to the gym in lower Manhattan where he himself had learned to twist and turn on the parallel bars and swing on the rings. There, some unknown tough Irish instructor would lace gloves on to his olive-sized fists and make a slugger out of him. They'd develop his left jab, teach him the right cross, nifty footwork, feints, how to clinch and how to break. That would fix everything. Albert could see himself matched against the ogre Zetz (or for that matter a peer like Bimbo). How brutally they would ignore his fancy footwork and proper textbook jabs! They'd bloody his nose with the first punch.

"Sure, that would have fixed the kid up!" his father went on. "Cooney made a man out of me when I was a dumb greenhorn, he could do it for him!"

"Albert is *not* a dumb greenhorn," his mother said. "He has the highest IQ in the history of P.S. 133."

But that won't stop Zetz from spitting in my eye, he said to himself.

He lingered, listening to their argument about his ability to contend with his environment. It was a relief in a way, even though it made him feel like a zoo animal being discussed by two impartial spectators. Moreover, it was a pleasure to be useful in terminating his father's despair—even by replacing it with a conversation about his own physical failings. But he remained haunted by his father's account of that frightening drive around Brooklyn streets—looking for a hospital he knew so well.

At first he had drowned in pity—bottomless, engulfing compassion. He was sorry for his father, terribly sorry. Then he was frightened. Something was awry in the old man. Something had gotten out of control. And as his own helplessness dawned on him, his utter inability to succor the doctor, he had become annoyed, almost angry—not with himself, but with his suffering father. He had wanted to yell from the screened window: *Why can't you find your way to a hospital? You are supposed to know where Carrollton Hospital is! Not only that, you are my father! As such, you are required to be tough, rugged, a leader, a man who knows his way around!*

Selfish, selfish. That's what his unspoken protest was, and he knew it. For it boiled down to this: if the old man couldn't cope with the world, where did that leave him? *He* couldn't even get into a punchball game. He suffered humiliations at the hands of monsters like Zetz and Bushy. Now, if his own father, on whom he leaned for support, encouragement, help, couldn't find his way to a hospital, what hope was there for *him*, in his weak, uncoordinated, unmuscled state? No, his father was no ally. Boxing lessons, indeed.

It was peaceful in the summery backyard. His father's flowers, lush foliage, perfumed the air. Above them, the pleached branches of the cherry tree and the sour apple formed a bower. So thick and close grew their robust leaves that the horrid naked backsides of the houses were obliterated. He understood his father's love of the yard: his retreat. Maybe he loved it too much. His colleagues in medicine who were rich and successful did not spend hours spreading horse manure on peonies. *Perhaps I shall build a hut here someday, and live out my life running the Continental League. . . .*

His parents conversed casually about minor matters. No reference was made to his father's ordeal. His voice had returned to its natural register. Albert was almost disappointed. Eavesdropping had filled him with a hideous fascination for his father's "fits"; he had felt the need to witness one at close range. It was like a certain scary drawing of a giant in the *Book of Knowledge*. As a small boy it had terrified him. Yet he often took the volume and played the game of opening the pages haphazardly, hoping that the frightening image would suddenly appear and scare him silly.

But his mother's sedate voice—and his own soothing presence—had blunted the doctor's hysteria. Relaxed, Dr. Abrams
got up and began poking at the roots of his rose bushes with a
rusty hoe. *Bowed by the weight of centuries.* . . . Edwin
Markham had been one of the doctor's boyhood heroes.

The front doorbell buzzed, buzzed again, and then violated
the rustic peace in a sustained scream. "Lunatics," the doctor
muttered. "Stick their fingers in the buzzer and try to break our
eardrums. Don't they have any consideration for anyone in the
world?"

He threw the hoe away and trudged down the garden path
toward the house. "Hah! Probably some idiot who cut his
finger, or a *tunkele* who drank too much soda pop."

Albert fidgeted. So? So what if it were? They needed
patients to eat. They needed the buzzer, and for their general
welfare it should have sounded frequently and been a joyful
noise to the old man's ears. Instead it drove him nutty. What
did he want? What in the world did he want? No buzzer? No
patients at all? He wanted to cry after his father: "But you need
them! That's your business, being a doctor! You're supposed to
take care of them and get their money!"

When his father entered the house, Mrs. Abrams looked at
Albert critically. She could slaughter him with the minutest
expressions of disapproval—an eyebrow arched in pique, a lower
lip, ever so faintly tucked in, an almost invisible movement of
the head. These minuscule manifestations of reproach maddened him, upset him much more than his father's rages.

"I don't think you're making enough of your summer," she
said.

"How come?"

"And don't use that expression. It is grammatically bar-
barous. You aren't reading enough. Or doing enough cultural
things. When you learned that we couldn't go to Rockaway this
summer, you should have planned better. Museum trips, a
reading list, visits to interesting places."

"Ma, I have been to the Brooklyn Museum forty-eight
times. The mummies sit up and wave to me when I walk in."

"Then it is up to you to find other diversions. We don't appreciate your being underfoot all the time. Your father and I have matters to discuss that in no wise concern you. . . ."

No wise, no wise. Who—who??—in Brownsville used the expression *in no wise?* And what good did it do her?

"You always seem to be poking around, sneaking in and out, sticking your two cents in, when you're not wanted."

All innocence, he pushed his drooping eyeglasses up his nose. "What do I care what you and Pop talk about? I couldn't care less."

"I wonder. You have big ears."

"And weak ankles."

"Stop that at once. Your father should undertake disciplining you now and then. It wears me out."

Why, why these interminable minor arguments? he wondered, when our world is going up in smoke, down in ashes? His father in mad rages; himself, butt and prey of the savage outside world—and they sat there sniping at one another. "Ma, could you do me a favor and stop referring to Pop as 'your father'?"

"Well, he is."

"Yeah, but he's also your husband. Would I call him 'your husband'? I don't know, maybe it's the way you say it. You give it a certain emphasis that bothers me. You inflect it in an unusual manner. I don't know if I'm making myself clear."

The faintest movement of her head agitated him—the slightest turning of face and neck, a lifting of eyebrows. It made him cringe. Deeply he felt all his sins, failures, shortcomings, ingratitudes, his essential worthlessness. Curse that tin alligator she had bought him when he was five! That had been the first of his Giant Sins. And from then on—downhill, damned, rejected, a pariah among men.

"They're intent on driving me to my grave," the doctor muttered. Blindly, he charged toward the street door. Some brutish caller had jammed a finger into the buzzer. The harsh alarm split his skull. Flinging the inner door open, he saw that the vestibule was empty. A genuine primitive, a stoop-stander, unaware that the outside door was open. Still the night bell screamed. "Stop the goddamn noise," hissed Dr. Abrams. "Tear my guts out, suck my blood, eat my brains—but stop the goddamn ringing." He cursed softly, as if pronouncing a spell, and opened the street door.

Summer heat, the awesome light, staggered him. Before him stood the great overripe form of Yussel Melnick. At the sight of the physician he withdrew a gloved hand from the doorbell. (Gloves? marveled Dr. Abrams. In July, gloves?)

"Hooi, doctor."

"Hooi yourself."

The teacher wore a shiny plug hat and a shinier below-the-knee "elpeckeh" coat. He rested his bulk on a silver-headed cane. His beard had been combed and parted; it appeared charged with unearthly electricity.

"Who are you supposed to be with that walking stick?" demanded Dr. Abrams. "Fred Astaire or Ted Lewis? Maybe Jimmy Walker?"

Melnick tapped the cane twice, as if calling the younger man to order. His vague eyes squinted accusingly at the doctor. Had they once witnessed the deliverance of the temple from the barbarians? Had they watched the Red Sea part, the bush burning, spied on Susannah, shuddered when Holofernes' head was displayed?

"You will come by the parade," Melnick said.

"I'm not in the American Legion."

"Don't make jokes. The parade is for our Torah."

On the street below, Melnick's parade had come to a halt beneath the shade of the doctor's poplar. They awaited the leader's return with the new draftee.

"What are you doing out of bed?" the doctor barked. "Didn't I warn you about making parades in Brownsville in July? Who do you think you are, Tom Longboat? Captain Spalding, the African explorer?"

"I am in good health at this moment. God understands. He gave me strength to honor the Law."

"He should give you some sense also."

162

Dr. Abrams shaded his eyes and studied the parade. What a stirring line of march! At the head was a teen-aged Yeshiva boy, some recent arrival from middle Europe. White-skinned, faun-eyed, he bore the sacred scrolls, looking queasy beneath their holy weight. The imperishable words were clothed in dark blue velvet, the rich cloth emblazoned with yellow and red letters—stars on a summer night. Above the blue coverlet protruded twin ivory handles, like the horns on Moses' proud brow. The young scholar bore his burden dreamily. Weak in the knees, he drew sustenance from God's testament.

Why kid about it? asked the doctor. *I eat pork, but I understand.* What a *shlep*, dragging those words, those notions, the ideas, the rules, all the way from the Holy Land, into captivity, in and out of places like Spain and England and France and Poland and who knew where else, and here it was, on a filthy street in Brownsville. "You got to hand it to them," he mumbled, looking at Melnick's crisscrossed face. The teacher looked like one of Hype Igoe's drawings of prizefighters —thousands of tiny intersecting lines.

Behind the fluttering student stood Rabbi Malamud, whom Dr. Abrams had never particularly fancied. He was a small trim man with a black beard trimmed in the manner of King George V, and he had once switched his allegiance from Dr. Abrams to a "young snot" of an internist who wore a white coat. Reason enough to damn him!

In back of the rabbi, however, loomed a flabby giant whom the doctor actively hated. A soaring, spreading man in a white linen suit, a white whale, this was the legendary Benny Otzenberger, the political boss of Brownsville. Benny the shrewd, the tough, the fixer, the deliverer of ninety-five percent of the vote for the Democratic Party, the scourge of Republicans and Communists, blood enemy of reformers and radicals, voter of gravestones, finder of jobs, protector of hoodlums, the grease that kept the wheels going.

"With that *goniff*, I don't march," the doctor pronounced. Melnick tsk-tsk'd. The physician's intolerance bothered him.

"Look at the size of him. Fat with bribes."

163

As huge as Otzenberger was, his suit had been cut a size or two bigger. As a result he seemed to roll and lurch within the linen sheets, assuming strange shapes, a thoroughly unformed and suspect man. But above the linen, there was nothing uncertain about the political boss's face. Eyes crinkled in false jollity; a predatory nose hooked importantly over a thatched gray mustache; pendulous ruddy cheeks advertised Otzenberger's excellent health. It was well known in Brooklyn that Benny the Boss could not read or write, either Yiddish or English. But he delivered the goods. Once they had named him Commissioner of Cultural Affairs (when good old Jimmy Walker was Mayor—LaGuardia had temporarily put Benny into eclipse). *Cultural Affairs!* Otzenberger could be seen in his chauffeured LaSalle around City Hall, "reading" his *New York Times* upside down.

"Hiya, Doc!" called Otzenberger. He waved a huge Panama hat. "Get inna parade!"

"If I do will you get me the easement for my sidewalk?"

"Hah! That's Sol Abrams! Mad at the woild! Never forgets nothin'!"

Years ago against his better judgment, the doctor had sought Otzenberger's help in securing an easement from the city to allow him to construct a low brick wall in front of his house. ("To keep the galoots out, and besides I can't stand the stink of that privet bush.") One of Otzenberger's underlings had dealt rudely with Dr. Abrams, referred to him as "Jackie," and hinted at a bribe. The doctor had threatened to knock his block off.

"Pay no attention to the *unterferer*," Melnick said. "We need him, for that is the way of the world."

"Yeah, but I don't need him."

"No," said the teacher. "But you need the words."

Behind Otzenberger the rest of the processional rested in the melting heat. There were three stooped musicians, a trap-drummer, a cornet player, a clarinetist, whom Dr. Abrams recognized from local weddings. Beyond were a dozen members of the congregation, most of them elders, bearded and caftaned,

164

perspiring holy buckets. Bringing up the rear were six more of Melnick's students in elaborately embroidered yarmulkes and prayer shawls. Their navy blue knickerbockers were newly pressed.

"Well, I warned you. You'll kill yourself in this sun."

"God is giving me strength for this honor."

"If you fall down dead, I won't be responsible."

"No, Abrams, learned friend. I would never blame you. I know I am sick, but I am not sick in my heart. I have seen real sickness in men, in their souls, but thank God, I do not have that sickness." The old eyes glowed with ancient memory; they had a life of their own.

The doctor was marveling at his plug hat. The top was threadbare, worn, the brim green. "All right, take your walk," he said.

"Only with you."

"C'mon, Doc!" hooted Benny Otzenberger. "Join the poddy! I paid for a big spread at the *schul*. I'll tear a herring wit' ya and ya can give me a bawling out! What a guy, that Abrams!"

Dr. Abrams disregarded him. "What have I got to do with this?" he asked Melnick—almost plaintively. "I eat *tref*. I haven't been in a synagogue in twenty years. I couldn't *dovvin* if you personally taught me."

"I know all that. In medical college the *goyim* forced you to eat vile clams—"

"Nobody forced me. I like them."

"You were with bad companions. We'll absolve you, as surely as I will finish my work."

"What work?"

"All I ask is that you help me down the steps and we will march off."

"Okay, okay," Dr. Abrams said. Melnick had wheeled about, pulling the doctor with him, his arm hooked in the doctor's. The physician sniffed the old man's aroma—rotten, dying. The sun doing its work. Putrefaction. Assisting the oxidizing of animal matter. Heat- and light-burning protein,

165

devouring amino acids. And his madness. Was the decay of his body accompanied by a failing of the mind?

"Attaboy, Doc!" Benny Otzenberger cried. "Now we got the medical profession represented!"

"Walk next to me," Melnick puffed. "In God's eyes you are blessed even though you sin. You are a learned man. With the gift of healing. Wisdom is a joy to the Lord as much as piety. He will forgive your evil habits."

Melnick drew Dr. Abrams to the head of the procession, directly in back of the Torah. "Go, go, Yankele," Melnick ordered the Torah-bearer. "With the man of learning at my side, I'm not afraid. Walk."

"Yeh. I can also pick you up if you fall down."

"Also."

The band struck up a melody in a minor key. Serenade to the Torah? Dr. Abrams asked himself. As they walked off, the doctor had a shuddering memory of himself in blue velvet shorts and high-buttoned boots, his parents dancing small apologetic steps at a country wedding. A barn in the background? Cows staring over a wooden stile at bride and groom?

"What matters, truthfully, is what God puts in your heart and your mind. Not the pork in your mouth."

"Wisdom from the Talmud, Reb Yussel?"

"My own, doctor." Backward he rolled his mad eyes until they vanished. Only the stained yellow whites remained. Backward he thrust his ancient head. As the beard rose, Albert's father expected to see small birds flutter from its recesses. Like in the limerick Albert used to recite: *Two larks and a hen have all built their nests in my beard.* . . .

Melnick chanted in a high, almost inaudible voice. Divine inspiration made him warble like a child.

"And now you're Rudy Vallee," Dr. Abrams said. Melnick rested his weight on him, unhearing, carried away. They trod the littered street together. Under sheltering catalpas and maples they promenaded, as little boys danced alongside them, clapping in time to the bouncy music.

"Pretty shrewd you are," Dr. Abrams said. "All that speech

about how smart I am just because you wanted your own doctor in the parade. Am I right?"

"For both reasons, I wanted you."

"You'll regret it. I won't let you get drunk in *schul*."

"I will be drunk, but not with wine."

A faster tempo celebrated the Torah's arrival. The Yeshiva boy tried to keep in step and wobbled. Melnick touched his shoulder: "Slow, slow, dumbhead. We have had the Law for five thousand years, so we can wait a few minutes more."

Someone placed a black skullcap on Dr. Abrams' head. It perched atop his shock of Indian-black hair. He mused: We pick up a lot of rules in five thousand years. But what does the Torah say about *loyzers* who don't pay their bills? Or the bastards who run off to the clinics or specialists without a word of thanks? Or this whole *fekokteh* depression when a man can't earn a dollar doing what he knows best?

The students began to sing—a wailing, high noise. In Dr. Abrams' mind there again fluttered shifting and vague memories, like poorly focused images on a screen from a wobbling slide projector. *The muddy street—the wooden houses—a blacksmith—charred flesh—and clang of anvil—himself in fur hat—feet in muddy snow.* He wanted to spin Melnick around and confront him with the awful truth: What did the Torah and the Talmud ever do for us? Get us murdered by Cossacks and now by Hitler? Or maybe that's why we survive. No matter how you slice it, it makes us different. He decided not to bother Melnick.

"What terrible lies they tell about me," Melnick muttered to the doctor.

"I never believed a word of it," the doctor said.

Crazy as a bedbug, he thought. All those years simmering inside of him. Still, he's different, he's something else. He was pleased to walk beside Melnick, pleased with a new identity, something to bolster his morale: physician, husband, father, American, and now, a no-bones-about-it Jew. What's inside that lush blue velvet cover? He wished he knew—even a little bit of it. Part of me and I'm part of it. Why am I so ignorant? Some months ago he received in the mail a circular offering a special rate on a six-volume *History of the Jews.* He'd tossed it out: too expensive. But maybe he'd find out who was offering the books and order them. Why throw away five thousand years?

Behind the screened windows of the waiting room, Albert and his mother watched the parade move away. Reedy music tinkled back to them, the thin sounds mashed in street noises, kicked cans, eternal yells, a dog's ki-yi.

"Well, a new facet of your father emerges," she said. "If there is a more irreligious man in Brooklyn, and now look at him."

"What's wrong with what he's doing?"

"I don't know. He's always poking fun at that sort of thing. The old guys with the spinach as he refers to them."

"He does that because he likes them. Ma, you don't understand him at all."

"Perhaps. But he's also guilty about the whole thing."

"That should be the least of Pop's worries."

They turned from the window as the music dribbled away in silence through the violence of the street. His mother walked calmly to the kitchen. Her day was orderly. It was time to prepare the evening meal. She always kept a book in the kitchen, or a magazine, so that in between work she could read. "Orderliness is the hallmark of good sense," she had once told him. Or, on discussing kitchen labor: "A place for everything, and everything in its place."

Once again, he returned to *Batter Up!* The game had been suspended when he had overheard his father's recital of the frightful search for the hospital. The man had seemed on the edge of collapse; Albert resented the way he had smiled, laughed, buried his misadventure at the sight of his beloved son. *Me. Me, myself and I.*

The metallic *whirrr*, the clanging stops of the game soothed him. Imaginary world, imaginary players, his own limitless power—all these dulled anxiety. Let Zetz do his worst. He was the boss of the Continental League. He tuned the redoubtable Philco in time for a newscast. The smartly read information also afforded him a sense of time, place, events happening that did not really concern him. *Them, not me.*

Madame Curie had died of anemia. The disease had been brought on by exposure to radiation. A great woman. Pity. In Vienna, the Austrian Nazi Party was renewing its attacks on Chancellor Dollfuss. There was a puzzler. He knew the Nazis hated Jews, but so did Dollfuss. He was no pal. What was the argument all about? They should have been able to agree. Or maybe the argument was which one hated Jews *more*. That always seemed to be a good ground for discussion in Europe. Well, he pitied the Jews in Austria and Germany, but something would be worked out. They'd all stop buying German products. That would fix 'em. Look what happened to Spain. Federal troops in San Francisco were ready to end the dock riots. The Nazis in Germany had forbidden the funeral of some general and his wife. Let 'em kill each other.

The news gave him solace—a world of sorrows of which he was not part, and sorrows that would resolve themselves. The Panthers were locked in a two-two tie with the Corsairs. He'd try to arrange for Mulqueen to belt one over the right-field wall. That would be the ball game.

"HE's nuttier than a bag of filberts," the doctor said later. "The sun did it to him. That new Torah. Believe me, it was a perfect example of Jung's theory of myth. That old guy is living in a religious memory older than I want to think about!"

They were eating supper in the backyard, on a bridge table covered with yellow oilcloth. It was cooler. The savage noises of the street were hardly audible. Peace, tranquility, surcease—these boons seemed to have mellowed and buoyed the doctor's outlook. He was actually pleased by his stroll with Melnick.

"I had to hold him up half the time. That's why he wanted me, I think. He was afraid that *shtunk* Otzenberger would come to his side!"

"Sol, you needn't be so hard on Benny Otzenberger. He could have been helpful to you, if you hadn't been so stand-offish."

"He's a punk! A cheap politician! He votes all the names in the Beth David cemetery!"

"Yes, and he's a personal friend of the President. There's a photograph of Roosevelt in his office. Signed, to my dear friend Benny."

"Roosevelt'll live to regret it!" the doctor cried. "Melnick had the right idea. He didn't want that crook in his fancy white suit helping him walk, that four-flushing tinhorn!"

"Why'd he pick you, Pop?"

170

"Why not? Who better than a doctor in case he pooped out? He's no chump." The doctor ate with unnerving swiftness, as if ready to fly off to the hospital, or to his office, or worried that some anxious patient, tired of waiting, would vanish, flee to a clinic, a professor, a drugstore, with his crumpled dollars and his ailments unless he nailed him. "Yeah, but the old guy made it. Wobbling, wheezing, stinking like a tannery. But he's losing his marbles, I can tell. He makes less sense as he gets older. Or was he joking with me?"

The doctor lingered, sipping his iced tea. "Oh, he's a great joker. He should be one of the Marx Brothers." He laughed easily: Albert's heart jumped—*happy, happy, for once happy.*

"Yeh, right into *schul* he dragged me. We all stood around the ark, and they put the Torah in. Lots of prayers. The rabbi, Melnick. Funny, the way Malamud deferred to him. I guess Melnick has some kind of priority with God. Maybe he's known him a lot longer than the Reb."

"Did you know any of the prayers, Pop?"

"Oh, I hollered a couple of Aw-mains. The heathen delegate. An emissary from the Gentiles. Listen, I wasn't the only dope there. Benny Otzenberger didn't know them either. Stood there like a circus tent, grinning, shaking hands. He knows where the votes are."

"You have *guilt* feelings," Mrs. Abrams said primly.

"Me? Withdraw that charge, woman."

"You do, Sol. Why can't you accept the fact that we are not religious people, that we are modern? It doesn't bother me in the least. I was brought up in an Orthodox house by a father who was such a tyrant I still hate him. I had absolutely no sense of guilt when I abandoned the rituals. Why bother with all that nonsense dreamed up by a desert tribe? When I die, Sol, no one will be required to say *kaddish* over me."

"Look who's talking about guilt! Woman, the first day I tasted an oyster I liked it! Mr. Cooney treated me. 'Abrams,' he said—he kind of talked through his nose like that—'Abrams, this goes against your faith, but it is good for your red blood corpuscles.' He was right. That reminds me, we haven't been out to Lundy's for a long time. We could take Yussel Melnick—"

"There you go again!" his mother cried.

Albert grinned; hugged himself.

"—and tell him, tell him"—Dr. Abrams dissolved in laughter—"tell him that the deviled crab is—is—hah—gefilte fish!"

Mrs. Abrams turned her head. "I fail to see the humor of that. I think the jokes are a cover-up for your sense of shame."

"It is not!" Albert protested. "Ma, you can't tell when Pop is joking. You take everything too seriously!"

"It comes from reading all those *fekokteh* English novels!" cried the doctor, joining the attack on his wife. "Yes! That's it! Life in Upper Ipsquitch, England, somewhere in the Kentish Downs! Your mother thinks we all have to have stiff upper lips!"

"There is a good deal to be admired in the English."

"What did they ever do for me?" the doctor asked.

"Are people required to do things for you? Is that the basis on which you judge them? Perhaps that explains your bitterness toward Benny Otzenberger—"

"Ward heeler. Shakedown artist."

"—who could have helped you."

"Ma, there you go!" Albert pleaded. "Pop said that about the English as a joke. J-o-k-e. You don't think he really expects Ramsay MacDonald or King George to send him a check for a thousand pounds, do you? He made his comment as a *joke*, but right away you jump on it and attach great earth-shaking importance to it."

"Many a jest has certain inherent truth in it," she said. "I don't deny your father's sense of humor, but there's more to it than the surface comment."

"Hah. You've been reading my Freud! Wit and the Unconscious!"

"Well, you claim to be his disciple. Physician, heal thyself."

"Pop doesn't need healing."

"Attaboy, Albert! Stick up for the old man!"

"I can see I'm being ganged up on," she said. But there

172

was an edge of happiness in her voice. For a few moments they had enjoyed bantering, teasing—instead of the abrasive outbursts they had come to expect.

"And how, woman! And do you deserve it!"

From an alley several houses down, a ranting, muddled voice shouted through a megaphone.

"Friends, comrades, fellow workers! Please note that we fly the American Flag and have secured a permit from the Police Department for this official meeting of the Communist Party of the United States, Brooklyn Chapter. . . ."

"Windbag," the doctor grumbled.

". . . and we are here as American citizens to alert you to the inevitable Fascist state that Franklin Delano Roosevelt is determined to turn our country into, under the disguise of the Blue Eagle, the NRA. For what is Franklin Delano Roosevelt? He is a rich man. And who are in his Cabinet? Rich men. Are these men truly friends of the working people of America? I do not think . . ."

The voice ranted on, a wailing, ill-favored voice, violating the night air. The sky had turned lavender-dark. It was cooler in the yard.

"What I don't get," Albert said, "is how come the Communists are attacking Roosevelt. I mean, when I read the newspapers I get the idea Roosevelt is almost a Communist himself. Well, if he is, why do the Communists attack him?"

"They stink," Dr. Abrams said. "Bolsheviks. I know that shtunk who's making a speech like Lenin. It's that weasel Margulies down the block. He still owes me for a GI series. Send him bills, he never pays them. No wonder he wants Communism."

". . . I tell you, fellow workers, Mr. Roosevelt is no better than the Hearsts and the Pattersons who made him President. The NRA is a trick to perpetuate the capitalist system that makes slaves of us, a scheme to pull the wool over the workingman's eyes and to deceive the proletariat . . ."

"Deceive the proletariat!" Dr. Abrams shouted. "He'd better tone down his language for that mob of illiterates out there! Listen to him. The voice of revolution. He couldn't make a revolution in a candy store. They all stink. We should have elected Norman Thomas president. He's a real man, a real intellectual. Better than the whole lot of them!"

Albert shook his head. "I don't get that either. The newspapers say the Socialists are just as bad as the Communists. You don't like the Communists, but you like Norman Thomas."

"Your father's politics are not models of consistency," Mrs. Abrams said, as she stacked the supper plates.

"Norman Thomas is a gent!" shouted the doctor. "He's a *mensch*, a man of stature!"

It occurred to Albert that Mr. Thomas, that oft-defeated candidate for the Presidency (who had won the election in class 6B at P.S. 133 in 1932), was the only person about whom his father had had a good word in many months.

"Holy smoke, Ma!" he cried. "We found somebody Pop really likes!"

The doctor smiled. Albert silently damned the Depression, the ungrateful patients, for rendering him miserable all the time. His face had changed—lines of defeat became crinkles of pleasure. The gray hollows under his eyes softened, the mouth surrendered its bleak appearance and curved smiling.

"That had all the earmarks of a dirty dig," Dr. Abrams said playfully. It was a favored expression; it meant he was happy. Albert was delighted to hear it, although he had no idea what an "earmark" was or why a "dirty dig" should have them.

"I like lots of people," the doctor said slyly.

"Name one!" Albert cried.

"Edwin Markham. I shook hands with him once. And Jack London. Great guys. I never met him but I liked Debs, and I liked John Peter Altgeld. I'm getting to like Roosevelt also. And I also like General MacArthur."

Mrs. Abrams' head swiveled. "MacArthur?"

"Sure. Why not? I like the way he parts his hair, and the way he waves to the crowd, that kind of stiff-armed salute." And the doctor spun on the bench, tilted his head, stuck out his jaw, and waved—looking uncannily like MacArthur.

Albert laughed out loud. "Pop should have been an actor!"

"Yeah, a medical Thomashefsky!" Dr. Abrams cried.

Mrs. Abrams frowned. "Sol, you are a mountain of inconsistency! All the people you named—Socialists or Liberals—people you like and suddenly you throw in a reactionary like General MacArthur. Why?"

"I told you. The way he waves." He imitated the general again; Albert whooped. "Woman, I'm my own man. If I want to like Debs and MacArthur, I'll do it. It's my America also, and I'll like who I want to like!"

"Pershing?"

"He was okay. I liked the way he rode a horse. But a lot of generals are bastards, I guess."

"Sol!"

"Don't reprimand me, woman. The kid here listens to a lot worse in the street. Those galoots don't recite poetry."

"Genius does."

"Who? Grubman? Well, he's a horse of a different color. It's a miracle he's alive. I don't know how he gets from day to day with that heart of his." The doctor ran his hand through his hair, his face was solemn. "I told his parents that years ago, that the kid didn't have long to go, that he couldn't go to school every day like other kids. So what did those ungrateful Litvaks do? Off to the professors they ran! Who told them the same thing!"

Albert slumped in the chair. He liked Genius Grubman and was disturbed that his parents had acted like ingrates toward his father. He hoped the old man didn't hold it against Genius. At all costs, the conversation had to be maneuvered from those treacherous shoals—patients, clinics, professors, and all the other trolls, kobolds and hobgoblins that haunted his father's life. Old Socialists like Jack London, and snappy generals like MacArthur were more suitable subjects for after-dinner talk.

"What kind of a guy was Jack London?" Albert asked.

"Looked you right in the eye and grabbed your hand in an iron vise," the doctor said. He extended his massive right hand

and shook the absent mitt of the Sailor on Horseback. "Husky, tough, but with a first-class mind. He had the right idea."

"About what, Pop?"

"Everything."

"There you go again with your rash generalizations," Mrs. Abrams said.

"It's not a rash, it's an infection," the doctor said, winking at his son.

"You worshiped Jack London, and as a result he can do no wrong in your eyes," she went on. "As a matter of fact, he became something of a racist in his later years, and was not altogether a very admirable person."

"Who could blame him? Maybe he went a little haywire. He saw what was happening. Any intelligent man would go a little off his nut."

"I don't get it," Albert said.

"It was building up," the doctor said darkly.

"What was, Pop?"

"A sickness, a national sickness. Crap-artists and whore-masters taking over—"

"Your language. . . ." She shut her eyes.

". . . yeah, it's true. You could sniff it in the air. I did. Was I surprised when the stock market crashed? I was not. I expected it. I knew in my bones we were headed for disaster. All those years after the war, bootleg booze, easy money, real estate swindles, stock swindles. You can look at some people, or listen to them talk and you know they're swindlers. But the public wanted it. Every slob and his kid brother in the market like they knew what they were doing. Regular J. P. Morgans! Hah! All those cake-eaters in yellow shoes and double-breasted vests! We used to see them in Rockaway at the boarding house before 1929! I knew there was something wrong somewhere. Deep down, there was something rotten and cheap."

"You were derelict in your duties as a citizen, Sol. You should have informed President Hoover if you knew so much."

"I'd have given him an earful! All of them—Harding and Coolidge too!"

176

"Oh, that's a whole career you missed," Mrs. Abrams said. "Why you could have replaced Bernard Baruch."

"I'd have told him off, also! Listen, those people like Harding and Coolidge and Hoover, they weren't bad guys. They were just like some specialists I've known, *fekokteh* professors in white coats, who can't even read a thermometer, who can't take a pulse properly!"

"Who could before the Depression?" she asked.

"Me! I knew it had to happen! I knew that crap couldn't go on forever. Why do you think I never put a thin dime of my hard-earned money in the stock market? I knew it would happen! All those cake-eaters jumping off buildings!"

"Ah, the great economist speaks. Didn't we invest a hundred dollars in Frootsie?"

"Frootsie?" Albert's eyes widened.

"Do I remember it?" roared Dr. Abrams—but not in anger. "How could I forget! Frootsie! Triple distilled mare's urine, that's what it was! And tasted worse! Hah! A whole folder of beautiful engraved certificates we bought from that rhumba-dancer in the pearl-gray suit and spats! Waxed mustache and a ring on his pinky! And he was a friend of your brother's, let's not forget!" He jumped from the bench and started toward the house. "I got a good idea to find them right now! I think I saved them—gorgeous purple and gold engravings! You couldn't even wipe your—shoes—on them!"

"What the heck is Frootsie?" Albert persisted.

"Now, actually, it was a very good idea," said his mother calmly. "It was a fruit juice concentrate in cans. You mixed a little with water or seltzer and made a soft drink. They were very good flavors."

"They tasted like bichloride of mercury mixed with asafetida!" the doctor crowed. Albert was overjoyed: the old man had found an ancient enemy he could joke about. Nothing terribly serious, but a good way for him to blow off steam. "Oh that cheat, that charlatan, that rascal who sold them to us!"

"But if you paid a hundred bucks for them, how could they be worth nothing all of a sudden?"

177

"The product never caught on," his mother said. "It wasn't popular. The company went out of business, and there went our stock, down the drain."

"Just like that?"

"You bet, kiddo," his father said. "Never trust the stock market, a politician or a newspaper."

"You're overdoing it, Sol. They happened to have been excellent flavors." She seemed to be trying to salvage something out of their lost dreams, their wild flyer in the market. Who really knew? With the breaks here and there, Frootsie might have become another Coca-Cola. Their hundred dollars might have become a hundred thousand. A small fortune. A house on President Street.

"Formaldehyde. Valerian. Hydrogen sulfide. They were the worst goddamn things I ever tasted. Alum. Wood alcohol. Ipecac."

The voice of revolution drifted toward them from the alley. ". . . and, comrades, what is this New Deal? What does it really mean for the workers of America? I'll tell you what it means. It means enslavement for the workers under the heel of capitalist tyranny! A step toward Fascism and the police state. Look and see who are the close advisers of Mr. Roosevelt—capitalists, generals, financiers, the very people who brought on this terrible depression, this slough of despond, the very people who at this moment are plotting to . . ."

"Noisy bastards," grumbled the doctor. "I swear, they'll bore us to death before they're through. How anyone can listen to those loudmouths and still believe in them. Between them and that *goniff* Otzenberger, I'd have to choose Otzenberger."

"I don't like their methods or their manners," Mrs. Abrams said cautiously. "And I don't care for the way they want to fight about everything and denounce everyone. But some of their accusations are valid, and they occasionally come up with a criticism that merits attention."

"They stink. They stink because they think they have all the answers. Nobody has all the answers. And anybody who says he does is a crap-artist or worse."

178

"Does Norman Thomas have all the answers?" Albert asked.

"He does not. And he'd be the first to admit it. Norman Thomas is a *mensch*." Suddenly the doctor stopped his pacing—he had been moving up and down the garden path, as if in search for the misplaced Frootsie certificates—and rubbed his chin. "I'm going to the hospital. I have to look at Glogauer, the old *kocker*. I want to make sure he's draining properly."

Mrs. Abrams leaned forward. "Must you go?"

Albert sipped at his iced tea. He held the glass up to drain the lees and stared at his parents through the amber bottom, spying.

"Of course I have to go. What else is there for me to do? Sit around and listen to Trotsky over there? Or discuss how we made a fortune in the market with syrup that tasted like green soap?"

"Shall I go with you?"

"Nah, what's involved? A ten-minute ride." He turned abruptly and left them, walking in short swift steps, a man forever fearful that a patient would run out on him.

Albert exhaled noisily. "What's wrong with Pop?"

"What do you mean?"

"How come he couldn't find the hospital this afternoon?"

"Mr. Big Ears. I knew you were snooping around. It's none of your business."

"It most certainly is. I'm over twelve. I'm a member of this family. I have a right to be informed. Primogeniture affords me certain inalienable rights."

"Spare me your literary locutions."

"I will, if you tell me why Daddy couldn't find the hospital."

She stroked her unwrinkled neck. "Your father is upset. A lot of things worry him."

"That tells me nothing. Ma, it sounded to me like Pop was going nuts. Crazy. Loco. Out of his mind. He was losing control of himself, nothing more or less." His voice quavered; he struggled to get it back on the track.

179

With unworried dark brown eyes, she looked at him in the gloom. Never, never would she betray fear, apprehension. The world might have scared her stiff, but no one would ever know it.

"Your father is not feeling well."

"Ma, we've been through this. Stop saying *your father*. He's also your husband. Sounds like we're in church. *Your father* which art in heaven."

"I'm not sure any of this is necessary. I'm under no obligation to pursue this conversation."

Albert leaped up and clapped his hands against his ears. He hopped around the bridge table, ducking in and out of the trunks of the surrounding trees. "I'm sick of that! I demand my rights as a dues paying union member! NRA, we do our part! Boy, the way you two exclude me from your lives, as if I committed a crime or something! It's enough to drive any sane person to booze or dope!"

A prim smile—that was all she would give him. His performance was funny—dancing in and out of the trees and bushes, threatening to become a drunk or an addict. "Your interest is appreciated, Albert. I concede that. But aside from being a good boy, doing your lessons, developing your mind, and staying out of trouble, what else can you do to help?"

"That's exactly the point. Nothing. I can't do a thing to help. Useless. Worse than useless. I can't even help Daddy clean up the backyard. He won't let me burn the cornstalks with him, or rake out the beds."

"He enjoys doing it himself."

"Well, in his work . . . if I could do something. . . ."

"Your fa—Daddy has reached the point where only he can help himself. He is frustrated, Albert. For some people, frustration is unbearable. Others make an adjustment and learn to live without having all their hopes and dreams realized. I have learned to accept life as it is given to me, and not to protest. I wanted a career, but I never had the chance. I accepted that. But Daddy refuses to adjust to his own limitations."

Cats battled with horrid sound effects in his father's cornfield at the rear of the yard. Albert shied a stone at them; there was a scrambling, scratching sound, then silence. The backyard cats were evil monsters. Ears missing, noses blunted, hides patchy, they roamed in packs, unafraid of dogs or people. Albert hated them. They left their reeking filth in the cornfield and vanished, thieves in the night.

His mother was stacking dishes when he got back from his duty as guardian of the crops. "Ma, what you were saying about limitations. Maybe it isn't Pop's fault. Maybe it's the world that's limiting him. You know, the Depression and everything. Maybe he isn't getting a fair chance, and he's got a right to be sore all the time."

"I'm not sure I agree. Why is he different from anyone else who is having a hard time? He will have to learn to accept the world, or else . . ." The unfinished sentence agitated him.

"Or else what?"

"Or else nothing."

He followed his mother to the house, each of them balancing stacks of dishes. "I know," he said. "I know. Or else he'll get worse and worse, and keep going around in circles not able to find the hospital, or his own house, or the few patients he's got left. He'll go nuts, Ma, admit it, plain nuts. Bughouse."

"That will do."

They entered the kitchen's harsh yellow light. Moths and night bugs sizzled against the screen door. He put his dishes in the sink and took a towel from the rack.

As he awaited the first clean dishes, a film of tears, involuntary, unwanted, embarrassing, pointless, clouded his eyes. He turned his head, but soon he was sniffling idiotically, trying to stem the flow. He removed his eyeglasses and dug the towel into his eyes. "Why's he so mad all the time, Ma? Sore at the whole world. Doesn't he ever stop being sore?"

"There is no need to cry." She poured soap flakes into the sink. "These things will work themselves out without your tears."

"You're always the optimist because you're so calm all the time. You got low blood pressure and low metabolism and you

181

control your temper. But not Daddy." His tears flowed softly, discreetly.

"He will have to make an adjustment," she said. "His behavior these days is the culmination of a series of frustrations, and he will have to learn to live with them. Years ago, Daddy wanted to be a surgeon. But how could he do graduate work, when he was penniless, when we worried about every expense? So we stayed here in Brownsville, and he made the best of being a good general practitioner. Since 1929, that has been a very hard life, even for as fine a physician as your father. All those dreams of glory—they've gone—and now, it's even difficult to make enough for everyday needs. You might as well know it."

Albert thought of the framed photographs of all those eminent Protestant professors at medical school who had encouraged him. Could they have all been wrong? "Ma, he's still got a good future!" he cried. "You almost sound as if you're glad he's a failure!"

"Hold that plate more firmly," she said. "And stop that carrying on." He wiped assiduously. He could always get a job in a restaurant kitchen if worst came to worst.

"Admit it, he's a failure."

"I will not tolerate such nonsense from you," she said. "He is a brilliant diagnostician. I've heard some of the biggest men in Brooklyn praise him to the skies. Financial success is not the only yardstick, try to remember that."

"Yeah, but it's all people care about." Tears turned to sniffles. His nose sucked in moisture; his eyes dried. He'd show them. He was hard as nails when he had to be. "How come he doesn't make more money?"

"He's too honest for one thing. Not just about money matters, but as far as his work is concerned. He tells people the truth. He refuses to involve them in a lot of needless medical expense if it's unnecessary. And I'm afraid he antagonizes a lot of people. He's always been that way, and I'm afraid he'll never learn."

"He better learn. We'll be in the poorhouse."

"That is our concern, not yours."

He polished a glass, admired its sheen in the harsh overhead light. Deftly, he picked up a platter, tossed it, caught it, flicked at it with the towel.

"Never mind the juggling act or artistic flourishes, just dry," she said.

"I'm extremely artistic. I'm the Picasso of dish-dryers. When we go to the poorhouse I can work in the kitchen."

She sprinkled Dutch Cleanser into the sink, sloshed water around it. "Your humor eludes me. Don't tell me I have no sense of humor. I may not make atrocious puns like Daddy, but I appreciate wit and a well-turned phrase."

He stored the last of the dishes in the high cabinet—its gnarled doors never closed properly, despite endless adjustments by his father. They were simply destined never to close; just as the old man appeared destined to be thwarted. Pensive, he flopped into the kitchen chair and studied his worn sneakers. Old Reliables, they had taken him through a wild day. And there was still the night ahead—ringalevio, a review of the day's baseball scores.

"Ma, what were you saying before about how you wanted a career and couldn't have it?"

She turned from the sink. "It's not important. I've mentioned it. I wanted to be a writer."

"Why didn't you?"

"Many reasons. I went to work as soon as I left business school. And having to help Daddy go to medical school. Still, I shouldn't look for excuses. Being poor and occupied with other tasks never stopped other people from a career. I'll set a bad example for you. You shouldn't get the notion that outside forces conspire against you all the time. That's a destructive form of self-indulgence, which I hope you'll spare yourself."

"Did you ever publish anything?"

"Only in school magazines."

"Was it good? Could I read it?"

"Oh, it's vanished. With my dreams of a career. But I like to think I had a little talent. Miss Kelly was the one who encouraged me. Do you remember those two books I gave you by Myra Kelly? *Little Citizens* and *Little Aliens?*"

"Sure." He remembered them vividly. But where were they now? Probably stuffed deep in the recesses of the all-purpose hall closet, buried beneath his *Boy Allies, Baseball Joes* and *Gary Graysons*. Or lost, misplaced, vanished. He should have taken better care of Myra Kelly's books.

His mother rested against the counter, her brown eyes misted in some gentle recollection of the beloved teacher who had encouraged her. Her early years in America, it seemed to Albert, were filled with good-hearted, generous Christians like Myra Kelly who helped her, took an interest in her, guided her. There was a mysterious woman named Miss McIntyre (for some reason his father always referred to her as Miss Flat Tire) who had been her superior at her first bookkeeping job. Miss McIntyre had introduced her to literary lectures, to the works of Emerson and Thoreau, to museums, to a chilling evening listening to the Swami Vivekananda. But Myra Kelly was the most dearly remembered of these heroines.

"The loveliest person I ever knew," Mrs. Abrams said. "She was not tall, but she had admirable posture, natural dignity. Her voice was soft. She was like a Gibson girl, with beautiful soft skin and fine features. I can remember her coming into the classroom on a winter's day with her cheeks ruddy from the cold. And snowflakes in her auburn hair, like a princess in Hans Christian Andersen. Her eyes were like Wedgwood blue. I adored her. It was so sad when she died."

"What did she die of?"

"I'm not sure—pneumonia, probably. She was so young, in her thirties. But she had lived such a beautiful life, making immigrants like myself happy, and writing those understanding stories about us."

As his mother spoke, the stories of Myra Kelly revived in his mind. Funny, sad, touching sketches about a teacher's life on the Lower East Side—Morris Mogilewsky, Sadie Steinberger, all the greenhorn kids. Perhaps she had cribbed a little from O. Henry, but what did it matter? On his tenth birthday, when he was already an omnivorous reader, his mother had given him *Little Aliens* and *Little Citizens*. It had taken him three days to devour them, but he returned to them again and again. In a few years though, Jack London loomed on the horizon, and Myra Kelly could not compete with that Klondiking, South-Sea-ing soldier of fortune. And right in step to a college marching band had come Ralph Henry Barbour, William Heyliger, Leslie Quirk and the deathless Lester Chadwick, creator of the equally immortal *Baseball Joe*, Big Joe Matson himself.

A twinge of guilt nibbled at Albert. His mother talked on about Myra Kelly. He had no right to abandon the books. They should have been honored on his bedroom bookshelf. He recalled a story that had moved him to tears. Of all the immigrant kids in Miss Riley's class (the fictional Myra Kelly), none was more gentle, lost, devoted than Morris Mogilewsky. Came Christmas, and the children each brought the teacher a present. (One, Albert recalled, was an old blue Bromo-Seltzer bottle.) When it was Morris' turn he gave Miss Riley a pink paper slip with something scribbled on it. Miss Riley realized it was a receipt for the month's rent on the Mogilewskys' tenement. Puzzled, she asked Morris why he had given it to her. Morris explained: every month, when his father showed that piece of paper to his mother, his mother would kiss him. So he knew the paper was something precious, and he wanted Miss Riley to have it.

He had read the story, intrigued. It took him a little while to figure out why the pink paper was so valuable, why it induced Morris' mother to kiss his father. But when the import dawned on him, he was stunned. *What a notion! What a story!* It had to be true. It had to have really happened to someone.

". . . then, when I was in the upper grades in public school, I still used to drop by and see Miss Kelly all the time. Usually it was to show her something I had written. She liked a story I did called 'A Walk in Central Park.' It was about how I had been entrusted with the care of my two younger brothers for the day, and the idea I was trying to convey was the way they were utterly dependent upon me and had complete faith in me to lead them, when I myself was frightened, and couldn't even speak English very well. I tried to point a moral of some kind, I suppose, about the need for *pretending* to be courageous and sure of oneself. Miss Kelly sent it to *St. Nicholas* magazine, but they rejected it."

She talked about further hobbles to her ambitions—work, a demanding family, caution, lack of confidence, and finally marriage. She hardly wrote anything after high school. Business courses occupied her time and soon she was keeping books for the Anthem Tract and Bible Society, where she met the arcane Miss McIntyre, the confidante of Hindu swamis.

Albert slumped deep in the chair. He was a little annoyed with his mother's quiet confessional. She had no right to have problems. She was the calm and adjusted one. Only the old man was permitted this kind of self-examination.

"And then of course, there were your father's needs." She rubbed at a stain on the kitchen counter. "It always seemed that his requirements took precedence. Of course that was how it should have been. I always had to be on hand, listening, advising, soothing him. Hardly a proper atmosphere in which to be creative and develop my own desire. But I have never once complained, and don't get the idea that I'm complaining now."

"The breaks of the game, Ma."

"Yes, you might phrase it that way. But I certainly have no intention of spending the rest of my life feeling sorry for myself. The way certain people do. You might profit from my example. I notice you seem to be doing a good deal of mooning about these days, with calf's eyes. As if the world were in conspiracy against you. Well, the world conspires against all of us and there are limits to our capacity to unmask the conspiracy. But I have learned that wallowing around in self-pity never changed anyone's life."

"No, but knowing how to roller-skate might."

"No you don't! I won't get involved in that old chestnut. I was trying to give you some good advice, but you, Smarty, have to keep returning to irrelevant issues. You are your father's son."

"Ah, forget it. If you can't understand what roller skating or riding a bike means to me, you don't understand anything."

How marvelously miserable she had made him! Pity for her—pity for the old man—and now a great sickening wave of pity for himself, the most miserable of all. Why did he have to listen to these sad stories of her aborted ambitions? She had no right to problems. That was *his* department, his father's. It had been uncalled for, all that sorrowful nostalgia about Myra Kelly. Nothing could be gained by prolonging the morose dialogue. (Although he was forced to admit his mother had told the story with great warmth and dignity, never once getting maudlin or weepy. He had to hand it to her.)

His mother walked to the screen door. The light illumined the edge of the garden. Beyond, it was dark and cooler in his father's oasis. "I'm going to rest in the garden a bit," she said.

"I'm going in the street," he said. The night beckoned—a new adventure. *Danger Is My Business* by Captain John D. Craig. *Roping Lions in the Grand Canyon* by Zane Grey. He hungered to see Bushy's bruised face.

"Must you wear sneakers?" she asked. "You've been in them all day. You'll succeed in ruining what little strength you have in your ankles."

"No!" he cried, skipping around the kitchen. "Oh no, Ma, not at the end of a day! I got the greatest ankles in the world. My ankles never felt better."

She muttered something about arch-supporting shoes and walked into the yard. He skipped away—a modest victory. A man had to count every advantage.

Emerging silently and slyly into the night, Albert saw that the political agitator was droning on. A moist crowd stood around his ladder, his drooping American flag. Above, night bugs wove a buzzing halo around the yellow street lamp. A single bored cop arrived at the edge of the audience.

Margulies, the revolutionary orator who had cheated his father, saw the policeman.

187

"Ah, the police, the police have arrived. Welcome, comrade, fellow member of the working class. No, we have no argument with the police, and our permit is in order. In the Soviet Union, police and citizens are true comrades, working together to produce the first genuine Socialist state. . . ."

"Dun't use it deh void Susshalist!" an old man cried. "*Ferdamteh* Communist, you make it rotten by everyone! Is different Susshalism, is not rotten Stalin Communism!"

"Attaboy, Pop!"

"You tell 'em!"

Margulies lowered the glasses that mangled his black eyes. He was a tubercular type, a scarecrow who hardly seemed capable of getting through a day's work, let alone starting a revolution.

"Ah, my friend, I see you are one of the reactionary crypto-Facists of our time! Out with it, my friend, is it the traitor Trotsky you support? Or the reactionary Social Democrats, or that tool of the capitalists, Mr. Norman Thomas, the Methodist minister? No, no, my friend, don't trifle with my superior intelligence! Yes, and I can see you are a supporter of that Judas, Franklin Delano Roosevelt, leading the workers of America down the road to a business-run Fascist state, with his clever NRA's and WPA's and CCC's. For what are these but echoes of Mussolini's repressive corporate state? I ask you, comrades, why . . ."

The crowd hooted, stirred, applauded occasionally. Only the old man who defended Socialism seemed bright enough to take on Margulies. Trotting past the meeting, Albert noticed that the vaporous Daisy and the Yankee-loving Cowboy were among the listeners. What, what in the name of heaven could they make out of Margulies' call to arms? And, indeed, if Daisy and Cowboy were his "fellow workers," the soldiers in his plan for Great Revolution, who was he kidding? All his life Albert would marvel at the blunt stupidity of radicals, their naïve assumption that virtue, courage, intelligence, honor and propriety abided solely in the working class. Why should a ditch-digger or a bricklayer be any more virtuous or moral than his father? It would have been a nice question to throw at Margulies, but more enticing enterprises beckoned.

At the ice-dock the Raiders appeared to have regained their normal dimensions. All afternoon against the Hawks, they had been shrimps, midgets at the mercy of monsters. Now they looked big and strong—big enough to bully him again. Even Bimbo Wexler had broadened. He was being trounced at boxball by Bushy. "On the line, on the line," Bushy snarled at his inferior.

"Ah, come on, Bushy, it was out by a ninch, at least a ninch."

Give up, give up, Bimbo, Albert murmured to himself. There is no conquering the likes of Aaron (Bushy) Feinstein, the greatest punchball center in the history of the game. Foolish Bimbo persisted in his argument—whining, pleading—until at length Bushy threatened to ram the Spalding down his throat. The game resumed. Bushy toyed with his opponent—slicing, cutting, slamming shots past him—the way Jack Johnson played with Ketchel before laying him out.

Albert settled on the ice-dock next to Teddy Ochab and enjoyed the show. It was pleasant not being the butt of Bushy's cruelty. What an artist he was!

"Hah!" Bushy cried. "Y'almost made a point!"

Was there no punishing him? No one who could make him bend, lose, surrender? Even his father's rod had not appeared to have harmed him. It bordered on the occult the way Bushy had absorbed those thwacks with the broomstick—and yet showed not a mark, not a bruise on his face or limbs! Nothing, nothing touched him.

Bimbo crushed, Bushy held up the ball. "Who's next? Who wants their lumps?"

No one had the energy to contest him. Even Teddy, who was his equal at boxball—and almost anything else—had no desire to further his lunatic plan of conquest. He was the Tamerlane of fourteen-year-olds.

Hopping, skidding, Little Artie plunged into their midst. He leaped on and off the ice-dock, vaulted a hydrant, climbed on Big Artie's broad soft back. Little Artie was in perpetual motion, like the chimp in the Prospect Park Zoo who threw orange peels and excrement at visitors. He had trouble in school because he was forever leaping from his seat, taking brief sprints around the classroom, throwing arms or legs about. He was a free soul. He had no father; his mother worked. She left a lunch for Little Artie and his younger sister and returned late at night.

Albert envied Little Artie his free run of the streets, his parentless abandon, ever since the day Little Artie had told him proudly: "My muddah goes to work and she leaves a can a Moose-a-bec sardines for me, and a can of Moose-a-bec sardines for my sister, a pear for me, and a pear for my sister, a Hoishey bar for me, a Hoishey bar for my sister, an' a quart of milk for the two of us." He envisioned Little Artie and his kid sister sitting alone, free as two rhesus monkeys (she resembled him), eating their splendid lunches without benefit of elders. How could he ever brag to Little Artie that in his own house they sat around an oak table, mother, father and son, and ate mashed potatoes, spinach, carrots, roast chicken and sliced cucumbers?

"I seen Zetz! I seen Zetz!" chattered Little Artie. He ran along the edge of the ice-dock, giving each of his friends a fast one-two. "Hey, Bushy, he says he's gonna lay chiggy for ya!" Away he skipped, ducking, dodging, evading tacklers, sliding into third.

They began to review the feverish game. It passed into the unrecorded annals of Brownsville—the freakish way in which the Hawks had lost their winning run, the unfairness of Mutty Zetzkin backing his kid brother, cowardly Fleishacker bending to the killer's will. The world had conspired against them.

Albert said little. He had really been out of it—a sideline spectator, a noncombatant, a rear echelon clerk pecking at his typewriter while others were up front dodging bullets and grenades. What admirable courage they had shown in confronting the Hawks! Some day he would write a lead for the *Journal*, something to set the nerve-ends tingling. *In all the annals of organized punchball there have been fewer examples of raw* unadulterated courage, of pure valor, than the hot afternoon in July 1934, when a band of young Brownsville athletes challenged, and almost subdued, the bruising bullies known as the Hawks. . . . Bill Corum might write it that way. Or Dan Daniel. Albert admired them beyond just about anyone in the world. There was something about the way Dan Daniel described a World Series game that made your blood race, your heart pound. Your eyes kept flying ahead, driven by a hunger for Dan Daniel's next magic word. Corum was no slouch, either. In all his life, Albert had never been as thrilled by a single sports story as he had been by Corum's report on Columbia's victory over Stanford in the Rose Bowl that year. The Columbia back who had scored the winning (and only) touchdown was named Al Barabas. He had scored on a tricky sneak play (Lou Little, there was another man to revere) that left the bigger, meaner, favored, Stanford Indians gasping. And Bill Corum's opening sentence! *And Barabas was a thief.* Now had anyone, anyone in the history of sports, ever said it better? It was the kind of thing that made Albert feel that life was worth living. Some day he would shake hands with Dan Daniel, Bill Corum and Al Barabas.

Little Artie rummaged through a burlap wastebag and found a tin can. With anthropoidal hands he peeled off the green Del Monte wrapper and pressed in the jagged edges. (*If I did that,* Albert observed to himself, *I'd get cut.*)

"Kickety-can, kickety-can!" Little Artie cried.

The game assembled in the gutter. They played on a court traversing the street, rather than along its length, as in punchball. Rules approximated punchball. The can was kicked, had to be fielded, thrown to bases. It was a dull pointless game—the slow movement of the can did not make for sensational plays— but it raised a fearful racket. *Another twilight game,* mused Albert. *When cars line the street, kickety-can will vanish. I am a somber witness to the slow death of ancient street games.* They awarded him the outfield (where no can was ever hit) and he lolled absent-mindedly against a wrought-iron fence wondering if the god-awful racket was bothering his father. No, his father said he was off to find the hospital. Was he lost? Wandering?

The can skidded, bounced, clattered. Runs scored, players collided. No one took the game seriously, but the noises were pleasurable.

At the ice-dock two of Albert's compeers wandered into view, materializing softly in the warm night. Gorilla and Mockey, mythic figures, loomed in the yellow glow, observing normal members of society shriek, bellow, curse. Half-wit and greenhorn, they stood like Bowery bums peeking into a Park Avenue dress ball. Gorilla's tweed cap was more jaunty than ever, yanked clear to the side of his great skull. He dug an elbow in Mockey's peasant hip.

"Boy, dey could play all night," Gorilla said. "Dey got lotsa games. When you learn English you could play too, Mockey. You gotta strong built."

With loving eyes Mockey admired his misshapen friend. Albert, watching them from across the street, had a disturbing thought. Suppose Mockey were to grow up thinking all Americans were like Gorilla? Gorilla was obviously his closest friend, his confidant. *Dear Folks in the Ukraine,* Mockey would write, *Americans are funny, sort of slow-talking people with big heads who wear their caps way on the side and have a crazy way of shuffling on bent legs and their voices are thick like sour cream. . . .*

Tired of kickety-can, they switched to Johnny-on-the-pony. Albert liked this game. No score was kept. It was not searingly competitive. It was merely a stupid collective effort involving no skills. Two teams were chosen: Teddy, Albert and Big Artie against Bushy, Bimbo and Little Artie. However, a seventh, non-playing man was needed—a "pillow." The pillow stood with his back against a wall. His belly was served as a rest for the first player's head.

"The new guy can be pillow," Little Artie said.

"G'wan, Mockey," Gorilla said. "It don't hoit."

Bushy had not noticed Mockey. The punchball game had

192

so inflamed him he had little time for normal brutalities. "Who is that guy?" Bushy asked angrily. "Where'd he come from?"

"Off the pickle boat," Bimbo said.

Bushy grabbed Mockey's arm and pulled him toward the brick wall of the ice-dock. "Stand here," he commanded. "G'wan, nobody'll sock ya."

Mockey muttered something in Ukraino-Yiddish. No one understood him.

"We go first," Bushy ordered. Bending over, he rammed his head into Mockey's gut, bracing his arms on either side of the greenhorn. Bimbo shoved his head into Bushy's behind and grasped Bushy's flanks with his arms. Little Artie did the same to Bimbo. All three braced for the assault. Mockey laughed.

"Hey, he makes a neat pillow!" Gorilla laughed. "And he's my pal!"

Across the street, the other team readied for the charge. Teddy, feather-light, ran, picked up speed and leaped on Bushy's back. Bushy held his ground. Albert was next. He ran and jumped, landing half on Bimbo, half on Little Artie. He barely budged them. They had saved Big Artie—all one hundred and seventy pounds of him—for last. Big Artie thundered across the gutter and hurled himself on Albert with an elephantine roar. Albert groaned (one was supposed to) and then succumbed to the peculiar warm pressure of Big Artie's motherly bulk. He wasn't quite sure why, and he was a little ashamed of it, but it was comfortable, pleasurable—almost exciting—being squeezed to a pulp by Big Artie's heft.

Bushy shouted the time-honored incantation: *"Johnny-on-the-pony, Johnny-on-the-pony, Johnny-on-the-pony, one, two, three, all off!"*

All six players tumbled to the pavement in a laughing muddle—arms, legs, bodies entwined. They sniffed one another's sweat, belched, unloosed farts, cuffed each other, goosed undefended rears. Mockey roared. What fun America was! Way more fun than the Ukraine, where they called him *Zhid* and threw rocks at his parents! Mockey clapped his blunted hands—a spectator at the Bolshoi.

The teams reversed positions. It was Teddy's turn to stick his head into Mockey's belly. Albert jammed his own head into Teddy's rear end and grasped his hips. Big Artie held down the rear.

"Don't nobody cut one," Big Artie said. "Except me." They all laughed.

"Yeah," Albert said. "Ailey-Bailey a bundle of straw, farting is against the law."

Little Artie sped down the street, leaped, and landed between Teddy and Albert. They steadied their legs and held. Bimbo landed on them next and they wobbled slightly. Albert felt grim, fulfilled. He wasn't much at punchball, but by God, he could hold his own at Johnny-on-the-pony.

Screaming, Bushy soared over them in a high leap, plummeting on Albert with all his muscle. Not content with that, Bushy bounced twice, digging knees and elbows into Albert's sagging back.

"Johnny-on-the-pony, Johnny-on-the-pony, Johnny-on-the-pony," Teddy counted. "One, two, three, all off!"

The supporters swayed, bent, groaned, and collapsed to the sidewalk grime, pulling the others with them. Gooses, punches, grabs were exchanged. Mockey applauded again: tribute to Stalin. In the tangle of arms, legs, torsos, Bushy pinned Albert with an iron knee.

"Is that really necessary?" Albert asked.

"That's for nothin'. Now do somethin'." His eyes gleamed; the blood madness was in him again. Albert saw it and dropped the discussion. Someone would have to pay for the fight with Zetz, for the humiliation at his father's hands. Bushy's face rotated. The hidden eyes fixed on Mockey.

"Who's that guy anyway?" Bushy asked.

Gorilla limped toward Mockey. "Don't pick on him, Bushy. He don't understand nottin'."

They roared, howled, fell on one another.

"Look who's talkin'!" Bimbo laughed. "Smart feller, fart smeller!"

194

"Yeah, yeah, dat's right," Gorilla said stolidly. "He's my friend. Leave him be, Bushy."

Bushy walked stealthily toward the two—leopard stalking baboons. Lunch.

Assuming a tough stance, Gorilla jiggled a wise guy's thumb at Mockey and spoke gangster-style from the side of his fishy mouth. "He's stupid. He ain't learned nottin'. I gotta show him everything."

Bushy bent double laughing. The others laughed less forcefully; Albert did not laugh at all.

"*He's* stupid! *He's* stupid!" Bushy shouted. "Look at his *teacher!* A coupla cockamamies!"

"Yeah," Gorilla said defiantly. "I'm his best friend. He likes me better than anyone." Gorilla spiffed out imaginary suspenders and walked around Mockey's grinning face.

"Let's see what ya taught him, if he's so great," Bushy said.

"Plenty, plenty," Gorilla said. The dimwit blew on his fingernails and polished them on his breast pocket.

Bushy fixed his slits on the new boy. Mockey smiled at him.

"Ya know how to play church-on-fire?" Bushy asked him.

"Chuchafaya?" Mockey asked.

"Oh boy, this'll be neat," Bimbo crowed.

"Ah lay off," Teddy said. "The guy don't understand anything." He bounced his Spalding and leaped on to the ice-dock. "Who wantsa play stoopball?"

"Me, I'll play," Albert said. No, he could not inflict church-on-fire on Mockey. Nor would Teddy. But the others gathered around the immigrant.

"Don' play wit' 'em," Gorilla begged. He plucked at Mockey's shirt. "C'mon home, Mockey, don' play wit' 'em."

But Mockey was ecstatic. He let himself be led to the sloping sidewalk in front of the ice-dock.

"Butt out, Gorilla, or I'll mopilize ya," Bimbo warned.

"Ah, he don' understand me anyway," Gorilla said sadly.

"He's stupid." Shaking his blurred head, Gorilla limped to the ice-dock.

"Why dey pickin' on him?" he asked Albert. "It ain't fair."

"Look at it this way, Gorilla," Albert said. "Everybody has to get church-on-fire sometime in his life. It's like an initiation." He and Teddy started to play boxball. But the ceremony was about to begin; they were constrained to watch.

The other boys gathered around the baldhead. "You got the easy part," Bushy said slyly. "Just stand here and holler 'Church-on-fire.' Get it?"

The others giggled. Little Artie punched Big Artie, sliced his ham, goosed him.

"Vus?" Mockey asked.

"Jerk. Dummy. Lissen to me." Bushy grabbed his arm. "You holler loud, real loud." He forced open Mockey's mouth. "Wit' ya mouth. Holler. Like this: Church-on-fire! Church-on-fire!"

Mockey responded in Yiddish. Bushy explained again, with gestures, shoves, yelling the words into Mockey's pale face. At last the new boy understood. He hopped in armored shoes, muttered, "Yeh, yeh."

"You guys ready?" Bushy asked. Bimbo and the two Arties were suppressing laughter. Giggles and snorts escaped their mouths.

"Go on, Mockey, now!" Bushy yelled. "Loud! Sprech!"

Beaming, Mockey opened his mouth; his eyes glowed. In a sweet singing voice, as if chanting in a shtetl choir he cried: "Chuchafaya, Chuchafaya, Chuchafaya!"

On the final rising note, the four boys ripped open their flies and urinated on Mockey. The victim stood still (most boys ran away from the ordeal) and the elated expression on his face gave way to stunned sorrow. His coarse European clothes and his starchy body absorbed the hot yellow streams. In steaming jets, the bladders discharged on him and still he did not run. Final drops were shaken free, flies were buttoned. Mockey's eyes searched their faces, seeking some clue, some hint.

"What a sucker," Bimbo said. "Did he fall for it."

196

"A real *shmuck*," Little Artie added. But he spoke without conviction.

Mockey smiled helplessly and walked away from them toward the ice-dock. There was no sense of elation, no high triumph. Once they had peed, they had been drained. A victim was supposed to run, shout, escape, fight. But the loving baldhead had taken his soaking without protest.

Gorilla limped toward the new boy. "Dat's how dey show dey really like ya, Mockey," he said.

Mockey kept fingering his embroidered shirt, his knee breeches. He was like a man in a strange new garment.

At once, the four persecutors began a chicken fight. Big Artie carried Little Artie on his shoulders, Bushy bore Bimbo. They slammed and crashed into each other, Little Artie and Bimbo trying to unhorse one another.

"They're embarrassed," Albert said to Teddy. "That's why they started the chicken fight. To forget about it. Right, Teddy?"

The noble Polack bounced the Spalding against the ice-dock.

"Why pick on a guy who can't fight back?" Honor and decency were bred in his thin bones.

Gorilla led Mockey away, mumbling consolations. In the street, the chicken fighters tumbled to the asphalt. How good to wallow in grime and spit, old chewing gum, horse-piss and eggshells! Bimbo bounced to his feet and saw Mockey departing. He raced after him and jumped on his broad back. "On and off the ice-dock!" he shouted.

A wild shriek came from Mockey's mouth. Like a dog emerging from a pond, he shook his body. Bimbo went flying; the baldhead came after him. A savage light glinted in Mockey's eyes. With fierce cry he kicked at Bimbo's behind with his steel-prowed boots, cursed, kicked him again. Bimbo rolled away, jumped to his feet and danced comically, hands on his butt.

"Wow! What a temper that guy has!" But he did not

pursue his attack. Something in Mockey's assault had given him pause. Mockey shook his fists at the prancing Bimbo.

"That guy made you run!" Bushy taunted. "Look out he don't sit on ya!"

"Yeah, with that ass he'd squash me into a blintz," Bimbo said.

Ah, but he is afraid, afraid of Mockey, Albert realized. And at once he was ashamed of his own cowardly retreats before Bimbo's bullying. Mockey, in one swift counterattack, had established for all to see that he was no scapegoat, no fool.

"That guy's okay," Teddy said. "He ain't scared."

"He's tougher than he looks," Albert said admiringly. Then a shudder of guilt silenced him. How many times had Bimbo Wexler tormented him, challenged him to combat. And how many times had he hedged, retreated, made excuses, refused to fight? Had he on one, solitary, single occasion risen on his hind legs and fought back? Not once. Never. And behold Mockey: baldheaded, unlearned, alone and unprotected in the savage new land. Mockey had struck back. He had sent Bimbo his message on the toes of his Ukrainian shoes: *Don't tread on me.* Certain mitigating circumstances did exist, he assured himself. Mockey was a sturdy oak. He did not have weak ankles nor eyeglasses, and he was hardly underweight. But he took no satisfaction in these excuses. His own wretched cowardice was never more evident to him. Mockey, of all people in the world, had reminded him.

"That guy could make a good athalete," Teddy said solemnly. "He got a built like a rock. Bimbo wouldn't last ten minutes if that guy really got sore."

Like a shadow, thoughtfully picking his nose, Frankie Udo appeared. He joined the boxball game with Teddy and Albert. "The Yankees won two," he said. Like all Italians he was a fierce Yankee fan. The Raiders, Dodger fans to a man, except for Teddy, who for obscure reasons rooted for the Pittsburgh Pirates, regarded Frankie's athletic preferences as part of his exotic Italian nature—of a piece with the Roman Catholic Church and pizza.

"How'd Pittsburgh do?" Teddy asked. It was puzzling but admirable to Albert that Teddy should stand so loyally by unimaginative ballplayers like the Waner brothers and Arkie Vaughan.

"They got beat," Frankie said.

But they lost fairly and squarely, Albert felt. Like Teddy would lose. They were a team of fast runners, naturals, men not given to bullying or foul tactics. Teddy's Pittsburgh Pirates would never fall under Cowboy's heading of dirty ball clubs.

"Hey!" Bushy shouted. "We got enough for ringalevio!"

He leaped on Big Artie's back, a trained baboon. Their bodies came together, Albert thought, like varieties of primitive ocean animals, drawn to one another's cousinly forms in a symbiotic relationship. They were really not bad guys, although he wished they had not urinated on Mockey.

"Choose ya sides, Teddy!" Bushy cried.

They hurled fingers at each other; Teddy won. Alternating choices, Teddy selected Big Artie and Frankie Udo. Bushy took Little Artie and Bimbo.

"Left out again," Albert said.

Bimbo hooted at him: "You're playin' with ya mudder's broomstick!"

"Can't you change that record?" Albert asked wearily. "You're a bore." But he was relieved the taunt was mild. Bimbo had been known to use a disgusting variant, substituting "bloomers" for "broomstick."

Bimbo cuffed the back of his neck. "Ya can't go in the gutter at night, ya can't jump fences, ya can't go in backyards, yer scared of boogies. So how can you play? Yer old man'll mopilize ya if he sees ya runnin' around the streets at night. Sister Mary."

Albert appealed to Bushy. There was no use protesting Bimbo's insults. "Can't we play three and four?"

"Yer old lady's prob'ly layin' chiggy for you at the window right now," Little Artie explained, without malice. "You'll get caught the second we start."

The injustice of it all! Why did his parents, with all their worries, have to be dragged into his own personal problems? An idea occurred to him. "Hey, we'll ask the new guy to play!" He pointed to Mockey, drying out in the shadows, consoled by Gorilla's wisdom. What stimulating conversations those two must be enjoying! His heart warmed at the thought of their comradeship—half-wit and greenhorn. Desperately, he yearned to be as decent to Mockey as Gorilla was. All three were blood brothers in the great fraternity of the insulted and the injured.

While the others pondered his suggestion—studying Mockey's stumpy figure—Teddy settled the issue. "Yeah, if the guy wantsa play, why not? I'll take Albert. G'wan, Bushy, take the new guy."

Pantomime, Yiddish, tugs and prods were employed before the baldhead would leave his sanctuary. Drenched once, he was wary of these new Cossacks.

"Gaw 'head, Mockey, dey won't hoit ya," Gorilla said. Mockey walked toward the boys.

Again Teddy and Bushy shot fingers at each other, again Teddy won. His team would run away, hide, attempt to evade capture. Bushy's men, each matched against a quarry, would have to catch them.

The teams went into strategy huddles. As Albert bent low, luxuriating in the stink of his teammates he reflected on the magic of the game. He composed a learned essay.

"The ancient slum game of ringalevio," wrote Professor A. A. Abrams, Ph.D. in American Studies, "is of obscure origin, although certain scholars believe it derives from native American games such as hare-and-hounds or chase-the-baron, these in turn being of English origin. The name of the game, however, remains to this day a total mystery. No etymological explanation, not even the remotest hint, tells us of the origin of the wild haunting cry—ringalevio! What does it signify? Who invented it? We are in a wilderness, a linguistic labyrinth. Like Basque or Magyar, we are confronted with an enigma, a puzzle that defies and mocks us.

"Inasmuch as the game is most frequently encountered in Jewish quarters of New York City (see attached Map B showing distribution of ringalevio in five boroughs of New York) and is played largely—though not exclusively—by boys of Jewish origin, one might be led to suspect a Yiddish, Hebraic or Yiddo-American basis for the word. But nothing in any of these languages or their variant dialects, including Ladino, offers us a clue. We must therefore reach the sober conclusion that the name *ringalevio* is a nomenclatural freak, a mutant. Possibly the best explanation—admittedly a weak one—is that the word has a certain euphonic appropriateness. It sounds right. It sounds like something one boy would yell on discovering another. It carries with it a ring of flight, escape, search and discovery. It trumpets itself forth on the night air in the same triumphant manner as *tally-ho!* or *view halloo!*

"Concerning the game itself, there exist no written rules to guide us. There is no mention of the game in the general literature on sports and games, and as far as this scholar is concerned, nothing in fiction. This lacuna is understandable. The game as currently played varies from neighborhood to neighborhood and the rules are vague, shifting and often arbitrary.

"Stated simply, ringalevio is a variety of mass hide-and-go-seek. But there are certain differences. To begin with, there is no home base, no countdown on the order of 'anyone-around-my-base-is-it,' no provision for 'home-free-all.' Still, the structure is similar—flight, pursuit.

"A game proceeds as follows: two teams of equal number are chosen. A team should comprise at least three men, and preferably no more than six. Larger groups tend to become chaotic, and the game at its best is of a disorganized nature. One team runs off into the night. (Ringalevio is never played during the day.) The fleeing team may break up into groups or run away singly. Ideally, a four-man team will split into two two-man subgroups.

"Flight must be characterized by deception, false leads, feints, other wily tricks. But oddly, the escape routes taken by players are, by tacit agreement, known to the pursuing team. What is required is a touch of ingenuity in hiding, a clever ruse

201

to mislead the pursuer. Each member of the pursuing team is charged with catching an opposing member—usually by clutching the fugitive with both hands, or sometimes merely by sighting him. (As indicated earlier, rules are flexible and subject to local custom.) Some ringalevio games, however, are 'wide open,' which is to say, any member of the pursuing team can apprehend any member of the running team.

"The moment of high drama comes when the fugitive is sighted and the chaser gives vent to the cry: *ringalevio!* Players of the game regard this as a stirring mystic climax, a startling sound in the city night. The word rings out loud and clear, echoing across tenement, schoolyard, backyard, street. It conveys adventure, the occult, boyhood secrets hidden from the adult world. The battle cry is usually accompanied by identification of the prey, as follows:

" '*Ringalevio!* Frankie and Bushy in the junkyard, back of the old iceboxes!'

"A game ends when all fugitives have been caught. But the rules are elastic. Games are often suspended (when players cannot be found or parents intervene at a late hour) or dribble off to incompletion. Often, to speed up a game, players who have trapped their men join in the hunt for the remaining hiders. When all have been caught, and if the hour is early enough, roles are reversed.

"No score is kept. There is rarely a big fuss over winners and losers. The main burden of the contest, it would seem, is the *game itself*, the manner in which the teams comport themselves, the variations and adornments that are added. In this respect it resembles certain ritualistic war games of the American Indian or the sub-Saharan African. Contestants are at pains to dramatize their roles, to involve their environment by seeking exotic hiding places, undergoing discomfort to elude their hunters, to court dangers outside the sport itself, such as hiding in Negro territory, where there exist threats far greater than apprehension by the enemy.

"One may also compare the game to Old World contests in which the dress, formalities and rules are more important than the question of winning. These would include the Eton wall game, and medieval athletic contests still practiced in Florence and Siena where procedure, rhetoric and tradition are of greater moment than the matter of victory or defeat. How curious that these ancient attitudes should find an echo in the slum streets of Brooklyn!"

Professor Abrams concluded his treatise as he scampered down Longview Avenue, trailing Teddy, Big Artie and Frankie Udo. Halfway down, under a street lamp, Teddy stopped them for another strategy meeting. The thrill of the chase rippled Albert's narrow chest. Already, he was breathless, apprehensive.

"We break up," Teddy whispered. "Me an' Big Artie, Albert an' Frankie." A natural strategist, he outlined their plan of escape. "Me an' Artie'll cut down Rower Avenoo, back of the lots an' through Kalotkin's place, an' hide in Junkman John's lot. There's a new hole in his fence. Bushy don't know about it. . . ."

Albert admired him—fearless, he would brave Kalotkin's savage dog, the junkman's drunken wrath, Bushy's pursuit.

"Albert, you an' Frankie split from us 'round the corner, shinny over the fence, and hide in the schoolyard. Frankie, you go to the door inta the basement, and Albert by the Chinese handball wall. If the other guys come, one of yez break for it."

Albert tried to look brave: the schoolyard. Scene of their ambush that morning by Lee Roy and his pals. Where he had caught the fly ball, but had his glove and softball stolen, had been bombarded with rotten eggs and stale bagels. But he would have Frankie with him. Frankie was not very tough, but at least he was an Italian, and that might give Lee Roy pause. Italians were supposed to fight, get tough, carry knives, although all Albert could remember Frankie Udo doing was picking his nose or daydreaming.

Yet there were rewards in Teddy's plan. Mockey, of course, would be assigned to him. He would make a monkey of the baldhead, feint him out of position, beat him over the fence and run away. At long last, he had a ringalevio opponent whom he could best.

They fled the enemy. Ahead of Albert, Teddy ran lightly. Big Artie bounced daintily on tattered sneakers behind him. Release! Freedom! How marvelous a game it was! No scores kept, no winners or losers—only a long night of hiding in urine-rich alleys, in garbage-bright empty lots, in alcoves, hallways, fine and private places.

It was still hot. Men in soiled undershirts, baggy women leaned on windowsills. (Most of them hate my father, Albert thought. They gossip about him, spurn him, and refuse to pay their bills.) From a secondhand clothing store window depended the red-white-and-blue banner: NRA   WE DO OUR PART. In the window of a bookstore owned by a reputed Communist was displayed a large cardboard placard reading: WE ARE PROUD TO BE AMERICANS. How proud? he wondered. Prouder than me? Prouder than President Roosevelt? And why advertise it? It made him think of his father's comment whenever they rode by COHEN'S TOOL WORKS. "So does mine," the doctor said, "but I don't advertise it."

On Rower Avenue they were in enemy territory. They passed the sagging synagogue. A light burned feebly in a basement window. Melnick? Some remnants of the Old World debating the subtleties of Rambam or Rashi? Soon they were in a no-man's-land of vacant lots, junkyards, squat, soiled brick buildings where old men knitted sweaters, or rammed pickles into barrels, or put together artificial flowers. The occupants of these dirty buildings seemed to Albert to be forever in transit. One week would find bearded elves cutting cloth for ladies' handbags, silent workers with shears and huge needles. A few days later these craftsmen would vanish, and in their place would appear burly red-faced clods in white coveralls squirting milk into paper bags to make farmer cheese. Industry on Parade. What Brownsville Makes the World Takes. What Brownsville Makes Makes Brownsville. But why didn't any of these free enterprisers last long?

Under the summer moon, the schoolyard was more hide-

204

ous, more forbidding than by daylight. Did its irregular playing fields, the lunatic boundaries serve some dread nocturnal purpose? Were Black Masses and animal sacrifice performed under the full moon on the truncated basketball court, the sloping handball walls, the fetid pavilion?

"G'wan, Albert, you an' Frankie git in," Teddy ordered. "If the other guys catch yez, one lead 'em away, and the other guy gits over the fence. Whoever gets out, meet us by the junkyard."

Albert was tempted to ask Teddy what they were to do if Lee Roy showed up. And the tall black boy with the hairy horns on his skull. But Teddy and Big Artie were gone and he was left with Frankie who was pensively picking his nose.

He admired Frankie's aplomb. But Frankie could run fast and he couldn't. And what words of advice could Teddy Ochab have offered anyway? Teddy did not know fear. Lee Roy was just another street boy, black perhaps, but just another adversary, not a dark menace.

"I guess we better go over," Albert said.

"Where ya wanna hide?"

"Teddy said we should break up. But we can hear the guys coming. That new guy wears those iron shoes."

Frankie hoisted himself over easily. Albert backed up to the gutter, took his running start, pulled himself over the spikes and hit the ground. Side by side, they halted in the schoolyard. It was eerie, deserted. Empty, it still stank of unwashed bodies, urine, dog turds and sour odors Albert could not identify. The stench was laminated, layer upon layer of foul smells. They walked softly across the concrete.

"Them guys'll come here," Frankie said. "They know someone always picks the schoolyard."

"Then we got to beat 'em to the fence."

"I can beat Bimbo any day of the week," Frankie said. "He got lead in his ass."

In the alcove the boys squatted amid the ammoniated stink, like lion cubs in the Prospect Park Zoo. The locked doors were painted a vomitous olive-green, mottled in a presumed decorative style. The upper parts of the doors were of thick frosted glass, reinforced with wire. They were horrid doors, jail doors, doors designed to imprison the criminally insane.

The doors made him think of the Ungraded Class, that collection of half-wits and unteachables (Gorilla was a veteran member) who strolled dull-eyed through the corridors and languished in a basement room amid primitive tools, under the stern eye of Mr. Morris Shapiro.

Whenever Albert thought of his alma mater, it was not of the pleasant teachers, the windows decorated with pumpkins or Pilgrims or George Washington, the assembly where they pledged the flag, but of the terrifying Ungraded Class. What a convention of spooks! Gorilla, who by tenure was its unofficial president, was an Albert Einstein, a Nobel laureate, by comparison to most of them. There was, for example, a mountainous fat boy named Zoog, a pinheaded, sack-bellied ogre who clomped around in high-button shoes. Zoog specialized in hiding stolen objects in the vast pouches of his elephantine gray knickerbockers. Once Albert had seen this apparition blundering down a hallway with the clear outlines of an ax jouncing against his knee. Zoog had cached the tool in his pants—for what sordid reason? No attempt was ever made to retrieve stolen goods from Zoog's bloomers. Those confiscatory pants were his own secret; no one dared enter them to search and apprehend. Perhaps, Albert reasoned, his parents had an agreement with the school to return anything brought home in Zoog's bottomless buckled trousers.

Oh, the depths unplumbed, the nameless horrors of the Ungraded Class! Like the case of the giant Sumatra rat, this congregation of the depraved was a story for which the world was not yet prepared! They were case histories in misery, creatures worse off than himself. In the urinous miasma, the night gloom, he studied Frankie Udo's secretive face—high blank forehead, drooping nose, recessive mouth. The boy's head had been shaved for the summer, but the reborn hairs studded his dome like tiny black bugs. Frankie bore an unnerving resemblance to his older brother Angelo, a long-time sand-paperer of the Ungraded Class.

"How's your brother these days?" Albert asked pleasantly.

"Ah, okay."

"What does he do all summer—when there's no school?"

"Whaddya tink he does? He sits by the window."

"Oh." A sadness descended on Albert. Everyone called Angelo Udo "Duck" or "The Duck." He carried his arms like bent wings; his feet were splayed and he waddled. "Is he getting any better, Frankie?"

"He loined to write his name last year."

"Maybe you could take him to a special hospital, certain doctors." Outside the schoolyard, bronze voices clattered in the night. Albert shivered. *Sheeet! Yo' ass, yo' ass!*

"No doctor ain't ever gonna touch *him*," Frankie said. "The doctor rooned him when he was born. He put iron t'ings on his head and squashed his brain. That's what made him crazy. He woulda been okay except the doctor rooned him."

"Hmmm. I'm not sure that's scientifically accurate." He was impelled to defend the medical profession. His father was always leaping to the defense of the American Medical Association, even though he had no use for it, except Dr. Morris Fishbein.

"He c'n count up ta twenny," Frankie mumbled.

"Yes, he seems to be a pretty nice guy, Duck." Thank God it was not *his* father who stood accused of turning Frankie's brother into a waddling winged moron. Other doctors evidently had problems also. Imagine saddling the Udo family with such a burden! He could remember calling for Frankie at their flat—exotic garlicky smells, a shimmering vision of a grape arbor in the backyard, a kitchen wall hung with haloed saints and a red velvet bleeding heart framed in filigreed silver.

Their noses grew accustomed to the stench. They awaited Bimbo and Mockey like anxious lovers. That was part of the fun of ringalevio. It was not a hateful or vicious game. One anticipated being caught; the players all knew one another; flight and search were carried out on a friendly basis.

A firecracker or cherry bomb exploded in the schoolyard. Both boys hopped to their feet. Across the crazily lined court another explosion sent up a puff of smoke. Penny paper torpedos.

"Chaaaage d'enemy!"

"Follah me, men!"

"H'yah comes Gen'ral Madison!"

Over the spiked fence, sailing effortlessly, they saw the dark forms of Lee Roy and his tall tufted friend.

"Holy smoke," Albert whispered. "What if they see us?"

Frankie shrugged. "So what? Just two boogies."

Frankie's contempt was almost worse than his own shuddering fear. "We better be quiet," Albert whispered. His voice trembled. "I know that Lee Roy. He's not such a bad guy." That was the ticket: if he kept thinking about Lee Roy Pennington as a swell fellow, Lee Roy might even become one. Mind over matter.

"Ah, dey all stink," Frankie said. "Dat boogie stole ya softball, dint he?"

Unassailable reasoning, Albert realized. He did not pursue the debate over Lee Roy's character. Torpedos exploded everywhere—against walls, the cement paving, the pavilion roof. Two night spirits in the savage state, Manitou and Whamba, Lee Roy and his horned friend flew about the schoolyard, at war with the world.

"Gen'ral Lee Roy, Ah orders yo' attack dat m'sheen gun nes' and kill all dem Krauts!" Madison was a rather good actor, Albert conceded. His emphasis was proper, his liquid voice was loud and clear.

Lee Roy was shirtless. Pale blue suspenders glistened on his mahogany chest like fourragères. Gurgling, Lee Roy sprinted across the schoolyard.

"Chaaaaage d'enemy!" Lee Roy shouted. He slammed a torpedo against a slanting wall. It exploded with hellish noise. How odd that nobody in the neighborhood seemed to care. Everyone (except his tortured father) accepted the noise, the screams, the blasts as natural. Perhaps they were. Perhaps his father was the only nut.

"Feex baynets," Madison ordered.

Lee Roy whipped a pocketknife from his trousers and flicked open the blade. Madison held a stick in front of him. "Does yo' wanna live fo'evah?" Madison inquired. "Follah me!"

They galloped across the schoolyard.

"I'm gittin' the hell outa here," Frankie announced. He watched the colored boys pound across the paving.

"Can we make it?" Albert asked.

"We better," Frankie said. He flew from the alcove toward the fence. Albert felt his throat clot with ashes, and took after him. Lean and swift, Frankie was on the fence and over in seconds. Behind him, Albert stumbled, got to his feet and made for the railings. But he did not have enough impetus. His foot missed the crossbar.

"Who dat?" shouted Lee Roy.

"Who runnin' deah?" cried Madison. "Who sneakin' in our te'tory?"

Back they flew across the yard. Fear coated Albert's hide— grease on a channel swimmer. His heart constricted, jumped, slammed at his ribs. Once more he flew at the fence, hooked his right foot in the bar, pulled himself up and started over the spikes. He saw Frankie vanish around the corner—an ally gone. Hot hands grabbed at his ankles. He was trapped, caught, finished. He gasped, struggled, surrendered, was dragged down by four black hands.

Why worry? he assured himself. Good sense, logic, calm reasoning, and he would emerge unscathed. Or would he?

They handled him as if he were an infant. Shoved against the railing, he saw their molten eyes goggling at him and he was deathly afraid.

"Know who dat boy is?" asked Lee Roy.

"Yeah. He deh one."

"Dat deh one Ah tole you 'bout," Lee Roy added.

"Aw-w, cut it out, Lee Roy," Albert said. Where had his voice gone? Why were his knees liquefied, his stomach full of gaping holes? "You certainly know me. Albert Abrams in Four-B? Don't you remember when I helped you with arithmetic once?"

" 'Rithmetic? Whut 'rithmetic?" demanded Lee Roy. Both captors held their small arms languidly—Lee Roy his knife, Madison his club—as if the smallness of their game did not require weaponry.

"It was n-n-n-nice running into you two fellows again, after seeing you this morning during the softball game. I-I-I got to go."

On jelly legs, he tried to climb the fence. Hands like grappling irons seized his belt. He floundered.

"Cut it out, Lee Roy, you know darn well who I a-a-a-am." He ordered himself to stop shaking; the order was disobeyed.

They spun him about, held him against the railing.

"Wh-wh-what's this business about my being th-th-the one?" he asked plaintively. "Why am I so special? The one what?"

"Man, you jes' deh one!" yelled Madison. "Hee-hee-hee!" What obscure secret did they share? When Madison laughed the tufts on his head jiggled. Horns, growths. Did his hair grow that way naturally? Was it trained? Did those two sprouts endow him with some witch doctor's knowledge? Or were they (wondered ethnologist A. A. Abrams) related to Michelangelo's "Moses" who possessed similar horns? Was Madison a Semite? A member of the lost tribe of black Falasha Jews of Ethiopia? If so, why was he persecuting Albert?

"Madison, whut we gon' do wit' dis boy who steal our baseball?" asked Lee Roy.

"Cut his gizzard."

"Will you gu-g-guys please cut the comedy? My gang is looking for me right now, six guys. We were playing ringalevio and me and Frankie Udo were hiding here when you happened along—"

Madison grabbed his polo shirt, yanked it free of his trousers, and lifted him off the ground, slamming him against the fence. "Cut it out!" Albert wailed. The first show of tears blurred his eyes: he saw Madison and Lee Roy like melty chocolate babies.

"Y'all got money?" Madison asked.

"Yes! Yes! Anything you want!"

Lee Roy's hands ferreted through his pockets.

"Sebben cents," Lee Roy said disgustedly. "Ain't dat deh sheeet. Doctah's son an' he ain't got but sebben cents."

"Will you guys let me go? Okay, you got the money, now lemme go." He was sniveling. Now, through the raindrops inside his glasses he saw them as underwater shapes. "If you hurt me you'll get in trouble. Knives are illegal, and the police'll—"

"Poleece *sheeeet*," Lee Roy said. But he snapped his knife shut, tossed it in the air, and returned it to his trousers. Odd pants, they were too, truncated men's woolen trousers, flapping at midcalf on Lee Roy's bandy legs.

"Who need a knife wit' him?" Madison asked.

Was he free? He hauled himself up on the fence, the hardest way to get over. He prayed for swift infusions of adrenaline. Lee Roy grabbed at his dangling right foot and clung to it like a limpet.

"Look whut Ah got, Madison."

"Whatchoo got, man?"

"Sebben cents."

"Fellahs, come on," he pleaded. Lee Roy's strength was too much for him. Sliding, his hands scorched on the iron posts. Madison leaped at his behind—not roughly, but playfully, in the way a large dog will assault its master. Amid their rich jungle odor, he landed on the paving. The knee of his knickerbocker ripped. His palms were on fire.

Reason and calm were indicated. His eyes had stopped tearing. What did tears serve against these agents of Pluto? "You ought to let me go," he said. "My gang'll be here."

"Yo' gang?" asked Lee Roy. "Yo' gang don' skeer us. We ain't skeered ef yo' got fifty in yo' gang."

"Yeah. We cut dem up too."

Should he scream? Of course not. The slum dwellers across

the street, lounging on stoops and windowsills would ignore it. They ignored disaster, too much concerned with their own troubles. Everyone yelled in Brownsville. At night, in his room, he heard yells in a lunatic symphony, a tone poem of shrieks, from nearby, a block away, a neighborhood away. Why yell? He appeared to have reached some unavoidable destiny, some confrontation that was preordained for him, like an original sin. There they were—black, fleet, free, wild, powerful, fearless, noble savages in rebellion. And look at him! What an adversary—slow, underweight, four-eyed, overintellectualized, well-read, cursed with weak ankles.

Four eyes like freshly opened oysters regarded him contemptuously. In the moonlight, the whites were stained yellow, as if in the summer heat, the furry pupils had melted and run. Like chocolate ice cream melting into the vanilla. The pupils up close were like Krasne's jumbo-sized black olives. In his terror he still had to marvel at those liquid orbs.

And the odor! His nose twitched. Hog bowels, pig meat, frying bacon fat. The captors sizzled with aromas from some choking kitchen. On the other hand, Albert reasoned tolerantly, I probably smell god-awful to them, with my sickly-sweet white vapors. With proper lack of prejudice, he recalled a study by a Columbia physical anthropologist who had boys of different races sprinting around an outdoor track in sweat suits and then, with scholarly care, sniffed their armpits to identify the various racial odors.

"Dis boy got to fight one of us," Lee Roy announced.

Madison thrust forward his lips. "Yeah. Hit look dat way. He got to make his choice. Ah deh oldest, Lee Roy, but you meaner."

"Yeah, Ah de meanest man in Brooklyn. He gon' have to fight me."

"I've no desire to fight either of you," Albert quavered. "I have nothing against you fellows. Honest. In-in-in-in fact I'd like to be friends with you. I'm not one of those white people who dislikes colored persons. Quite the opposite. I think you've had a rotten deal, and we owe you something."

212

"Hey," Lee Roy said, bending his great head, so that their foreheads touched. "Ain' choo deh guy what call me *black* oncet?"

"*Never!*" shouted Albert. "Never! I've never called you black in my life! I'd never dream of insulting anyone in the world because of his race or religion!"

"*Sheeeet,* Ah heerd you. You call me *black.*"

"Lee Roy, I swear it. I would never do such a thing. You know darn well, Lee Roy, the only time you and I ever had any dealings was in the 4-B when I helped you with arithmetic. Now admit it to me, Lee Roy."

"Yeh." Lee Roy mulled this old association a few seconds. He stretched his pale blue suspenders, then snapped them against his naked ebony chest. "How 'bout today?"

"How about today?"

"You stole mah ball."

"I did not! It was *my* indoor baseball, don't you remember? It was you and Madison stole it from *me!*"

Somehow, his brave riposte appeared to have intensified the odor of frying oil—a biochemical response.

"Da boy jes' accuse us of stealin'," Lee Roy said gravely. "Reckon Ah got to whup him."

"I don't wanna fight you! I got nothing against you! Besides, you've got a good ten pounds on me!"

Hard as old bread, Lee Roy's hand slapped his mouth. Albert gasped and pressed himself against the iron rails. "*Haaaaaalp!*" "*Haaaaaalp!*"

Madison cuffed him again—the back of his hand against his cheek. Albert turned his head. Across the street he saw three adults seated placidly, sweating through the night, on a stone stoop. None looked at him. Not a one had budged. *Yell, shmell,* he could hear them saying. *All you lousy kids are the same, hollering all the time; shaddap and go home.*

"Donchoo go holl'in' fo' he'p," Madison said. He sounded betrayed. "We make it bad fo' yo', yo' keep holl'in'. We tryin' play fair wit' yo'."

Lee Roy backed off and began to box, throwing left jabs

213

and right crosses. He bounced, ducked, feinted, spun on his bare feet, a small black majesty of the streets. Yet even as he skipped about, Albert had the feeling that he wasn't serious. He was not really shadowboxing, but performing a satire of boxing. Was there still hope they would spare him? That his nose would not be bloodied, his head not split open by these fierce Masai?

"You guys have it all wrong," Albert pleaded. Madison was guarding him while Lee Roy danced in wide circles. "I mean, you don't have it right. I'm supposed to be persecuting you. You're not supposed to be persecuting *me*. You got it all backwards."

The tufts on Madison's narrow skull sprouted a little. Lee Roy peppered an adversary with a flurry of lightning left jabs, spun, and bounced back to Albert. With his marine eyes he stared at the frightened prisoner. "Huh?" he asked.

"I mean, you shouldn't be tormenting *me*," Albert explained. "It's supposed to be the other way around, only I'm not that kind of guy. In a million years, I wouldn't dream of harming you, either of you guys. I really want to help you. I want you to get a break of some kind, if only I knew how—"

Madison, though older, appeared to be a good deal more stupid than Lee Roy. He scratched his head. "Whut he sayin', Lee Roy? What dat boy talkin' 'bout?"

"Oh, he jes' tryin' to git outa fightin' me, but he stuck. His manjer arrange dis bout, now he got to fight. His manjer sign deh papers an' he got to go t'roo wit' hit."

"I don't have a manager. I'm a rotten fighter."

"Yeah, but you sign deh papers," Lee Roy said. "Madison, make deh 'nouncements."

Madison grabbed Albert's shirt and yanked him into the playground, halting him on one of the lunatic designs. Lee Roy took a position diagonally opposite him, and began pulling himself up and down imaginary ropes.

Hooking a hand in Albert's shirt collar, Madison dragged him center ring. Then, in a fair imitation of Harry Balogh or

Joe Humphreys, he called out: "In dis yeah co'ner, weighin' one hunnert pounds, deh cha'nger, he name—whut yo' name?"

"Oh for goodness' sake, does it matter?"

"Hit matter," Madison said. "You goin' get deh sheeet beat outen yo', we has to know who yo' is."

"Albert Abrams."

"Abbit Aibins." Then, pointing at the magnificent Lee Roy, skipping rope, tossing punches, bobbing, he called out: "And ovah deah, deh world champeen weighin' hunnert pounds, Lee Roy Pennington!"

Madison played the crowd also. He whistled, stomped his bare feet on the cooked cement, and applauded. Lee Roy kept gamboling around the ring; he was tireless.

"Y'all come heah," Madison ordered. He dragged Albert to face the executioner.

"This has gone far enough," Albert protested. "I won't fight. I'm a lousy fighter. I admit Lee Roy can slaughter me. . . ." He felt the involuntary tears blur his vision. His knees were water. His bladder, his rectal sphincter, ached for release. Home, home is where he should be. In bed, reading, listening to the radio.

"De people pay money fo' dis fight," Madison said peevishly. "Yo' cain't dis'point dem."

"Das right," Lee Roy added. White teeth, yellow-white eyes, skin like burnished mahogany. He was blinding.

"Y'all know deh athaletic rules," Madison said. "No hittin' in deh nuts. No rabbit punchin'. No ass kickin'. Dis jes' a nice sociable fight. All dem things is not sociable, so keep dis a sociable fight. Ass-kickin' ain't sociable. Shake hands an' come out fightin'."

He shoved Albert away, waited, then whistled. "Dat deh bell fo' deh first round."

Bottom had been reached; the depths of a dark, terrible day. Degraded, helpless, naked, he raised his puny fists. Let it come, let it come now. He could sink no lower.

Madison appraised his stance. "Dat boy a killer. He got

215

deh killer look in his eye. Lee Roy, he gon' beat deh pee outen yo'."

"Ah skeered." Lee Roy, in classic boxer's pose, the left forward, jabbing, the right cocked on his naked chest, hopped toward his opponent. The adversary got a whiff of frying oil, saw Lee Roy's football head jouncing at him, and stumbled backward. Lee Roy jabbed the left at Albert's fading head and purposely missed. Then he jabbed the left again, but stopped it an inch short of Albert's nose. Then he feinted once, threw the left and touched Albert's nose lightly. He was playing with him.

"Get it over with!" Albert bawled. "I know you can murder me if you want, so do it!"

"Nah, yo' got to hit me, man. Das deh way hit is. Yo' manjer say you tough." Lee Roy giggled.

A solemn referee, Madison shook his head. "Ah gon' declare dis no contest, if dis boy don't git in deah an' swing." He circled Albert, lifted him off the ground with one iron arm and threw him at Lee Roy. Albert shouted, bounced against Lee Roy, then gasped and grunted as Lee Roy drove his fists into his gut. The blows were not hard, but they carried a message: *It will get much worse.*

"Hit at him!" Madison commanded Albert. "He ain' so tough!"

Straight up and down, a marionette, Lee Roy was soaring on ebony wings, a death bird. Off the cement rose his pointed chocolate toes, his lovely petal-pink soles, in a charming ballet. After the fifth entrechâtisse, Lee Roy sprang forward and slammed the flat of his palm against Albert's nose, the same brutal tactic Zetz had used that afternoon. Stinging pain spread from nose to cheeks to mouth. Salt dribbled into his mouth; his nose was bleeding.

What was left? Why did they not kill him and have it over? He could no more fight Lee Roy—that elusive spirit—than he could Jack Sharkey. The blood dribbled down his lips and he licked at it. Lee Roy was studying him pensively—almost sorry he had made him bleed.

"Now look what you did, Lee Roy," he sniveled. "What a friend you turned out to be. I tried to understand you and help you, and look at the way you rewarded me." He lowered his useless fists and backed away.

"Uh-uh," Madison grunted with high disapproval. "Dat boy don' wan' fight." Shaking his long head, he stood shoulder to shoulder with the bouncing Lee Roy. They studied the bloody victim.

"Ah, you guys don't understand anything at all, it's useless," Albert sobbed. "I know about the rotten deal you have, your homes aren't so hot and your parents have trouble getting a job, I understand all that and I'm sorry for you. But why take it out on me? What'd I ever do to you? Why my father takes care of lots of colored people and he never asks them to pay when they can't. . . ." Babbling on, he hated himself more with each whining word. In his heart, he wanted to murder both of them, to pump hot lead into their black bodies. But he chattered on, logician, reformer, sidewalk sociologist to the bitter end.

"Dat boy sure lak to talk," Lee Roy said.

"More dan he lak to fight."

"No, he tough, Madison. You see dat right cross he t'row at me?"

"Yeah. He skeer you good wit' dat."

Lee Roy scratched his furry head. "Let's see can he run."

"Yeah. Mebbe he run better dan he fight."

"Know whut? He gon' race me in deh hunnert-yart dash."

Albert wiped his nose on the bottom of his shirt. "If I race him, can I go?"

"Mebbe," Madison said archly, "and mebbe not."

Lee Roy was already warming up, making fast getaways from a crouch, practicing short sprints. Did he ever stop? Did he ever tire? Albert marveled at him, hated him, envied him. Of course, Lee Roy would leave him in the dust, but what matter? They'd be good sports about it. Suddenly he was furious with his father for ramming all those vitamins and minerals down his throat. Fat lot of good it had done him! He couldn't fight, he couldn't run, he had weak ankles and no muscles. And look at Lee Roy—raised on white bread and collard greens!

"Now dis heah deh startin' lahn," Madison said. He was a fine organizer. "Runners git down. Dat deh finish lahn out deah."

"Oh man, Ah in great shape," Lee Roy said. He flew about the schoolyard—a black whirring blur. "But dat boy a great runner also."

"Onyomox," Madison announced.

"What?" Albert asked.

"Ah said Onyomox. Das what dey say when deh race starts. Yo' cain't hear me, Ah slice yo' ears off."

"He mean git down on yo' hands," Lee Roy explained irritably.

"Oh, on your marks." Squatting, he set his seared palms on the cement. As he lowered his head, the blood dripped again from his nose. Coin-sized spots decorated the ground below him. He wished it were midwinter. January. Streets piled high with filthy snowbanks lavish with charred and exploded garbage bags. He yearned to be warm in galoshes and a Tim cap, trekking to school, briefcase over one shoulder, a Jack London sourdough in the Alaskan gold fields. In winter, the likes of Lee Roy rarely ventured forth. He imagined himself settling into his warm bed in his private room, listening to the steamy knocking of the radiator and the soothing hum of his Philco, offering him endless cheering newscasts and weather predictions. As it droned through the winter's night, he would work his way through a pile of McIntosh apples and the collected works of Rudyard Kipling.

Madison kicked him in the rear end. He sprawled face forward. Lee Roy and the tuft-headed boy were skipping around him. Had they tired of him? Was he such a hectoring, logical fellow, so helpless with fists and feet that he wasn't worth the game? Yes, he was a worn-out tire, a grapefruit squeezed dry.

"He no fun," Lee Roy said. "He too easy. Ah wan' ketch dem tough guys."

218

But they never would. The tough guys could take care of themselves. On those levels of terror, there were no cowards. Bushy, Zetz—they did not retreat. Had not Zetz once so ravaged a Negro assailant that the black boy's eye had dropped from his skull to the floor of the Alexander Hamilton High School locker room, and was sewed back in? Zetz and Bushy would never countenance such humiliations. But he was low man, the bottom of the barrel, fair game, everybody's patsy. "And quite frankly," he told himself, "I'm getting sick and tired of it."

"*Halloi! Halloi!*" Was it Krazy Kat who called him? He turned his bruised head and saw Mockey outside the iron fence, hopping on thick legs, ecstatic that he had found his man. The Royal Jewish Ukrainian Mounted Police had done it again! Albert felt good for him: three days in America and he could play ringalevio. A flood of swallowed Yiddish riffled across the schoolyard. Mockey was bubbling with joy.

Albert's captors flew off to new sport at the distant end of the schoolyard. He ran for the fence. Madison and Lee Roy were engaged in a game of bodily insult with an old fruit crate. The game consisted of smashing the crate over each other's skulls. They had lost interest in him.

Sensing deliverance, he hurled himself at the fence, vaulted over it, and fell into Mockey's arms. The greenhorn crushed him joyfully against the ruching of his *shtetl* shirt. His wide eyes glistened, his breath was soiled. But to Albert it was essence of hyacinth, attar of roses.

"Halloi," Mockey said.

"Halloi yourself."

Mockey studied the crusted blood under his nose. He offered guttural sympathies.

"*Schwarzers,*" Albert explained.

"Oi, oi," Mockey commented. Miserable underdog, refugee from the Cossacks' knout he knew how to sympathize with victims. He released Albert and peered into the schoolyard. Lee Roy and Madison pursued their game, smashing the remains of the crate on one another's head. It didn't seem to bother them;

the crate splintered, split, and they remained unharmed. Mutiny among the blacks! Jack London would have handled it—a Winchester and a bullwhip and a few sharp commands in pidgin English. *Bigfeller leave littlefeller alone bimeby selfsame otherwise firestick b'long me cry out and make big hurt. You blackfellers topside cry out bimeby when bossman make firestick talk too much.*

"That's my trouble, Mockey, my head is filled with trivia. It's full of irrelevant facts that impede my capacity to act. Get it?"

Mockey was staring at the Negroes. Sights and wonders of his new home! Around and around went Lee Roy and Madison in measured steps, smashing the protesting boards over each other's polls. Impervious to pain or hurt they made a gavotte of their combat.

"Look who I have to explain it to," Albert said. He touched his upper lip: almost dry. "You, the lowest of the low. Friend and counselor."

Mockey grabbed Albert's arm and led him off. He had captured him. America, land that teaches me church-on-fire and ringalevio! Like lovers, they strolled down the street, turned the corner, and walked toward Longview Avenue.

Albert looked into the boy's round eyes. Trust, affection, faith shone in them. The very sweat on his shaved head spoke of his love for Albert.

"We'll see to it that you change," Albert said emphatically.

"Vus?" Mockey queried.

"Mockey, we'll arrange it so that you can get angry, horrified, frustrated and selfish. Know what I wanted to do tonight when Lee Roy and Madison were beating me up? I wanted to *kill* them, Mockey. As simple as that. That's twice today I had the killer's urge, but wasn't man enough to follow through. I wanted to drill Zetz right between the eyes with a Winchester. I would have mowed Lee Roy and Madison down with a Thompson submachine gun if I could have. I mean it, Mockey, there was no mercy in me, none at all. There are times when I could murder people, I admit it. Oh, not Bushy and

220

Bimbo—I only dream of just beating them up. But Zetz and those two guys in the schoolyard, I could shoot them down in their tracks."

"Yeh, yeh," Mockey commented.

"Fortunately these murderous impulses pass. In a little while I will overcome them, although I admit I'm scared stiff of Lee Roy and Madison. Scared to death. It's because they don't care—about *anything*. It's like somebody wiped out their brains and their hearts and put something else in there, a battery, just to keep them going. I know it's not their fault. But that doesn't help me be *less* scared of them, or want to kill them every now and then. Luckily you haven't understood a single word I've said."

Mockey opened wide his mouth in a silent laugh. Did he know more than he showed? Impossible. He was the best of friends, a faithful dog, a listener. The confessional had been a tonic for Albert. He had told him things he would not have dared tell anyone in the world. Certainly not his parents. He could hear Bushy's screaming sarcasm if he dared confess his murderous sentiments.

"But what's worse," he went on, "is that when I'm finished hating Zetz and Lee Roy and Madison and wanting to murder them in cold blood, I have only myself left to hate. Because of my inability to face up to the world. That's even worse, but I suppose I can get over it by reading a book. It's like my father's problems, I guess. Mad at himself after he gets mad at the world and can't do anything about it. I hope, my boy, you will be spared these sufferings."

"Yeh, yeh."

Thrilling conversationalist! But he would have Mockey no other way. Once he learned English he would be useless as a confessor.

A peace of sorts descended over Brownsville. No blossoms scented the air (only in Dr. Abrams' backyard), but the hot calm, the conglomerate odor of sweat, ripened potato peelings, ordure was almost pleasurable. The city was tired and resigned. Albert was much relaxed. Freed of the black terror, comforted by Mockey's stoic presence, he was feeling pretty good. For this relief much thanks, as Genius would say.

"Hey, what's your real name?" Albert asked.

"Vus?"

"Your name, your name. *Nammen*."

"Ahhhh."

"Look, we can't go on calling you Mockey. It isn't right. Now that you're in the Raiders."

"*Nammen!*" Mockey hopped up and down. Then he pointed a finger at his stitched shirt. "*Ich bin Label*."

"Label?"

"Label Gurevich."

"Label, that's Lev, or Leon or Leo or Leonard. That's how it will come out in school. Maybe we will have to refer to you as Union Label."

"Hah?"

"I can see long evenings of witty repartee and gay banter with you. We will have some mighty deep discussions you and me." But he had a feeling Mockey would fool them all. He would learn English, get a scholarship, and go on to make great discoveries in organic chemistry.

"*Und du—Al-bare?*"

"Close enough. So long as you don't call me Four-eyes or Sister Mary. I get enough of that all day."

The greenhorn locked his arm in Albert's again and they walked on. At the corner, a meeting of some kind was in progress. They walked toward it.

Beneath a street light, a speaker had mounted a ladder. But it was not the Communist Margulies who earlier in the evening had accused President Roosevelt of being hand in glove with the capitalists.

Under the golden globe, a much larger crowd than the revolutionary had drawn had assembled. There was a good sprinkling of Italians and Negroes among the Jews. Margulies himself, the fiery denouncer of the New Deal, was in the front rank. As previous speaker of the evening, he enjoyed certain rights. None of the Raiders was present. Frankie Udo, escaped from the voodoo ritual, had probably run home. He felt a passing annoyance, an envy for Frankie who had escaped and left him to be humiliated. He gently fingered his insulted nose. The blood had caked thickly below it and on his upper lip. *Among things to be grateful for,* he thought, *I congeal well. I have a high fibrinogen content. I will never be a hemophiliac.*

As they strolled toward the street meeting, Albert mused over the possibility of Teddy and Bushy and the two Arties ranging far and wide into the night. Ringalevio games sometimes went on past midnight—endless chases through backyards, empty lots, streetcar terminals, deserted factories. Boys still talked in awed tones about a game played in August of 1931 in which a team captained by a certain Futka Wisnofsky (later to gain fame as an all-city forward for Boys High) fled through Brownsville, East New York, Canarsie and Rockaway Inlet, ending up beneath a salty marsh near the Island Park Bridge. The chase lasted until dawn and Futka, the last survivor, was not apprehended until seven-thirty in the morning as he was about to row across the inlet in a commandeered rowboat. Such was the glory of Futka Wisnofsky, hero of history's greatest ringalevio game! Today, Albert reflected bitterly, this same hero could be seen shouting the praises of his oranges and tangerines from a stall on the market block, his glory preserved in that one mad night in the salty marshes of Jamaica Bay. It saddened him. Futka deserved better.

"I am heah to deliver you from dirt," cried the new speaker. The man on the ladder was a pale tan Negro in a turban. He had a pencil moustache, sharp features. Beneath the street light he appeared menacing. "I am sent by the Angel of Cleanliness Hisself, the most honorable, mystic Abracadabra Allah Bah-Ooyah."

Albert and Mockey elbowed their way to the foot of the ladder. On the lower steps, the haranguer's assistant squatted— a chocolate-colored Negro carrying a huge cardboard box.

"Who, you may ask," the speaker went on, "is the mighty, holified Abracadabra Allah Bah-Ooyah? He is a sage, my

223

esteemed friends, a wise man, a scholar of the mystical East, where I make my home."

"Yeh! East New York!" a wit cried out. The crowd laughed.

"Joke not, serf. Abracadabra Allah Bah-Ooyah has bestowed on me his ancient wisdom. I speak ten languages including the Hebrew, the Yiddish, the Eyetalian, the Greek—"

"*Shmuck*, say something in Yiddish!" roared Kalotkin the mighty roofer. In undershirt and dungarees, he looked like a sea cook, a hairy beachcomber washed up on the Brownsville littoral.

"Yes, mah fat friend," the turbanned Negro responded, "I shall oblige. *Shalom Aleikim. Zeit Gezint. Gay in dread.*"

"Ah, you could loin that anywhere," Kalotkin scoffed.

"Yer a phony," added Margulies. "Class warfare turns up lumpenproletariats like that."

"Don't lump me, there, or limp me," the Negro said coolly. "I am nonpolitical. Karl Marx was a heathen Chinee. He stole every word he ever wrote from the Book of the Dead. I, on the other hand, represent all religiosities and religified religions." He displayed a golden Star of David depending from his neck. "Behold, I cometh."

"A Yid?" Mockey asked Albert.

"I am inclined to doubt it, Mockey. It's part of his sales approach."

"Now then, my friends," the pitchman went on, "before I impart to you the wisdom of my mentor, teacher and guide, the late and great Abracadabra Allah Bah-Ooyah, I will, for your divertissement and edification perform several acts of the occult and unseen, forces unknown to ordinary mortals, but which were revealed to me when I served in the Riff wars against the accursed Spaniard. I need a volunteer to assist." He pointed a sorcerer's finger at Albert. "You down there, Four-eyes, get up here."

Now who told him about me? Albert wondered. *Why me?*

"Yes, I mean you, Glasses, you bespectacled young man with the blood drying under your nose. That's right, don't look over your shoulder as if to evade my magic call. You know who I

224

mean, standing next to Baldy right down there. As the Bible sayeth, Go down, thou baldhead; but in this case, it is climb up, thou four-eyed one. *Now!*"

The crowd snickered, stared at Albert, amused by the mountebank's fun at his expense. *Why should I deny them their pleasures?* he asked himself. Wearily, he climbed two steps of the ladder. As he did, the black assistant at the bottom gave the pitchman a copper pot and a milk bottle filled with water. At a level with the turbanned fellow's fly, Albert saw how stained and creased his trousers were. He couldn't make much of a living at this sort of thing.

"Behold the ancient wisdom of the East!" cried the tan Negro. "Four-eyes, take this empty copper pot and display it to our friends out there."

Dutifully, Albert took the pot, turned it upside down, around, and returned it.

"Behold!" the pitchman cried. "I fill this selfsame pot with water from this battle—*aqua pura, vasser, eau, agua.* Thus." On the ladder, Albert suddenly got a whiff of cheap strong perfume. It came from the cardboard box below. Peering into it, he saw soap cakes wrapped in green paper. So that's what it was! A medicine show! And he was reduced to playing stooge for them! What a comedown for the manager of the Pittstown Panthers!

"Now then, I don't care who you is or who you *are*," the Negro said, "whether you is rich or poor, black or white, Jew or Gentile, who you is or who you *are* is immaterial. You will all be mystificated and confusified and occultized by the magical powers of my teacher, Abracadabra Allah Bah-Ooyah."

"Your grammar could stand improving," Albert volunteered. Why did he have to put up with this charlatan's insults? "Who you is or who you *are* makes no sense. It may sound impressive to you, but it's incorrect."

Beneath the scarlet turban, cold black eyes studied the impertinent one. "Indeed, Four-eyes? Who you is or who you *are*? You dast to correct the mighty Abracadabra? Proceed with your devotions and leave the usages of language to us." He

225

shoved the pot of water at Albert. "Grab that, Glasses. Teach you to correct me. Now, pour the water into the street, but try not to dampen any of these good people out there with your limited vision."

"You can cut out the wisecracks. I don't have to stay up here."

"Yeah? Who you is—"

"I know, or who you are."

"This boy is in need of punitivizing and chastitation." He winked at the mob. They snickered. They were united against Albert's truth-seeking, his calm rationalism. They wanted to be had, to be deceived, to be cheated. *I am the Enemy of the People, trying to save them from their own folly.*

"Nuts," Albert said. He turned the pot upside down. The water sloshed on to the sidewalk, splashing Mockey's steel feet.

"Now then, Four-eyes, gimme back that magic urn," the mountebank said. "Behold how I turn it up and down, round and round. Not a solitary drop of water remains. Look, I rub my hankie in there, and it is dry! Drier than the vast Sahara where once ruled the mighty sage who taught me, the all-powerful Abracadabra Allah Bah-Ooyah, who once advised—"

"Enough awready!" cried Margulies. "What is this? Give us a show? Enough of these cheap bourgeoisie deceits!"

"A doubter of the magical powers! You shall be shown, friend; your eyes shall be opened wide."

"You are a fraud!" Margulies shrilled. "Look, look every-one what happens to minorities under capitalism! See, they're reduced to cheap performances, instead of having dignity and gainful labor!"

"Labor me not, Lenin," the Negro cautioned. "I got mine. You is yet to get yours. You is a seeker. I is a gotter. But you will never learn that in your Marxicated mind. Now then, we proceed. I have demonstrated through logical abstractifying that this here copper pot is evidaciously unfilled, empty and dry. I now give it back to our grammarized young friend, Four-eyed Filbert here." He shoved the pot at Albert. "Now then, Glasses, hold that there pot over your head and illustrate to our assembled dignitaries that it is utterly empty and that it possesses a total absence of water."

Sighing, Albert held the pot over his head. Nothing happened. Around him goggled slum faces—expectant, upturned, happy that he was the butt of the dark one's jokes. There was Margulies, the revolutionary FDR-hater, squinting through mangling lenses that reduced his eyes to a pair of humming concentric circles. Kalotkin loomed behind him, furred like the mammoth. Mockey beamed with admiration. Old ladies in babushkas clacked gums. At the edge of the mob, Cowboy, obsessed with dirty ball clubs, helped support Daisy, whose fumes hung heavy in the air. Some distance down the street he saw the Raiders running toward them—Bushy, Bimbo, the two Arties.

"Shake that pot, Weak-eyes."

Albert shook it.

"Shake it again, rap it, my half-blind friend."

Albert complied. How idiotic he felt! He affected a bored, annoyed look. *I am above all this.* He rolled his eyes to the top of his head, a cool customer. Let them stare; he was superior.

"I now pronounce the mystificating words of the holy prophet—*Abracadabra Allah Bah-Ooyah!*" So saying, the Negro thrust his fingers at the pot several times.

Water—magically, marvelously—flowed from the overturned pot, drenching Albert's head, running in rivulets down his forehead, nose, chin, mingling with dried blood and street dirt. It trickled down his neck, slid into his polo shirt, found its meandering way into his pants. Stunned, he pulled the pot away from his insulted head too late. The pitchman took it from him.

"A splendid performance, Glasses," he crowed. The mob roared, applauded. They nudged one another, pointed at Albert. They knew he was a freak: *the doctor's son.*

"Marx foresaw it all," Margulies cackled. "The revenge of the lumpenproletariat. Taking it out on the bourgeoisie. Boy, was that beautiful."

"Very funny," Albert said. "A million laughs." He descended the ladder. Actually the water was not that unpleasant. It had been rather refreshing to have his aggrieved head doused. With great curiosity, Mockey was touching his soaked head. *America!*

"You thought that was just hilarious, didn't you?" Albert asked his new friend.

"*Vus?*"

"Yeah, *vus*. You sure are a help." Unadulterated love bathed Mockey's face. Both he and his friend had been baptized: Mockey with church-on-fire, Albert with the ancient wisdom of the East.

The Raiders, who had witnessed Albert's humiliation, shoved through the crowd.

"What a sucker," Bimbo crowed. "Jerko."

"Hah, he really got you," Bushy laughed. "Some trick. How'd he do it? That was neat."

"I'm glad I was able to furnish you some amusement tonight," Albert said. He shivered a little. Strange, how the water chilled him despite the heat. "Anything for a few laughs."

"Hey—and look!" Bimbo yelled. "Mockey caught him! Boy, that's a hot one! Can't even git away from that dumb Mockey! What a weak-a-ling!"

No response came from Albert. Forever reconciled to last place, to the cellar, the lowest rung! Bushy declared the ringa-levio game over. Bimbo had found Frankie Udo lolling on the stoop of his house. Reluctant to mess with boogies, Frankie had quit. Only Teddy remained on the loose and Bushy was reluctant to pursue the Polack. Teddy would show up when he was good and ready. They turned their eyes toward the fakir.

"What awready are ya sellin'?" demanded Margulies. "Yer a disgrace to yer race, as a matter of fact. The proletariat shouldn't be reduced to freak shows because of capitalism's failure to supply an altoinative. No cultural or occupational outlets leads to debasement of the woiking man!"

"Shaddap!" shouted Kalotkin. "Let him talk!"

The turbanned gent lofted an eyebrow at Margulies. "You

down there, Four-eyes Senior, watch your radicalized tongue. I need not your Marxificated philosophy. I my own man. Is you?"

"Tell 'im, *schwarzer!*" bellowed Kalotkin.

The pitchman took a bar of soap from his black assistant. Unwrapping it, he held it aloft. "I have heah an ordinary soap purchased at your corner grocery or drugstore, not the mystic brand in which I deal. This here soap which you buy from your local emporium, I say unto you, with which you wash face, hands, and more personalized parts of your body, with which you bathe your beloved *kinder*, this soap is laden with vile, dirty, and poisonous impurities! I shall prove it."

The crowd edged closer. This promised to be even better than seeing Dr. Abrams' sissy son soaked with water.

"The poisons in this innocent store-bought soap can kill your red blood cells, diminuate your sex drives and cause loss of hair, not to mention inducting skin diseases and cancer. I say unto you, and I don't care who you is or who you are, you are slowly assassinating yourself every time you wash!"

"Ah, yer a phony," Kalotkin shouted. "Whaddya handin' us, ya jerk? A bar soap could kill us? Cah mahn!"

"He may have a point," Margulies said—shrewdly switching sides. "Adulteration of commercial products with poisonous elements is a standard aspect of American capitalism. Go on, comrade!"

"Don't comrade me, Trotsky. But I appreciates your support. Yes, friends, sooner to later the scoffers come around. Behold the proof direct, given me by the wise Abracadabra Allah Bah-Ooyah—proof that this here soap is killing you, inch by inch!"

A small brown bottle appeared in the medicine man's right hand. "Behold the essence. Seeing is believing."

On to the white bar of soap he dribbled a clear liquid from the bottle. "Watch carefully. Be elucidated."

As the crowd gasped, sighed, recoiled, nudged one another, the bar of soap turned a hideous deep purple.

Truly they were witnessing a miracle, an act of revelation. They understood. They believed. (They did not believe Dr.

Abrams' advice, indeed they hated him for it, Albert mused, but this nonsense went down well with them.) They had faith. They had been won over.

Bushy gasped: "How'd he do that? Man, what a trick!"

"Poisons, poisons!" cried the Negro. "Vile poisons showing in that purple stain!"

"It's a simple chemical reaction," Albert said. "Like litmus paper. There's phenolphthalein or something like that in the bottle and it makes the alkalis in the soap turn purple. It isn't poison at all. No mystery."

"Ah, ya full of it," Bimbo said.

"Yeah, how'd you learn so much?" Bushy added.

"Well said, young friends," the pitchman offered. "Four-eyes is still smarting from my pleasantries."

Mockey was pointing—enchanted—at the livid purple soap which the pitchman kept rotating in his hand. "*Oi, gib a kuk!*" No end to miracles!

"Fake," Margulies said. "I'm opposed to you now."

"Fake is it?" the turbaned one asked. "We will see how fake! Abdullah, hand me a bar of our own Iroquois Vegetable Oil Soap, the rare and lovely product I offer at an introductory first-time-only price of ten cents a bar, after which it goes up to the regular mail order price of twenty-two cents. Thank you."

He removed the green wrapper from his own product. "Behold! Iroquois Vegetable Oil Soap! Four-eyes, and the rest of you young trash, stand back, so's the grownups can see. You, too, my leftward friend, come closer. Observe—milled, ground, boiled, reboiled, strained, shaped and purified, according to a formula handed down to me by the great Abracadabra Allah Bah-Ooyah hisself—Iroquois Vegetable Oil Soap—from the mystic East, good for man, woman, child and beast. I don't care who you is or who you are, this soap will make you cleaner, healthier and happier, and enable you to gain worldly success!"

So saying, he poured liquid from the brown bottle on the pristine cake. "I say, let there be *white*, and it stayeth white." The soap remained white; it did not turn the deathly purple. "Is that not proof? Proof positive and eternal, friends? Does

230

that not silence the criers of Fake? Little Four-eyes there telling his friends that I am using a cheap chemical trick? Yea, behold how they are silenced and their lying voices turned to dust by the terrible white light of truth! This here soap is pure, clean, germless white! Undefiled! Rich in vegetable oil and vitamins! Buy, buy—while the offer lasts—a dime a bar—before the price goes up!"

Several people in the front rank edged forward offering dimes to take advantage of the generous offer.

"Hmmm," Margulies said. "I don't approve of this kind of devious retail trade. In the Soviet Union profiteering is not permitted. The state sees to it that trade is conducted on a fair and dignified basis. Everything costs less, because the middleman is eliminated. You know what I'm talking about, Kalotkin?"

The roofer pushed him aside. "Ya talk wit' yer ass, Margulies. Hey, Rastus, give us a coupla bars that there soap! My wife could use it. Attaboy, Sambo, thanks. Yer awright for a nateball."

"That's right, encourage him," Margulies said. "Make him more of an Uncle Tom than he is."

"Git lost," Kalotkin sneered. "You had your meeting, let him have his. Give the guy a chance to make a buck. Right, Bojangles? Give us that big smile again, Satchelmouth! Boy, you sure are a lotta porkchops!"

"Right, right, and no offense there, whoever you is or whoever you are, Muscles." The racial insults bothered him not at all; he was too busy making change. "Yes, thank you, thank you, madam, and may a lovely sweet complexion be yours. Thank you, four did you say? Ah yes, ten cents back out of the half dollar! And beware that radicalized man there mocking me, that critic of what makes America strong, such as free enterprise and individual initiative. Yes, capitalism is twentieth-century Americanism and don't nobody here ever forget that!"

Impelled by patriotism, by common sense, they pressed forward—fat housewives, aromatic Negroes, a Chinese laundry-

231

man, young girls—all eager to try that magic nonpurpling white Iroquois Vegetable Oil Soap.

"Folks, you're making a big mistake!" cried Margulies, as the crowd inundated him. "This man is a freak, a vestige of an antiquated system! You encourage him in his cooperation with decadent capitalism! He should be gainfully employed in a state-run cooperative, performing useful and satisfying labor!"

"Go home, Lenin, go home," the Negro said loftily. "Go home to your dreams of revolution, dirty Bolshevik. How dare you counterdict the great all-seeing middle eye of Abracadabra Allah Bah-Ooyah?"

"Fascist," muttered Margulies. "Toady. Lickspittle, bourgeois counterfeit!"

"To the Finland station with you, midget, in a sealed train."

As the crowd pressed around the ladder, eager hands extended to buy the magic soap, Albert decided that Margulies and he were among the losers, the outsiders. *We are scoffers, doubters, and the world wants belief.* Spurning the superior wisdom of the charlatan, they had been shown up, Margulies betrayed by the unheeding masses (so it would ever be with trusting Bolsheviks) and he himself humiliated, turned into a comic stooge. *Some joke! Negro Cheater Amuses Crowd With Bespectacled Small Boy; Helps Him Sell Fake Soap!*

"Thank you, thank you, sir. Take three while you in a buying mood. This offer may be withdrawn at any moment."

Dimes flashed, a carton was emptied, the assistant ripped open a second.

"He's a phony," Albert confided to the Raiders. "Why does he call it Iroquois soap? He says he got it from the mystical East, Persia and so on. But Iroquois is American Indian. Good thing he's got a bunch of dopes to talk to, or he'd get shown up."

"Ah, you know everything, doncha?" Bimbo snarled—and punched him in the small of the back.

They drifted back to Longview Avenue. Little Artie

danced crazily on the curb; Big Artie hurled his great hulk against shuddering iron fences.

"Boy, how people eat up that nonsense," Albert continued.

"He fooled you," Bimbo said.

"That fake? He didn't fool me for a minute."

"Peed all over ya. You and that jerk Mockey, two of a kind. I swear, Abrams, yer a disgrace to the block."

Mockey, clomping along, smiled when he heard his name.

"You can stop calling him Mockey," Albert said. "His name is Label. If you don't care for that, call him Union Label." No one laughed. "He's a pretty good guy. At least he has good manners."

Bushy spun around. "Ya wan' him?" he screamed at Albert. "Ya got him!" Roughly, he shoved Mockey against Albert. The baldhead thought it was a game; he laughed silently, enfuming Albert with garlic and love.

"Can it, Bushy," Albert pleaded. "Is that all you can do, pick on people? I swear you're as bad as Lee Roy."

He went on to describe his martyrdom at the hands of Lee Roy and Madison, but he tried to make it sound funny—humor to soften the fear that still constricted his gut. In his account, he made a folk hero of Mockey, Mockey to the rescue, knight in plated shoes. But even as he lied, embellished, fictionalized, he was ashamed of himself. He had been scared to death of the black avengers. Who could predict when next they would ambush him?

". . . Lee Roy took one look at Label here with his baldy head and big shoes and he turned white! That was when they made me fight Lee Roy and I got a bloody nose. He's got ten pounds on me easy, but I landed a few good ones. . . ."

Lies, lies. How low can a man stoop?

"Yer ass, too," Bimbo said. "You couldn't fight ya way out of a terlet. He musta mopilized ya. A boogie just looks at ya and ya run."

"I don't deny it. He got the best of me. But I socked him a few times."

Disdainful, disbelieving, they ignored him. Little Artie

233

began chalking giant circles in the street. Inside them, he lettered: KICK ME HARD and I STINK ON ICE and FARTING IS AGAINST THE LAW.

Under the yellow globe of a street lamp, they rested. The long hot day was dribbling to its end. It had claimed too much of them. Albert collapsed on the curb. How totally exhausted he was! Drained, enervated, boned and stretched on a drying board. His skinny frame whimpered, his chest heaved. Gently he probed his upper lip. The dried blood had formed a hard crust. Those warlike Othellos! They had seized the circumcised dog by the throat, toyed with him, discarded him. A fat lot they cared that he felt sorry for them, that his father never collected bills from colored patients! In their stained eyes he had seen something awful, a hate over which they had no control, an involuntary need to hurt someone, anyone. Why? Why? What did he ever do to them? How could he make it up—whatever it was?

Big Artie skipped in and out of Little Artie's cabalistic circles. When he touched KICK ME HARD, Little Artie booted him in his great behind, but in FARTING IS AGAINST THE LAW, Big Artie had his revenge: he cut a barrage, then lumbered away from his cousin's blows. How energetic they were, how untroubled! Nothing bothered them. And he, rogue and peasant slave, had spent the day in dubious battle—but on no plains of heaven. Were his only victories to be in Algebra and Civics? Was the sweet taste of triumph to elude him forever, except in the rigged results of *Batter Up!* Or through deceits like his false account of the Agony in the Schoolyard? Perhaps someday he would really learn to roller-skate. That might help. He would never get off his skates. He would live on them. That dumb Ruthie! Calling them ball-bearians! No matter, she could skate. A barbarian on ball-bearians.

Had the day's horrors matured him a little? He rested his aching back against the base of the lamp post. *I survived. I got there.* The watery trembling in his bowels had ceased. Watching Mockey undergo kicks and shoves from the two Arties, he

234

gave some credit to the greenhorn. Mockey's existence alone was enough to cheer him up; some people were worse off than he was. Ah, but give him a few years. Soon he would be blasting a punchball two sewers, twisting his arm behind his back, and calling him Four-eyes. But maybe not. One could hope. And there would always be Genius Grubman and Gorilla, and the Public Library and Jack London.

Now they were playing slice-the-ham, flicking one another's behinds wickedly with the bottom of their limp open palms. It delighted Albert the way Little Artie got in four shots for every one Bimbo gave him. But Bimbo was pretending he was just as skillful, grimacing, threatening, yelping, as he tried to circle Little Artie. They sped past Albert; Bimbo landed hard on Albert's sneakered right foot. Pain made him gasp, but he was beyond protest. Just like Bimbo—to take it out on him because Little Artie was getting the best of it.

It was odd, odd beyond explanation the way Bimbo, redheaded son of a seltzer-wagon driver, had turned into his tormentor. Once they had been dear friends. Once Bimbo had worshiped him, played with him in the backyard, shared homework with him at the oak table in the Abrams' dining room. "That redheaded boy certainly spends a lot of time here," his mother said. "I'm glad he's such a nice boy." Nice boy! But that was a year ago. He had wanted to say: "He's here all the time because he lives in a small dirty apartment with no hot water." The Wexlers were the poorest white people Albert had ever known—a houseful of redheaded, chunky kids in patched clothing. Still, they were neat, and they got good grades in school. The oldest Wexler boy, Heshy, was a nut on figuring out miscellaneous ways to make money—bundling up mounds of old newspapers to sell to Junkman John, working nights for Western Union (Albert used to see him in his olive-green uniform and brown leather puttees and envy him) or selling Concord grapes from an old baby carriage.

And then Bimbo's love had turned to contempt. It was really the fault of Miss Pivarnik, their teacher in fifth grade. A stringy bird, she wore her hair boy-short and affected dangly earrings. A Holy Terror, the kids in P.S. 133 called her, a tiger, a hard marker. At one time she had been a patient of Dr. Abrams. One day in her class, and Albert understood why that relationship could never have lasted. Opinionated, shrill, she probably had told the old man how to practice medicine, and he undoubtedly had informed her to mind her own lousy business. One more patient down the drain!

Yetta Pivarnik was a fiend for cleanliness. She inspected them daily for nits, bedbugs, dirty fingernails, unshined shoes. Boys in her class had to wear white shirts and red ties; girls were forced to dress in white middies. Her high standards of purity proved to be Albert's downfall and led directly to his rupture with Bimbo. Half-asleep at the lamp post, he recalled how it had come about. Miss Pivarnik hated dirty fingernails and unkempt hair. And he, the doctor's son, was a perpetual failure on both counts. How explain it? How was it he flunked fingernail inspection and haircomb, when he was a whiz at Arithmetic and Reading?

"I am biologically deformed," he explained to his mother, after a third note from Miss Pivarnik. "Ma, it is a basic fact of my life, and I can't get Miss Pivarnik to understand it. First, my hair will not stay combed. I can't part it. I can't put Vitalis on it. It's like wire, only in all directions. *It cannot, in any way, be combed.*"

His mother nodded mechanically. She understood, but there was nothing she could do to help him.

"As for my fingernails, this sounds even crazier, but I swear on a stack of Bibles that every day when Miss Pivarnik found dirt under them, they were absolutely spotlessly clean when I left the house. Here's the horror of it, Ma. *They accumulated dirt while I walked from our house to school.* My fingernails are abnormal. They're constructed like lobster traps—dirt gets in but can't get out. They have a secret magnetic force which attracts and secretes dirt. *They can never be kept clean.*"

Mrs. Abrams' head moved rhythmically from side to side. She was not amused, nor was she distressed. "I don't think you clean them very strenuously. Personal cleanliness is not one of your strong points."

Hopping, he flew away, circled the living room and returned. "Ma, you're as bad as Miss Pivarnik! I washed, polished, scrubbed my fingernails. I dug a peck of dirt out from under them! And an hour later, when she inspected them, the dirt had sneaked back in! I am biologically doomed to have dirty nails and uncombable hair! You got to tell her that!"

"I will do nothing of the sort!" And she returned to her J. B. Priestley novel. Or was it Sheila Kaye-Smith?

Yetta Pivarnik was relentless. Three more times Albert flunked inspection. His mother was summoned to school to answer for his sanitary failures. But Mrs. Abrams demurred. Once she had been Miss Pivarnik's partner at a bridge luncheon. The teacher had treated her cruelly—a tongue-lashing over a wrong bid. She had no stomach for confronting the virago in the classroom. The task fell to Dr. Abrams. Slumped against the lamp post, watching his friends in a mad game of leapfrog, Albert recalled the awful day his father had to trek to P.S. 133, and while he, lummox, was forced to watch the humiliation, Miss Pivarnik threw the whole mess in the doctor's face. Of course his fingernails were dirty that day. Of course his dull brown hair was uncombed.

Later his father had raged and roared about the house. "That goddamn *petchetcha!* That lousy little dried-out old-maid bitch!" But he had sat there during the audience, his face dark and preoccupied as Miss Pivarnik's tweety voice damned his son and heir. Finally he had sighed and said: "I got a man dying of leukemia in Carrollton Hospital and a woman in her eighth month who needs induced labor, and a kid around the corner with pernicious anemia, not to mention a desk full of unpaid bills, and is this all you can bother me with?"

But his plea—which embarrassed Albert until his ears turned hot scarlet—did not sway her. "We all have to confront our problems," Miss Pivarnik sniffed, and for a moment, Albert, seeing his father's shoulders twitch, thought the old man was going to haul off and belt her one on the snoot. But he only

237

walked out of the room, mumbling something about maybe it's more important that Albert gets straight A's in everything, jammed his battered hat on his head, too weary to prolong the debate on why his son's hair was uncombed, his fingernails filthy.

Miss Pivarnik wasn't through with him. Somehow, she must have gotten word about the doctor's fulminations. The old man had popped off about her in the drugstore. A relative, a friend must have snitched: *Oi, what that crazy Abrams said about you, Yetta.* . . . And so, a few days later she launched another lecture on personal hygiene, starting gently, fixing her birdy eyes on Albert.

"There are certain of us here," Miss Pivarnik piped, "who have the advantage of coming from privileged homes, homes where there are more cultural benefits than in the general run of Brownsville homes, and certainly these children, above all, should know better than to be dirty and unkempt. Neatness is important. We are obliged to be clean. I can understand slovenliness in a child from a poor household, but those of us who have educated and wealthier parents have not the slightest excuse. And it speaks poorly of parents as well as child when . . ."

Pecking at his heart and soul, she chirped on. Her dangly Greenwich Village earrings glinted in the winter sunlight. Albert tried staring at the cutout pumpkins and turkeys on the steamy windows; her voice was killing him. *Unfair, unfair,* he wanted to shout, *leave my family out of it!* How terribly he wanted to explain to everyone that he was a mutant, a biological sport, a freak, a man with unruly hair and dirt-attracting nails!

"Yes, and especially when a parent is a professional person, a person engaged in a scientific career, it is doubly shameful that a child from such. . . ."

It was at this point that Bimbo Wexler, his dearest friend, seated across from him, held a hand to his freckled mouth, and side-lipped:

"*She is referring to you, Albert.*"

238

Bimbo liked his discovery so much, he repeated it, this time louder, so that the students surrounding Albert heard it. A girl giggled. "It's Albert she means," someone said. His neck turned vermilion, crimson, his ears deep purple. The heat of humiliation burned his cheeks. Soon, all in the class knew the identity of the offender, that ingrate, that scion of wealth and power, that young Rockefeller, who betrayed his parents' esteemed position in life by flunking cleanliness.

The morning crawled by, four hours of stares, asides, giggles, pointed fingers, peeks at his nails, his hair, his wax-stuffed ears. At recess in the snow-whipped schoolyard Bimbo stood in front of him, his former pal, who shared homework with him, and had joined him in sly peeks into his father's medical books, and chanted:

"She was referring to you, Albert!"

Others took up the cry—a jury of peers in lumberjackets, Tim caps, leggings, soggy mittens. In snowy circle they surrounded him, delighted to have a victim. And what a victim!

"Cut it out!" Albert cried. "She was not!" Tears, half-formed, froze in his eyes; snowflakes melted on his tongue; his protests vaporized in the chilled air. Then he charged Bimbo. But laden with slung briefcase, cocooned in two sweaters and the heaviest lumberjacket on the block, he missed, tripped, and Bimbo was on him, pumping a thousand blows and pushing his face into a snowbank. The others cheered for Bimbo; all united against the leisure class. Bimbo washed his face with fresh snow, shoved his head down once more for good luck, and rose from triumph.

"Stick it under his nails!" somebody shouted. "That'll keep them clean!"

Weeping, he stumbled to his feet. To what avail all those hundred percents in arithmetic? What value in those elaborate book reports, jacketed with colored paper? Shuffling home through the swirling snow, he whimpered, utterly perplexed by a defeat so complex, so uncalled-for, that it stunned him. Pivarnik—Bimbo—the other kids—his helpless parents—his hair and his nails.

That had been two years ago. From that day on Bimbo had been his enemy. No longer did he share the backyard, join him in homework. Bimbo became Bushy's stooge—toadying to the tyrant, whispering in his ear.

Chicken-fighting, the Raiders bobbed and flopped around him. He had withdrawn from the violence. Enough for one day. He longed for his bed and peace. Silently Teddy Ochab had returned. He had not been caught. He was too sly. Now he joined the chicken fighters, bouncing higher, more expertly than any of them, dodging, ducking. A scrawny Polish chicken, Teddy hopped away from the onrushing Bimbo. Wobbling on one foot, Bimbo came after him. They bounced passed Albert, half-asleep at the lamp post. Teddy skipped lightly over him. Bimbo came down viciously on Albert's right foot, fell on him and pressed him against the base of the street light. Albert's lungs constricted, his back shrieked.

"You did that accidentally on purpose!" he protested.

"Watcha gonna do about it?" Bimbo got to his feet and hopped away.

A blow for the dignity of all men had to be struck. Albert got to his feet. He was convinced a small metatarsal bone in his right foot was fractured. He could take no more. There was no way back.

"I had enough!" Albert cried. "I had enough!"

Chicken-fighting stopped. All of them studied him. "I can't take it anymore! I'll kill all of ya! I'll kill you, Bimbo! You got to leave me alone!"

Trembling, he stood in the geometrical center of the circle of yellow light. "Something's got to be done!" he shouted—and gave his folded eyeglasses to Teddy.

"Ah, he's havin' a fit," Bushy said. "Lookit the crazy look in his eye. He's gawn nuts. Let's sit on him."

The tyrant advanced. He could destroy Albert with one hand tied behind his back, but he wanted some fun. Yes, it would be great fun if they all sat on him, ignored him, talked about him as if he weren't there, and let him shriek out his lunatic seizure under their combined asses. They had done this to him before.

"Not you, Bushy, not you!" Albert cried. "I gotta fight Bimbo! I had enough of his crap! I'll kill him!" His lips curled. "You stay away, Bushy—I—I'll kill you too!"

Gun blazing, he would have shot Bushy down in cold blood. No regrets. No remorse. He would have laughed to see the blood spurt from Bushy's mighty heart; snickered as Lee Roy and Madison stumbled in the dirt as the bullets struck home; danced as Zetz, plugged neatly between his marble green eyes, pitched forward. But he would have to settle for Bimbo, a member of his own age group.

"Fight, fight!" Bushy screamed. Other people's violence intoxicated him. He waxed fat watching others bloody themselves, grind fists into eyes, scratch, gouge, feel pain. Already he was shoving Bimbo toward the yellow circle.

"He's nuts," Bimbo said. Was there a hint of resistance in his voice?

"Kill him, kill him!" Bushy cried. He attempted to hurl Bimbo at Albert, but Bimbo had halted. "I can fight him any day of the week and twicet on Sundays." He hitched his belt, walked on the edge of the circle of light, and made a "screwy" sign at his temple—index finger rotating. "But this guy is crazy, he's loony."

"I'll murder you!" Albert shrieked. He put his scrawny arms up, clenched his apricot-sized fists.

"Ah, you and what army?" Bimbo asked.

"Me, myself and I!"

"Give 'em room, make a circle!" cried Little Artie. Dutifully, they arrayed themselves in a circle around the gladiators. Bimbo appeared puzzled; Albert was not himself. The Albert he knew and appreciated was the sucker. Madness in this weak-a-ling was something to be considered very carefully.

"Swing at him!" screamed Bushy—infuriated by the delay in the bloodletting. Again he shoved Bimbo toward Albert. Teddy whispered in Albert's ear: "Jab, jab, Albert. Stay away when he swings!"

"I had enough!" screamed Albert. Like windmills, his arms rotated. Emitting feral noises, he flew at Bimbo. The redheaded boy was unprepared. Blows settled on his cheeks, his neck before he got his guard up; they bounced off his thick arms and shoulders. Stunned, he staggered backward.

"Okay, he asked for it. He wants it, he'll get it." Breathing heavily, Bimbo jigged on his toes. He looked more professional, more sure of himself.

Adrenaline and unreasoning fury were Albert's allies. Once more he lunged at Bimbo, his arms flailing. Backing away, Bimbo's guard dropped. Albert's right fist struck his left eye. It turned red and began to close.

Bushy grabbed Bimbo by his belt and all but lifted him off the ground. His fishy mouth was an inch from Bimbo's ear.

"*Swing!*" he screamed. "*Swing!* Make him *bleed!* Make him *hoit!* Ya can't win if ya don't *swiiiiing!*"

Bimbo shook himself loose. Bushy's frenzied advice was making him uneasy. Far from encouraging him, it made him realize that he and Albert were both suckers—luckless animals pitted together to satisfy Bushy's blood lust. But he jogged back, fists up, teeth bared. Albert flew at him once more. But Bimbo was ready. He struck Albert soundly in the gut, again on the temple, once more on the side of the neck. The blows hurt, but not quite as badly as Albert had anticipated. *All in getting used to it.* The pain was almost delicious.

"The battle of the cenchary!" Little Artie shouted.

"Tooney and Dempsey!" cried Big Artie.

"Schmelin' 'n' Sharkey!" responded Little Artie.

Both warriors stopped to gulp air, then milled again. There was no more hopping, posing, feinting by Bimbo. Savages, they charged, swung, missed, landed, retreated to catch their breath.

After the fourth exchange of blows, Albert saw that Bimbo's eye was closed. It was a sickly purple-black. *Did I do this?* he marveled. *Am I that great?* A joy beyond any ecstasy in Kipling or Jack London flamed in his chest. Even if he were destroyed, maimed, killed, he had known glory; a shiner hung on Bernard Wexler!

242

Bimbo took the offensive, charging first, landing hard uppercuts, abandoning defense. Once he smashed his right fist into Albert's mouth; he drew blood, cut his own knuckle on an incisor. Snarling, Albert spit blood and landed a clacking blow on the side of Bimbo's thick skull.

Again they parted and waited. It was customary for battlers to wait like this for the first acknowledgment of "enough." But neither would succumb, although Albert suddenly had had his fill of the affair. He was dreadfully exhausted, devoured by fatigue, convinced he could not raise his arms again. And Bimbo, loutish, one-eyed, was stronger, bigger, endowed with more endurance. Albert sensed some dire conclusion to his challenge.

"Git after him!" Bushy howled. "He's dead on his feet! Lookit him, he can't even lift his hands!"

"He's gonna faint!" Little Artie cried. "He's wobbaling!"

"All Bimbo's gotta do is fart and he'll go down. We oughta stop it," Big Artie offered.

Bimbo ran at him, struck him once on the nose, again in the chest. His strength was asserting itself. Albert swayed, stood his ground, took two more hard cuffs in the chest, a sidewinder that almost knocked his head off. Eyes bugging, the yellow globe of the street lamp shone brightly in each dark pupil. A demon inhabited him. He was a boy transformed. He bent low, gulped air, set his arms in motion, and came at the unbelieving Bimbo. *She is referring to you, Albert.* A blow bounced off Bimbo's temple, another cracked at his chin.

"*Swiiiing!* Swing, ya bum!" screamed Bushy. "Make him *bleeed!*"

"You cut it out, Bushy," Bimbo begged. "Lemme fight my own fight."

"Yer a disgrace!" shouted Bushy. "Anybody can beat him!"

"Ah, he stinks on ice," gasped Bimbo. "He ain't hoit me once. He hits like a powder puff."

Arms on hips, Albert rested. He was finished, licked. His chest was scorched; his lungs burned; his heart sought release from the rib cage. Bushy raced across the circle and began to shriek at him:

"Then, you git after *him! Swing!*"

Sucking air, sensing a tremor rise in his feet and shiver his limbs and his chest, Albert found what was left of his voice:

"You go to hell too, Bushy. I had enough of you, you bull-thrower."

"Ya both stink!" Bushy howled. "Yer both yellow-bellies! Sister Marys!"

"Lay off, Bushy," Teddy said. "He's doin' good for a guy who never fights. Let's call it a draw. Come on, you guys, shake."

"No, no, no!" Bushy howled. "*One guy's gotta go down!*"

His senseless rage deterred both of them. They rested, gasping, spitting blood, weary beyond belief. Albert's breath whistled in and out his nose. How could he go on? All Bimbo needed was to rush him once more and he would be dead. But Bimbo was resting, his chest heaving, one hand tentatively fingering his closed left eye. A burst of intelligence illuminated Albert's mind. *He doesn't really hate me, but I hate him.*

"They stink! They both stink!" Bushy wailed. "They oughta be killin' each other! No draw, no draw, let 'em fight it out!"

An interior voice whispered to Albert: *Settle for a draw, go home, shake hands, favor your weak ankles, avoid argument.* It was, of course, his mother's voice, a voice that lived in him. But he denied it. He spurned it. For once, once, in his miserable life, action would overcome thought.

"Look, they're dead on their feet," Big Artie said. "It's a draw, g'wan shake hands, you guys."

Albert shook his head. "Nope."

"Yay!" Bushy shouted. "Kill each other! Murder!" His lips peeled back. In a second he would bite them, nip at their flanks to force them into combat. He leaped behind Bimbo. "Take his eye out! Make 'im quit! One guy gotta quit!"

"*Bbbbbrrrrrt!*" Little Artie blew a Bronx cheer at Bushy. "Nobody quit when you fought Zetz!" The smell of blood—

anyone's blood—deterred Bushy from running after the monkey.

"I don't quit!" Albert screamed. Only dimly conscious of his acts, he hurled himself at Bimbo again. Bimbo struck back—once on the arm, once on the cheek. The blows exploded on him like electric light bulbs smashing. *Oh, but he doesn't hate me the way I hate him.* Face unguarded, Bimbo's fist crashed against his nose—that poor snubbed nose already maltreated by Lee Roy. The blood spurted for the second time that night. Rich, salty, it flooded his mouth.

"He gotta bloody nose! A bloody nose!" Bushy screamed.

"Stay away, Albert, stay away!" Teddy shouted. "Dance around him!"

Despair drenched him. He could barely move. Sighing, lighter than air, he struggled to get a headlock on Bimbo's freckled neck, hooked one skinny leg in back of the redhead. Both boys crashed to the gutter. In the sweet filthy smell of the street they rested like exhausted lovers—deep in the mingled aroma of horse piss, rotten orange peelings, motor oil. Legs locked, they thrashed, grunted, sobbed, squeaked. A wheezing noise kept issuing from Albert's tortured mouth; he kept his arms locked around Bimbo's neck while the adversary beat his chest and stomach with both fists. Besmeared with filth, they rolled, kicked, pummeled, in and out of the yellow circle, like wiggling bacteria trapped in the circular light of a microscope.

"Let's stop it," Teddy said, "they'll murder each other."

"Tie, tie," Big Artie said. "They can't even move."

At the edge of the street, hidden in the shadows, Mockey watched in hideous fascination. *"Oi, oi, shlecht."*

All but paralyzed, a delicious discovery dawned on Albert: he no longer felt pain. Bimbo's blows, driving into his unguarded gut, were like ping-pong balls, like soft waves at Rockaway. How wonderful! He was anesthetized, insensate. He could fight forever—if his body would respond. That was the problem. His arms and legs were drugged. Manfully, he tried to wriggle on top of Bimbo, but in exerting himself, he changed position, and the heavier boy, with a groan and a mighty heave, pulled himself above Albert. In a second he was on top of him, straddling Albert's chest, pinning him to the gutter, knees on Albert's forearms, fingers tightening around the victim's throat.

"Gotcha," Bimbo croaked. "Gotcha, ya bastid bitch."

"Yach, yach," Albert croaked. "Yach, no fair."

"Bimbo wins," Big Artie adjudged. "He got him pinned."

"No!" Bushy yelled. "Abrams gotta give up! Ask him does he give up? Make him say *uncle!*"

"Nah, nah," Teddy said. "He don't have to, he's licked." He patted Bimbo's heaving back. "Let him up, Bimbo."

"Say uncle," Bimbo said.

"Yach, yach, nah."

"Choke 'im!" Bushy screamed. "Choke 'im! Dincha know what it means to choke a guy so he can't breathe! G'wan, dig yer fingers in, deep, that's it! *Kill 'im, he'll quit!* That's it. Squeeze. *Squeeeeeze!* Harder, so he can't get no air!"

"Jeez, Bushy, lemme do it," Bimbo wailed. He looked over his shoulder, appealing to the leader to shut up.

"Ya stink, ya yellah," Bushy sneered. "I'd kill him, if it was me."

In the split second of Bimbo's distress, Albert wriggled his hands inside of Bimbo's grip on his throat. Instantly, he was able to relieve the pressure. It was peaceful beneath the bright globe, back flattened on the filth, licking the flowing blood from his nose and lip. Around him gaped the Raiders, puzzled by his bravery. He saw Mockey's bald head, Teddy's yellow mop, Little Artie's leer, Big Artie, fat and harmless, and Bushy, hungering for blood. No, he could not stay there forever, he had to make a move. Perhaps he would die. But at least he would die with honor.

"He won't quit," Bimbo complained.

"Never, never," Albert gasped. Then he arched his back, and with every fraction of strength, sent Bimbo's body upward, at the same time jerking his right knee under Bimbo's crotch. The bony knee struck Bimbo full force in his privates.

"Aaaaaaagh!" shrieked Bimbo. Pain coursed through his

crotch and his abdomen like an injection of sulfuric acid. Convulsed, he released Albert's throat, and in the instant of release, Albert rolled away, scrambled to his unsteady feet and assumed the boxer's pose—Bat Battalino, Jimmy McLarnin.

Agonized, Bimbo whimpered, stumbled to his feet, and began to walk away. In mincing, pained steps he limped off. "Lousy dirty fighter, dirty fighter. . . ."

"Not finished!" howled Albert. In lunatic elation, he flew across the circle and leaped on Bimbo's back, screaming. The others had to pull him off. He was clawing for Bimbo's throat.

"Ya won, ya won!" Teddy said. "Lay off him!"

Bimbo was crying. "Right inna nuts. Right inna nuts. Bastid bitch!"

"I'll kill him! *I'll kill him!*" Albert shrieked. But Teddy and Big Artie restrained him. Bimbo—deserted even by Bushy— kept limping into the darkness until he was across the street. Against a wrought-iron gate he rested, favoring his bruised crotch. His weeping came to them in a thin, wet line. No one went to console him. They knew that justice had triumphed, that the persecutor deserved what he got.

"Go over an' shake with him," Teddy Ochab said. "You guys can be friends again. It was only a fight."

"Ah, bullshit!" wailed Bimbo. "Lousy dirty fighter. . . ."

Albert's heart leaped, his blood raced. How marvelous, how exhilarating to be a lousy dirty fighter! Someday, someday he would be mean enough to battle Bushy, or even Zetz, or maybe Lee Roy. Yes, that was it—dirty fighting was what was needed, not intellect. Ah, he had learned, he had grown. With eminent satisfaction he licked the salty blood from under his nose, wiped his grimy hands on his soiled polo shirt, fingered his bruised arms and chest.

"I'll shake with him anytime," he said.

But Bimbo was walking toward the ice-dock.

In silence they dawdled down Longview Avenue. The night was not over. Certainly the two Arties were far from finished. They were ripping at one another's flies, trying to score

247

runs. One button open was a single, two a double, three a triple—the whole fly ripped apart—a homer. Ahead of them Bushy leaped, spun, taking practice runner-ins, tossing his Spalding and catching it, tireless, unbeatable. He had abandoned his protégé. To hell with Bimbo; he had not cared one way or the other who won. Bloodletting was all that interested him.

From the shadows, a solemn Mockey emerged. The battle in the gutter silenced him. More of America! What murderous world had his parents brought him to? And his best friend, the boy with the eyeglasses, Al-bare, why did he have to have fights with the *reute*?

Aloof, winner for once in his life, once during that awesome day, Albert felt no bubbling sense of victory, just an elegant detachment. *I am above all this.* And he found himself pitying Bimbo, youngest son of an impoverished seltzer-wagon driver. He wanted to run to him and say: *Look, Bimbo, we can do 'rithmetic homework again. You can play in the backyard. We can look at the pictures in my father's books. We can match baseball cards. We can go to the Brooklyn Museum together and look at the mummies. We can do all the things we did before you made fun of me in Miss Pivarnik's class.*

Albert saw Mockey goggling at him.

"I don't hate him anymore, Mockey, I mean Label," Albert said softly. Mockey was a splendid audience—no arguments, no wisecracks. The others could not hear him. "That must be a sign of maturity. I used my hatred of Bimbo to defeat him, but now that it's over, I can accept him again, when he's ready to act in a humane manner toward me. I still hate Lee Roy and Zetz, but who knows? Someday I might have my revenge, and then I won't hate them either. Get it?"

"*Vus?*" He stared at Albert's trickling nose. "*Oi, gib a kuk.*"

"You're a great help."

He held his head high, puffed out his narrow chest. And *drunk delight of battle with my peers far on the ringing plains of windy Troy.* There was bounce in his step, a flutter in his heart. He wished his two Conradian cronies, Gorilla Fisloff and Genius Grubman, had been there to see his famous victory.

"If you wait long enough, things even up."

"Vus?"

His boots struck sparks, lightning bugs in the night. Ally, admirer, he walked beside his dear American friend.

THE progression of noises signifying the doctor's return roused Mrs. Abrams from the Priestley novel. First, she heard the Chandler come to a coughing halt at the curb. Then a scuffing, tinkling noise—the doctor kicking a tin can off the sidewalk. Then the outer door opening and slamming. This was followed by the doctor's key rattling the inner door. Finally, she heard his heavy tread as he walked toward the rear room. Did she also hear a *bastard* under his breath? A *son-of-a-bitch*? She sighed; the curse words dropped softly around her like a schoolboy's spitballs. Even when they were unspoken she fancied she heard them. She helped herself to another sprig of grapes and settled back with her book. The English soothed her—sensible, well-mannered people. Most of her evenings were spent in this manner. Once a week she played bridge, not in the neighborhood but with a group of lady schoolteachers in Crown Heights. On Fridays she and the doctor and Albert went to the movies. The doctor liked Wallace Beery and she was partial to the Barrymores. All three loved Laurel and Hardy.

In the area around Longview Avenue she had no friends at all. What could she discuss with accented, waddling *bubbas*? Had they read Trollope and Fielding? The friends of her youth, with whom she had attended college, listened to poets and reformers, had moved to Crown Heights or Flatbush, away from the stench and racket of Brownsville. Only she and the doctor remained. He had no choice; it was where his patients were. She was a little jealous of her schoolteacher friends. They had no overhead, were paid regularly, took long vacations, and suffered no aggravations. Their lives were manageable while hers got less and less so every day. But she never complained. Not a word of protest ever reached Dr. Abrams' ears. Long ago she had set down the rules. All protest, outrage, fury, profanity and resentment were his. No one was allowed these indulgences. Albert's problems were to be brought to her. If she had frustrations they were to be kept to herself.

On summer nights she sat in the glow of a baroque bronze lamp (serpents, eagles, deer) and read her novel. Her deep brown eyes were untroubled, her powdered face motionless.

"I do not believe in interminable combat with everything in the world," she told her son. "Why must some people always be raging against their lot, acting as if they are the only ones who are cheated or mistreated? The world is not a fair place. It is unjust, and once we accept that fact the better off we will be."

"For Pete's sake, Mom, you mean, Pop, doncha?" he would ask.

Her head would nod, that faint agitation, substitute for exercise, involvement, anger.

Wild screams from the street never distracted her from her reading. The foulest odors never reached her nostrils. The stink and swarm and noise of Brownsville, the vengeful acts of their predatory, jealous neighbors were lost on her. Deep in her novels of English country life, of thatched roofs, vicarages, high teas, croquet, she was deaf to each crashing garbage can, each drunken shout, the inane clatter of the slum. And as she sat and read and nodded, Dr. Abrams grew more frenzied. A stench of burning mattress ravaged his nostrils, smoked his brain for a week. The yells of colored boys kicking a can ricocheted in his skull far into the night. She ate another grape.

She anticipated rather sadly his footsteps in the hall. Visits to the hospital were always followed by an acting-out of recent events. There was always an argument, a raw abrasive encounter to report—nurses, rivals, patients, specialists. Someone invariably snubbed, cheated, insulted or challenged him. They were not visits. They were skirmishes, forays into enemy territory. Years ago as a vigorous young GP, he had been a founder of Carrollton Hospital. The big shots, the "K-nockers," had talked of him as a potential chief of medicine. *Sol Abrams is the best medical man in Brooklyn; got a mind like a steel trap, keeps up with all the literature. If only he'd control his lousy temper, stop fighting the world. Who's he think he is, a Nirishman? Got that way from hanging around all those goy gym teachers when he was a kid. . . .*

In her mind, her eyes rising from the printed pages and fixing on a noxious oil painting of a New England farm, she recalled his failures. After a few years at Carrollton it became evident that Solomon Abrams, M.D., for all his brilliance as a diagnostician, could never be a chief of medicine or anything else. He argued too much. He made jokes at the wrong time. He insulted his superiors and showed disrespect for the chief surgeon. Besides, how could a hospital promote a man to chief of medicine if he didn't cut his hair or shine his shoes? Worst of all he sometimes smelled of manure. Fresh from gardening, he would come to the hospital redolent. "So what?" he protested. "It's a goddamn lot richer stuff than most lousy vitamins."

Oh, how he had missed, Mrs. Abrams reflected, by a mile, ten miles. The Longview Avenue address had been held against him. Other doctors graduated to Crown Heights; he lingered amid the racket, the grime, the sodden Negroes. Failure fed on failure. Patients vanished. Doctors ignored him. Specialists stole from him. Younger men undermined him. And he cursed, antagonized, learned nothing. He remained at Carrollton: the hospital eccentric. Nurses particularly appeared to be in league against him. His wife contended he was more to blame than they were. It was inconceivable that every nurse in the world was stupid, cruel, unfeeling and conniving. No visit to Carrollton passed without some fracas with a nurse, often a chief nurse. The curses reverberated in her ears: "*I told that old bitch* off once and for all! Me, me, she wouldn't let into surgery! Me, a founder of that flea-bitten, cockroach palace of a dump! Why, I was on the first staff they ever had there, the only one worth a damn, and she tells me I can't go into surgery! Why, that lousy old . . ."

On and on. The litany never changed. She expected it. Having heard him enter, she missed his step, his ascent to her sanctuary. In violent tones, he would smash the glass enclosing her world of English novels, rage against the world, curse nurses, damn specialists, consign patients to hell, denounce the entire practice of medicine.

She closed her book. Where was he? She placed it on the leather lamp table, next to a deformed ceramic ashtray Albert had made in second grade. The boy had no manual dexterity like his father. Dr. Abrams could upholster furniture, wire lamps, build a cabinet, plaster a ceiling, lay bricks, paint a window frame, build a picket fence. Albert had difficulty driving a nail. She walked to the head of the stairs and called into the darkness below. "Sol? Are you back?"

There was no response. From the street, a mélange of noise emphasized the silence within—a mongrel ki-yi'd, a garbage can lid was rattled, a mother howled for her errant son:

"Yussel, come home!"

"No. You'll kill me."

She walked down the stairs and entered the hallway. Halfway down the corridor she heard a peculiar heavy breathing. Gasping? Crying? She quickened her pace down the dark corridor—nothing to indicate anxiety, of course—and entered the consultation room.

The doctor was stretched out in the Morris chair. His shoeless feet rested on a rude leather stool that he himself had fashioned from a dining room chair she had discarded. In the half-light of the desk lamp (another of his concoctions, assembled from an old reading light and a candlestick) he looked pale. The substance beneath his skin appeared to have melted; the skin was loose and bloodless. With a sickening regularity his

253

mouth opened and closed—like a beached fish—and the noise he made was half a gasp, half a moan.

"Sol?" she asked softly. "What is wrong? What happened?"

"Nah. Nothing." His voice was surprisingly strong when he spoke.

"I'll call Dr. Moscowitz."

"To hell with him, the punk." Moscowitz was a younger competitor, a "comer," a tiny sleek man who charged double what Dr. Abrams did, and somehow, somehow—*how? how?*—had twice as many patients.

"You don't look well. Can I get you some water? Or tea?"

"Nah, the hell with it. The hell with everything."

His eyes rolled, pupils and irises vanished, leaving only two ghostly whites. The awful voids made her tremble, but she showed no fright, walked over to him and sat alongside him, drawing up his swivel chair. It was frayed and worn, but it rolled noiselessly; he always kept it oiled. With a shudder, his eyes rolled back, the terrible white spaces were filled. Some dreadful spasm had seized him, ended.

"Well, if you don't like Harry Moscowitz, I could ring up someone else, Meyer Klug or someone you like a little better . . . one of your old friends. . . ."

"Hell with all of them. Listen, kiddo, I've had these before." He sucked air again. "Never told you. I didn't want to bother you."

"But what is it? What's wrong?"

"Neurotic collapse of some kind. Vagatonia. Vagus nerve. I diagnosed it already. Had them for a year already. I get dizzy, palpitations, trouble breathing. What do you care?"

"I have to care. I must help you."

He began to moan again—a weary, lost sound. She had the shivering feeling that he was making it worse than it really was, embellishing, acting, drawing every ounce of terror out of whatever pain he had.

"Sol, what is hurting you? Your chest? Are you having trouble breathing?" *He has always helped others; no one can*

254

help him; he will not permit it. "Can I get you some aspirin? Some codeine? Or an injection?"

"Nothing. None of that crap. It passes. Lousy pressure, can't get enough air. It'll go."

"But the pain. . . ."

"Easier now, only trouble is getting enough air. Vagatonic type, I knew it long ago. Had four or five of these already, but that's none of your business." He patted her hand. "I'll get these on my own time, don't need any audience."

"Something must have brought it on. What was it?"

"Lousy hospital. That bitch of a chief nurse. I had it out with her once and for all." He seemed to be controlling his moaning now that he was purging himself, the inevitable struggle with the enemy. His disputes were like masses, confessionals. "Dirty old kraut, that Strohmeyer, that white-haired one, complaining about Glogauer, my patient, saying he rang the buzzer too much. So I said, Lady, if your ass was as painful as his, you'd be on the buzzer also, and she opens a big yap to me and I—"

Mrs. Abrams closed her eyes. The grim perfection of his life! In a morbid way, she was almost fulfilled, now that she knew what had brought on his seizure. An argument with a nurse over old man Glogauer, patriarch of a long line of four-flushers who owed him bills since the Year One, who aggravated, tormented and abused him, but kept calling him because he never made any effort to collect what was due him! And now he lay in collapse, Sir Solomon Abrams, Crusader, who defended Zayde Glogauer's God-given right to ring the night bell.

"Why do you have to involve yourself so deeply, Sol? Maybe the nurse was right for a change. And even so, can't you just shrug these things off?"

He was gasping again, sucking air, moaning, his powerful chest rising, falling. "They all stink," he pronounced in between moans. "Stink to high heaven."

Yes, perhaps they did—patients, nurses, other doctors, and even she and Albert. What could any of them do to save him? She got up, walked to the desk, and turned off the crude lamp.

255

Outside the screened window (more of his handiwork, frames and screens built one spring afternoon; she could remember him in dirty workman's clothes which he loved, whistling, flexing his iron muscles in the backyard while Albert, an awed and undersized six-year-old, watched in fascination and handed him nails), night insects chirped their pleasure at the succulent feast in his garden. *They eat his leaves and blossoms the way all of us eat his heart.* She was terror-stricken now, but nothing showed on her unlined white face. The humming and clicking outside suggested Walden Pond and she felt dismayed that she and the doctor had never made the trip to Massachusetts that they had been promising one another for years. They would go. They would have to go. Just pick up and leave for a week— Lexington, Boston, Concord, the Emerson house, Walden Pond, the rude bridge, the Alcott home.

"Are you feeling any better?"

"Yeh, yeh, a little."

She stroked his arm: the power was still in it, a hardwood arm, corded with years of giant swings, Swedish calisthenics, barbells. Moonlight diffused the small room; above the desk, it illumined the photographs of boyhood friends, teachers. The eminent Gentiles who had educated him. Fellow school-teachers. Confident phys ed majors. Tribal gods like Freud and Maimonides. Why it was perfectly ridiculous for a man with so much in back of him. . . . She had trouble saying "fail" to herself. But it *was* ridiculous, utterly incomprehensible that his life should have dwindled into a hash of relief calls, unpaid bills, runaway patients, and arguments with nurses.

"I quit," the doctor mumbled. "I quit."

"You certainly do not. That is the silliest thing I ever heard."

He did not respond. His breathing was softer, more sub-dued. The moaning noise had stopped. Was there still a chance? Of course, there had to be. That's what Mr. Roosevelt was there for. Things would get better. People would have jobs and money. They would need a good family physician again.

She studied the motion of his mighty chest under the

sweaty yellow shirt. (Yellow shirt? What doctor in Brooklyn, in all of the United States went around in a short-sleeved yellow shirt with a green tie improperly knotted, so that tie and collar were one mangled ruffle?) Much of his disaster had been self-inflicted. A man could somehow learn to wear a starched white shirt, a neat tie, shined shoes and, at minimum, get his hair cut regularly.

"You seem to be feeling better."

"A little."

"I'll get you something. Tea?"

"Nah, just sit here." His need for her was more upsetting than his affliction. A dependent note—almost a *whine*—had crept into his voice. Raging alone, he was his own comforter. But now he needed an audience.

"Where's Albert?"

"In the street, with friends. He should be home any minute."

"Ah. Is he all right?"

"Why shouldn't he be all right? Sol, you confound me. Here you are gasping for breath, and all you can do is worry about him. If you stopped being so concerned about every step we take, you might be better off. Now that you seem to be feeling better, I think I'll call Moscowitz and ask him to—"

"He can go to hell. *Fekokteh* specialist in a white coat. The ladies like his moustache."

He had to be feeling better to denounce Harry Moscowitz. He was back in his own half-mad world of stern judgments, moralistic pronouncements that weakened him, absorbed his strength, took his mind off the necessities of life. But the odd thing was, he was right, *dead right*, one hundred percent right. Harry Moscowitz *was* a fraud. Of late, Moscowitz was affecting an English accent, and he adorned his office with not one but two specious nurses, local girls decked out in starched white dresses. Once, in the early years of Dr. Abrams' practice they had decided to try a nurse. What a disaster! She had been a fat, straw-haired German woman, ill-tempered, silent, clumsy. She lasted a week. Why, why? wondered Mrs. Abrams, do some people manage these things so perfectly, yet they elude us forever? Neither of them, she realized—and she saw the signs already in Albert—had what was needed to "get along."

With a sudden display of strength, the doctor raised his back to a sitting position. He kicked the stool away. "The insurance papers, they're in the strong box at the East New York Savings Bank." He spoke brusquely, almost as if in response to a question.

"What has that got to do with the man in the moon?"

He put a hand over his eyes. "In case something happened to me. I wouldn't want those bastards to do you out of it."

"Why should anything happen to you? You're not even fifty."

"Oh, who knows."

"What are you talking about? You are in excellent health. You said so yourself the other day. Your problems are in your mind, Sol, the way you eat yourself up. You must make some kind of treaty with the rest of the world."

"No lectures."

"It's the truth."

"Listen, Hannah. Don't get frightened. I'm telling you this for your own good. If anything happens to me, you have the insurance, and those lice better pay up! You could get a good price for this house, considering the tip-top shape I've kept it in. You and the kid could get a small apartment in a good neighborhood, and you could even get a job, not a tough one, but something easy. It might be better for all concerned."

Trembling, she withdrew her hand from his. It would be better to feign ignorance, to pretend that she had no idea what he was talking about. "What can happen to you?"

"Do I have to spell it out? You want a diagram? I'll arrange it so it'll look natural." He gasped again. "Natural causes."

"Stop that. Don't talk that way."

"When I got lost in the car this afternoon, I knew something was giving, something was coming apart. Something going in me, no control. Me, the toughest guy that ever graduated from Cooney's school, but I couldn't find the hospital. I knew it was coming apart. . . ."

"And this is your way out? And I'm supposed to be the coward of the family?"

"Oh, lots of people are finding it the easy way. You have enough, you end all the crap. Look at your rich Uncle Nate, in Providence . . . the big knocker, the all-rightnik. It didn't keep him from . . ."

"You are five times the man he is!" she sobbed. But as soon as tears started, she stifled them. Tears were not her privilege. Then she rested her head on his chest. He stroked her hair. Beneath the shirt, she could hear the gymnast's heart pounding. He was still an athlete who had not run to fat. It was inconceivable that he should—willy-nilly—want to crush the life in him. She would not acknowledge such nonsense. *Nonsense!* That's what Myra Kelly would have said to a worrisome pupil in P.S. 1. It was not very long ago that she and Sol Abrams, medical student, had walked through meadows reciting Whitman, climbed hills to shout the Rubaiyat at the sunset, rested by mountain streams and quoted Tennyson to one another. *To seek, to strive, to find and not to yield.*

"Yes, a small apartment. Better for both of you."

"I will not permit you to talk that way. That is utter nonsense, and you know you have no intention of carrying out these—these *threats*."

"Never mind, kiddo," he said, stroking her hair. "Never mind, it'll be easier for all of us. You won't have to listen to my screaming and yelling and getting mad at the world."

"Things are getting better. The Depression is over. A few months more, business will pick up."

"For everyone else, not for me. I won't sell apples. Too old for the WPA."

He said no more; his breathing was quieter. Outside, the night insects hummed and clacked, a chained dog howled, and cats screamed over prior rights to discarded garbage.

Mockey, now a quasi-member of the Raiders, was being subjected to his first "Chinese haircut." Surrounded, his bald head shoved down, he writhed and shouted Yiddish curses as his new friends took turns grinding their fists into the nape of his neck.

"A Chinese haircut for a Russky-hooey!" Little Artie cried.

"Don' rub too hard, ya'll start a fire on the wood!"

"Wood? It's like eye-ron!"

After the Chinese haircut, they subjected him to "Indian wrist-burn," grabbing his arms and twisting the skin in opposite directions. This was even less painful, but the greenhorn obliged by wailing mournfully, a Ukrainian wolf cub. As he shrieked, he looked lovingly into Albert Abrams' eyes.

"No brains, no feelings," Albert told the others. "This guy is the original nerveless wonder. He isn't hurt at all."

"He's makin' believe," Big Artie said.

"A smack in the snoot'll make him cry," Bushy said—but half in jest.

"He's okay," Teddy said. "Built like a rock." Admiringly he squeezed Mockey's muscles. Albert joined him in appraising the new boy's heft. His arms were like white gristle, reminiscent of the pale chunk of "choon-gum" in a veal roast.

Big Artie thudded away, returned to bend low in back of Mockey. Little Artie then pushed the baldhead, ass over tea-kettle, over Big Artie's back. As soon as Mockey got to his feet,

Little Artie sliced his ham. Albert, emboldened, danced in front of him and ripped a triple off his fly.

Underdogs needed, no Irish need apply, Albert thought. Mockey had taken his place on the lowest rung of the ladder. Beating up Bimbo, he had won his spurs; status had come to him after a long painful day. How good it felt not to be lowest of the low, at least for the time being! And poor Bimbo! He avoided Albert's eyes, he lurked in the shadows of the ice-dock, he touched his insulted crotch every now and then. In his manner, Albert perceived, there was not only an admission of defeat, but a sense that he knew he had brought it on himself, that his persecution of Albert had been cruel and unnecessary. Now Mockey had come into their lives—dumb, trusting Mockey, a gift from Mother Europe!

Exhausted, they collapsed against the ice-dock. Unbuttoned once again by Little Artie, Mockey worked on his fly. Iron buttons, solid iron, Albert noticed. The boy was made of hard stuff—armored shoes, iron fly, steel head, flesh and bones of gristle. Someday he would make a great running guard for Alexander Hamilton. A long happy period of Americanization lay before Label; someday he would win the John Wanamaker drawing contest for children and perhaps a medal from the Police Post of the American Legion for a speech on the Obligations of the Citizen.

"Yes, you have a great future, Label," Albert told him. Mockey nestled next to him, like a great stupid dog.

"Yuh?"

"Yuh. Soon you will master the English language. Then on to high school, a football scholarship to Princeton, and three years of varsity ball as a running guard under the tutelage of the wily Fritz Crisler. You are a Princeton man if ever I saw one. Then, on to a brilliant career in Wall Street, Label Warshofsky, king of the speculators."

Big Artie smiled serenely at him. "You got some imagination, Albert. You oughta be a newspaper reporter."

There was a brief discussion of careers. Teddy wanted to be an airplane mechanic, Bushy wanted to go into business—real

261

estate or something. Big Artie liked the notion of coaching somewhere, but Little Artie hadn't the faintest idea. Albert could not envision him at work anywhere. He was born to race around the streets, on and off ice-docks, in and out of parked cars, over fences, down alleys, up stairways. As soon as the conversation bored him, he started a boxball game, dragging his cousin into it.

Bushy watched them. The bouncy Spalding evoked memories of the afternoon. "Tomorrow I go see the Hawks. We're gonna challenge 'em again."

"You mean you're gonna talk to Zetz?" Albert asked.

"I ain't afraid of him." He spit into the gutter. Albert knew he spoke the truth; he was not afraid of Zetz or of anyone else.

Teddy pushed his glasses up on his nose. "We all better go, Bushy, everyone."

"They won't start nothin'," Bushy said. His eyes vanished. "They couldn't beat us an' they know it." Albert marveled at him: the undefeated. No eyes. That was his miracle. You could not reproach a man with no eyes, frighten him, stare him down, discipline him. No wonder his father had to flail at him with a broomstick; Bushy was impervious to anything less. He was jealous of Bushy. Someday, he might develop a puffed eyeless face, a face nobody could stare down, a fearless, impregnable face. Not even Lee Roy would dare attack him!

Luxuriating in bruises and wounds, the scars of battle, he stretched full-length on the splintery ice-dock. Yes, he was arriving. He noted that Teddy had included him in the delegation to challenge the Hawks. *I am ready for them.* He would stare insolently with iced eyes at the beast Zetz. No fear would shiver his fragile limbs. Tongue flicked at upper lip: dried blood. Was it blood that spurted under Lee Roy's quick jabs, or blood from his triumph over Bimbo? It was heavenly blood. A lump on his forehead throbbed deliciously. On his chest, where Bimbo's fists had landed, he treasured each bruise. Fingers probed lovingly at his filthy polo shirt, still wet with Abracadabra Allah Bah-Ooyah's mystic water. He was happy now, happier than he had been in months. Above the tenement cornices, the sky was frantic with stars. The dampness had evanesced from the air and a faint breeze stirred. How good to be twelve years old on a July night in Brownsville! And to-morrow—new adventure. Hitching belts, sneakers padding softly, he envisioned them striding toward the nest of the hated Hawks, through alien streets, to confront the bad guys and hurl the challenge in their teeth.

A surge of love for his friends made him tremble. He was madly in love with them. It was disheartening that they would all have to grow up, go their ways, never meet again. Generously, he included Bimbo in his affection. The redhead sat alone, coated in grime, his head lowered. For a moment, Albert was tempted to play the good fellow, extend the hand of friendship to him; but that would come in time. He was terribly sorry for him; he could not hate him anymore. Bimbo wore clothes that often seemed a collection of patches. He had his hair cut at home "*kok-teppel*" style—as if a chamber pot had been set on his round skull, and his mother had snipped everything that showed beneath it. Whenever Mrs. Abrams had offered Bimbo fruit or candy, he had blushed, turned away, mumbled, and had taken a very small piece. Yes, he and Bimbo would have to make up. All in time, all in time.

Drowning in euphoria, he forgave Bushy. Was this mad leader, this crazy king, nothing more than a mirror—or a reaction against—his hot-tempered, bearded terror of a father, that angry wielder of broomsticks, who, *tsitsis* a-flying of a summer afternoon, came charging out of a tenement to basti-nado his son? Did the myths of the Greeks, yea, the very Hebrew Bible its holy self ever produce such a stirring father-son encounter? Daedalus and Icarus; Abraham and Isaac; Aeneas and Achates—what were they alongside the awesome legend of Bushy Feinstein and his savage progenitor, Menahim Yussel Feinstein?

A world of wonders. Miracles. Visitations. Portents. He embraced it all. (If only his father's income would rise, if only he would stop losing patients, everything would be splendid.)

Across the street a lamp burned in the basement flat of the Grubman family. The Genius sat at his books. It was summer vacation, but that did not stop Genius. His mind absorbed everything. The teachers gave him assignments for the summer. He raced the clock; everyone knew death went to bed with him every night, that his fragile heart could not last. On ballooning knickerbockers, propped up in high laced boots, he fulfilled his brilliant destiny. A short race, but a magnificent one, Albert thought. Cursed with his malformed heart, he aroused Albert's sympathies so deeply that he felt the tears forming on his battered eyes. Genius, do not die, do not die!

"Old Grubman," he murmured. "Lookit him study."

All paused from their games to pay tribute to the doomed brain who padded softly among them, quoting Milton, Shakespeare, theorems, formulas. How often had he bailed them out of algebra homework? Or compositions? If only they all could offer him a bit of their vigorous, tireless lives!

The last boxball game of the day ended. Little Artie beat Big Artie. The monkey leaped on the ice-dock. A mite of energy still bubbled in him; he began a crazy dance, leaping sideways from one brick wall of the dock to the other. Spinning, pivoting, he seemed to stop himself in mid-air. "Hey look! It's all red! The sky—way over there!"

"Wow!" shouted Big Artie. "Somethin' boinin'!"

They turned their heads toward Rower Avenue, beyond the school. A flickering glow colored the night. Smoky reds and orange painted the sky a livid shade. Magentas merged with indigos like the running paints on a child's palette.

"Fire, fire!" screamed Little Artie. "Fire! Waaaaaayoooo!" He shrieked like a fire engine, flew from the ice-dock, and raced toward the glowing sky.

"Near the *schul!*" Bushy shouted.

The others took off in Little Artie's wake. First they trotted, then they sprinted. Suddenly the orange glow grew brighter, leaped, billowed, as a great cone of smoke soared upward. Sirens screamed; they heard shouts, cries. Distantly, the clanging of the fire bell, the sound of another siren. Whistles, the noise of trucks and police cars.

Albert ran to the rear. He puffed with exhaustion. The day's deeds had enervated him; he could barely lift one foot after the other. Mockey kept pace with him. The clodhoppers struck sparks on the paving. Albert wondered: how did he ever run away from Cossacks in gunboats like those?

Windows slammed open; there were more shouts, cries. People came from the tenements in pajamas, undershirts. A crowd was converging on Rower Avenue, drawn to the disaster. Albert, gasping his way down Longview Avenue, bumped into Daisy. It was like hitting a sack of pressed grapes. Daisy and Cowboy were strolling serenely toward the fire. In no hurry, they knew it would be there when they arrived.

"Now you look at dat Cleveland," Cowboy explained. He spoke with great authority. "Dey a dirty ball club. Averill and Trosky and Kamm, dey dirty ball players, but only 'gainst deh Yankees."

"Yeh. Look hit dat fah."

Albert detoured around them and bumped Gorilla, shuffling on deformed legs.

"Dah schul, dah schul," Gorilla said to Albert. "It's boinin' opp. Boy, somebody's gonna get a sin for makin' a schul boin."

"Maybe it was an accident," Albert puffed.

"Dat don' matter," Gorilla said wisely—a sage in his dimwitted way. "Den everybody gets a sin. Dat's maybe deh biggest sin in de woild, boinin' a schul. It's woister dan tearin' opp a Hebrew book."

There was no time for theology; Albert sped by him. Streets blurred past his excited eyes. Now a mob poured from the tenements—fat ladies in bathrobes, old gaffers shuffling in slippers, a horde of howling brats. The sirens shattered the night. The grand City of New York was coming to the rescue! Mayor LaGuardia himself might show up!

They flew past the great dark hulk of P.S. 133—more than ever a jail for the criminally insane—and turned the corner on to Rower Avenue. Louder wailed the sirens, closer came the ding-ding-ding of the fire bells.

The fire was not in the synagogue but in a narrow yellow brick building adjoining it. Great spurts of flame, crowned by billows of mauve and orange smoke issued from a basement workshop. The proprietor of the tiny shop was one of those mysterious dwarfs, a certain Gotbetter. As long as Albert could remember, N. GOTBETTER CAPMAKER had labored in that underground warren, a fixture on Rower Avenue, unlike his fellow trolls who seemed to be forever in transit, hauling knitting machines and bales of rags in and out of store-front ateliers. In fact his mother had purchased several snazzy tweed caps from this very Gotbetter. A bandy-legged, potbellied midget, Albert knew him not only for his handmade caps, but for the alarming habit he had of thrusting out his false teeth at teasing children as he scurried to and from his workroom. Once, many years ago, Albert, standing near some kids who had thrown a road apple at Gotbetter's feet, had been frightened out of his wits by those protruding false fangs and wet lips, hurled at him from behind a gray beard. For years he had been terrified of the gnome and when his mother took him there to be fitted for a cap, he shuddered a little, wondering if the fearsome choppers would be thrust at him. But no. In the shop, Gotbetter was a gentleman. He had patted Albert's head, given him a hard candy, and referred to Mrs. Abrams as "*Frau Doktor.*"

Beneath the veil of smoke, Albert could see the lettering in gold leaf: N. GOTBETTER CAPMAKER. Rhythmically, tongues of flame leaped from the opened door. In counterpoint, the smoke soared, great pillows of ruddy stuff. A crowd agglutinized in the gutter at a safe distance from the heat and smoke, but close enough to savor fully Gotbetter's disaster. With Bushy in the lead, the boys pushed their way to the front rank, halting behind the sentinel figures of two policemen, who, with bland contemptuous faces, watched Gotbetter's livelihood—happily it seemed to Albert—vanish in smoke and fire. It fulfilled, he decided, their policely need to see others in misery.

They almost seemed to have set the fire for their own amusement. In between the two cops, half their size, a stunted figure in yarmulke and woolen undershirt, leather apron and baggy black trousers, N. Gotbetter, Capmaker, wailed and wrung his artisan's hands. In the excitement he had forgotten his false teeth, and his rubbery mouth assumed undersea shapes as he sobbed his misery to the unheeding police.

"*Gonovim!* Gangsters! Crooks!" he bawled. "Dat somobitch Zetzkin, dat doidy son from a Galitzianer! I'm not afraid it from him, I'll break by him de head he comes by me again!"

"Hold it down, willya, Shorty?" the older of the two cops asked rhetorically. He had white hair and ruddy unlined face. Perhaps he was as old as Gotbetter, but he was far better preserved. Oh, Albert thought, how I would like to punch him right in the schnozzle, make him bleed for being so cruel to Gotbetter! Why was he smiling? Was it so hilarious that the capmaker's shop was burning? The older cop sweated healthily in the heat. His younger partner, a bovine man with sleek black hair, nodded wisely. "Lookit it boin. It's really goin' now." They agreed; it was really going. Narrow-eyed, they watched and approved, manifesting their evident superiority over the slum animals surrounding them, lower forms of life stupid enough to labor over caps in basements and then lose their entire kit and kaboodle in a fire.

"Aaaaah," sighed the mob. A bigger jet of flame leaped from the store front. Gotbetter howled. The crowd pushed forward.

"All a yez, back!" shouted the older cop. "Git back, deah, Moe, or I'll belt ya. The engines are comin'!"

With undulating moan, incessant clang of bronze bell, the hook and ladder rounded the corner—on two wheels it appeared—and roared toward the fire. Rubber-coated firemen, helmeted, booted, leaped from the vehicle. Like their brother police they were the lords of the earth. They seemed to be taking their time.

"Whaddya havin', a conference?" a young man shouted.

267

"Whadda we pay ya salaries for? Look, it'll spread to the *schul* by the time you guys are finished!"

"Dat's right!" bellowed roofer Kalotkin. He stood in the midst of the mob—half-naked, hairy. "Look, it's woister and woister—go awready start the hoses!"

"Shaddap and git back!" snarled the older cop. He and his partner braced their clubs and started moving the spectators away. Albert stumbled pleasurably, drowning in smoke, stink, the softness of other bodies. He rested against Big Artie's hulk. N. Gotbetter was also shoved away—protesting, weeping.

"Bestids! Somobitches! Doidy gengsters! Lissen by me, policeman, what I'm saying. Dat Zetzkin, vat dey call Mutteh, *trombonik, paskudnyak, loyser,* doidy bestid! He vanted I should pay it him money, *gelt,* so he should protect me. Vat I need your lousy protection, you bestid, I told him? Get hout from my place, odder I'll call a cop! Not a nickel, not a penny I'll give you! So he did it! He made it deh fire, because I vouldn't pay him!"

"Can it, Shorty," the white-haired officer said.

"Know what?" Little Artie asked Albert. "Betcha don't know what happened."

"I can guess."

"Mutty Zetzkin did it. They don't pay up, *whooooosh,* he boins 'em."

Big Artie nodded. "Yeah. He stuck a stink bomb in Ratner's bakery a coupla weeks ago. Stunk up all the bread for a week."

"Nobody fools around with Mutty," Little Artie said reverently.

They sounded proud of the hoodlum, pleased with his evil works. Was there no justice? Albert wanted to lecture them, explain to them that there was nothing admirable in Mutty Zetzkin's career. Why wasn't anyone feeling sorry for N. Gotbetter? Albert thought: I never should have begrudged him the right to scare me with his false teeth. The poor guy deserved an edge over somebody in the world, even if it were only me.

"Wow! Wooooooah! Lookit go now!"

"Somethin' musta caught inside!"

"Back, back!"

"Waaaah—way up in da sky!"

"Dah whole block'll go up!"

"Lookit deh colors—all orange and yellah!"

Great searching cones of flame roared from the basement, licking their way up the side of the building, which had long been emptied. By now the hoses were in play, shooting hissing streams into the shop, turning fire into more choking clouds of smoke. Enraged, the smoke formed turbulent patterns, puffed out, turned gray and black, lay in a heavy blanket over the hot street. People coughed, spat, wiped tears from their eyes, staggered away. Albert pressed a handkerchief to his mouth.

Kalotkin informed the hardier spectators: "It's dat cleaning fluid he keeps. It's like turp. No wonder."

N. Gotbetter, howling like an injured dog, tried to hurl his undersized form through the police—who had now been reinforced with four more members. He was pushed back unsympathetically. "Moe, when I tell ya to stay back, I mean it! Ya wanna singe ya whiskers?"

"Mine place!" the capmaker wailed. "Mine place, mine whole life!"

No one seemed to hear him; no one cared. Let him burn. Let him roast. Let him be destroyed. They were safe.

The street was jammed; the crowd roared as the hoses played against the building and the smoke gushed upward. Albert turned his head—all of Brownsville had come out for the fun. In the dark background, perched high on the school fence he saw black figures—Lee Roy, Madison, their friends. They hooted louder than anyone, shrieked joyfully.

"Burn hit up! Burn hit all!"

"Fahman, fahman, save mah chile!"

"Save yo' ass!"

There was a moment when the smoke diminished under the pressure of the hoses. Two helmeted firemen, axes on shoulders, entered the basement.

"About time, ya bums!" Kalotkin shouted.

"Yeah, about time!" echoed Margulies. "Some civil servants! Whose interest do they have at heart anyway?"

"Pipe down, ya squirt, ya lit—"

But Kalotkin's admonition was lost in a mighty, terrifying roar from the capmaker's shop. The firemen came running out. Quickly they went into consultation with a white-capped chief who had arrived in a snappy red sedan.

"Wow, lookit it now," Little Artie said.

"Dat'll loin him, dat'll loin him," Kalotkin said wisely. "Ya gotta play ball. Ya gotta grease the skids. Did I ever have trouble with Zetzkin? Never. Why? I play ball. He understands me. I understand him."

"Mine place! Mine place," moaned Gotbetter.

"Ah, ya brung it on yasself," the roofer bellowed. "Whaddya expect from a dope like Gotbetter? He don't know how to talk to a guy like Mutty. Mutty's okay. He's wit' us. But whaddya expect from *alta kockers* like him? They make it hard for all of us." He looked, for some reason, at the Raiders. "Know what I mean?"

Albert coughed; the smoke was scorching his throat. He returned Kalotkin's glance of wisdom. "No, I don't know what you mean at all. What's Mr. Gotbetter supposed to do? Pay that gangster for nothin? Should he be happy his shop's burning?"

"Look, the doctor's son!" Kalotkin growled. "Like his old man, a mouth on him!"

"And proud of it," Albert said.

The jets of water hissed, the smoke poured out, and still the miserable workroom would not die. It seemed to Albert that all of Gotbetter's insignificant life had accumulated in the dark cavelike room—hours of pattern-making, stitching, basting, fastening brims to crowns, sewing linings, affixing neat buttons, trimming leather sweatbands, storing silk, tweed, worsted, stacking up boxes, bills, unsold stock—and now these small lost acts were determined to go out in a blaze of glory. Ferociously, they burned and smoked, protesting Gotbetter's rotten gnomelike life, defying the dull-witted cops and firemen

270

and Gotbetter's cruel neighbors wallowing in the mud of his defeat.

"It sounds like a goddamn wall went out in the back," Albert heard one of the firemen say.

"The synagogue's gonna go also," another said. "Them old walls are made of paper."

Mysteriously, wisps of smoke were issuing from the barred and wired basement windows of the temple. The crowd hummed and stirred.

A tall straight-backed man, close-cropped, with a white spade beard had appeared in the official group outside the burning building and conferred with the police and the fire chief. He was, Albert knew, the austere "Captain" Feigenbaum, *shammes*—sexton—of the synagogue. He had, at one time, like many local characters, been a devoted patient of Dr. Abrams, a long-winded recounter of vivid adventures in the Austrian Army in the First World War. ("A crap-artist of the first water," the doctor told everyone, "thinks he personally won the Battle of Caporetto.") For a while the doctor had indulged him, sat patiently and listened to his tales of heroic deeds in the service of Franz Josef. But when "Captain" Feigenbaum had appeared in the office one day, placed an old service revolver on the desk, and informed Dr. Abrams that "they" were after him, and that he wanted the doctor's help in fighting "them" off, the friendship ended. (Dr. Abrams' exact words were: "Get the hell out of here, you nut, before I shove that dime-store gun down your throat." The half-mad "Captain" had retreated in disorder, pausing only to spit a gob of mucus onto the doctor's hall runner.)

"This old guy says the building's empty," the younger cop told the fire chief. "He's the caretaker."

"Caretaker!" yelled Kalotkin. "Hah! Whatsa matter ya don't know General Feigenbaum? Hoy, General, give us a goose step, or a right shoulder arms!"

Feigenbaum, ramrod stiff, eyes glinting under white eyebrows, glared at the roofer. Happily he would have run him through with a bayonet. "Pfui," he spat. *"Ferdamter blut."*

"Hoy, Feigenbaum, left, right, left, squads right, assholes tight!" Kalotkin shouted.

A delegation of synagogue elders, bearded relics, gathered around the sexton. They pleaded with the police and the fire chief to be allowed into the synagogue to rescue the scrolls. The new Torah, paraded that afternoon, rested in the ark!

"No one moves his ass in there, unless it's one of my boys, understand?" the chief asked. "Tell 'em that, Whitey." He dug "Captain" Feigenbaum in the ribs. "Besides, it's prob'ly only smoke. It ain't boinin' in deah." He winked at the older policeman. "Not yet it ain't."

God of our fathers will punish you, Albert thought.

Abruptly the flames ceased. Gotbetter was destroyed, his lifework, as miserable as it was, his hopes, his art, billowing into the street in great gusty clouds of smoke. A great coughing chorus went up, throats hawked oysters, tears ran—but nobody left. A curbside river of soiled water coursed down Rower Avenue. Albert felt his sneakers drenched. He wiggled his toes wetly.

As soon as the flames had stopped, the firemen reentered the capmaker's shop. In a few seconds, the crowd heard the crackling shattering sound of their axes. Gotbetter leaped for the white-haired cop—who else could he appeal to—and grabbed the blue arm.

"Royined! Royined! Nottink! Not a penny insurance!"

"Hands off, Jake," the cop said. He unfastened Gotbetter's midget hand. "Whaddya want me to do, light a candle?" And now, to Albert's visceral horror, the cop smiled. It was a flat, wide smile, and for many years to come, Albert would recognize that same bloodless, unfunny smile on storm troopers, SS guards, young men selling *Social Justice*, and the crowds keeping Negro children out of Southern schools.

Still no one consoled the capmaker. *If I try to, they will laugh at me,* Albert thought. *It's no use. This is the way the world is sometimes. Like the day I pushed Gorilla into the mud puddle. Should never have done it. Should tell Gorilla I am sorry. Mr. Gotbetter, I will wear your tan tweed cap forever,*

272

*until it is a shred; I will wear your cap always. Your worktable is
a charred ruin, but your caps will go marching on.*

"Hah, all it's good for is to speak fresh to me!" wailed
Gotbetter. "I'm tellink you vas dat lousy gengster Zetzkin, dat
fekokteh Galitzianer made it deh fire!"

"File a complaint, Moe."

"Und you vudn't help me?"

"I wouldn't give ya the time a day." Booze-red, ruddily
smooth, he was a lord of the earth—untouchable, a privileged
person, who could not be hurt, insulted, offended, bested. With
a monarch's heavy tread, he walked the earth, striking terror.
On flat feet, he strolled away from the bawling capmaker,
jerking a thumb over his shoulder, addressing his compeers.
"The old guy's gone bananas."

"Pipple!" Gotbetter cried to the mob. "Pipple! Vat did
I do it wrong? Pipple know me—Nathan Gotbetter, Capmaker!
Tvenny years I am making caps here by deh *schul!* Vat I ever
did it wrong to anyone?"

With neutral eyes and slack jaws the mob studied him.
They caressed him with their indifference, embraced him in
their contempt. They oiled themselves in his disaster. Oh, how
good to have it happen to someone else! How exhilarating was
the suffering of others! How lucky they all were not to be
destroyed by fire and flood!

A despair more wasting than any of his private terrors
wrenched at Albert. Indifferent eyes, gaping mouths surrounded
him: nobody cared about Mr. Gotbetter. The very sweat that
oozed from their bodies—neighbors, artisans, fellow-sufferers of
the great Depression—was tainted with their terrible joy.

"Who made it de fire?" howled the capmaker. "Did I make
it?"

Iron hearts and stone ears—they heard nothing.

"Ya brung it on yaself," Kalotkin said. He spoke for all of
them. "Ya can't fight City Hall."

"He did *not*," Albert said with annoyance. "Whyncha shut
up for a change, Mr. Kalotkin?"

"Man, lookit the smoke from the *schul* window," Bushy

said appreciatively. The temple reminded him of his father. Let it burn.

A fireman emerged from Gotbetter's ruined store. Albert saw him gesturing toward the temple, heard a word here and there. "Whole wall went down . . . back room . . . spreadin'. . . ."

The back room. A secret place, Albert knew, a place forbidden to curious boys, padlocked, windowless, the sanctuary where Yussel Melnick performed his hidden wonders. "Captain" Feigenbaum was summoned again. He walked as if on parade, some old military insanity bright in his eye. In the presence of police and firemen, he felt as an equal among equals.

"Lissen, whiskers," the old cop said, "it's in the back of the choich now. You sure nobody's in deah?"

A convocation of elders was summoned. Under a pall of smoke they argued, gestured with thumbs, wailed, stroked beards. Ancients of the temple, Albert thought, Sanhedrin, Tzadiks, learned doctors, amber-eyed oldsters steeped in Talmudic marginalia.

The shammes informed the cop: "It could be Melnick is in there, but usual he tells me when he goes."

"Yeah," the officer said. "Usual."

"Dat's all we need," the fire chief muttered. "Otzenberger'll be on our back forever we lose one of dem beards."

A new expectation of disaster fluttered the crowd. The word spread through the ranks: Melnick was in the schul; if he wasn't out yet, he was surely dead, suffocated, boined opp.

"Well, if he was dumb enough to get caught there," Kalotkin pronounced, "he's deader than Kelsey's nuts."

"Boined to a crisp," Margulies added.

"Boy you two guys give me a pain in the neck," Albert cried. "You sound like you want him to die!"

"Shaddap, Four-eyes, I'll give ya a roost in the ass," the roofer grunted.

"A professional man's son," Margulies added cryptically. "What a disgrace."

274

A savage chant rose in the night air. Dark caryatids ensconced on P.S. 133, Lee Roy and his friends had learned that there was someone in the synagogue. Voices rich in Ibo and Yoruba accents wailed a witch doctor's curse.

"Dey burnin'! Dey burnin'! Yah, yah, yah!"

"Dey all sheeet, dey all gon' burn!"

"Roast dem good!"

"Burn hit up!"

The synagogue door was forced open. A hose was brought in. Smoke still poured from the basement window, but the fire appeared crushed. The second fireman came out and Albert could hear him conferring with the chief.

"He's there all right. Some old guy, out cold . . . when the wall went down, he got stuck. . . . I think he's breathin', but I couldn't budge him . . . jammed. . . ."

"Jesus, and I thought we'd git off clean."

". . . big fat guy . . . whiskers. . . ."

". . . breathin'?"

". . . think so. . . . I dunno . . . maybe he's gone. . . ."

". . . ambulance?"

"Yeah, we done it already . . . but you know, July . . . they're all out pickin' up boogies. . . ."

". . . better git a doctor. The old sheeny must have a doctor. . . ."

My father! Albert wanted to shout. What deterred him? Would his father unleash some unreasoning rage at being disturbed?

"There's a guy on Longview. Levine?"

"No!" Albert shouted. "He's my father! Dr. Abrams!"

The two cops and the fire chief looked at him with unemotional eyes. Lords of the earth!

"Well, g'wan get him, kid," the cop said. "Is it far?"

"No, I can run faster 'n' a car can get there." And he was off. As he pushed his way through the mob, he heard the fireman say: "I don't think no doctor is gonna help. He looked pretty cold."

"Maybe we oughta try to lug him out."

"I'll need help. He weighs a ton."

"Treat him careful. Might be some big Yiddish salami. Otzenberger'll be on our ass."

He was a Jack London sourdough, mushing his way across the Klondike with serum; Kit Carson on a dash through the Sioux lines; a Kipling subaltern on secret mission on the Northwest frontier. Never had he run so fast; his sneakers squished and squirted on the hot pavement. He raced past eager latecomers, faces shining with expectation, ready to be happy in someone else's death.

Al Abrams, the Phlying Phenomenon, the World's Fastest Human—Ben Eastman, Ralph Metcalf, Paavo Nurmi. Tenements, two-story homes, the rows of poplars and maples all rushed by him until he reached his father's great tree—harbor, landmark, canopy of beauty rising from the filth. He skidded like Pluto in the Mickey Mouse cartoons, stumbled, bounced up the steps.

Gasping, he plunged through the outer doorway, noting that the window light under the glass sign SOLOMON ABRAMS, M.D., was not on. In the foyer he jammed his finger into the buzzer. No answer. He did it again. There was a pause. Then the inner vestibule light went on. His mother opened the door.

"Oh, it's only you." She looked weary.

"Ma! They want Pop right away!"

"Your father is not feeling well. He's resting."

He flew by her. "There's a fire, Ma! Dincha hear the engines? It was in the capmaker's and then in the synagogue! Yussel Melnick's in there! They need a doctor!"

She followed him down the corridor. "Now don't go bothering your father, Albert." Nothing he had said appeared to have reached her.

He blundered into the consultation room. No lights burned, but a milky light reflected from the yard—moonlight, neighbors' lamps—suffused the room. "There was this fire, Pop . . . and they need a doctor. . . . Yussel . . . he's trapped. . . ."

Words crumpled in his throat. His father looked like the one who needed help. He was stretched out in the Morris chair, feet on the stool. An instinctive terror stopped him: his father looked dead.

"Pop?"

"Ah, how are you, kiddo?"

"Can I switch a light on?"

"Sure, sure." And crazily, the old man sounded happy, buoyant. *It is me, my miserable presence,* Albert told himself as he flicked on the homemade desk lamp. *One look at me and he is at peace with the world. If I asked him to take me to the movies right now, he would.*

The lemon walls were singularly hideous in the dim light—whorls and waves, foisted on his parents by some cunning painter, costing a lot more than flat paint or wallpaper. They were all born suckers, a family of suckers.

The hooded metabolism apparatus stood to one side of the chair where the doctor lay motionless. It had a sinister look—like a bad priest, an evil magician, casting a spell on his father. The old man's face was pale. It annoyed Albert that it looked soft, kind of mushy. All the hard lines, the strong forehead, the Indian nose, the sharp chin had gone melty. Worst of all, he was speaking in that high voice, the voice that Albert felt was not his.

"What about a fire, kiddo?"

"It started in Gotbetter's. . . . Look, Pop . . . we have to go right now. . . . I'll get your bag. . . ."

Dr. Abrams sat up—with great effort. His eyes flashed bright, angry. He was staring at Albert's bloodied shirt, the dried maroon clot under his nose. "What happened?" he said—his voice growing louder. "Who hit you? *I'll murder the bastards!*"

"It's nothing, nothing, Pop. . . ."

"Lousy ruffians!" shouted the doctor. "Dirty bullies! Scoundrels! I'll teach them a thing or two!" He lurched forward, inspecting his son's nose, seeking clues to the vile perpetrator. Mrs. Abrams padded in softly. "Sol, stop exerting yourself over nothing. Albert, let your father alone."

"Lice! Vermin! Picking on a kid like that!"

"Pop, please I'm okay! I'm OKAY!" he shouted at full throat. "I won a fight, for once. So what if I got a bloody nose? Pop, we got to go to the *schul!*"

"To hell with them all! Who did this? I'll find the bastards and make them suffer! You, Hannah, bringing him up like a mollycoddle so he can't fight a lick. Scum of the earth!"

"Sol! You were passing out a minute ago!"

"Someone else will pass out when I get my mitts on them! Who? *Schwarzers?*"

"Pop, once and for all, will you please stop worrying about *me?*" Albert cried. "I had enough! I'm trying to tell you somebody needs you. Melnick might be dead, and you're worried about some blood on my nose! *I won a fight!* Finally, at last, I won a fight, and you sit there staring at my nose like it's the only nose in the world." He grabbed his father's arm: *iron.* "Come on!"

"Albert! Your father is sick!"

Dr. Abrams got up; some kind of realization was dawning on him. "You won a fight? Who'd you knock the stuffin' out of? Some *tunkele?*"

"Bimbo. We had this fight. But nuts to that." He dragged his father across the room toward the office.

"Haddya like that, Hannah? The kid won a fight!"

"Is that so important? Where are you going?"

But he did not hear her. "You socked him good, hey kiddo?"

"Pop, I'll tell you later. But we got to go—honest—the cops, the firemen, they asked for you—"

"Don't let 'em crap you up, kiddo!" his father said. Thank goodness the crazy high notes had left his voice. "Fight back! Boxing lessons!"

"There'll be an ambulance there," Mrs. Abrams pleaded. "Some younger doctor—Moscowitz maybe. . . ."

"To hell with him also!" roared Dr. Abrams. "To hell with all of them! I'll show the lice a thing or two!"

What lice? wondered Albert. Show who what? Why? He picked up his father's scuffed black bag. The two of them walked through the office rooms. Mrs. Abrams called after him: "And a minute ago you were passing out! Threats . . . arousing my sympathy. . . ."

"That was a year ago!" Dr. Abrams shouted. "I'm fine, I'm fine!"

"You were not so fine before."

She followed them to the waiting room. The doctor paused at the door. "Listen, *ketzeleh*," he said, "I'm sorry, all that nonsense. A little bit of the crap-artist in me. After all, Melnick is my patient. I've kept the old bum alive this long—can't run out on him now!"

"But your own health—"

"Strong as an ox! Let's go, kiddo!"

At the window, she watched her husband and her son start down the dark street. "Be careful," she said.

He did not hear her. But she heard him—loud, confident, aroused. "I'll show those *kockers* a thing or two! Just let some young snot off an ambulance try to fool around with a patient of mine! So you really knocked the tar out of that redhead, hey kiddo?"

Curses, denunciations, testimonials to his own strength and knowledge fluttered behind him—like a child strewing petals. *Bastards* and *bitches* littered the air. Mrs. Abrams listened to his voice until it became indistinct, then settled slowly into one of the ancient waiting room chairs. Perhaps it was better this way; in any event, it was the only way they knew.

He paraded pridefully alongside his father. A salty breeze riffled the night air—a gift from Coney Island, the Rockaways. Oceans pounded around them and they never knew it. There was even a neighborhood called "Ocean Hill" nearby. Crazy, how you lived in dirt and cement and never knew how near the mystic sea was. But on a summer night like this, if you sniffed

279

hard enough, you smelled it. Some day if things got really bad, he would run off to sea like O'Neill or Conrad.

Smoke issued fitfully from the basement of the temple, from the open doors of the darkened building. Dr. Abrams and Albert made their way through the clotted mob.

"Ya too late, Doc," Kalotkin boomed. "I hoid 'em say he's gone."

Water sprayed backward from the *schul* and the capmaker's shop. The street was flooded; dampness settled over everyone.

"Lousy bastards," the doctor muttered. "Leave things worse than when they find it." A ricocheting stream of water left droplets on his face. "They all stink." Albert did not press him on the point. "Ruin everything they get their paws on."

Firemen with paws? Albert marveled at his father's irrelevancies. Dalmatians? Why should he be so sore at firemen?

The Raiders watched him in silent admiration. None of *their* fathers could come to the rescue. The white-haired cop walked toward Dr. Abrams. "Where ya goin', Mac?"

"Where the hell do you think?" the doctor asked. "To a fire?"

"Oh. Doctor. Took ya time, dincha? No fee, no call, hey Doc?"

"Yeh. I was busy bribing a dumb cop. Who's in charge?"

Startled, the ruddy face tried the flat smile. It didn't work with Dr. Abrams. "Smart guy. I think I had to straighten you out once before, right?"

"Don't try it again, McCooey. Stick to taking money under the table. Where's the chief?"

Dr. Abrams spoke swiftly and professionally with the fire chief. There were no words wasted, no insults traded. The older cop had inflamed him—red flag and bull—but the chief displayed a modicum of courtesy. He explained that part of a rotting wall between the buildings had tumbled on "the old geezer" in the basement room. Smoke poured in; he had fainted and had fallen between a worktable and a bolted door. Two firemen were inside now, hauling debris from him, trying to dislodge the swollen form of the teacher.

"Yeh, he's my patient. Runs the Hebrew school for the kids. It's a miracle if he's alive."

They walked toward the synagogue. Albert followed them. He was puzzled about a certain difference in the way his father and the others—firemen, cops—discussed old Melnick. It was not merely that the teacher was his father's patient, and that they did not know "the old geezer." It was—he searched for the subtle distinction—it was that his father was worried, concerned, troubled, and they, lords of creation, did not give a damn. They discussed Melnick's situation coldly; in their indifference there was a certain power.

"Let's go," the doctor said. "Can the kid come with me? He can give me a hand."

A young fireman on the doorstep shrugged. "Safe enough now."

Albert followed the doctor and the fireman up the steps. The fireman's lantern threw a wide cone of yellow light ahead of them. On the street, they heard the older cop warning an elder: "Git back when I tell ya, Moe. Doncha understand English?"

As they sloshed through the synagogue, the doctor delivered a homily. "Moe. Izzy. Ikey. That's a great career some people have. They all deserve a good punch in the snoot."

Jordan's waters lapped at their feet. Cascades rippled down the narrow stairs. Water from the rock. Parting of the Red Sea. They splashed their way through the smoke of battle—Joshua, Gideon, the Maccabees. The doctor had come abreast of the fireman.

"Ain't you Dr. Abrams?" He had a wide pale face, blond hair.

"That's me, sonny boy."

"Doncha know me? Tellefsen family on Bushwick Avenue. You delivered my kid sister."

"Oh sure. Your father is a carpenter."

"He was. Sold the shop, like everyone else. He works for the city now, like me."

"Give him my regards. Nice old guy."

Albert, trailing them in the smoky gloom, was impressed

with the way the essential stink of the synagogue asserted itself above the choking pall. It was an unmistakable odor, layer upon layer of aromas, old men's sweat, snuff, moth-balled clothing, worm-eaten books, disinfectant, smoothly rubbed benches, a musty venerable stink. The odor of sanctity? It intrigued him that neither fire nor flood could prevail over that ancient mélange, that century-old perfume.

Above them loomed the ark of the covenant, crowned with the two mystical hands, thumbs and index fingers touching. Below, in the locked and curtained cabinet, the scrolls slept.

"Funny," Dr. Abrams said. "I was here this afternoon, when the old *kocker* made me march in his parade. What a sport. I haven't been in a *schul* for years, and now I go twice in one day."

"Down here, Doc."

They followed the fireman down a narrow staircase, through a low-roofed corridor. Albert knew it well. It led to Melnick's room. A second lantern illuminated the teacher's workshop. They could hear firemen talking.

"Jesus, he's fat. Like a whale."

"I can't budge him. Stuck right in there."

"He sure looks dead."

Dr. Abrams followed Tellefsen's beam of light across the flooded threshold. Albert paused; this was about as close as he wanted to get. The room was narrow. Most of the space was occupied by a long worktable. It was covered with an ancient stained canvas, rising and drooping over whatever secrets old Melnick stored under it. There was a ramshackle bookcase, a chair—and that was all. On the side of the room next to the capmaker's shop, a huge section of wall had collapsed. Ancient bricks, powdery chunks of plaster, rotten lathing, had tumbled on the teacher—the walls of Jericho felled by the mighty axes of the City of New York.

The firemen were squatting alongside Melnick, tossing chunks of plaster and bricks from his body. A great beached whale, the *melamed*, chalked with white plaster, lay motionless. *And I only am escaped alone to tell thee.* No, he wasn't Moby

Dick. He was more Ahab. A Jewish Ahab. Hmm. But wasn't Ahab Jewish to begin with? A bad king? When the lantern came closer, Albert was terrified by the sight of the teacher's beard. It had wilted. Once it had been wiry, sprouting, an iron-gray bush. Now, in smoke and water, it lay flat on his drowned face. And under the buttoned caftan his great belly was still.

Tellefsen and the doctor knelt beside the other firemen. In helmets, rubber cloaks, they looked like Macbeth's weird sisters. Visitors from somewhere else. He was glad to hear the ringing Brooklyn nasalities of one of the firemen. Nobody who talked like that could be an other-worldly creature.

"Ain't budged since we been here, Doc. I tried artificial resp'ration, but he don't come to."

Stethoscope in ears, Dr. Abrams knelt in the water. He unbuttoned Melnick's ghetto coat, ripped open his shirt, the holy *tsitsis*. He found the ancient flesh, placed the stethoscope against it, listened for the thump of life. "Nah, not a chance. But we'll try. Who knows. If we can't work a miracle here, we can't anywhere. Gimme some light, sonny boy."

Yellow beams flooded the teacher's parchment face. "Blue," the doctor said curtly. "Suffocation. His lungs were no bargain anyway. And not much of a heart left. So he had to go walk in a parade, and then come do his homework in this dump. Well, he lived a long time. Let's get him on his stomach."

Gently, they rolled the huge flaccid figure. The doctor turned Melnick's head, placed it in the crook of a folded left arm. "A lost cause," he said. "But we'll try it." With strong, slow strokes he began pressing his hands against Melnick's sides. He straddled him—like a jockey on a Percheron. He worked slowly, rhythmically, like the former playground instructor that he was, worked with the authority of a gym teacher giving a high school class a first aid lesson. Every now and then he stopped and put his ear to the teacher's mouth.

My father, my father. My old man. Let them gossip about him, and tell stories, and say he's crazy, and call him names, and run to the specialists and the clinics and the chiropractors. He is

283

my father and he can save somebody's life, or at least he can try. . . .

A rush of pride and love swept over Albert. He wanted to embrace his father, cheer for him, help him, but he understood the rules: the matter at hand involved only Melnick and the old man—and death. So it had been a hundred times, and would be a hundred times more. *No wonder he's so unhappy all the time. . . .*

"He's through," Dr. Abrams said. "Not a chance in the shape he was in. Even a younger man . . ."

"Your patient?" Tellefsen asked.

"Yeah. One of the old-timers. Vanishing American. A real sport."

"Them old boys with the beards," Tellefsen persisted. "They all rabbis?"

"Nah. It's kind of a club. The House of David, you know."

Dr. Abrams dismounted from the teacher's body. His trousers were drenched. "What I can't figure out is, what was he doing here all by himself in the middle of the night, with the door locked?"

"It was his workroom, Pop," Albert said. "He was always down here. Nobody could get in."

The doctor mopped his forehead. "Nobody except the Angel. He couldn't keep him out."

"That stuff on the table," Albert said. "That's what he was making. The guys peeked through the keyhole one day and sneaked a look."

The firemen turned their lanterns on the long canvas-shrouded table. At one end of the surface, where the stained covering ended, there was a clutter of tools—calipers, rulers, protractors, small hammers and files, a tiny saw, brushes, pots of paint. They had a foreign look—ancient artifacts that Melnick had brought from Europe years ago. The tools were clumsy, crusty, purchased at the turn of the century in Vilna or Lodz or Kishinev, or wherever the teacher had come from.

The doctor picked up an earthen pot and sniffed it. "Oil paints," he said. "Smells like he was using it recently."

284

"Let's look at it," Tellefsen said.

"Yeh, no secrets anymore," said the doctor.

Tellefsen held the lantern high. The others peeled back the tarpaulin.

Under the wide yellow light, a magic city appeared before them, an ancient town in miniature, in perfect proportions. It dazzled them, silenced them. They stood like Pizarro and his men above Cuzco, transfixed, marveling. It was fantastic—towers, walls, battlements, streets, a palace, spires, blocks of ordinary homes, shops, water wells, stables, courtyards. Everything had been lovingly carved, painted, decorated. There were even tiny trees—palms, cedars—cunningly fashioned of wire and bits of colored cloth.

"That old guy made this?" Tellefsen asked incredulously. "What was he—in the toy business?"

The doctor studied the miniature city below them. "That's no toy, sonny."

All stood around the long table—silent, in tribute to the ancient. "Man, that's some woikmanship," the other fireman said. "The guy was an artist. Lookit the way them doors are carved."

"Yeah," Tellefsen said. "And the decorations. He even got the bricks on the buildings. And the Joosh star."

Above the main gate to the city, a Star of David, perfectly carved, nested in the archway. Columns on either side were meticulously fluted, each capital exquisitely turned.

"He was in here all the time, Pop," Albert said. "When he wasn't teaching. I bet we're the first ones ever saw it."

The doctor walked around the table. He appreciated craftsmanship. "A lifetime, a lifetime of work," he said. "Who ever thought that old *kocker* could even hold a screwdriver or a paintbrush?" He inspected the row of pots. "I figured he spent his life rummaging around books—and look what he did."

At the rear of the room was a canted bookshelf. The firemen had opened some of Melnick's volumes—yellowed, flaking works.

"Hey, look—they got diagrams in them. Like architects'

drawings. Ain't that somethin'?" He shook his head, confounded by the mysteries of those strange Hebrews. Once again the lantern turned on the magical city below. It was noon in the desert. The streets seemed to live; the trees bloomed; Sadducees and Pharisees strolled in loose robes. Kenabites, Rechanites, Essenes, Midianites and Nabateans.

There were voices outside, footsteps sloshing through the water. Another fireman appeared in the doorway, followed by an intern carrying a pulmotor.

Tellefsen looked up from the table. "Too late, Charlie. The guy packed in."

"Ah, tough. What's that on the table?"

The intern walked to Melnick's dead form, knelt over him.

"Take my word, sonny, he's through," Dr. Abrams said. "He's been dead a long time. But he lived a long time also."

"Holy smoke, what a job," the new fireman said admiringly, as he walked around the city. "Looks like Macy's window at Christmas. Look at them houses. And trees."

The intern listened for Melnick's heart, felt his wrist, got no response and shook his head. "Might as well wrap him."

A rubber sheet was brought in. The firemen began to wrap the teacher's sodden form in it.

"This here thing," Tellefsen said to the doctor. "What's it supposed to be? I mean it must be worth a fortune. All that stuff is hand-carved."

"Something out of the Bible," the doctor said.

Albert circled the long table. Beneath a clutter of rusty tools he found a sheaf of drawings. Faded, barely discernible, they were part of the plans from which Melnick had built his scale city. He squinted at the Hebrew letters. "It's Jerusalem," he said triumphantly. "Look, Pop—it says so right here."

Dr. Abrams adjusted his glasses and peered at the diagram.

"Y'rushaloyim," he read. "Yeh, that's it all right. Building Jerusalem in a dirty basement in Brownsville."

Rubber slapped on rubber as they tightened the shroud around Melnick. "He weighs a ton," one of the firemen grunted. "Easy, Charlie, watch it when you git up. The floor's flooded. Don't strain yer milk."

"The doorway, the doorway, Eddie, step over it. *Step.*"

In the strong arms of two loyal *goyim*, Melnick, enrubbered, was carried out of his Jerusalem. His secret had been revealed. The treasure had been seen by the barbarian, the egregious Gentile (and two of his own faith). Albert and his father could hear the firemen laboring, groaning, as they bore the teacher's body up the stairs.

"He got it from these books," Albert said. He had taken a stack of them from the shelf. At his touch, little clouds of dust had risen, flakes of crumbled dried leather and paper tumbled. "He must have been collecting them all his life—they're ancient."

An odor of centuries rose from the venerable books—strong enough to be detected through the sickening smoke. The books smelled of dark rooms in a Polish ghetto, of snuff, decay, knowledge, sweet wine, sweat, mystery, and old Melnick's whiskers. Albert set them on the edge of the table—opposite the main gate to the city. A caravan of undulating camels could have walked through any minute. Frankincense and myrrh? They turned the pages—tiny Hebrew lettering, ancient drawings, occult symbols, an architectural mishmash, spiced with misinformation and wrong guesses, from some Melnick in Jerusalem, to the Melnicks of the Diaspora, to a Melnick in Poland to the late eccentric teacher, several thousand years in passage, information sold, bartered, donated, from bearded sage to furry *tzadik*, in forgotten villages, precarious *shtetls*, books miraculously preserved amid fire, pogrom, flood, famine, the bad tempers and hard fists of the Gentile, denounced as Satan's work by clerics, yet read and remembered. Peeling, wormy, crumbling books from which old Melnick had summoned up his vision of Jerusalem.

"So that's how he spent his spare time," Dr. Abrams said sadly. "Well, it kept him out of the poolroom."

They walked around the long table. Alabaster towers, high gates, carved doorways gleamed under the lantern. "The old guy was no amateur. Those soft hands—who'd guess they could handle tools like this."

Above them the floor creaked, swayed. Booted firemen struggled with the sodden corpse of the late builder of new Jerusalem. The dead weight resisted them. Who would build God's City with the teacher gone?

"One of the giants before the flood," Albert's father said. Water dripped from the ceiling, pinging off the city walls. "But the flood caught up with him, I suppose."

"I found a book in English, Pop." Albert opened a coverless volume. From the creased title page, he read: "*The Ancient City of God, Being a Treatise on the Old City of Jerusalem; Walls, Fortifications, Gates and Other Features in the Time of Solomon,* by Hartley Croft, D.D., J.S.D., Professor of Hebrew Rhetoric, Cowell College, Salisbury."

"Why, the son-of-a-gun," said the doctor. "And I thought he couldn't read English. It took him long enough to figure out my bills."

Tellefsen was inspecting the gouge in the basement wall: the fortress breached, the place where the Roman soldiers had broken through to sack the sanctuary. "Have to board this up and keep the boogies out. They'll rob every one of them models." He paused again to admire Melnick's Jerusalem. "Longer you look at it, the better it looks. I guess it was kind of a hobby, hey, Doc?"

"Yeh. These old guys are real hell-raisers. If he hadn't been working on this, he'd have been running after Clara Bow or sticking up grocery stores."

"Ya kiddin' me, Doc."

"It's the truth. Back in the old country, he was two-gun Yussel, the Terror of Glebocki."

"He's fooling you, Mr. Tellefsen," Albert said, with some annoyance. "Pop, you push your jokes too far."

"Ah, I don't believe yer old man anyway," the Viking said. "He's a great kidder." Everygoy himself, he raised his lantern and led them up the stairs into the smoky temple. Dr. Abrams scowled, muttered a few irrelevant "lice" and "scums of the earth"—to whom? At whose malign head was he hurling his thunderbolts? Albert wondered. At the whole world? At the world that had assigned Yussel Melnick to a sordid old age, squinting at his miniature Jerusalem far into the night, after hours of beating Hebrew into resisting young skulls more concerned with Tony Cuccinello? But Melnick hadn't been *that* unhappy, or *that* frustrated. He hoped his father understood.

They stepped down the synagogue steps into the flooded street. It was like a steamy outdoor stage. The crowd murmured and shifted. They were almost sated: Melnick's rubbered corpse had filled them with what they really wanted: somebody else's troubles.

The mob gaped at them. Albert's friends pressed around him.

"Didja see him dead?" asked Bushy.

"Was his eyes open?"

"Did he make any noise?"

"Was he boined?"

Eyewitness to recent history, he answered their questions freely and fully. *Richard Harding Abrams.* As he did, his father spoke to the fire chief and the cops. They listened to him for once; no backtalk, no wisecracks. Albert had a desire to see his father forever chasing fires, forever saving people in burning buildings, working alongside police and firemen instead of waiting in his office for patients who never came, for bills to be paid.

"Artificial respiration, but it was too late," Albert told the Raiders. "He suffocated. You should see what he had in there. Artie, remember when he socked you for peekin' in? He's got this long table, and under a canvas, he's got a whole miniature city. It's Jerusalem—little models—better than any of us could carve. He must have been working on it all his life."

"Doc, thanks for givin' us a hand," Albert heard the fire chief say.

"Any time, Feeney."

Feeney! How appropriate a name, Albert thought. And

289

how reassuring that his father knew the chief's name and could address him familiarly! His old man was part of the world, an important functioning part—not a semi-invalid collapsed on a Morris chair in a dark room, moaning with self-pity. So what if he couldn't find the hospital that afternoon? Who cared? Old Melnick was dead. But his father, no two ways about it, was alive. He and Feeney. A couple of the boys. *There is my real father—that's my Pop*—Albert thought. *He is strong, capable, tough, tougher than any cop or fireman. He does not lie gasping in a chair wondering why he cannot find his way.*

The crowd wandered off. The hoses stopped. A party of elders led by "Captain" Feigenbaum were permitted to enter the synagogue. Certain strict procedures had to be followed to cleanse the temple after the death. Old Gotbetter, weeping lost tears, crying out his misery to an unhearing world, was led away by a neighbor. What would happen to him? Was there no justice? A hard place, the world. A bad business, the Depression. He was ashamed of his own elation, of his father's renewed strength.

"G'night, Albert, see ya tomorra." Teddy Ochab skipped off—inviolate, heroic.

Bushy, the two Arties, Bimbo, meandered away. Little Artie had leaped into the schoolyard. He raced swiftly along the wall, jeering at Lee Roy and Madison. They would never catch him.

Like a nighttime spirit, the monkey-face buzzed by the gargoyles. "Eight-ball, eight-ball!" Little Artie hollered. The colored boys followed his fleet figure with glazed eyes. "Who dat?" asked Madison. "Jes' some sheeet. We git him," responded Lee Roy. And Albert told himself: *No, not him. Not Little Artie. That is also the way of the world. Some never get caught. Some get caught. Like me. But not always. I can win, too.* Against his wishes, he found he was feeling sorry for Lee Roy and Madison. Sorry! They had degraded, abused, mortified and threatened him—held a knife under his throat, bloodied his nose, made him the butt of their voodoo games. But now seeing them isolated on their perches, silhouetted against the sky, he was sorry. *Dope*, he said to himself, *don't be sorry*. But he was terribly sorry for them, sorry that they could not do their arithmetic homework. Misplaced Watusi, poor Masai herdsmen not meant for classrooms, they were objects of his pity, not his scorn. He recalled Lee Roy's pitiful trimmed pants, the ragged suspenders against his black chest, the mystic tufts on Madison's head. *Lee Roy, I saw you weeping one day in fourth grade, hiding your head behind your "joggerfy" book.*

It was a good thing, Albert thought, as he and his father made their way through the thinning crowd, that Mockey did not understand his murderous declamation against the colored boys. He withdrew it, every word of it. The problem was, how to get across to them that he didn't really hate them, and therefore, they had no reason to hate him. Fair? Of course. But how could he make that clear to those dark spirits?

The hook and ladder clanged past them in the night. The doctor and his son turned on to Longview Avenue. Tellefsen waved to Dr. Abrams.

"Nice fellah, that Swede. They paid their bills. I was wondering why they hadn't called me in so long. The old man went broke. Bastard Depression took some of my best patients away." But he added: "I still have an enormous practice."

He doesn't, Albert said silently. *But what's the difference if he wants to think he has?*

Summer filth glowed in the yellow light—egg crates, cantaloupe rinds, puddles of pee. The detritus of a great battle. All day long, the war had raged up and down Longview Avenue. *Myself among them.* Metallic clanking reverberated in back of them. Albert turned and saw Mockey. Like a mongrel stray, he followed.

"Who's that?" Dr. Abrams asked. "What a cueball!"

"That's a new kid. He can't speak any English, not a word."

Mockey drew abreast of them. He smiled shyly at the doctor.

"He'll learn 'em soon enough," the doctor said. "All the

291

dirty words and maybe a few dirty tricks. He'll be one of us all right. *Vus machts du, boychick?*"

The smile distorted Mockey's gleaming face. "*Dein zin, Al-bare?*"

"*Yeh, yeh, mein zin.*"

"*Mein freund. Mein bucher.*"

"You got a friend," the doctor said.

"He's becoming my shadow."

"Well, don't be mean to him. He looks like a harmless *shlemiel.*"

They walked in silence for a while, father, son, baldhead. Then Dr. Abrams started to reminisce. "You know when I got sore at the cop before, there was something else bothering me," he said slowly. "It was the hoses."

"Hoses?"

"Yeah. When I saw them *shpritzing,* I began to think of something I hadn't thought about for years. I wasn't mad at that dumb cop, I was mad about something I saw when I was a kid on the East Side—a little greenhorn like your friend here."

"Ah come on, Pop—that far back? And you're still sore?"

"The *schul,* and the cop, I could see it plain as day. There was this old guy on the East Side who died, chief rabbi, Hymowitz. Boy, was he holy! He was so religious you could hardly hear him talk. They used to come to touch his *kaputa,* to ask him about everything from childbirth to the stock market. Anyway, he died, and the Jews had this big funeral for him. He was a Galitzianer, but he never did anyone any harm. Even the Litvaks and the Romanians came out for the funeral.

"Well, there was a procession—thousands of greenhorns praying and crying and singing—the old guys in the beaver hats—the *bubbas* in the handkerchiefs—and a mob of kids—and we started down East Broadway. Hot as hell. July or August. A bunch of old guys from Hymowitz' home town were carrying the coffin. Lots of hollering. Did they pray up a storm! So they got on to East Broadway and started to walk past the Malone Pipe and Valve Works. It was a weekday afternoon. The factory was full of tough *goyim*—I mean *tough*—boilermakers, hod carriers. You know what those bastards did? *They turned the factory hoses on the parade!* Big joke! Hah-hah! Right out the windows, as if they were pissing on the funeral, the hoses going full force on the old people, the rabbis, the kids, the women, and all over the coffin! Did you ever hear of cussed meanness like that? I can still see those red-faced *loysers* laughing at us! *Sheeny! Kike! Mockey!*"

The new boy looked up, intrigued at the sound of his nickname, fascinated by the doctor's narrative.

"Not you, Label," Albert said.

"Those hoses really hurt when they hit. People were knocked down, sloshing around in the gutter. They dropped the coffin. It was a miracle it didn't smash open. All the old guys got soaked, they couldn't run. Some big laugh—all those wet Jews. That's what I got so sore about before—the hoses—they got me thinking about Hymowitz' funeral. Hadn't thought about it for years."

"They got away with it?" Albert asked. "Couldn't you do anything? Couldn't you tell the cops?"

"The cops! *Hah!*" Dr. Abrams cawed. "Those old *yiddlich* were afraid of their shadow! Fat chance they'd have telling the police that the bastards at Malone's *shpritzed* them! They'd spit in our eyes! Oh, they would have sure helped us. But we took care of those *paskudnyaks* in our own sweet way!"

His father's voice was loud and triumphant. Memories of an old victory stirred him.

"The next day all of the kids in the neighborhood got together. We made slingshots. From our suspenders. Those old elastics, they made good slingshots. But even a rubber band would do or a garter. Then we filled our pockets with stones, stuffed them in our shirts, under our yarmulkes. In the afternoon we gathered on East Broadway outside the Malone factory. All the bastards were inside working, probably telling jokes about the way they soaked the *Yiddlich*. We lined up, like artillery. Then we let 'em have it! Did we give it to them! We fired on signal, reloaded, fired! And we busted every lousy window in the place! I bet we hit a lot of those galoots with the stones and the broken glass. I was never sorry a minute. Then we ran like hell—they never caught one of us. We could hear those lice yelling inside! It served 'em right!"

"It sure did."

"The old guys didn't want us to do it. They sat around mumbling that we'd all get punished—but nothing ever happened. What were we supposed to do? Stand around crying for God to help us? God is okay, sonny boy, but you got to handle some things by yourself. This was America, and you had to stand up on your hind legs or get killed."

Mockey stared at Albert's father in awe. Here and there he had caught a Yiddish word, but the burden of the story had been lost on him. However, Dr. Abrams' dramatic rendering of the adventure at Malone's had fascinated him. He had grasped the notion that his friend's father was intelligent, brave, forceful, and possibly rich. He was a man of rank and authority who ran into burning buildings to save people.

"Can't go through life being afraid of your shadow," Dr. Abrams said. "Like Baldy here. He'll learn. Give him a few months, he'll learn."

As I have learned, Albert thought.

"You get your lumps now and then, but it's better than ki-ying like a kiyoodle with your tail between your legs." The doctor nodded, with evident satisfaction. "Boy, I'd like a chance to punch Hitler in the nose. Why do all those other lice keep having meetings with him? Don't they understand what he really is?"

Mockey started to cross the street. He looked appealingly at Albert. "*Morgen? Kenst shpielen?*"

"Sure, *morgen,*" Albert said.

"Get a load of him," the doctor said. "Clothes by Rogers Peet. Don't ever be mean to him."

"I'm not." Albert giggled. "But he sure is a dopey green-horn." He laughed as Mockey darted into his tenement. *If I have had a day of marvels, what of him? What miracles have shivered his thick hide, what wonders have penetrated his hard hairless pate?*

294

At Lieberson's candy store, the doctor stopped. "We'll surprise Mama. Mel-o-rols and ginger ale." His father entered the store, Albert lolled against the wooden news stand. The first editions of the *Daily News* were neatly rolled inside the slot.

IT'S STILL HOT;
NO RELIEF DUE
Three More Die at Coney

He hoped his mother would react favorably to the ice cream and soda. You could never tell with her. She was unpredictable where the doctor's surprises were concerned—as if she begrudged him little acts of generosity. It seemed to him that what she really wanted was for him to stop cursing and spuming and moaning all the time, not to bring her gifts, that the gifts were to her mind substitutes for a more tranquil life. Once his father had surprised her by buying a radio for the car. It was one of the first models, a pentagonal black box, bolted to the steering wheel and trailing wires into the guts of the Chandler. Albert had giggled when he had seen it. He and his father winked at one another: *conspirators*. They were on the way to Brighton Beach on a call. Slyly the old man had turned it on. Music drifted to the back of the auto where his mother sat coolly. Then she heard the jazz band.

"Oh, you did what I told you not to," she pouted. "Sol, you know I regard a car radio as a menace to safe driving. Why did you go ahead and buy it?"

"Ah Christ," his father had mumbled and switched it off. For months they refrained from playing it when she was in the car. But the two of them alone—Albert and his father—kept it humming stringily all the time. Albert had even heard the Rose Bowl Game on New Year's Day on it—feeling the joy course through his veins when Al Barabas had sneaked over with the ball and Columbia beat Stanford, 7–0. It ranked among the greater thrills of his life. A snowy cold evening, riding on a call with his father to East Flatbush and hearing the excited account of the New Yorkers' famous victory. It was sunny and warm in Pasadena, and cold and dark in Brooklyn on New Year's Day, but he had been part of it. He would never forget.

As his father chatted in the candy store with Mr. Lieberson (once he had been his patient, had argued, left him, come back), Albert relaxed in the warm night. His body ached pleasantly, but his mind was clear and concentrated. A giant's capacity for absorbing the entire block, all the people on it, all events, all future possibilities, bloomed in him. Across the street he saw Genius Grubman peering into his books, burning in the night. Grubman was part of him. Grubman might die but he, Albert Abrams, would never, never forget that mighty brain, floating about on inflated knickerbockers, quoting verse and equations. "Listen, God," Albert said softly. "It's essential that Genius not die. He has to live. He must learn everything he wants to learn and become rich and famous." He had an urge to shout across the street to Grubman to take heart, to be brave, to be assured that the predictions of his imminent death were false rumors.

Beneath the Genius' window on an up-ended milk crate sat Gorilla. Gorilla was eating an orange. His prehensile teeth picked the seeds out daintily and spat them on the sidewalk. He ate exactly the way the big chimpanzee in the Prospect Park Zoo ate—with long incisors nipping the pits, red tongue and curling lips ejecting them. Poor stupid Gorilla! But he was part of it also; he had to be understood, fitted into some general plan. The tweed cap, rakish as ever (was it not one of Gotbetter's?), was yanked to the side of Gorilla's rattling dome. As he sat outside Genius' window his head tilted backward, his eyes on the heavens, he recited:

"I see da foist star,
Da foist star sees me,
God bless da foist star,
God bless me."

"Hey, Gorilla," Albert called. "That can't be the first star. The first star was out a long time ago."

"Oh yeah? Well it's deh foist one I seen tanight."

Unassailable logic; Gorilla had him there. Someday he would have to take Gorilla aside and confess to him that it was he who had shoved him into the mud puddle on the first day of school. Someday, but not now. That sin would have to be expiated; he knew Gorilla would forgive him. It took very little to make Gorilla's day joyful; only that morning a roasting dead dog had delighted him.

"Let's go, kiddo," Dr. Abrams said. "We'll make great big ice cream sodas."

They walked by an admiring Fleishacker, who called to the doctor: "Too bad about the *melamed*, hey, Doc? I hear he got boined to death."

"If you're going to feel sorry for him, get it right," the doctor said. "He was suffocated."

"What a lousy shame." *Confidant of gangsters, stooge of the killer Zetzkin, where were you that afternoon when my friends were victimized and I was humiliated?*

"I bet he knows," Albert whispered.

"Knows what?"

"That his pal Mutty started the fire in Gotbetter's store." He hurled a silent curse on Fleishacker's head.

When they reached their home, the doctor made his final sanitary tour of the sidewalk. It was a dance, quadrille, gavotte or schottische, the way he stepped smartly around the plot of cement, kicking off a tuna fish can, scooping a dog turd with a cardboard, flicking at fallen leaves. When he had skimmed the surface trash, he stepped back and admired his tree. It never failed to cheer him up.

For Albert this was his last look at the street—*his* street— before bed. It was dreadful—yet he loved it. He loved it simply because it was there, there to torture him, challenge him, embarrass him, entertain him, arouse him, offer him the hot meat of life. Dirty, crowded, noisy, the horrid arena where he would always be Four-eyes, Sister Mary, The Doctor's Son, he loved it nonetheless. How could he not love it? It was to him as the Congo had been to Paul DuChaillu, that intrepid hunter of the highland gorilla. It was to him what the Grand Canyon had been to Zane Grey, roper of mountain lions. It seethed, bubbled, stank and rumbled, but it was his, and he was part of it, and he was duty-bound to accept it, learn from it, and be able to handle the trolls and giants and dragons—Bushy, Zetz, Lee Roy—and understand Daisy and Cowboy and Gorilla, and honor the noble Teddy and the brilliant Genius.

Mrs. Abrams was waiting for them in the kitchen, reading the *Ladies' Home Journal*. The doctor made a solemn presentation of the brown paper sacks. "Ice cream sodas, please," he ordered. "The kid and I earned them. In that *schul*. Melnick is dead, but there wasn't a thing we could do."

He told her about the fire, the arguments with the cop (were they any different from lousy nurses?), the death of the teacher, the discovery of Melnick's Jerusalem.

"Incredible!" she said.

Unwinding Mel-o-rols from their circular wrappers, pouring foaming ginger ale over them, she was wonderfully calm. So she didn't let him roller-skate or ride a bike (he would have to overcome *that* particular prejudice, and very soon). But what woman in the world could reduce Melnick's death to the level of a complaint over a rotten tangerine sold by a pushcart peddler? Life's greatest sorrows (and who knew how deeply she felt them) could always be distilled to a frown, a lateral movement of her head, a pursed lip, a cautious comment. *Perhaps I am a little bit like her. It explains my resiliency. I bounce back. After many a defeat, I come up scrapping.* An improvement, perhaps, over the doctor's eternal rages. He was doubly blessed! He had in his genes the best of both! If only he owned the old man's mighty biceps, his enormous pronators and supinators, the leathery deltoids! In time, in time. Barbells, setting-up exercises, boxing lessons. Nothing could stop him. He would be a young Doc Savage—brain and brawn in one pocket-sized figure.

In chemical fury the ginger ale bubbled into a creamy crown. It was not a bad life after all. It was better than lying drunk in the street like Cowboy, or running around barefoot like Lee Roy, although Lee Roy's life had enviable aspects. But there was little doubt that the ball was taking favorable bounces. He was fielding his position like Travis Jackson. His triumph over Bimbo was perhaps the first of a long series. The start of a winning streak. Someday he would bulge with muscles and be gifted with speed. He would challenge Lee Roy. He would bloody Lee Roy's nose, make him cry Uncle, and then reason with him. Through books and kind treatment he would guide Lee Roy to a better life. Dr. Livingston Abrams, he would lead safaris into darkest Brownsville, carrying enlightenment and seeds to the impoverished Bantu.

They retired to the consultation room with their ice cream sodas. Albert switched on the desk lamp and turned off the glaring overhead chandelier. Subdued lighting was indicated, a pastoral mood. The room glowed warmly. Even the noxious yellow swirls on the walls looked cheerful. From mahogany frames, Freud, Maimonides and assorted Gentile professors stared down at them. He took his first sip of the soda. It was a taste of heaven—nectar, mead, aged brandy.

With a flick Dr. Abrams turned on his desk radio. From somewhere in Westchester County, up there in a land of lawns and Tudor houses, oak trees and shaded drives, a band played a soupy waltz. Up there in upper middle class America, something they could all aspire to, well-dressed couples glided effortlessly over varnished floors in the soft July night. Serenade of syrupy saxophones and liquid clarinets! Lullaby of non-Depression people! Japanese lanterns cast romantic tints on Norway maples and red oaks—on a greensward untainted with sardine tins. Someday his father would have such a lawn, such trees, a place free of filth and noise.

His parents talked softly of what had happened, of Melnick's death—had he a family to notify? Anyone in the world? They discussed Mutty Zetzkin—his parents were nice people, Mrs. Abrams said, forever salvaging virtue.

The dance music ended with a *bump-bump-de-bump*. On came the announcer reading consoling news bulletins:

"President Roosevelt is resting tonight in San Juan after a triumphant tour of Puerto Rico . . . all day long huge crowds cheered the President. . . . police were unable to hold back the enthusiastic but orderly crowds in Mayaguez who . . .

". . . a sixty-two million dollar deficit in the state and Governor Lehman says new taxes are likely . . . special session of the legislature will hear the governor's appeal for . . ."

Albert adored newscasts. They were the best things on radio. They told you bits and pieces about the real world. Then you could go to a newspaper or a magazine and devour all the other information. How had people lived before there were newscasts?

"British Prime Minister Stanley Baldwin told Commons today that the forthcoming visit of French Foreign Minister Louis Barthou . . . military link . . . denied Liberal and Socialist charges that such an alliance was . . ."

". . . a new move by Chancellor Hitler to reduce the power of the storm troops after last week's massacre of dissident members of the uniformed organization . . . purged soon by Herr Hitler to enable him to carry out . . ."

It wasn't just Mutty and Bushy and Zetz and Lee Roy to be afraid of. There was a vast world outside filled with terror, terrible people. But you did the best you could. You tried to understand; you prepared; you resisted; you survived. The way Melnick had survived.

"Yeah," his father was saying quietly, "if he could live, so could I."

If he could live, so could I. He meant Melnick. Not everyone could build Jerusalem, but life could be lived bravely and honestly. (It did no harm to have muscles and know when to kick someone in the crotch.)

Albert sucked the last of the soda. The dregs were as soul-satisfying as the first sip. The shlurping noise drew a reproving glance from his mother and his father's smiled comment: "It tastes better when he does that." He walked out of the office into the warm kitchen, through the screen door into the backyard. A sweetness charged the night air, hundreds of the old man's flowers ejecting perfume into the miasma. He saw his father in faded overalls, black hair wispy in the breeze, raking

300

amid dahlias and peonies. His father raked and hoed the way he took somebody's pulse, eyes solemn, shoulders hunched.

Beneath the pleached trees Albert sank to the slatted bench. How he would sleep tonight! He ached everywhere. Pains darted and leaped in every fiber, every ligament. Muscles moaned; tendons trembled. But he loved each tremor. For tomorrow it would begin once more—more terror, more adventure, perhaps more triumph. But nothing was beyond him; everything could be handled. As he had managed Bimbo. As Teddy had confronted Lee Roy. As his father had faced up to the cop, and then looked death in the face. As Melnick had built Jerusalem. Suddenly he was furious with those English Socialists and Liberals the man had been talking about on radio, those Englishmen who were worried about an alliance with France *against* Hitler. *Didn't they really understand what Hitler was and what he was going to do?* Holy smoke, he was twelve years old, and he understood *exactly* what Hitler was up to! All you had to do was look at those uniforms and read what he said, and you'd know that he meant to kill everyone he could lay his hands on! He could tell them a few things. So could his father. Hitler was no ordinary politician whom you made treaties with and exchanged diplomats and signed papers. And why be so polite and call him "Herr Hitler"? If *he* could figure that out, why couldn't they?

Around him window lights blazed, flickered, dimmed. In each window was one more mystery, a dream, a nightmare, a hope. Maybe not as awesome as Melnick's, but a story worth knowing. Grubman, for example. Or Mockey.

"It is past your bedtime, Albert."

Not *it is time to go to bed,* but *it is past your bedtime.* *That's right, phrase it so that I am guilty, delinquent.* He forgave her. Shoulders braced, head erect, he limped down the garden path. House, garden, office, parents, street—all his. Old Jack London, back from a run on a South Sea pearl lugger. Wounded, sun-seared, cursed, his name whispered, left for dead on nameless beaches, half-drowned in a lost lagoon, he had come back.

They had stayed but a short time on Longview Avenue. Now through dark streets Abrams and his children walked to the subway. The visit had not been a success. His daughter kept whining that she had really wanted to go to Chinatown. He had to stop in a dusty candy store and buy them Life Savers.

It was colder. Slouching Negroes, their tropic blood jelled by December's wind, passed them noiselessly, insulated in shapeless overcoats and Army surplus hats.

"Those boys you used to play with, Daddy?" asked his daughter. "Do you ever see them?"

"Not any more."

The war had dispersed his friends. Before that he had gone off to college. After the war the old residents began to leave Brownsville (how ironic that his father, deemed the block's "rich man," lingered in the slum the longest and died there). Teddy Ochab was killed in the Pacific. Fearless Polack, he had leaped on a tank on Saipan, dropped a grenade down the hatch and was blown apart by machine gun fire. Abrams recalled attending a Mass in St. Stanislaus' Church for Pfc. Thadeusz Ochab. He had no idea what had become of his swift brothers. Or Bushy. Or the two Arties. Now and then he saw the name B. J. Wexler in the real estate pages—a successful builder of split-level homes in Nassau County. Bimbo? He hoped so. He hoped his old enemy had prospered.

During the war the newspapers reported the discovery of the burned corpse of Morris (Mutty) Zetzkin in a salty swamp on Jamaica Bay. Rude justice! Gotbetter's nemesis had gotten his come-uppance, as Mrs. Abrams would have said. The newspaper described Zetzkin as a "petty hoodlum, gambler and shakedown artist." He had loomed much larger in Abrams' youth; he was sorry that the Times had cut him down in importance.

"Didja ever see the little girl who taught you to skate?" asked his daughter.

"She died."

It was curious the way Cousin Molly and Ruthie died within a year of one another. When? Ten years ago? Fifteen? They had been each other's world. The older woman had died first. He was vague on the details. TB? Diabetes? Ruthie outlived her by less than a year. A symbiotic relationship, his father would have said. Host and guest, dependent on one another. Molly gone, Ruthie could not live—even though she knew how to roller-skate. Abrams was wroth with himself for not having thanked her for teaching him to skate. It was too late now.

They passed a corner drugstore, the kind of doomed ill-lit place designed to attract holdup men. In the window a grimy antipasto of faded Dr. Scholl placards, rubber baby-pants, Ex-Lax ads, displays for Ipana, Bayer's, Gillette. How many of these stores had his father frequented? And how many times? Abrams peered into the dim interior. His heart thumped. Foolishly he half-expected to see his father within. On so many cold evenings he had sought him—a call, a patient in the office, someone needing him. His eyes sought the lumpy gray fedora, the unbuttoned black overcoat, the scuffed satchel. His father would be arguing with the druggist. He liked them (except for the lice who practiced medicine on the side). He wasted a lot of time (Mrs. Abrams said) standing around and gabbing with them. "So what?" his father responded. "I never buy a lot of razor blades or cigars at once. It's more fun to have an excuse to drop into Shapiro's or Laufer's and buy a little something. It gives me an excuse to chew the fat."

Abrams was tempted to walk into the store and ask the pharmacist: "Do you remember my father? Sol Abrams on Longview Avenue?" But he caught a glimpse of the man behind the counter. He was a young man. He could not have remembered Solomon Abrams, M.D., who had died sixteen years ago, climbing endless steps to give an injection to mad "Captain" Feigenbaum. The doctor was stricken at the last landing, staggered into Feigenbaum's flat, gave him the shot, had the "Captain" call an ambulance, and had died that night. (The "Captain" and the physician had resolved old grievances during the war. Albert suspected they sat around arguing military strategy.)

On the subway train, the children dozed. It was an off-hour. They rode in privacy except for a few dazed Negroes.

Abrams' mind swarmed with images, visions—people of his youth, smells and sounds, deeds half-remembered, words barely recalled, notions entertained. Was Harry Lauder Jewish? As a small boy, he was convinced that the great music-hall entertainer was. His parents had several scratchy records—"It's Nice to get up in the Mornin'," "Roamin' in the Gloamin'." Abrams remembered himself in woolen pajamas listening attentively to the thick accent, the peculiar foreign mumbling at the end of each song. Jewish, that's what Lauder was. Sounded just like the old garment workers in his father's office. Years later, he was terribly let down to find out Sir Harry wasn't. But he still had his doubts.

And were there still sheep in Prospect Park? A blinding vision came to him: a spring day, straddling his father's iron shoulders (was he four?) high on a green hill, watching an advancing herd of gray sheep. "They keep the grass cropped," his father said. "Fertilizer, too. Smell it—best in the world. Nature's work." But were there still sheep in Prospect Park?

His children had no need of sheep. They lived on a wooded hilltop, rode in a red station wagon. They were surrounded by oaks and hemlocks and Norway maples—and did not care. But his father's Lombardy poplar was dead, stripped, felled, burned, replaced by an aluminum lamp post.

Abrams' eyes wandered to the advertisements above him. One double-length placard caught his attention.

NEW YORK CITY TRANSIT AUTHORITY
MONTHLY POLITENESS WINNERS

Do you know a NYC Transit Employee who has been especially courteous and helpful to you? Write his name or badge number on a postcard and mail to Box 1008, NYC. He will be rewarded!

Beneath this heading were three large cutout photos of this month's winners. Beneath the heads were tiny cartoon bodies—uniforms, shined shoes. Abrams read the identifying captions.

SALVATORE FILARDO
Transit Authority Policeman, Queens

DENNIS F. BOYLAN
Bus Driver, Manhattan

L. R. PENNINGTON
Platform Attendant, Brooklyn

Abrams blinked. He leaned forward and scrutinized the black face of the last winner. Could it be? Was it his own Lee Roy? The football head! The sad eyes! Could there not be other L. R. Penningtons? But the longer he stared at the vast half-smiling face, the more he was convinced that the Monthly Politeness Winner was his ancient foe Lee Roy.

He was happy. The trip to Brooklyn had been more than a success. Something had been saved, some destiny fulfilled. He forgave Lee Roy everything, including the stolen pencil box.